GLYNN STEWART

FAOLAN'S PEN
PUBLISHING
faolanspen.com

This edition published in 2018 by:

Faolan's Pen Publishing Inc.

22 King St. S, Suite 300

Waterloo, Ontario

N2J 1N8 Canada

ISBN-13: 978-1-988035-30-7 (print) | 978-1-988035-72-7 (epub)

A record of this book is available from Library and Archives Canada.

Printed in the United States of America

1 2 3 4 5 6 7 8 9 10

First edition

First printing: July 2018

Illustration © 2018 Tom Edwards

TomEdwardsDesign.com

Read more books from Glynn Stewart at faolanspen.com

1

"THE WORMHOLE STATION IS OURS."

The transmission from the Marine boarding parties that Vice Admiral Isaac Gallant's people had spent *weeks* infiltrating onto the Eridani Wormhole Station echoed loudly across the flag bridge of the Confederacy battlecruiser *Vigil*.

"Do we have a stable communication wormhole?" the Vice Admiral asked calmly. If his Marines had seized the station, then the die was well and truly cast. The Rubicon was crossed.

Battle Group *Vigil* was now unquestionably in rebellion.

"Brigadier Zamarano has her people holding the line," his communications officer replied.

"Put her on," Isaac ordered. "Kira, what's your status?"

"We have secured all key engineering and command segments of the EWS," Kira Zamarano said crisply. "Resistance has been minimal. We have some casualties but no fatalities on either side. Overwhelming force pulled its usual trick."

"Well done, Brigadier. Pass my regards on to the Marines of the 77th," Isaac ordered.

EWS had roughly a battalion of Marines as security. Zamarano had

infiltrated her entire 77th Brigade aboard the station. That kind of imbalance of forces was useful for avoiding losses.

"Inter-system communications?" he asked his Marine commander.

"Locked down. We now control all communication and travel out of Epsilon Eridani," she confirmed. "What are your orders?"

"Move to Phase Two," Isaac replied. "The Battle Group will be on our way momentarily. 35th Brigade will bring your transports with theirs. How many Marines will be needed to hold EWS?"

"By the time you get our transports to us, I'll have everything locked down enough that we can leave a battalion behind and bring the other three to Sol," she confirmed instantly.

"All right, Brigadier, we'll see you shortly," he told her.

He rose from his chair, striding up to the main holodisplay as his flag deck crew watched, waiting for him to say what they knew was coming.

"Rhianna, hit the Rebellion channels," he told his com officer. "Inform Archangel that Bombardier is moving."

It would take several hours for the message to percolate through the network of wormhole communicators that linked the Confederacy together, but that was fine. It would take fourteen hours for Battle Group *Vigil* to reach the wormhole station.

By the time they were ready to transit to Sol, the Rebellion would be activating cells across human space. Most of those were irrelevant to Isaac—he cared about the cells in Sol, the ones that were supposed to take over Earth Fortress Command.

"Cameron." He turned to his operations officer. "Please inform all Captains that we are initiating Bonaparte. They are to set their course for the Eridani Wormhole Station, matching *Vigil*'s maximum flank acceleration."

He smiled.

"Officers, it's time to retake the Confederacy for her people."

His orders set the entire flag bridge into motion—and thousands of people throughout the hull of the battlecruiser as well. The big holographic tank in the middle of the flag deck showed the icons of his battle group, twenty-five strong.

Eight of those icons were useless in a fight. Two hundred and twenty meters long and carrying a battalion of Confederacy Marines apiece, the Orbital Attack Transports technically weren't under his command.

Brigadiers Zamarano and Michaels had thrown in with his rebellion long before, though. Eight battalions. Two brigades. A tiny force to fling against the might of the Confederacy, but it was what he had.

Ten ships, smaller than the OATs, moved around them. Those were his destroyers, speedy little ships that were designed to make high-speed attack runs at ships like his *Vigil*.

Two missile cruisers flanked the main formation, his snipers that would try to take out destroyers before they closed on the battlecruiser flagship.

Four warp cruisers led the way, their vulnerable drive rings making them the only ships in his rebellion that could outspeed light on their own. Everyone else required the wormholes, and the warp cruisers couldn't carry the battle to come.

That would fall on *Vigil* herself, the four hundred and thirty-meter-long behemoth at the heart of the battlecruiser group. Two full battle groups guarded Sol, and while Battle Group *Vigil* out-gunned either of them individually, the fight to come would test them to their limits.

"Battle Group is in motion," Commander Cameron Alstairs told him quietly. "Estimated time of arrival at EWS is sixteen hundred hours Greenwich Meridian Time, June fifth, 2386."

There was no *need* for Alstairs to give him the full date, but the weight of the moment was on them all. Only once before had units of the Confederacy Space Fleet turned on their government.

The result of *that* was what Isaac Gallant was going to fix.

"We have confirmation from Archangel," Rhianna Rose told Isaac. "All plans are now in motion, and Archangel has double-confirmed activation of Dynamite and their cell."

A cell-based structure made sense to Isaac, but it made the kind of massive, multisystem plan they were executing cumbersome. As "Bombardier," he was in the second tier of cells, but he didn't know

Archangel's true identity—and all Archangel knew about Bombardier was that they were a battle group commander.

That would probably have been enough to get a lot of people killed. The Confederacy only had twenty-six battle groups, after all.

In many senses, though, Dynamite was even more key to their plan than Isaac. Dynamite was a division commander in Earth Fortress Command—there were only *six* of those, and Isaac was pretty sure he knew which one Dynamite was.

Dynamite would deliver the EFC to the rebellion and, almost more importantly, neutralize *Liberty*. Isaac would back Battle Group *Vigil* against any of the Confederacy's other battlecruiser groups, but his force could not fight the Confederacy's dreadnought.

"77ᵗʰ Brigade's transports are rendezvousing at EWS," Alstairs reported. "Brigadier Zamarano reports the last of her people who are going will be aboard in twenty minutes. Colonel Nguyen is retaining command of the station; he gives us thirty-three minutes to wormhole activation to Sol."

"Have they had any problems with the communication lockdown?" Isaac asked.

"Nothing," Alstairs replied. "No questions, even. That seems…odd."

"That's *very* odd," the Admiral agreed. The Eridani Wormhole Station was responsible for all outgoing interstellar communications from the Epsilon Eridani System. It had been silent for over thirteen hours. The rebellion had an excuse and a reason for that, one that should have passed muster, but they hadn't even been asked for it.…

"Sir?" Rose asked quietly.

The word hung in the sudden silence on the flag deck.

A moment later, Captain Lauretta Giannovi appeared on the computer screen tattooed into Isaac's left forearm. His Italian-born flag captain looked…uncomfortable.

"I can't put my finger on it, sir," she told him. "But something doesn't feel right."

"I know," he agreed. He rose from his chair, studying the holographic display.

"We've already initiated," he told his flag deck crew. "We can't abort now—if we do, thousands are going to die for nothing." He shivered. "Once Archangel's messages start arriving, half the Confederacy is going up in flames.

"We can't stop now," he echoed. He studied the position of his fleet. Currently, they were decelerating for a nice, calm wormhole transition. One that wouldn't draw attention when they arrived in Sol for anything other than its size.

"In fact, Cameron—order all ships to cease deceleration. Bring up engines at full, straight at the wormhole target zone. Have Colonel Nguyen prep the wormhole for immediate activation. We're going to hit it as fast as we can and punch clean through."

"We'll draw all kinds of attention when we come out," Alstairs noted.

"Surprise would be nice, but the positioning of Sol's battle groups is what we're actually relying on," Isaac reminded him. "Pass the orders. Let's punch it."

———

THE WARSHIPS and transports flipped in space, no longer slowing as they approached the wormhole station but blazing toward it. The smaller ships matched *Vigil*'s acceleration, keeping pace with the battlecruiser that would have to carry the heaviest fighting once they reached Sol.

In some ways, it was almost a relief to Isaac when the other shoe dropped.

"Admiral, we have wormhole energy signatures," Captain Giannovi said flatly over the link from the bridge. "Dropping them to the tactical feed now."

Signatures. Plural. That was *definitely* not good.

"How bad, Cameron?" he asked quietly as the data filled in on the display.

"No details on who's coming through yet, but we have nine individual wormholes forming," his ops officer replied. "Wait…I have emergence."

The battlecruisers led the way. *Enterprise*, from Alpha Centauri with her overstrength battle group, the Confederacy's other strategic reserve force.

Dante, the previous flagship here in Eridani.

Calypso, from Conestoga.

Athena, from Tau Ceti.

Zulu, from Erewhon.

Victoria, from New Soweto.

And *Glorious* from Sol itself.

Eight battlecruisers. Only *Glorious* was *Vigil*'s equal; the other ships were older, smaller to various degrees. *Vigil* could take any one of them—but there was no way she could take all of them.

"Sir, the last wormhole…" Alstairs trailed off as the data codes propagated.

Liberty. As long as the battlecruisers but eight times as wide and carrying six particle cannons to the battlecruisers' one apiece. The Confederacy's only dreadnought, with a ninth battlecruiser for escort and an entire battle group to support them.

"IFF codes confirm the First Admiral is aboard," Isaac's operations officer concluded. "What do we do?"

Ten capital ships versus one. Nine battle groups versus one. If they were here, Isaac could be almost certain that Dynamite had failed, and Earth Fortress Command was still in loyalist hands.

"Sir, *Liberty* is hailing us," Rhianna Rose told Isaac. "…It's the First Admiral herself."

Of course it was.

They could run. They had enough of a velocity advantage that Battle Group *Vigil* might be able to pass through the gauntlet and make it into the outer system.

It wouldn't help them. If Nguyen tried to generate a portal, *Zulu* and *Athena* were positioned to disable the station's exotic-matter projectors. They couldn't leave the system. Any other option was just…wasting time.

"Admiral Gallant is repeating her hail," Rose told him. "What do we do?"

Isaac exhaled and nodded.

"Cameron, order the battle group to cease acceleration," he said quietly. "Rhianna…put my mother on."

The ships around him shut down their engines, coasting on inertia toward the entire fleet that was waiting for them as the image of First Admiral Adrienne Gallant, the unquestioned military dictator of the Confederacy of Earth, appeared in the main holotank.

Isaac had inherited his merely average height from his petite mother, even if his dark coloring took after his father, a native of New Soweto.

Adrienne Gallant was slightly built and pale-skinned, with hair that had faded from gold to silver over the course of the last twenty-plus years of dictatorship. She didn't *look* like the bloodyhanded tyrant who'd ordered the deaths of hundreds of thousands to maintain her power base.

Looks were deceiving. Isaac's mother had blasted her way into Earth orbit and "temporarily suspended" the office of President when the President and his cronies had become too openly corrupt for anyone to tolerate anymore.

Like most revolutions, she'd had popular support. When that had faded, she'd had the Fleet.

"Isaac," she greeted him. "Are we going to play games about what's happening here?"

"No," he said stonily. "You wouldn't be here if you didn't have enough information."

"I would not," she agreed. "Commodore Trevelyan was your mistake, if you wondered. He was doing *such* a good job, too, until he tried to co-opt the wrong person and panicked." She smiled coldly. "In his place, I'd have made better arrangements to kill Captain Pratchett if she was uninterested.

"Instead, your entire house of cards has come crumbling down. So, tell me, Isaac, are you going to run the gauntlet?"

He was eyeing the math. *Vigil* was the newest battlecruiser in the fleet—there were perks to being the dictator's only child—which meant he had a slight but measurable range advantage with his particle cannon over the rest of the Confederacy Space Fleet battlecruisers.

Vigil could potentially kill at least one, possible even two or three, of her older sisters.

But then *Liberty* would end Isaac's revolt.

"No," he finally admitted. "I'd ask you to guarantee my people's lives, but we both know how often those guarantees have been ignored."

That was probably a low blow, but it was true nonetheless.

"I have done what I must," Adrienne Gallant said coldly. "I thought you understood that."

"I did. It was everything *else* I objected to," Isaac replied.

"Order your ships to stand down and prepare to be boarded," the First Admiral told him. "Your rebellion is over."

Isaac nodded and killed the channel.

"You heard her," he told his people. "Stand them down. Stand them all down."

He waited there, in his command chair on his flag deck. Watching the red icons of Confederacy assault shuttles swarm over the fleet he'd hoped to free his people with.

He waited there until the Marines came to arrest him.

———

2

"Miss Amelie! Miss Amelie! Can I get your autograph?"

There was something both precious and stereotypical about the girl running towards Amelie Lestroud down the street of Nouveau Paris. She was all of maybe twelve years old, probably hadn't been allowed to see more than half of Amelie's movies yet and had a mother closer to Amelie's own age trailing behind her, desperately trying to impose decorum.

Amelie smiled at the girl as she stopped and turned to face her.

"Of course, miss," she told the child. "Do you have something for me to sign?"

The girl blinked in confusion, but her mother managed to produce a flimsy copy of *Stars of Honor*, last year's big blockbuster action epic, for Amelie to scrawl her signature across. The sheet of paper-like material contained the entire three hour-long three-dimensional production, but it was really only the size it was to allow for exactly this purpose.

"I'm sorry, she just loves your movies," the mother told Amelie. "I'm sorry to interrupt."

Amelie's companion was manfully refraining from rolling his eyes, but Amelie had known Archie Dresden for a *very* long time.

"It's not a problem," Amelie assured the mother and daughter pair. "But we are in a hurry, so I can't stick around."

The mother offered profuse thanks as Amelie and Dresden moved on down the Nouveau Parisian street.

"In a hurry," Dresden muttered. "That's a bit of an understatement, isn't it? *Archangel*?"

"Shut it, Artemis," she replied out of the side of her mouth. The tall blonde actress had long since mastered the art of speaking without anyone hearing or seeing her lips move that she didn't want. "None of this is *that* time-sensitive, not until Bombardier is actually in Earth orbit, and children like that are why we do everything."

Movies. Appearances. Autographs. Armed multisystem revolution. All of these were things Amelie Lestroud did for the future and the children who would live in it.

Stepping off the street into the apartment building, they quickly reached their destination. Amelie lived in the penthouse apartment at the top of the seventy-three-story tower—and owned the building, so no one would ever question her arriving there.

Instead of her luxurious penthouse, however, she and Dresden entered a rundown apartment on the twenty-third floor. The security cameras on this floor had been glitchy for years. That they hadn't recorded the two of them in the hallway wasn't unusual, even if it was intentional. This time.

Amelie let the door close behind them and then tapped the light-control panel in a specific pattern. A piece of cheap plastic paneling slid aside, allowing a *very* modern communications setup to slide out of the wall as the blinds closed and the door locked behind her.

"What updates do we have?" she asked Dresden as she took a seat at the console.

Officially, Archie Dresden was her bodyguard. Anyone who'd noticed his earbud would have dismissed it as part of his job.

Unofficially, he was Artemis, the right-hand man of the leader of an armed revolution.

"All of the B-tier cells have reported in but one," he told her. "I've heard nothing out of New Soweto. Buzzard hasn't checked in."

"Damn. What about the secondary?" she asked.

"I've thrown a note in the dead drop for Cherry Bomb, but I haven't heard back," he said grimly. "We may have to temporarily write off New Soweto, move in later once we've secured the other systems."

"I'd be more okay with that if New Soweto wasn't the CSP HQ," she pointed out. The Confederacy Secret Police were exactly what they called themselves—and the biggest obstacle to Amelie's revolution. "What about battle group tracking? Do we know who's moving? Not that I'm really questioning Bombardier, but I'm curious who they actually are."

"That's the odd one," Dresden replied. "We've got a lot of movement in the battle groups, more than usual but not entirely out of the norm…but the first to move was Epsilon Eridani."

"Gallant's *son*?" Amelie said. "That's not a good sign. There's no chance in *hell* that Battle Group *Vigil* is Bombardier."

"Except Eridani's wormhole coms also went down exactly on Bombardier's schedule," her bodyguard pointed out. "The Iron Bitch's son might actually *be* Bombardier."

"Great. Because we need more complications at this late an hour," she snapped. "What about Dynamite? Have we heard from their control?"

"Final confirmation codes. Nothing more. We shouldn't hear anything more until after it's all over."

Amelie nodded, drumming her fingers on the console. "So…what do we do now?" she finally asked.

Dresden laughed.

"Unfortunately, my dear Amelie, we wait," he told her. "We've spent ten years arranging this, contacting the factions, assembling the Bravo cells and making sure the money and weapons went where they need to be.

"And you, Miss Lestroud, made it all happen. Which means now you wait to hear how it all comes out."

She grimaced.

As one of the Confederacy's top actresses, she had every reason to travel across star systems and meet with thousands of people. Her trips had been the perfect cover for meeting and negotiating with rebel organizations in every star system. She'd bribed and laundered and blackmailed and—though she didn't like to think about it—murdered her way to assembling the largest prepared revolution in history.

Now it was time to throw the dice and see where her carefully assembled plans landed.

————

"STILL NO RESPONSE FROM CHERRY BOMB?" Amelie asked, checking the com systems.

"Nothing," Dresden confirmed. "Our entire New Soweto network is down." He shook his head. "With it being the CSP's headquarters…"

"We've probably lost everybody," the actress-turned-revolutionary half-whispered. The nature of a cell-based organization meant she had only the roughest notion of how many people they'd had on New Soweto…but Buzzard had been planning on assaulting the CSP's main facility.

That meant hundreds, if not thousands, of armed volunteers. All of whom were now off her network, potentially arrested or dead. It wasn't a good first step.

"Fleet movements are getting…hazier," Dresden said as well. "Our contacts in the wormhole stations are saying that a lot of the interstellar Fleet coms are going black. *Very* black."

That wasn't good. They'd relied on their ability to see what Fleet was doing to keep Bombardier warned if the CSF was moving against him. But if the…

"Wait, what the hell?"

"Archie?" she snapped.

"I just got an emergency pulse from Chariot—and then the entire Sol network went offline," he told her. "All Chariot said was that Bastard was down and they were compromised."

Red icons started to flash up across Amelie's system and she stared at them in horror.

"Our coms are down," she said softly. "All of our wormhole station people just went offline."

She now had no idea what anyone outside of the Nouveau

Versailles System was doing. "Is it just us or did all communications go down?" she asked.

The Confederacy had only done that during the purges, when entire system governments had risen up against the central government. They'd shut down all of the communication wormholes.

"Everything is down," he told her. "They've gone to full blackout. That should have taken hours to get into play. *How*?"

"They knew we were coming," Amelie said flatly. "Someone fucked up. I don't know if they're ready for us everywhere, but they knew it was coming."

She hit a button.

"Bartholomew," she barked into a microphone. "Everything's busted. Go *now*."

Bartholomew was the primary cell leader on the planet of Cherbourg, the man charged with organizing the rebellion's seizure of government houses and the planetary defense centers.

"We need to move," Dresden said grimly. "Bartholomew" was also Barry Wong, Archie Dresden's boyfriend. "We need to go to ground while our people try and pull what they can out of this mess."

"I can't abandon—"

"Yes. You can," her minder snapped. "If they haven't flagged you, your connections are the only chance of pulling anything out of this disaster."

"And if they've flagged me?" she demanded. "They seem to be waiting for everything *else*."

"Then *my* job is to make sure you get out alive," Dresden told her. "That's what you've paid for me for for fifteen years, Amelie Lestroud. It doesn't change just because you dragged me into this revolt!"

She swallowed hard. The communications setup was worthless now. Worse than worthless, in fact, because if any of the Bravo cell leaders were compromised, the Confederacy Secret Police would be able to follow the trail back to it.

"You have a plan?" she asked meekly.

Dresden smiled brilliantly at her.

"Of *course* I have a plan."

———

AMELIE'S BODYGUARD went to the same lighting-control pad she'd opened the coms setup with and typed in a different sequence of lights —one she hadn't been aware was in there.

A dusty bookshelf that had probably never seen a book in its lifetime swung away from the wall, exposing a man-high metal cabinet. Dresden crossed to it and plugged a code into the safe's keypad to open it.

He pulled out a pair of armored vests and passed one to her. Somehow, she was unsurprised that it fit perfectly over the tank top she was wearing under her blouse and disappeared neatly when she put the blouse back on.

By the time she'd put on the armor, Dresden had finished emptying the cabinet. He passed her a small concealable pistol with a shoulder holster to go under her blazer as he strapped a slightly larger weapon to his own waist.

Amelie had starred in enough action movies that she recognized the final weapon he pulled from the cabinet.

"A pulse rifle?" she said softly. "Seriously?"

"The Confederacy Secret Police has access to every piece of gear that the Confederacy Marines do," he pointed out. "If they come after you with battle armor or combat vehicles, we need to have some method of taking them down."

She shook her head but didn't argue. The pulse rifle was a vastly scaled-down version of the pulse guns that formed the main armament of warships these days—but those had entire fusion plants feeding them plasma.

The pulse rifle was disturbingly energetic for a hand weapon, but it could take down just about anything the CSP sent after them.

Dresden checked something in the cabinet as she was shaking her head at him, and cursed.

"We're in trouble," he said grimly. "CSP just sealed the front of the building. I guess they tracked us faster than I expected."

Amelie went cold.

"They're here *already*?"

The rebellion had been more compromised than she'd ever thought if the secret police were already *there*.

"Hopefully, they'll go to your penthouse," Dresden reminded her. "But I have an override on the elevators for just this occasion. We're out of time; let's go."

It seemed Dresden had prepared for everything. They charged out of the apartment and into the empty corridor, and made it to the elevators uninterrupted. Her bodyguard checked his military-style tattoo-computer and then tapped a command on his wrist, activating the car without using the regular controls at all.

"They've got aerial coverage, too," he said grimly. "I'm in the Nouveau Paris Police network…they'll lock me out pretty quickly, but the back door should give me about ten minutes of oversight."

"If they're above us, where are we *going*?"

"Down," Dresden told her as the elevator car lurched into motion. "One of the main storm sewers runs eleven meters from the basement of the building. I had a tunnel dug years ago."

She was shaking her head at his preparations again when the elevator doors slid open and gunfire echoed in the confined space of the basement. Once again, the CSP was one step ahead of them.

"Stay here!" Dresden barked. She didn't even have time to argue before he was out of the door, the terrifying *hiss-CRACK* of the plasma rifle overwhelmingly loud in the confined space.

The plasma rifle fired four times in rapid succession, and then the basement was silent.

"Come on," her bodyguard ordered, his voice…strained.

Amelie was familiar, if nothing else, with how fake injuries looked in movies and she was expecting the horror she saw as she came out.

The secret police hadn't been expecting a pulse rifle. Four plasma bolts had wiped out a ten-man squad, but not before they'd managed to shoot Dresden repeatedly. The body armor had stopped some of the rounds, but the CSP had used armor-piercing bullets.

"There's nothing you can do for me," he told her. "I'll…cover you."

Amelie didn't think he was going to live long enough to make any damn difference.

"I can't leave you," she hissed.

"Yes. You can," he replied, wincing at his wounds. "The tunnel is through there"—he gestured—"in the janitor's lockers. Third locker from the left has a keypad. Code is five-five-five-six.

"There's a hover-bike at the end of the tunnel, next to the storm sewer." He coughed. There was blood in it. Dresden was fading fast. "Follow the storm sewer out of the city and head for Ile de Bonita." He coughed again.

"Joey's Marina," he gasped out. "They…were never part of the rebellion. A backup. They'll know where to go.…"

He was gone.

———

THE HOVER-BIKE WAS a few years old, but someone—probably Dresden —had clearly been maintaining it.

Tears burned at the corners of Amelie's eyes as she ran through an abbreviated start routine, bringing up the bike's antigravity generators and fans simultaneously. It might not be safe or smart, but she was in a hurry.

And if she smashed herself to a pulp against the roof of the storm sewer, that might be better for everyone.

She dashed the tears from her eyes with the back of her hand and then slammed a helmet onto her head. There was a second bike, a harsh reminder that she wasn't supposed to be alone. That she could never have made it this far on her own.

The sounds of shouting behind her focused her mind and she kicked the bike into gear, leaping off the ground and down the storm sewer. She was lucky it was midsummer there in Nouveau Paris and the spring snow melt and storms had passed.

There was enough space in the sewer for her to fly the bike, screaming down the tunnel at a speed that was insanely unsafe. She knew, in the back of her mind at least, that she was walking a fine line between taking unreasonable risk and being outright suicidal, but she didn't care.

If the Confederacy Secret Police had known enough to come for *her*, then everything was doomed, and all her life's work had achieved was to get tens, possibly hundreds, of thousands of people killed. She'd watched some of the videos of the mass executions from the last round of purges.

That was what she'd led her followers to.

The storm sewer was perfectly straight, angling down toward the ocean at enough of a gradient to guide the water. She blasted through over twenty kilometers of tunnel in under six minutes before bursting out onto the open sea.

Ile de Bonita was almost five hundred kilometers away, just under two hours at the bike's maximum speed. Now she was out in the open and above water, sustaining that was harder, but the bike's screens protected her. Mostly.

They didn't protect her hearing, however, and she missed the approaching aircraft until they flanked her.

Black-and-red assault shuttles, Confederacy Marine spacecraft pressed into duty as high-speed interceptors, flew on either side of her. She ignored them, trying to find the nerve to bite down on the poison tooth she'd had implanted without telling Dresden.

If they took her alive, they could end the entire rebellion…but it looked like they'd already done that.

She tried to evade, diving for the surface, only for an EMP blast from one of the shuttles to cripple her hoverbike.

Amelie Lestroud had enough time to realize that there were easier ways to kill her before she heard stunners whine and blackness swept over her vision…still at least three meters away from the water.

———

3

THEY'D LEFT him his uniform. There was a bitter irony in that to Isaac Gallant.

In fact, the only clothes he had in his luxurious cell were his Vice Admiral's undress uniform. The guard at the door still treated him with respect when they delivered his meal. Everyone acted like he remained a senior flag officer of the Confederacy Space Fleet as opposed to a condemned traitor.

The cell itself was incredible. They'd locked him in what he was reasonably sure were the visiting VIP quarters for Earth Fortress One, the central command facility for Earth Fortress Command. An entire wall was transparent aluminum, allowing him to look out over the surface of the planet below.

Like the rest of the command centers, EF-One was in geostationary orbit above Earth's equator. North and South America spread out beneath him in a glittering array of nighttime lights and immense megalopolises.

He was reasonably sure he could pick out New York City from there, the central capital of the Confederacy and home to the Senate. That had been where the plan had been *supposed* to end, with him dissolving the Senate and calling new elections.

Things hadn't gone according to plan. He didn't have access to news or datanet feeds, but if his mother had known enough to bring *Liberty* to Epsilon Eridani, she'd known enough to short-stop Archangel's entire rebellion.

As if summoned by his thoughts, the door to his cell slid open with a soft sound. Footsteps followed, a familiar fast, almost hyperactive, pace.

"I thought you, of all people, understood," Adrienne Gallant finally said.

"I trusted you for a long time," he replied. He didn't turn to face her, still looking at the planet below. "The coup was hard enough to swallow. I'm not even sure, anymore, how I convinced myself that the purges were justified."

"Order *had* to be maintained. If the Confederacy collapsed, everything we'd done had been for nothing."

"Everything we'd done," he echoed. "Mass executions of people who'd surrendered in exchange for their lives. Literal purges of the bureaucracy, the military. The mass imprisonments—the use of political prisoners as slave labor in facilities *you* owned.

"Where did it go wrong?"

She chuckled bitterly.

"It's hard to say, isn't it?" she replied. "I can't argue with any of that. It all made sense at the time, but you look at it in total and it's hard to justify."

"Then *why*?"

"Because it all made sense at the time," Adrienne Gallant repeated softly. "And then, eventually, you get to the point where you're holding things together with blood and duct tape and just praying someone will come along and help.

"Which was supposed to be you." She sighed. "I trusted you above the rest, you know? I *knew* you would avoid the slippery slope, that you could avoid the corruption.

"Guess I should have thought through what that might mean in the short term, huh?"

He was silent.

"What's the point of this?" Isaac finally asked. "I doubt our efforts aren't about to set off a new round of purges. Do you want to remind me how many people I got killed?

"I made my choice. Turn me over to the damn executioners."

The room was silent for a long time. If Isaac hadn't been able to see her reflection, he might have thought she'd left.

"I'm weak enough to admit that I don't have the stomach to order my own son killed," she said quietly. "And you're too much *my* son for us to play any games pretending you infiltrated the rebellion to betray them."

"Not a fucking chance," he snarled. "So, what, you kill everyone else and I get to live with that, huh? How long do you think it'll be before I swallow my own damn gun after that?"

She chuckled sadly.

"Not long. No longer than I would have lived if I'd failed and been spared. I am not prepared to order the execution of my own son, Isaac. I am *also* not enough of a hypocrite to spare you and condemn a million others."

"I weep for your ethical dilemmas," he told her. "Are we done?"

The First Admiral sighed.

"For now," she agreed. "There *will* be consequences, Isaac. But your involvement changes what I am prepared to do. We shall see."

He was silent, ignoring her now as he looked at the cities beneath him.

She waited for a few more minutes, then left. Her footsteps were slower this time, barely recognizable as hers.

———

IsAAC'S SUPPER that evening arrived precut, without even the intentionally fragile plastic knife they usually gave prisoners. That led him to take a second look at his quarters and come to the conclusion that, if he hadn't already been, he was now definitely on suicide watch.

There were no curtains for the observation window. The bed was an adjustable-viscosity gelpac with a self-warming canopy—no bedclothes to fashion into a noose. No rope-like objects in the quarters at all. No unsecured heavy objects. No sharp objects.

He was…reasonably sure he wasn't suicidal. Not yet, anyway. That could easily change once the full magnitude of his failure sank in.

Fatalistic, sure. He was prepared to face execution for his actions, to die along with the officers, spacers, and Marines he'd led into this mess. It seemed he was to be spared that, but…

The VIP quarters were a gilded cage, but they were a cage nonetheless. He had no way to check in on his people. Couldn't speak to Giannovi or Alstairs, or any of the dozen and more Captains who'd followed him into mutiny.

He *hoped* that Archangel and the rest of the planetary cells had realized things had gone wrong fast enough to flee to safety, but hope was all he had.

Watching through the observation window, he saw another set of glittering lights cross Earth's orbit. Ships of a dozen types and sizes moving cargo up and down the gravity well of the Confederacy's beating heart.

It took Isaac a moment to realize that several of the lights were heading toward EF-One. He had a flare of hope and then sighed. They were warships, but they weren't there to rescue him. It was, in fact, *Vigil* herself…being towed by a pair of tugs into a spot where she could be watched by the heavy guns of Earth Fortress Command.

Like him, his ship was a prisoner.

Somehow, that was as depressing as anything *else* he'd seen of late.

———

Nine days.

For nine days, Isaac Gallant sat in the VIP quarters, able to see his former flagship orbiting less than five kilometers away, going more than a little crazy.

His guards were unfailingly polite and respectful, delivering his meals—clearly prepared by the same chef who was responsible for the flag mess on the station—regularly and efficiently. The cleaners who came through his room were equally polite and efficient, in the way that only longstanding military NCOs can be.

Not that a man who'd spent his life in the military left much to clean, regardless of how much pampering his mother's influence had bought him. He'd gone through the Academy before Adrienne Gallant had seized control of the Confederacy, after all.

Like any citizen of the Confederacy, Isaac had a list of movies and books stored on his personal computer to go through if he ever had time. Unlike most civilians, his computer was physically installed on his arm—though it could also speak to the screen in the VIP quarters.

That helped keep him from going completely insane, but there were only so many books and drama movies one could watch. By the fourth day, he'd degraded into watching spectacle blockbusters starring Amelie Lestroud, everyone's favorite blonde action heroine.

By day nine, he was into classified research memos on gravity-warp-drive weapons. The grav-warp drive was an evolution of the original calculation by Alcubierre and came along with the inherent invulnerability while encased in the bubble of warped space.

Of course, a warp cruiser could no more fire out of its grav-warp than be fired upon, but there'd been research done on taking out a warp ship at full speed. The memo was inconclusive—but Isaac could tell from its tone that the researchers had been told to stop before they ended up with conclusive data.

Only the Confederacy, after all, had grav-warp drive warships. There were fewer than thirty gravity-warp-drive ships in human space. If you could fly up to a wormhole that could fling you three or four hundred light-years in seven point four two seconds—every wormhole trip lasted *exactly* the same length of time—why would you play around with ships that could go a "mere" four times the speed of light?

He'd made his own career with an unexpected and effective use of a warp cruiser, shutting down a potential civil war before it had begun. In hindsight...well, the irony wasn't lost on him.

The First Admiral, it appeared, hadn't learned to knock in the nine days since her last visit. This time, he looked up as his mother entered, his focus on his tattoo-comp, not the window this time.

"You know, there is pornography in the library I have access to," he said mildly.

"It wouldn't even be the first time I'd walked in on *you* watching that, let alone the first time I'd walked in on someone," she pointed out. "Besides, you *are* a criminal."

"Traitor and rebel, technically," he replied. "*Criminal* understates things so very drily."

"I see you continue to find this hilarious," Adrienne Gallant snapped.

"I have few pleasures left to me in life, it seems," Isaac told her. "I may as well mock you. The honesty is refreshing for me, if nothing else."

She visibly swallowed a snarl, then sighed at him.

"This isn't easy for me, you know," she said quietly.

"Was betraying every principle you overthrew our government to support easy?" he asked bluntly.

"No," she replied. "Sometimes, yeah, let's be honest. But not always. It came down to holding the Confederacy together or watching everything I had sworn to defend and sacrificed to preserve come apart in anarchy and fire."

"But after everything you did or ordered done, what was left of what we tried to defend and preserve?"

"I'm not here to debate with you," the First Admiral told him. "I accept what I did and why I did it. I wanted you to understand, once, but you neatly rendered that unnecessary, didn't you?"

"Why *are* you here?" he asked. "I won't pretend it's not good to have company or that I regret seeing my mother, but, fuck…just because I was leaving killing you to someone else doesn't mean I hadn't accepted it needed to happen."

Adrienne Gallant turned her back on him, walking over to the observation window and studying Earth below them.

"I know." Her voice was very small. "Just like I knew Franz would never understand."

Isaac winced. Franz Liebermann had been his father, Adrienne Gallant's lover and partner of over two decades.

And Vice Admiral Franz Liebermann had died aboard his flagship, defending Sol against his lover's fleet. No one knew if he'd known who was in command. Only that regardless of what he knew, Franz Liebermann had done his duty.

"But we are where we are," she continued. "Your rebellion has been crushed. Fewer fatalities than I was afraid of, but that just leaves me with more damned prisoners than I know what to do with." She shook her head. "Cohen, of course, would have us execute them all. I've been a bad influence on that man."

Fifth Admiral Cohen had once promised the lives of a surrendering rebel fleet—only for the First Admiral to order all of the officers executed.

"Given history, sparing anyone is inconsistent, isn't it?" Isaac asked. "We knew what we were getting into."

"I already said I won't execute my only damn son," Adrienne barked. "And I won't be enough of a hypocrite to execute five hundred thousand others and spare you. If you live, *everyone* lives."

"I suppose we have the prison space for that," he said flatly. "You can send us to work on those lovely exotic-matter plants you own. You know, that personal benefit you swore never to take from your office?"

She sighed.

"I already said I wasn't here to debate you," she reminded him. "I'm here to tell you what was decided, for your fate and the fate of your rebellion."

Adrienne Gallant smirked, and if Isaac could tell she was hiding pain behind the smirk, well, he *was* her son.

"It even gives us a benefit, in truth. Because we're being *merciful,* we can launch a far wider sweep than we were expecting. If we were just going to line you all up against the wall and shoot you, we can only sweep so wide. Active members of the rebellion are one thing, but families and sympathizers and college rabble-rousers are quite another. We can't really shoot them.

"We can send them with you, however."

"With us where?" Isaac asked carefully, trying to conceal the horror of the implications.

"I can't kill you, Isaac," Adrienne Gallant said. "I don't have it in me. I can't keep you prisoner—not a *flag officer* of the Confederacy Space Fleet. Not my son. You and I both know what an icon of rebellion you would become. You and Lestroud both are too damned famous to keep as political prisoners."

Lestroud? What did the actress have to do with this, Isaac wondered.

"That leaves us one real choice, and thankfully, one of our side projects has offered a spectacularly convenient opportunity."

She turned to face him. With Isaac seated, even his petite mother could glare down at him.

"The sentence is exile, Admiral Gallant," she said flatly. "You and everyone even associated with your rebellion, far beyond where you can ever threaten the Confederacy again."

———

4

Isaac sighed, still seated in the chair he'd been reading in, and leveled his best unintimidated look on his mother.

"Exile to where?" he asked. "Where could you even *send* us that's beyond the Confederacy's reach?"

The First Admiral chuckled, tapping on her tattoo-comp and taking over control of the screen in his quarters. The image of a star appeared on the screen. A strange star.

A *spinning* star…one of two.

"The J2222-0137 binary pulsar system," she explained. "A fascinating piece of astrography and one we've been investigating for years. It's at the very limit of the Confederacy, one of the first systems accessed with fourth-generation wormhole generators."

A fourth-generation generator could create a wormhole crossing three hundred light-years. If it had been reached with one of those, from the existing borders of human space when the fourth-generation platforms came online…it was almost nine hundred light-years from Earth.

Still not exactly beyond the reach of the Confederacy, though. Unless… Isaac vaguely recalled something about a station built at a pulsar, testing new types of wormhole generation.

"For the last twenty years, J22 has been home to Hermes Station, the Long-Range Wormhole Research Facility," Adrienne continued. "They've been experimenting with using the binary pulsar as a booster to dramatically extend the range of our wormhole generators."

"I'm guessing they succeeded?" Isaac asked.

"They succeeded in opening over twenty wormholes, Isaac, before they managed to identify a pattern that would allow them to open the same wormhole twice," she admitted. "We sent through a survey expedition of warp cruisers to investigate the other end."

She shivered.

"We missed the first damn pickup. They'd calculated wrong and opened the wormhole seventeen *thousand* light-years off target," she noted. "We grabbed them on the second scheduled pickup, though, with their survey data of the stars around the emergence point."

Adrienne Gallant turned back to the window looking at Earth...no, Isaac realized. Looking at *Vigil*. What did she see in his old flagship?

"We started assembling a colony expedition, and then the Hermes Station team finished rerunning their numbers," she continued. "We can open wormhole XL-17 one more time. Just one. The next opportunity to open it will be in over two hundred years—something to do with alignments of the J22 pulsar with another pulsar at the other end of the galaxy.

"We were debating still sending a colony expedition, made up of volunteers, but now...now, well, I have a few million dissidents that need to go somewhere *else*."

Isaac swallowed.

"How far?"

"It's hard to nail down the emergence location exactly," she pointed out. "We barely know anything about the region except what we can identify."

"But you know, roughly, don't you?"

"It's the other side of the galaxy," Adrienne told him. "The Hermes staff estimates seventy-five thousand light-years or so. Once you go through, you'll never be coming back."

Exile. That was pretty definitively final.

"Some mercy," Isaac replied. "Sending us that distance, I'm assuming the wormhole opens in deep space?"

Wormholes could emerge at planet-star Lagrange points or in deep space, a minimum of six light-months from a star. The one natural wormhole humanity had ever found was closer in, going from thirty-one light-hours away from one sun to forty-one light-hours away from the other.

But to open a wormhole across the length of the galaxy…

"Pretty much exactly two light-years from the nearest star system," she confirmed. "Of course, we had a solution for that even when we were planning on sending volunteers. They're calling it a 'warp cradle', a grav-warp ring big enough to create a bubble that can move an entire fleet."

"Which you'll need," Adrienne concluded. "I may need to get rid of you, but the thought of setting up a second basket for humanity's eggs has value of its own."

She gestured at the battlecruiser.

"We'll give you *Vigil* back. Your entire battle group, in fact. Crews, too. We'll see what our sweep of the rest of the Fleet produces, but I suspect you'll have at least a second battlecruiser, and I'll make sure you end up with at least six warp cruisers."

"You'll trust me and my people with warships?" he asked.

"Fuck, no," Adrienne snapped. "Your magazines will be empty and your particle and pulse guns physically disabled. Your munitions will be carried on one of the freighters accompanying you—you can arm once you're on the other side of the galaxy."

"So. Multiple capital ships. Freighters. Colony ships, I'm assuming." Isaac shook his head. "At least it will be a comfortable exile."

"I leave that to you," she told him. "You'll have all of the resources of a top-tier colony expedition. It's not like you'll be able to call home for help. Once XL-17 closes, you're done, Isaac."

"Out of your reach," he noted.

"Out of sight, out of mind, but not dead," she replied. "That's as much mercy as I can afford—it's not like you left me any choice."

"We won't be the last," Isaac said quietly. "The tighter you squeeze the Confederacy, the greater the risk it will implode on you."

"I have to take that risk," Adrienne told him. "Or watch it disintegrate. However much blood and fire I must shed to hold humanity together, I will shed it. But XL-17 gives me a chance to sweep up every dissident and troublemaker we know of alongside your actual rebellion."

She smiled coldly.

"If I'm going to be merciful, then I see no reason not to spread my mercy as wide as possible."

———

5

"MOVE IT!" the guard barked, a shock stick rapping against the walls of the cells as he made his way along the prison row. "Everybody up, everybody out. If you've got anything in there you want to keep, grab it now; you are all moving out."

Being the suspected leader of the rebellion had earned Amelie the grand luxury of a cell to herself with what she suspected was the most comfortable bed in the orbiting prison station. It only had *three* unavoidable hard lumps.

The cell doors popped open as the guard passed by, and she slowly obeyed orders. The bruises from her earlier attempts at actual disobedience were a reminder that the Confederacy Secret Police's prison wardens were *not* gentle souls.

A line of wardens was moving along the row of cells, using shock sticks for chivying anyone who wasn't moving fast enough. As usual, they were low-powered enough to merely hurt rather than disable.

A second line carried stunguns. If the prisoners tried to rush the shock stick-wielding wardens, they'd be laid out unconscious in moments.

It had happened while Amelie had been there. The prison was at least double capacity, stuffed full of people from her failed rebellion.

Since the real identity of Archangel had been a carefully guarded secret, she had all the guilt of being responsible for everyone being there without the danger of being blamed for it by the people around her.

There were people in the Nouveau Versailles System who knew who she was to the rebellion. Unless they were all dead, they were probably somewhere on this station.

Most of the prisoners around her were still wondering why the actress was in with the rebel scum.

The guards kept barking orders and Amelie fell into the line, following the stream of prisoners.

They were emptying the cell blocks. *All* of the cell blocks, she realized, as they moved into one of the larger prisoner-transfer areas. A massive open bay had been commandeered to hold most, if not all, of the station's prisoner population.

She stopped in horror at the edge of the bay. There had been, give or take, twenty-five or so thousand people in the rebellion in Nouveau Versailles.

This bay held at least twice that, crammed in like cattle. Presumably, some transports would be arriving soon to move them out somewhere…else. Probably a work site, but why would they be moving *everyone*?

"Hey, bitch, you ain't famous enough to not have to *move*," one of the wardens barked. Amelie turned in time to watch a shock stick flash toward her—too late to do anything about it. She braced herself for the impact…except it didn't happen.

The warden hit the ground instead, one arm tucked behind his back by a black-armored Confederacy Marine.

"She's in the bay, so she's ours," the Marine told the warden before he let the man up. "Go start getting the second batch ready if you need to get your sick jollies."

The warden bolted, and the Marine turned an assessing gaze on Amelie.

"Rebels or not, there are fucking standards," he noted calmly. "Not the first warden we've had to educate today, Miss Lestroud. Keep moving, please."

She nodded her thanks and joined the crowd. They might have traded up for a better class of jailer, but they were still prisoners.

———

"AMELIE!"

It took her a moment to place the person shouting through the crowd. One of the minor disadvantages of fame was that most of the people around her knew who she was, though, thankfully, that didn't seem to result in that many requests for autographs in prison.

Then she spotted Barry Wong, the tall man gently pushing his way through the crowd toward her. Wong had been in charge of their operations on Cherbourg, and enough of the crowd were members of his organization that they made way for him to get through and wrap her in a tight embrace.

"Archie?" he asked softly, looking around for his boyfriend.

"He didn't make it," Amelie admitted. "He tried to get me out, but... they were waiting for us."

"Everywhere," Wong told her. "They pretty clearly didn't know *exactly* what we were planning, but they knew something was coming. The precincts were all locked down, and the local CSP facility dropped an entire battalion of Marines from orbit the moment we arrived."

He shook his head.

"I don't think we actually lost that many people," he continued. "Overwhelming force convinced most people to surrender rather than fight it out."

"But now we have no control," Amelie whispered. "I led all of these people here."

The part of her brain that had helped write horror movies was noting that the bay was designed to hook up to a large transport...but could also simply be opened to space. If someone wanted to dispose of fifty or sixty thousand rebels and dissidents...

"These can't all be ours, can they?" she asked, looking around the chaotic crowd.

"I...don't know who 'ours' is, per se," a massive, older-looking gentleman nearby told her, "but I would guess not." He offered a hand

and she saw he was wearing an eyepatch. "I'm Professor Lyle Reinhardt, from the Nouveau Paris University."

He looked around.

"I got caught up in a sweep of the university," he noted. "I'm a *physicist*, Miss Lestroud. I won't pretend I haven't had my involvements with the student union and some of their more vocal protests, but I'm hardly a rebel."

"They must have been sweeping anyone they considered a dissident," she replied. "That's...not a good sign."

Reinhardt swallowed.

"I wasn't informed of any charges. Just stunned and woke up in a cell," he admitted. "This isn't *right*."

"No, it's not," Wong agreed. "That's what we tried to stop." He shrugged, gesturing around him. "They were waiting for us, Professor, and what you see around you is the Nouveau Versailles branch of the rebellion.

"So far as I can tell—and between Amelie and I, we should be able to tell—they swept up everybody."

"Everywhere," Amelie told the two men. "The entire rebellion was snapped up as soon as we moved." She shook her head. "And now we get to see if the Iron Bitch is feeling more merciful than usual."

If Archie Dresden's assessment that Bombardier had actually been Vice Admiral Gallant, that was...actually possible. For now, however, she was taking her reassurance from the fact that the Marines moving through and organizing the crowd weren't wearing vacuum helmets.

So long as there were Confederacy troops in the bay who'd die with them, they were going to live at least a few more minutes.

―――――

THE MARINES ORGANIZED people into rough rows, an approximation of lines waiting to board the presumably inbound transport through the locks at the front of the bay. There were tens of thousands of prisoners in the space and maybe four hundred Confederacy troops...but the Marines were unquestionably in control.

Several portions of the lines were made up of unconscious bodies dragged into place. The Marines were being gentler than the secret police had been, but they were perfectly willing to use whatever force was necessary.

Amelie stuck with Wong through the formation of chaos into order, ending up near the front of one of the lines as a woman in a sharply creased black-and-red Confederacy Marine Corps uniform stepped onto a platform at the front of the room.

Her hair was cropped short and she wore a golden eagle on each side of her high-necked collar as she looked down on the swarm of prisoners.

"Be silent," she ordered firmly. When the crowd continued to argue and shout, she tapped a command on her tattoo-comp and a screech of feedback tore through the room, silencing the last of the chaos.

"I am Colonel Amanda Hale," she told them. "I will be responsible for your security and transport from Nouveau Versailles to your next destination."

Hale did not look impressed with her job.

"You are all rebels, dissidents, traitors and scum," she noted. "You have betrayed the Confederacy in your deeds and your words, and were it up to me, you would be spending the rest of your lives at hard labor, repaying your debt to society with the sweat of your brow.

"In her wisdom and mercy, however, the First Admiral has decreed a different sentence for you. You will be taken from this penitentiary aboard the CMC transport *Starflower* and delivered to a classified location where you will be transferred to a colony ship.

"Once aboard the colony ship, you will no longer be prisoners so long as the ship follows the orders given to it by proper authority. Some of those of you with starship experience will be drafted to man the colony vessel, which will proceed from the classified location it awaits you to a different, also classified, location far beyond the Confederacy's borders.

"*Exile* is the First Admiral's sentence upon you all. Your final fate will fall upon your own skills and willingness to work rather than destroy what others have built."

The room exploded into noise again, until Hale activated the feedback scream again. That was insufficient to quiet the chaos, so she activated it a third time—and then gestured to the Marines.

The chatter of stunguns cut through the crowd's shouting, the loudest and most difficult speakers finding themselves sprawled out on the ground.

The Marines dragged the unconscious troublemakers out, laying them alongside the rest of the unconscious prisoners, making sure no one was accidentally trampled.

Amelie was silent, watching and waiting to see where things went. Exile opened possibilities, but only if they managed to *not* get killed along the way.

"Cooperation will see you safely delivered to your new home," Hale told them all after they'd quieted again. "Resistance will be met with all necessary force. I am expected to deliver you all intact and alive, but make no mistake: I will not risk my Marines to preserve your worthless lives.

"My Marines will direct you aboard *Starflower*. Do not cause me further troubles."

————

ONE OF THE oddities of her career was that Amelie Lestroud was actually quite familiar with the interior of the standard Orbital Attack Transport the Marines used for carrying battalions. She'd been in four movies that had the use of the military spaceships for sets in the last five years alone.

She wasn't as familiar with the Strategic Deployment Transport the prisoners were loaded onto, but many of the same principles applied. The mess hall they were supposed to eat in was absolutely identical. The only real difference between an OAT and an SDT was that one carried a thousand people and the other carried fifty thousand.

OATs secured the landing sites, and then SDTs delivered the armies to expand from the beachhead. An OAT could land. An SDT used slower space-to-ground transports to deliver their heavy gear.

Without the heavy gear of its usual two divisions, her best guess was that they'd probably packed the entire hundred-thousand-prisoner capacity of the prison station they'd just left aboard *Starflower*. That was a terrifying thought all on its own.

"We didn't have enough people on Cherbourg to fill this ship," she told Wong as they sat in the mess hall. "Where the hell did they find enough prisoners to fill her?"

"Cherbourg," her cell leader said grimly. "Based off our conversation with Reinhardt...they swept up *everyone* they had any reason to throw in a cell and they're shipping them all out."

"If they found a hundred thousand people on Cherbourg..."

Cherbourg was an average Confederacy world of a billion souls or so. Across the forty or so planets of the Confederacy...

"Millions," Wong concluded. "The Iron Bitch is exiling *millions*. A colony transport is what, three times the size of this ship?" He gestured around them.

"She can't possibly think this is going to be swallowed by the people," Amelie pointed out.

"She's selling it as mercy," her comrade replied. "And given the last round of purges and the fucking *orbital bombardment* at Waterloo... enough people will buy it to get her another decade or so of calm."

"And then the Confederacy comes apart; with no coherent organization between factions, the systems go their own way," Amelie told him. "I did the damn research, Wong. The Confederacy is *fucked*—the whole point of running a multi-stellar rebellion was to try and hold together a multi-stellar union when it was done.

"If she's exiling every dissident she can find..."

"She'll be gutting half the universities in the Confederacy, students and faculty alike," Wong agreed. "They'll never recover."

"And we'll be 'far beyond the borders of the Confederacy,' where we can't help or hurt," she said. "What a shit-show this is going to be."

"Aye. What do we do about it?"

Wong, it seemed, was still going to look to her for leadership.

"Find your cell leaders," she told him, a moment of decision crystallizing her thoughts. "Put out the word, put out the call. If they're sending millions of people into exile, at least a couple hundred thousand of them are ours.

"If even half of our old cells can be brought online, we may be the only chance these people have for some semblance of order—and if we're going to turn this exile into a new chance for us all, we *cannot* dissolve into anarchy."

Wong chuckled.

"Somehow, I knew you'd know what to do," he told her. "All right, 'Archangel.' The call goes out again.

"Let's see who answers."

———

6

SAYING a wormhole transit took 7.42 seconds was the equivalent of saying pi was 3.14. It was accurate enough for most purposes but ignored an infinite number of irrational decimals after that point.

The human brain processed those seconds strangely. Isaac barely registered them, where others felt them take subjective minutes or even hours. As their ship punched through into the J2222-0137 binary pulsar system, he blinked—and the wormhole passage was over, leaving them floating in the middle of a slowly assembling fleet.

Zulu was an older ship, one of the oldest battlecruisers in the Confederacy Space Fleet. Captain Ó Rodagh had been perfectly polite to Isaac, though there was no question that the Admiral was a prisoner aboard the younger woman's ship.

His staff was also being transported aboard *Zulu,* and they'd been allowed supervised time together, culminating in being on an observation deck as the battlecruiser arrived in J22, letting them see what they were getting into.

Hermes Station was at the edge of their vision, the starfish shape of a wormhole-generation station drawn at several times the usual scale. Isaac wasn't sure of the station's size, but he knew the battlecruiser orbiting under one of its arms far too well.

Vigil helped define the size of the station for him, marking just how big Hermes was compared to a normal wormhole station. A second battlecruiser orbited with her, and a small swarm of glittering fireflies marked the escorts he was being given.

Given was the right word, too. Isaac was all too aware that the expedition was being put together out of necessity and that the scale of it and the resources being provided to it really were a gift to *him*. His mother's final peace offering, a chance to start anew on the other side of the galaxy.

"Those are *huge*," Lauretta Giannovi said softly, studying the other set of ships. "I thought the dreadnought was big."

"You haven't seen a colony ship before?" Isaac asked, turning his attention to the true core of the fleet that was going to make the trip through wormhole XL-17.

"I might have, but I wasn't paying attention," the battlecruiser captain admitted. She tapped at her tattoo-comp , seeing how much information she could access. *"Twelve hundred meters long?"*

Isaac chuckled, studying the sixteen ships that dwarfed everything except Hermes Station itself.

"They carry a quarter million people each," he pointed out. "Plus frozen animals, vast quantities of seedstock, heavy machinery, light machinery... They're designed to found an entire colony on their own."

"That's enough transport for four million people," Cameron Alstairs noted. "I don't suppose they're going to be running part-empty?"

"No," Isaac confirmed. "From what my mother said, they're sweeping up anyone who's ever so much as called her the Iron Bitch and throwing them on those ships. It's going to be anarchy; even the *crew* will be prisoners."

"And we get to hold it all together?" Alstairs asked. "How exactly are we planning on doing that?"

"I don't know yet," the Admiral admitted. "I know we get to move back aboard *Vigil* before we jump out. At that point, we'll start holding staff meetings and planning."

He shook his head. "I don't know what resources we're going to have in the end. I don't think anyone's going to until we make the jump—my impression is that we'll be getting ships and cargo and prisoners delivered until zero hour."

"How long is that?" Giannovi asked. "They know, right, when they'll be able to open the passage?"

"Within reason," Isaac agreed. "Three to five days, if I'm reading the data they gave me right. About a forty-eight-hour window of possibility, and they expect to be able to hold the portal open for about eighty minutes."

His flag captain shook her head.

"And then?" she asked. "What do we do then?"

"You see that giant tube?" Isaac asked, pointing to a long silver line currently hanging in the middle of the colony ships. "Once we're through, we hit the activation button on that and it turns into a grav-warp drive ring that's seventeen kilometers across. It'll make a bubble big enough for the entire expedition fleet.

"It'll take us to our new home."

Giannovi studied the warp cradle in its dismantled form.

"I've never heard of anything like that," she noted.

"Why would you have?" Isaac said. "It'll move the fleet at four times lightspeed. That's all. Why would we use something like that when we have wormhole generators?

"But for a seventy-thousand-plus light-year jump? We can't target it accurately enough to be sure we hit a star system's Lagrange points. From what I've heard so far, we'll be coming out two full light-years from the nearest system."

"Six months in warp," Giannovi said. "That is going to hurt. Even a few hours sucked."

"Six months." Isaac nodded. "Six months with four million civilians and I'm not even sure how many Fleet and Marine Corps personnel."

Alstairs sighed.

"Am I allowed to hope that our collection of dissidents includes some damned good psychiatrists?"

"You're allowed," Isaac told him. "If only because I'm hoping the same thing!"

———

SHUTTLES SWARMED around *Vigil* and the other warships, delivering Isaac's crews back to their ships. His own shuttle was one of the last in the current batch, escorted for the entire length of the trip from *Zulu* to *Vigil* by a hovering destroyer.

That was overkill. Even the destroyers' secondary anti-missile lasers could have vaporized the unarmed spacecraft carrying the Vice Admiral, but they clearly wanted to be sure Isaac didn't get any ideas.

He was taking command of two battlecruiser groups, an entire fleet…but Fifth Admiral Cohen commanded the guard force there at Hermes. And Cohen had *four* battlecruiser groups—and unlike the two Isaac was joining, his were fully armed and operational.

Isaac knew, with absolute certainty, that no one from his crews had been aboard *Vigil* for more than twenty-four hours. That, it turned out, did not stop his people putting together a proper honor guard and boarding party.

Twenty-four Marines, unarmed but in full dress uniform, flanked a pathway to where Captain Lauretta Giannovi and Brigadier Kira Zamarano waited, both holding perfect salutes as Isaac crossed the shuttle bay to them.

"Exile Fleet, arriving!" a perfectly-turned out Chief Petty Officer barked loudly.

"Captain, Brigadier," Isaac greeted the two women, a study in contrasts. Giannovi shared his own merely average height and pitch-black hair, her darkly tanned skin only a few shades lighter than his own. Zamarano was as poorly matched to her Spanish surname as Giannovi was perfectly matched to her Italian one. She towered over both Captain and Admiral, a blonde Amazon who didn't need battle armor to intimidate.

"Admiral, welcome home," Giannovi told him as Zamarano dropped her own salute. "*Vigil* awaits your command."

Isaac sighed and nodded. "Walk with me, Captain, Brigadier," he ordered. "I know the way."

The Marines saluted as he and the two senior officers moved out from the flight bay. Memories of the two years he'd spent aboard *Vigil* rushed back. He knew the way from the flight bay to the flag deck without thinking—he could probably navigate most of the warship blindfolded.

"How long have you been aboard, Captain?" he asked Giannovi.

"Three and a half hours," she admitted. "They've been very careful about how many people were getting aboard and how quickly. I think they might have been afraid that we'd manage to unblock the guns before we made transit."

He chuckled.

"Any chance of that?" he asked. "I won't pretend I think we can fight Cohen's fleet, but options are always good."

"Commander Popovski says it's unlikely," she admitted. Vusala Popovski was *Vigil*'s chief engineer, and if he said it wasn't doable, it wasn't doable. "He came aboard with me and immediately went to check on the guns."

"What is our status?"

"We have no missiles aboard and every pulse gun is physically disconnected from both power and the plasma conduits." She shook her head. "From what Popovski has told me, we have a couple of corridors down in Engineering that have basically been re-floored with deactivated plasma conduits. We have the components, but getting more than a handful of pulse guns online will take days."

"And the particle cannon?" Isaac asked.

"Same story, give or take," she said. "Every cyclotron is disconnected from power and from the cannon chambers. Even if we *had* power, it takes twenty-six hours to warm up the cyclotrons from a cold start to standby."

He nodded silently. No battlecruiser in the Confederacy Space Fleet would ever have been caught dead without the cyclotrons that fed their primary weapon at standby. Cold cyclotrons were for ships in dry dock.

A standby cyclotron could fire one pulse while spinning up to full power, a process that took four minutes, but then could feed the cannon a packet of near-c charged ions every sixty seconds.

Vigil had seven cyclotrons attached to her particle cannon, one more than any other battlecruiser in the fleet.

"So, we can't fight," he said quietly. "Hermes is fully in their control, so we can't run. I guess there's only one thing left for us to do."

They'd reached the flag deck and the doors slid open. The main holographic tank was online, showing the dozens of spaceships swarming around Hermes Station. Between Exile Fleet and its guardians, there were over a hundred ships on the display.

"Speaking as the, ah, uneducated jarhead here, just what is that one thing?" Zamarano asked.

Isaac stepped up to the tank, studying the warships, freighters, and colony ships that would carry the former rebels to the other side of the galaxy.

"We do what they tell us," he admitted. "We go into exile. We forget the Confederacy ever existed. We forget who we leave behind and what we fought for here.

"We go into exile," he repeated, "and we build a better world than the one we leave behind."

———

7

"We leave you here, Miss Lestroud," the Sergeant leading the security detail told her. The towering man looked through the lock into the colony ship and shook his head. "Normally, these things have pretty solid order in place before anyone goes aboard, but now…"

He shrugged.

"I don't care much for the rebels," he admitted, "but I'm surprised to see you here. Who got you into this mess? You're too famous for this!"

Amelie smiled warmly at the man and dipped her head.

"They called me Archangel, Sergeant," she told him. "No one 'got me into this mess.' I led the whole damn thing—and if we need order in here, I think we will manage that ourselves.

"Without the Confederacy's help."

Even as the Marine was blinking at her, Barry Wong and half a dozen other men and women of a similar build to the Sergeant closed in behind Amelie as she held the man's gaze—and then stepped across the invisible line into the colony ship that would bear her into exile.

"Do we know who got stuck in command of this one?" she asked Wong as she strode deeper into the ship. The colony ship would be a maze of corridors and chambers, with about a fifth of its volume consumed by a large atrium intended to both transport plant life to the new colony and keep the colonists sane and oxygenated.

She wasn't sure how many colony ships there were in this mess. What she *was* sure of, however, was that she needed to get hooked into the communications networks and reach out to her cells on the other ships.

The rebels had the organization to make sure the ships ran smoothly and safely—and there were enough cases of colony ships turning into turf war-ridden gang territories inside of a few months that she knew some order *had* to be arranged.

"That would be me," a voice with a thick Indian accent interrupted their discussions. "And you have no idea how much it cost me to make sure I knew which transport you were on, Miss Lestroud."

Amelie looked at the broad-shouldered and dark-skinned Terran man standing in the hallway. Half a dozen others, wearing security armor and carrying shock sticks, accompanied him.

"I don't believe we've met," she told him. "I am Amelie Lestroud."

"The entirety of humanity knows who you are, Miss Lestroud," the stranger replied. "I am Shankara Linton, the Captain of this ship by grace of being a ship captain before this mess and, well, having men willing to follow me."

He gestured to the armed guards around him.

"Now, I bought the knowledge of your arrival time with the intention of offering my protection in exchange for certain personal favors," he said frankly, looking her up and down lasciviously, and then smiled brilliantly as he studied Wong.

"Instead, I find you with an entourage and an attitude I did not expect. So, tell me, Miss Lestroud, what would you have of the Captain of *Star of Delights*?"

"You weren't one of ours, I'm guessing?" she said flatly.

He laughed.

"One of the rebellion, I presume you mean?" he asked. "No. I was a smuggler, Miss Lestroud. Perhaps other things on occasion, but never a rebel. Certainly *scum*, though, as seems to be the criteria the First Admiral has used for her selection.

"You, then, were more senior in the rebellion than I expected.

'Archangel,' you called yourself to the Marine. He even seemed to know what that meant." Linton studied her. For all that he'd admitted he'd been planning to try and intimidate her into sexual favors, he seemed open to other possibilities.

"So, I repeat myself: What would you have of me, Miss Lestroud? And what would you offer in return?"

"I need full access to the communications between the colony ships —if possible, to whatever escorts and cargo vessels are coming with us as well," she laid out briskly. "Do you want to try and hold a quarter of a million people in line by force, Captain Linton? Do you have enough thugs and leg-breakers for that?"

He hesitated for a long moment.

"I can give you that access," he finally confirmed. "But what do you intend to do with it that could keep our passengers in line?"

"I was Archangel," she repeated. "The leader of the Alpha Cell of the rebellion. That means I know who all the Bravo cell leaders are and most of the Charlie leaders, too. If I can get communications, I can reactivate those cells. I can turn what was intended as a rebellion into some framework of authority and government to keep us all sane until we know what the hell is going to happen."

There was one Bravo leader she didn't know. She had her suspicions, now, who Bombardier had been...but she didn't even know if Isaac Gallant had survived his revolt against his mother.

Linton was still studying her. He wasn't looking at her breasts anymore, either, focusing on her face and her eyes. He was silent for longer than she'd hoped, seconds ticking by into nearly a full minute of their two groups of guards facing each other down.

Then he nodded and gestured to his men.

"Let's see what happens, Miss Lestroud," he told her. "For now, though, I am your man." He smiled again. "If only because you have a plan and I'm honest enough to admit that I don't."

———

LINTON LED her and Wong into the colony ship's command center, a space that drove home just how fragile the Indian smuggler's control of the ship was. The command center was a four-story spiral around a central display tank, designed for a crew of over two hundred to handle every part of the ship's affairs from balancing oxygen recycling to piloting the immense behemoth.

Linton had less than a dozen people manning key stations, enough to fly the ship and *maybe* make sure the life support didn't accidentally poison them all.

"You need help," Amelie told him.

"I know," he admitted. "They gave me a list of the people aboard with ship experience, but how do I know who to trust? Many of the people aboard are like me: criminals, not rebels with consciences. What would *you* do?"

"Barry?" Amelie said to her subordinate.

"We'll have to see who's aboard," the tall Cherbourgian said distractedly, studying the main display. "There were definitely people on Cherbourg who could work on a starship that I trust, and if we've got more than one planet's worth of dissidents aboard…"

"We've probably got another Bravo cell, you're right," the actress agreed, then realized that Wong hadn't trailed off to let her finish for him. She stepped out onto the edge of the platform, studying the holographic display showing everything around them.

"Where the *hell* are we, Linton?"

"I don't have a damned clue," the captain admitted. "I *think* that station is some kind of super-wormhole generator, how they're planning on sending us away from everyone else. As for the rest…" He shrugged.

"There's only so many pulsars out there, but I guess it doesn't matter."

Amelie wasn't entirely familiar with the iconography being displayed—she'd *seen* it before, but she didn't actually have to understand what the displays behind her in her movies actually meant—but she could read some of it.

"Captain, am I reading this correctly? Sixteen colony transports? Six *battlecruisers*?"

"You're reading it correctly," Linton told her. "Four of the battle-cruisers appear to be our guard dogs, though. The other two, though... well, the other battlecruisers have their main guns trained on them. I think they may be yours."

"Do we have a communication network with the rest of the exiles yet?"

"Officially, we're only hooked up to the other colony ships," the smuggler replied. "I, of course, have definitely not short-circuited the security on their systems and set up a direct laser with *Vigil*. I promise."

"*Vigil*?" Amelie asked. "It's definitely *Vigil*?"

"I know the ship. I haven't talked to any officers aboard, yet, just one of the communication NCOs who helped me set up the link."

"Damn. Is Gallant aboard her?"

"I don't know," Linton admitted. "You mean... the kid, right, not the Iron Bitch?"

Amelie laughed.

"Isaac Gallant is many things, including apparently a traitor to the Confederacy like the rest of us, but I'm not sure he counts as a 'kid.'"

———

THERE WERE over a dozen ships that Amelie should have reached out to. Forty-six Bravo cell leaders that she needed to make contact with, to establish a plan and a structure to hold them together as they jumped into the unknown.

She reached out to *Vigil* first.

"This is Chief Winther," a gruff voice answered. The only video feed she was getting was the unblinking eye of *Vigil*'s ship seal. "This channel should be secure, but I've got no guarantees as to what'll happen if the Confeds pick it up."

"Chief Winther, this is Amelie Lestroud," she told him. "You may have heard of me as Archangel. I need to speak to Admiral Gallant immediately."

The other end of the tightbeam laser was silent for several seconds.

"Yeah, all right, I see the point," Winther agreed. "I may not've mentioned that I had this channel set up to anyone on the bridge yet, you see. Flag deck and bridge have been swamped, trying to sort out what comes next, but Archangel…that's a name to conjure with, I hear.

"Let me see what I can do."

Amelie sat back in the chair on the communications floor of *Star of Delights'* command center. Behind her, she could hear Barry Wong arguing with someone over the ship's internal communicators. Sorting out *Star* was probably going to mostly fall on Wong and Linton.

Holding together the entire Exile Fleet, though, that was Amelie's job.

And, if everything broke right, Isaac Gallant's.

As if summoned by her thoughts, the image of *Vigil's* unblinking eye disappeared. In its place was the seated figure of a black-skinned man of medium height. His hair and eyes were even darker than his skin and the gaze he leveled on her was unreadable.

"Archangel," he greeted her. "You're not what I expected."

"Nor are you. Bombardier."

Gallant chuckled.

"I think even more people knew the name *Archangel* than knew the name *Bombardier*," he noted. "I wouldn't have guessed Archangel to be one of the Confederacy's most famous actresses, though I see the value and methodology now."

"And I never would have guessed that Bombardier would be Gallant's own son," Amelie said. "You stood to gain everything, Admiral. Why join us?"

"I stood to inherit dictatorship of a broken system," Gallant told her quietly. "I stood to inherit the debts and assets that irresistibly bound my mother to the corporations that broke the Confederacy the first time. I stood to step into shoes of a stronger person than I—one who *failed* to avoid the corruption that she raised her blade to burn out.

"What chains, do you think, would have fallen on 'the Iron Bitch's' successor?" he asked. "No, Miss Lestroud, I stood to gain *nothing*. And only by *breaking* the system could I fulfill my duty."

Even as she wanted to argue with him, his words ran down her spine with a fierce intensity she'd rarely encountered before. She'd triggered that feeling in others, she knew, but it was a rare man or woman who could make *her* spine straighten as they spoke.

"And we failed, Miss Lestroud. So, what do you seek now?"

"We need to hold these people together," she told him, letting the fire of his words fuel her in turn. "Sixteen colony ships, Admiral. Unless I miss my math, four *million* souls. And what plan did the First Admiral have for all of this?"

"She's given us every resource we could want, but she's throwing us to the other end of the galaxy," Gallant told Amelie. "However far you think we're going when they open that wormhole, Miss Lestroud, we're going farther.

"A light thrown into the darkness, to be a new spark for humanity far beyond where we could ever threaten or be threatened by the Confederacy." He shook his head. "Hold them together? Yes. How? Damned if I know."

"I have some thoughts," Amelie told him. "Are we actually getting those battlecruisers?"

"Two full battle groups," he confirmed. "No other flag officers but me, but full crews otherwise. Most of the support freighters are also manned by military personnel judged 'dissident.' I think I can keep them in line, convince them we have a cause, but I don't know if I can convince the civilians to follow.

"I'm a soldier *and* I'm the Iron Bitch's son," he said flatly. "Even if they would follow me, they *can't*. I *can't* lead them all without becoming everything we fought against."

"I can lead them," she said. "Not forever, but I can call on the cells and the rebellion, bring some order. I may need help bringing the ship captains in line, but I can get the civilians to follow."

"An interim government," Gallant noted. "We *must* hold elections once we're ready, to create what we promised."

"Agreed," Amelie said instantly. "People are confused and scared right now. I have the structure to give them hope, but we need to fulfill what we promised in the end."

He smiled.

"Good. I think we can work together, Miss Lestroud."

She laughed.

"If we're going to work together to lead everyone through this exile, Admiral Gallant, I think I must insist you call me Amelie."

His smile widened, and she couldn't help but return it.

"Then, Miss Amelie, I must insist you call me Isaac."

———

8

ENERGY FLICKERED along the arms of Hermes Station, exposed exotic-matter arrays glowing a strange blue as the oversized wormhole station's systems flared to life. Enough energy to power a world for a year blazed into space, and Isaac watched as reality *rippled*.

But, once again, nothing happened.

"Test pulse sixty-eight complete," Alstairs reported on *Vigil*'s flag deck. The battlecruiser was the closest ship in Exile Fleet to where the wormhole should open. *Dante*, the second battlecruiser, was the farthest ship.

Eight missile cruisers, six warp cruisers and twenty destroyers were positioned through the Fleet. None of them had functional weapons, but they were the only defense the civilian ships had.

Sixteen colony ships and twenty-four transports, including four Fleet munitions colliers, made up the true core of Exile Fleet. Seventy-six spaceships, a not-insignificant portion of the available ships in the Confederacy, waited for the wormhole to open.

"Test pulse sixty-nine, initiating," Isaac's operations officer noted as Hermes Station flared to life again.

Isaac checked. Sixty seconds, exactly, between test pulses. The forty-eight-hour window of possibility was going to consume an utterly insane amount of power before it was done, but Hermes Station's power cores and energy capacitors had been upgraded for just this mission.

"Dr. Schneider." The Admiral looked at one of the secondary screens on his flag deck. "Are we going to have any warning before XL-17 opens?"

The white-haired scientist-administrator running the test pulses looked exhausted as she shook her head.

"Nothing significant," she told him. "There's a reason for needing this many test pulses, Admiral. There's no sign, no warning, that the connection can be made. It depends on a specific alignment of the J2222-0137 pulsar with a second pulsar on the far side of the galaxy. We can calculate the rough window, but…"

She shrugged.

"Test pulse sixty-nine complete," she said calmly. "There is no question that we will be able to open XL-17 before the window closes. But there is no certainty inside that window at all."

"I understand," Isaac conceded. "You'll understand, Doctor, that I just want this over with."

"That's your choice," Schneider said sharply. "I cannot change the laws of physics—certainly not for a traitor. Be patient, Admiral."

Isaac shook his head as the physicist turned away, ignoring him to focus on her instruments. He muted his microphone for that channel and turned back to Alstairs.

"We're ready to go?" he asked quietly.

"Every ship has functioning engines and maneuvering control," his ops officer confirmed. "I have remote control of the warp cradle." Alstairs shook his head. "I still can't wrap my head around the distances involved. *Seventy-five thousand light-years*?"

"We don't get to come home afterwards," Isaac agreed. "We're going where only one set of humans has gone before."

Alstairs nodded.

"Pulse seventy complete," he reported. "This is going to take forever."

Isaac reactivated the channel.

"Any news, Doctor?"

"Only that I'm getting happier and happier it'll be over two hundred years before you can bother me again after this," she snapped. "It'll open when it opens, Admiral. And then good riddance to you."

The channel cut, and Isaac sighed.

"I don't think she likes me."

"Most of the people who agree with what we did are on those damned transports," Rose pointed out. "She's still sending the data channel, just cutting off the visual link."

"Anything interesting?" Isaac asked.

"No," Rose replied.

"Pulse seventy-one firing."

Nothing. *Wait…*

"Alstairs?" the Admiral asked.

"Something changed," the ops officer confirmed. "No wormhole, but I got a Cherenkov radiation feedback pulse."

"I guess Dr. Schneider may have some new data to play with," Isaac replied. "Pulse seventy-two?"

"Firing," Alstairs confirmed.

This time, it wasn't just a pulse. An entire section of space lit up in the odd blue of Cherenkov radiation, mixed with colors humanity had no name for as reality *tore*, a gateway opening to the other side of the Milky Way.

"There's our doorway," Isaac said calmly. "Is it stable?"

"All metrics read clean," his ops officer confirmed. "Giannovi?"

"We confirm," *Vigil's* Captain replied. "Everything looks good to go."

Vice Admiral Isaac Gallant exhaled slowly, rising to study the wormhole in the middle of his screen.

"Then I don't see much of a choice; do any of you?" he asked. His people were quiet and he smiled at them.

"Let's be about it."

———

IT TOOK all of Isaac's willpower not to hold his breath as the battlecruiser dove toward the portal. It didn't even *look* the same as a normal portal, with a strange purple-blue glow surrounding its edges in a way he'd never seen before.

But he needed his people to have faith, which meant that Isaac Gallant stood straight-shouldered as his ship entered the unknown. If he would never be able to return home again, then he would show the people sent into exile with him that there was nothing to fear.

The transition itself almost undermined that determination.

Until that day, he'd always thought that taking a wormhole transit at almost double the recommended speed would remain the worst experience of his life. He'd felt like someone had stabbed him with a sword that time, but his usual near-instantaneous subjective experience of the transit had spared him the worst of it.

This time, he felt like he was being pulled into quarters, each of his limbs trying to stretch away from his torso with brutal force. He managed to keep his reaction to a sharp inhalation…but the sensation didn't *stop*.

Seconds ticked by like eternities, and then it was finally over.

Carefully, as subtly as he could, Isaac released the breath he was now holding and checked that his limbs were still attached before turning to Cameron Alstairs.

"Ops," he said steadily. "Transition time?"

Alstairs blinked blankly for a few seconds, then swallowed and nodded, checking his systems.

"Seven point four two seconds, sir," he replied, then coughed to clear his throat. "Sure as hell didn't feel like it."

"No," Isaac agreed. "We'll probably want to record that for later analysis, get people's assessments of the transition."

He activated the intercom to the bridge.

"Captain Giannovi, how's your bridge crew?"

"Beaten and bruised," she replied. "That was one hell of a trip."

"Check in on your crew, Captain," Isaac ordered. "The reality is going to start sinking in on people quickly now. We need to be ready to support the colony captains and Miss Lestroud's people in maintaining order. Just in case."

"I know the drill, sir," Giannovi replied. "As I recall, *you* taught me it."

"*Tarantula* and *Scorpion* just made transit," Alstairs reported. "They're moving into escort positions."

Two warp cruisers. Isaac turned his attention back to the holographic display just as the first of the immense colony transports emerged, her engines sputtering in a way that told him everything he needed to know about her crews' experience.

"Alstairs, we're going to need to run traffic control," he told his ops officer. "None of these civilians and only a few of the Fleet personnel have made a high-velocity transit, and this is *worse*. They're coming through shattered.

"The *last* thing we need right now is a collision! There's no help for us out here."

NORMALLY, ships came through wormholes with their crews almost entirely functional. Even the gentlest wormhole transit was rough on a small portion of the population, but those people generally didn't end up on starship crews.

A seventy-five-thousand-light-year wormhole transit, it seemed, was a completely different situation. Ships' crews were disoriented, ships were flying off-course—in the case of one of the munitions colliers, the entire bridge section passed out.

Fortunately, *warship* crews self-selected for people who could handle wormholes better than most. Most of the ships of Battle Group *Vigil* and Battle Group *Dante* came through mostly in control of themselves—and all of the civilian ships could be remote-controlled with the right codes.

It took forty-five minutes, but every ship made it through intact. Finally, *Dante* herself flashed into existence, the battlecruiser marking the last transition of the Exile Fleet.

"Let's get *Dante* into a holding pattern with the rest of the warships," Isaac ordered. "We'll want status reports from everybody, especially the colliers.

"Currently, we are in the middle of nowhere by anyone's standards, but I want every warship fully armed and operational before we bring up the warp cradle," he continued. "Missiles loaded, cyclotrons on standby, pulse guns hooked up to the plasma conduits. I want us ready to protect the Fleet before we go anywhere."

"Yes, sir," Rose replied, the communications officer getting straight to work.

Isaac smiled and gestured Alstairs to where he stood by the holotank.

"Do we know where we are relative to the first expedition?" he asked. "I know they flagged four possible habitable worlds. Which one's closest?"

The ops officer looked past Isaac to the hologram. "Astrographics are updating as we speak," he promised. "My best guess is that we came out within the expected error radius: roughly a light-day. That means our closest target is Alpha."

"We're going to need a better name for it than that when we tell people what we're doing," Isaac replied. "How far?"

"We're still resolving and comparing back to the expedition's data," Alstairs replied. "But if we're where I think we are, about two point one light-years."

"Six months."

"Yep."

Isaac looked at the fleet in the hologram.

"That's going to be a foretaste of hell for a lot of these people," he said quietly. "I *think* Lestroud has most of the civilian side in hand, but we couldn't admit to much on the radio while we were still in Confederacy space."

"Sir!" One of Alstairs's technicians pointed. "The wormhole."

It flashed on the screen, one final pulse of blue energy, and was gone.

"Well, that's it, isn't it?" Isaac stated for everyone to hear. "No way home, people. Onward to Alpha."

———

9

Isaac was expecting the transmission from *Star of Delights* that linked into his office several hours later. He was, however, expecting a call from Amelie Lestroud and was rather surprised by the stuffy-looking bureaucrat type he found on his video call.

"Can I help you?" he asked slowly. "I don't believe we've met."

"Of course not," the man said rapidly. "I'm Werner Knutson, I'm the head of the Colonial Development Teams assigned to this project."

Isaac blinked at his speedy delivery, taking a second to process Knutson's words.

CD Teams were the technocrats who arranged and organized the implantation of governance structure, technology, industry...basically, *everything* at a new colony.

"I didn't think we were getting a Colonial Development Team," he noted slowly. "I didn't think that the Corps would have a great many dissidents for my mother to exile with us."

Knutson shrugged.

"We didn't," he replied. "We're all volunteers. Which means we were all at least sympathizers, though not openly enough to warrant being tossed on the ships involuntarily."

"Volunteers for...what, exactly, Mr. Knutson?" Isaac asked.

"Colonial development," Knutson replied, as if stating the obvious. "Each of the transports has a full two-hundred-person CDT in a secured section away from the general population. We'll be responsible for managing the deployment of the industrial and infrastructure base included on the colony ships and the accompanying freighters.

"We'll need your assistance, of course," he continued. "It's looking like it's going to be a bit of a mess by the time we arrive, but we'll need workers and backup to get our job done. We'll probably need your Marines to recruit the necessary labor force."

Isaac finally caught up, and he knew his smile was unpleasant.

"Let me make sure I understand what you're asking for correctly," he said slowly. "You are expecting me to use my Marines to basically acquire forced labor crews to complete your infrastructure projects?

"Does that not sound, Mr. Knutson, like *exactly* what we left behind?" Isaac demanded. "I will not rebirth the same dictatorial nightmare the Confederacy became in our new home. We will not use slave or forced labor to establish our new home."

Knutson paused, seeming to slow down to think for the first time since the conversation had begun.

"I'm not sure what alternative you expect us to have, Admiral," he told Isaac. "We have ships stuffed full of rebels and dissidents with only minimal organization or structure. Six months in warp is only going to create more chaos.

"I would prefer not to use forced labor, in fact, but it will almost certainly require the intervention of your Marines simply to maintain order when we reach Alpha."

They *really* needed a new name for the planet. Most of the ideas that had come to Isaac, however, were things like "Haven"—great ideas except for having shown up in famous movies and entertainment.

"I think we have an alternative you may have missed, Mr. Knutson," Isaac replied. "I have no intention of allowing the populations of the colony transports to fall into anarchy. Measures have already been taken, but we were obviously not being public about them while we were in J22.

"If I come aboard *Star of Delights*, will you be prepared to meet with me and certain others in person? I think we need to make a plan for how we're going to handle the next six months."

The bureaucrat looked taken aback, but there was something else in his stance and eyes. He slowly nodded, leaning forward and steepling his hands on the desk.

"Admiral Gallant, I would be *delighted* to handle this in a less… disastrous manner," he admitted. "We will open the CDT section of *Star of Delights* once you are aboard. Only a small contingent, please. We are technically still a branch of the Confederacy government. We have reason to be paranoid."

"Then that, Mr. Knutson, is one of the first things we're going to need to fix," Isaac told him. "You're here on the ass end of the galaxy with us. You're not Confed anymore.

"You're Exile Fleet now."

———

EVERYONE in the Confederacy knew what Amelie Lestroud looked like, Isaac reflected, but it was still something different to meet her in person. She'd been a famous actress for almost as long as he'd been a Confederacy Space Fleet officer, starting out in her teens before becoming one of the most sought-after performers in human space.

She was taller than he'd expected, too, towering a good ten to twelve centimeters over his own modest height, with braided blonde hair that reached halfway down her back. As she shook his hand in greeting, however, he found that his assessment of her lined up more with what he would have expected of Archangel than the movie star.

"Miss Lestroud—Amelie. It is a pleasure to meet you in person," he told her with a smile. "Whether we're talking the actress or the rebel leader, I've wanted to do so for quite some time. I'll admit I'm more impressed with Archangel than your performance in, say, *Stars of Honor*, but…"

He shrugged, and she laughed, a soft golden sound that sent a shiver down his spine.

"I have yet to meet any military officer who was overly impressed with any of my military films," she noted. "I could tell you a good thirty or forty ways we *knew* we were getting things wrong in the Honor films, but there's always what the audience expects."

Isaac shared her laugh.

"I know. I swear the first year in the Academy was always beating the movie illusions out of our new recruits' heads." He smiled. "I'm glad to meet you in person for more immediate reasons, too. How goes our provisional government?"

"Is that what you're calling it?" Lestroud asked. "Because I'm still regarding it as bullying everyone into line."

"Call it what you will, these people need a leader and it *can't* be me," Isaac reminded her. "So, how is it going?"

"We have…order," she told him. "Not everyone answered my call. About a quarter of the old Bravo cell leaders are dead, and at least half a dozen more are refusing to acknowledge my calls.

"But that still leaves me at least one Bravo cell on each colony ship. They've linked into the lower-level cells, and we're a good chunk of the way to assembling a police force across the fleet. A couple of the colony-ship captains are being less than cooperative, though. I think they thought they were going to be in charge."

"To a degree, they need to be," Isaac pointed out. "A starship captain has to be the master after god of their own ship. But…they also need to work with whatever governing structure we need to hold together. If anyone gives you too much trouble, let me know. I have a Brigadier who needs to work off some frustrations, and beating an idiot captain or two into line would make her feel *so* much better."

Lestroud laughed again.

"What brings you to *Star of Delights*, Admiral?" she asked. "Not that I'm not pleased to meet you myself, but…I would expect us to be getting underway shortly?"

"Thirty-six hours until the warships are fully reequipped and the warp cradle is online," Isaac said instantly. "We have some time, and it appears that we also have a set of Colonial Development Corps teams aboard the colony ships.

"They're all volunteers, and they're somewhat concerned about how to hold everything together until we get to Alpha."

"CD Teams?" Lestroud asked. "They could be very useful."

"Right now, I think they think they answer to me," he told her. "But they're civilians, not military, which means they answer to the provisional government—and CDTs are also the people we'll want to help us hold together that provisional government.

"So, they need to answer to you," he concluded. "That's why I'm here. We need that chain of authority sorted out now, not at the last minute in orbit of Alpha."

Lestroud pursed her lips.

"We need a better name for that planet."

"Part of me just wants to call it 'Exile,' but that may end up being too much of a reminder," Isaac agreed.

"A problem for later, I suppose," she said. "For now, shall we go inform the bureaucrats who they report to?"

––––––

THE SECTION that Isaac had been directed to turned out to be blocked off by what appeared to be a solid wall. As they approached, however, it slid aside, and a pair of Colonial Development Corps constables stepped out.

The constables would, in normal circumstances, act as bodyguards for the CD Team members and a training cadre for the new planetary police. In this rather more complex situation, they clearly expected to have to protect the teams from the rest of the "colonists" of Exile Fleet.

"Admiral Gallant," the older one greeted him. "Mr. Knutson is waiting. I know he asked for a small contingent, though."

The constables were eyeing the two fireteams of Marines that had accompanied Isaac—and he doubted the equivalent number of burly men in ship's security uniforms and shock sticks who'd accompanied Lestroud were helping their calm.

"Just three of us, constable," Isaac assured him. "Myself, Brigadier Zamarano and Miss Lestroud."

He glanced over at Lestroud.

"I'm assuming, I suppose, that *Star of Delight*'s security will let you out of their sight?"

The Admiral was reasonably certain that the men in ship's security uniforms were actually members of the rebellion assigned to keep Lestroud safe, but *Star*'s crew appeared to have fallen completely in line behind the rebel leader.

"Mr. Collins?" Lestroud asked, glancing back at her guards.

"We're yours to command, Miss Lestroud," the largest of them replied. "You want us to wait, we wait. You want us to shock this pair into submission, tie 'em up and frog-march 'em through the atrium as an example, well..."

Collins grinned wickedly. He was *trying* to make the constables think he was joking.

Unless Isaac was misreading the man entirely, he wasn't.

"Just the three of us, then," Lestroud said with a smile at the constable. "Let's meet this Mr. Knutson, shall we? It sounds like we have some work to do, going forward."

———

KNUTSON LOOKED MORE than a little surprised at the two women accompanying Isaac into the meeting room, but his largest surprise was clearly reserved for Amelie Lestroud.

"Miss Lestroud"—he inclined his head—"I was aware you were among the exiles, but I didn't expect to meet you directly anytime soon."

"Before we get any further, I think proper introductions are in order," Isaac said with a firm smile. "Amelie Lestroud is also Archangel, the leader of the rebellion, the woman who convinced *me* that she could field a Confederacy-wide armed revolution to backstop the coup I was going to launch in Sol."

From his expression, Werner Knutson hadn't been expecting anyone to be quite so frank about what had got them all exiled.

"Of the four million-plus people in Exile Fleet, only about three hundred and fifty thousand were directly or indirectly part of the rebellion," the Admiral continued. "Miss Lestroud has been attempting to run communications through her cell network and bring the former rebellion back online as a provisional government.

"My understanding is that she has succeeded sufficiently that I have no hesitation recognizing Miss Lestroud as the civilian head of government for Exile Fleet," Isaac said. "Which means, given that I intend to honor the principle of military subordination to civilian authority of the Confederacy's founders, she is now my boss.

"*Our* boss."

Lestroud seemed taken aback by Isaac's determination, which was a sign she didn't know him well yet. The last thing Isaac wanted to do was repeat his mother's mistakes.

Knutson was studying her carefully, then wordlessly gestured the two military officers and the once-rebel leader to seats.

"We did not expect there to be any form of civilian government beyond the minimal governance structure of the ships' crews," he admitted. "How...how much authority and control can your...rebellion exert?"

"We didn't get everyone to report back in," Lestroud told Knutson after a quick glance at Isaac. "But, as of my last check-in with my Bravo cell leaders, I've got between three and ten thousand volunteers on each colony ship.

"For the moment, I've mostly got them acting as citizen peacekeepers, but we'll need to move in the direction of taking over general administrative tasks as soon as possible.

"The rebellion provides us with a framework of hierarchy and people, but we need to make that a governing structure and not an army as soon as possible," she concluded. "We're working on getting the last of the starship captains in line—Admiral Gallant has promised us assistance there—but we need to find a way to make the rest of the exiles, the people who are stuck out here *because* of us, respect our authority."

"Provide leadership and they will follow," Knutson pointed out. "These people are scared, lost and confused. They have questions, and no one has answers. If we make sure your people do have those answers for them, many of them will fall into line.

"You need to decide how provisional this structure is going to be," he noted calmly. "I have a few hundred CDC people on each ship; we can work with your organization, set up the administration and policing frameworks to hold everything together if you can provide the authority and manpower.

"But…we'll do different things if we're going to be running an election six months after we land than if we're going to operate under this structure for a while."

Knutson looked perfectly calm. Not at all like he'd just admitted he'd help Isaac and Lestroud install themselves as permanent dictators of this exiled portion of humanity.

"If I was going to install myself as God-Empress of Alpha, I think the Admiral would find someone else to replace me soon enough," Lestroud said drily, and Isaac choked.

"That…might be in disagreement with the theory of subordination to civilian authority," he told her. "But yes, I would probably find some way to discourage you."

Knutson sighed in relief.

"I'd probably have tried to find some way myself," he admitted. "My first task, Miss Lestroud, Brigadier Zamarano, Admiral Gallant, is to make certain we all survive. To build a new civilization out here.

"It's not really my role to judge what form that civilization takes. If you want to set yourself up as the Empress of Alpha, my job description says I shouldn't stop you. But…" He shrugged. "We volunteered for this trip for a reason. You've probably got every idealist *left* in the Confederacy's Colonial Development Corps."

"We didn't plan a rebellion out of a lack of ideals," Lestroud told him. "Six months after landing sounds about right for an election to me. Admiral?"

"That, Miss Lestroud, Mr. Knutson, is entirely out of my court. And *staying* that way," Isaac said firmly. "I remain merely the commander of Exile Fleet. When we reach Alpha, I will simply be the Vice Admiral in charge of your defenses."

Lestroud chuckled.

"That just sounds silly, Admiral Gallant," she noted. "The sole flag officer of our new nation, a *Vice* Admiral? Don't you agree, Mr. Knutson?"

"I have learned in my career that it is never wise to disagree with your boss," the stuffy little man said firmly.

"I think you need to get yourself some new insignia, *Admiral* Gallant," Lestroud ordered. "Consider it a test of your submission to civilian authority, *non?*"

———

10

Isaac was about to re-board his shuttle to return to *Vigil* when his tattoo-comp buzzed and Giannovi's face appeared above his arm, his flag captain looking discomfited.

"What is it, Captain?" he asked crisply.

"We have a problem," she replied. "Well, several problems, really. Battle Group *Vigil* knows you, boss. Enough of *Scorpion*'s crew knows you that they're loyal too, and they've apparently talked *Wasp*'s crew around as well."

That was every warp cruiser, at least. But if Giannovi was implying what he thought, he was in trouble.

"And the rest of Battle Group *Dante*?" he asked carefully.

"I guess the word *mutiny* doesn't have much legal weight with JAG on the other side of the galaxy," she said with a sigh. "It's more of a sit-down strike than a mutiny. Some of the ships are just refusing to obey orders as a body; others just have chunks of their crew refusing to do anything.

"Most of *Dante*'s officers are with us, but the crew has simply stopped working," she told him.

"Any idea what they want?" he asked.

She chuckled bitterly.

"I'm not sure any of them know what they want," she told him. "What they *need*, Admiral, is a reason to have faith. Battle Group *Dante*'s crews weren't rebels, boss. Mostly, they weren't even crews. Their ship companies were randomly assembled from troublemakers and dissidents from the entire space fleet.

"They have nothing to believe in now. They were troublemakers, but they were Fleet. Now…now they don't know what they are."

"Now they're exiles and it's not even their fault," Isaac agreed. He considered for a long moment, then unclipped his vice admiral's insignia. He'd obey Lestroud's instruction and start calling himself an Admiral once this was over, but if he was going to fix this, it wouldn't be with hierarchy and force.

"Tell them I'm coming to *Dante*," he ordered. "Link the shuttle's exterior cameras to the rest of the military ships. Tell them that I am coming to listen, not to dictate, and if they have questions, they can bring them to me."

"And what happens if they bring pulse rifles, sir?"

"Then they will rapidly discover that Kira brought an entire squad along with me as an escort," he reminded her. "I *want* to listen. I *will* survive."

"You'd better. I might be able to lead Battle Group *Vigil*, but I can't lead the Exile Fleet for you, sir."

"They're lost, Captain Giannovi," Isaac said softly. "If I can lead them out of that fog, then I can lead them anywhere."

Amelie Lestroud could declare him an admiral all she wanted. But if he was going to command the warships of the Exile Fleet, then he needed these men and women, these mutineers, to obey.

———

DANTE's FLIGHT deck was full, packed with a watching crowd. More packed than was safe, in fact, and it was only by dint of extraordinary flying on the part of Isaac's pilot that no one was injured.

He was quite sure that more than a few of the gathered spacers got more of a face-full of ionic rocket exhaust than they'd prefer. Hopefully, any of them who acquired more than the equivalent of a bad sunburn would be sensible enough to seek the med bay.

Nonetheless, Isaac waited for the shuttle to land and for the area around it to cool, watching the gathered crowd through the cameras with a cautious eye.

"If there are pulse rifles or even bloody dart guns out there, you'll be dead before we can intervene," Zamarano noted. "Can I *please* send Marines out with you?"

"No," Isaac told her, straightening his plain black uniform. It wasn't a dress uniform, and he'd already taken off his insignia. Any officer, from the rawest Ensign to the First Admiral of the Confederacy, could have worn the same uniform.

"I need to earn their trust, Brigadier," he said calmly. "The first step to that is to show I trust them."

She chuckled.

"Look at their eyes, Admiral," she told him. "They know what you said—and they're still expecting my people to storm out of this shuttle with stunners and rifles, to force obedience and execute the ringleaders.

"It's what your mother would do."

"I am not my mother," Isaac reminded her.

"I know that," Zamarano agreed. "They don't."

"I know," he replied. "That's what I need to show them. You're all waiting here."

The Marine officer sighed theatrically—but nodded and hit the button to open the shuttle's hatch.

"Your adoring audience awaits."

———

Isaac Gallant walked down the ramp onto the deck of the battlecruiser. The silence in the open space was amazing to him. No starship was ever truly *silent*, but there had to be five hundred people crammed onto *Dante*'s flight deck, and no one was speaking.

He walked away from the shuttle, toward the densest part of the crowd and turned a calm glance on them.

"So," he said. "Are you going to make me stand here, or can someone bring me a chair?"

The confused arguments and side glances that followed answered his real question. No one was in charge there. This wasn't some grand conspiracy. It was exactly what it appeared like—a spontaneous gesture by a crew that barely knew each other and barely knew what they'd got into.

After a few seconds, a grizzled older man with a Chief's stripes brought him a folding chair.

"Sorry about this, sir," he said gruffly. "Not what you expected from Fleet, I'd guess."

"I don't know about that, Chief," Isaac replied as he took a seat and studied the crowd. "I don't see violence here. I don't see the Captain crucified to the wall over there. I see a bunch of very intelligent officers and spacers who have no goddamned clue what's going on. Was this the best way to handle those concerns?"

He shrugged.

"Hell, no," he told them. "But you could have done a lot worse." He gestured to the shuttle. "The shuttle's cameras are running. We're sending this to every ship in Battle Groups *Vigil* and *Dante*. You speak for thirty thousand spacers.

"I'm here to answer your questions, address your concerns. I have no moral authority here except what you give me. I *want* you to follow me. I will not make you.

"So, ask."

For all of the chaos they'd created to get him there, none of the sort-of-mutineers seemed to know what to say. The quiet stretched on for ten seconds, twenty. More.

Finally, the Chief who'd brought him the chair cleared his throat.

"Where are we, sir?" he asked.

"You all got the briefing, but it's one thing to see that package and another thing to understand just what has happened," Isaac agreed. "Best guess? We are somewhere between seventy-five and seventy-six thousand light-years from the J22 binary pulsar. We have no way of going home.

"This was First Admiral Gallant's idea of mercy, so she ordered every possible dissident they could find swept up and stuck on those transports. Four million troublemakers, protesters, rebels, smugglers… and us. Half of us rebels and mutineers, who raised our hands against the Iron Bitch.

"The rest of you? You didn't follow me into rebellion against my mother. But you're here nonetheless. You got flagged as troublemakers. Mouthy. Potential problems. And this was your reward."

He gestured around.

"We are roughly two light-years away from a habitable world that is designated Alpha," he told them. "We are going to call it Exilium."

The word came from nowhere, a remnant of decades-ago Latin courses. It *meant* Exile, but that step of removal might salve the wound in time—while keeping the memory. If Isaac had his way, this branch of humanity would forgive the Confederacy without forgetting what had happened.

"And we've got some kind of warp drive to get us there?" a new voice asked.

"Exactly," Isaac replied. "It's a one-shot giant device called a warp cradle." He smiled. "I hate to be the one to break it to you, but if you don't come with Exile Fleet, well, you aren't going anywhere quickly."

The warp cruisers were with him. That meant *Dante* was actually the only ship that had a chance of reaching one of the other systems. The closest of those was four light-years away, however. At best, that would take Dante somewhere between sixteen and twenty years. The battlecruiser could theoretically sustain her crew that long.

Theory was not practice. Most likely, they would kill each other long before they reached Charlie.

"We…What if we don't want to be Fleet anymore?" someone else asked. "If we're troublemakers, it's 'cause many of us were done with what the Fleet wanted us to do and be. What if we're still done?"

Isaac nodded and sighed.

"The problem is that those colony transports are packed," he admitted. "We have nowhere else to put any of you, and we need these ships to make it to Exilium. We need *you* to fly them to Exilium."

"And if we don't want to?" a voice shouted. "Will you make us?"

"No," he said flatly. "I won't make anyone do shit. But there's nowhere else for you to go, and if you don't have enough to fly the ship by the time we bring the cradle online...I would prefer not to leave anyone behind, but the choice is yours."

"That's bullshit. You may as well be making us!"

"That's fair," Isaac agreed. "I don't have a choice, so I suggest a compromise."

"What kind of compromise?" the original Chief demanded.

"Give me six months, people," Isaac asked them. "Give me six months and we can bring this fleet to Exilium, our new home. Then you can join the colony on the surface—all of you, if you want. I'd rather only have half our ships properly crewed than draft you, but I need you to bring those ships home.

"But for six months, I need you to be spacers still. I need you to follow your officers' orders and do your jobs. Keep your ships from falling apart around you."

He held up a hand to forestall further comments.

"We are no longer the Confederacy Space Fleet," he reminded them. "Beyond the obviously necessary, I see no reason to enforce the codes and regulations. Keep it clean and keep it off duty, and your officers will ignore booze, fraternization, whatever.

"But we've brought four million people to the far end of nowhere," Isaac said quietly. "These starships, these warships, are their only hope for safety. You don't owe me or these colonists anything, so I am *asking* you: please.

"Please give me those six months so that I can make certain our families are safe."

———

11

BACK ON HIS FLAG DECK, Isaac watched the warships of his fleet fall into proper defensive formation. Most of the weapons were back online, the components never having been entirely removed from the ships. The Confederacy had wanted to make sure they didn't try and shoot their way out of J22 while still allowing for them to defend themselves here.

"What's the status of the warp cradle?" he asked.

"We're beginning the initiation sequence now," Alstairs replied. "This isn't going to be fast, boss. The damn tube is fifty-five kilometers long. Just forming it into a circle is going to take most of a day."

Rockets mounted on the ends of the cradle flared as Isaac watched, the long snake they'd dragged through the wormhole with them beginning to move, its ends slowly drifting together.

"Do we have a course plotted for Exilium?" Isaac asked.

"Right, that's what we're calling it now," his ops officer replied, shaking his head. "More evocative than *Alpha*, anyway. It's not much of a course," he continued. "The cradle doesn't have a lot of maneuverability. Point at the destination, calculate the travel time, turn it on."

"That's it?"

"That's it. Don't turn it off until we're done, too. There's no second chance with this thing, Admiral," Alstairs pointed out. "I don't know how they managed to put it together to create a stable drive ring on this scale, but it's a one-shot deal.

"Once we collapse the warp bubble the cradle creates, it can never create another one. We should be able to mine the damn thing for exotic matter afterward, but no one in this expedition has a clue how to restore a seventeen-kilometer-across warp drive ring."

"Please tell me we at least have people who can maintain the drive rings for the cruisers," Isaac asked. "I know from bitter experience how rusty even the people supposed to be running the grav-warp drive sections can get with the things."

Alstairs nodded.

"Most of our grav-warp teams seem pretty competent, and I'm making sure they brush up on everything. We've got some volunteers from all six warp cruisers to go over to the cradle once it's live."

"That is not a job I'd take," Isaac murmured. "I hope there's at least *some* decent quarters over there?"

Once the cradle engaged, no one would be able to move between ships. The warp bubble wasn't stable enough for anything smaller than the starships to be able to survive. The volunteers manning the cradle would be trapped in the control center for six months.

"Looks like," Alstairs confirmed. "The folks who put this whole affair together knew what they were dumping on us. No idea how comfortable they are, but there's at least a set of apartments for them to sleep in."

"Going to be a long six months," Isaac said. "At least we can be relatively sure not much is going to happen during it."

"Assuming none of the ship crews or passengers devolve into cannibalistic anarchy," his ops officer replied. "It's been known to happen with ships lost for too long without rescue."

"Every ship has food, water, entertainment, friends," Isaac said quietly. "And Miss Lestroud's people making sure some order is kept. We'll keep our eyes open, but…"

"But there's fuck all we can do if one of the ships is lost along the way, Admiral," Alstairs told him. "If I may make a suggestion?"

"That would be your job, wouldn't it?"

The younger man chuckled.

"Split our Marines up, make sure there's a detachment on every ship that's working with Lestroud and Knutson's people," he suggested. "Hopefully, their presence alone will be enough to head off trouble—and if it's not, well…"

"Better for Lestroud's 'provisional government' to have real soldiers than volunteer militia," Isaac agreed. "Good call, Ops."

———

AMELIE LESTROUD NOW HAD AN OFFICE. She wasn't sure who the office was *supposed* to belong to—a colony transport like *Star of Delights* was supposed to have an entire corporate and governmental organization behind it that Exile Fleet lacked.

She didn't much care. Unlike many of the people around her, she didn't have a computer tattooed onto her arm—she'd had one faked for her military roles, but outside the Marines and Space Fleet, a tattoo-comp was a rare decision.

Most people just carried a tablet, though that simple description covered a vast variety of different portable computers.

Amelie's own was roughly the size of her thumb, a stick she could put down on any surface to project a holographic keyboard and screen. It would respond to voice commands in carry mode but was most useful when you were sitting down somewhere.

In her new office, it linked handily into the colony ship's computers, giving her full access to *Star*'s vast computing power and data-banks, as well as the starship's sensor feeds.

She was studying the warp cradle when Barry Wong stepped into her office, her new second-in-command looking exhausted.

"Hell of a show we're putting together," he told her. "Between me and Linton, we have *Star of Delights* humming along now. Pulled together a crew to keep her flying, got volunteers in armbands at every corridor crossing.

"Confed at least did us the courtesy of assigning rooms to people," he noted, "but just keeping people fed and sane for the next six months is going to be…frustrating."

Amelie nodded, gesturing to her own screen.

"*Star* sounds like she might be in the best shape," she told him. "But the captains have fallen into line and we've got everyone fully crewed and operating. Cooking rotations are probably going to be our first big project, mundane as they seem."

"Everybody's got to eat, and everybody's got to do something," Wong agreed. He sighed and took a seat. "What are we even *doing*, Amelie?" he asked. "We were supposed to be overthrowing a tyrant, not…whatever the hell this is."

"We were always going to have to build a new government," she pointed out. "We had plans in place. I'm leveraging them as best as I can, because we sure as hell weren't planning on using them to hold together an entire fleet of colony ships."

"That part was on you and Archie," the exhausted-looking man told her. "And now he's gone and I…I'm lost, Amelie. I'm going where you're pointing, but I barely see the path, let alone the destination."

"I know," she admitted. "Archie was…Without Archie, there never would have been a rebellion. I was the one who found people and talked to people and organized and connected and lied and…everything else.

"But it was Archie who had my back when I couldn't do it anymore," she told Wong. "Just as he had yours, always."

"He wouldn't want us to give up, would he?" Wong replied, brushing tears from his eyes. "Damn the man; just like him to be the highest-ranked rebel casualty!"

"He always had to be important," Amelie agreed, blinking away her own tears. Archie Dresden had been at her shoulder for years, over a decade. All of this…would have been easier with him. "But I think we honor him best by getting these people to Exilium and building a new home.

"We've got them looking to us to leadership. We just need to *keep* them looking to us until we arrive."

"What about Gallant?" Wong asked. "We all know true power flows from a barrel of a gun—and the Iron Bitch's son has most of the guns."

"I suspect he'd disagree with you there," she pointed out. "True power flows from the social contract, the will of the people. He's backing us, for now, because we need to keep these people safe.

"I'm not sure what would happen if Gallant thought I was going to set myself up as a dictator, but I don't think it would end well for anybody. I'm not sure, Barry, but I trust him. He doesn't *want* to be like his mother, to rule with an iron fist."

She shook her head, considering the average-looking black man leading Exile Fleet's warships with a smile.

"He has a job to do, same as us," she concluded. "If we work together, well…"

"Exilium awaits us," Wong replied. His cheeks were streaked with moisture, but he looked less tired now. "A new hope. A new dream."

"We'll make it right, Barry," Amelie promised. "If I have to build a new human civilization out here at the end of universe, then by all that is sacred, I will build it right."

———

"CALIBRATIONS COMPLETE. Cradle crew report self-tests complete. Colony transports in position. Freighters in position. Warships in position."

Alstairs continued his report, running down a checklist no one had ever used before and that would probably never be used again.

Isaac looked at the holographic tank, and then at the image of the woman on the screens next to his seat.

"Governor Lestroud," he greeted her, smiling as he gave her a title no one had officially dropped on her yet. "Exile Fleet is prepared to engage the warp cradle. Estimated time of arrival at Exilium is six months, seven days, thirteen hours and seventeen minutes after activation of the grav-warp bubble."

"I make that nineteen hundred hours on February first, 2387, Admiral," she replied. "Do we expect any problems?"

He kept the smile on his face. In truth, part of him half-expected the warp cradle to simply vaporize them all. It would be a neat solution to the Confederacy's problem—fling the Exiles to a place where no one was watching and have them vaporize themselves. On the other hand, it wouldn't have been *that* hard to fake an overly stressful wormhole transition and pretend they'd gone tens of thousands of light-years away, either.

It depended on how far he trusted his mother...and Isaac wasn't sure that Adrienne Gallant was owed even that much trust at this point.

"None expected," he told Lestroud brightly, though something in her gaze suggested she'd picked up what he couldn't say. Even if something *did* go wrong, there was nothing they could do. "This may not be a particularly efficient or fast method of travel compared to wormholes, Governor, but it's old enough that we know how it works."

Lestroud smiled.

"Do you have anything to say to the people of Exile Fleet?" she asked.

"I think that one is on you this time, Governor," Isaac told her. "I've only got one order left to give in this godforsaken corner of the void."

"I think we'll have plenty of time to talk to everyone before we reach Exilium, Admiral Gallant," Lestroud replied. "Give your order."

Isaac nodded and rose from his chair, crossing over to the holotank where Commander Catalan, once a direct subordinate of his and now the XO of one of his warp cruisers, waited. Catalan had transferred from *Tarantula* to the warp cradle itself, taking command of the team that would take them all.

"Commander Catalan, status?"

"Everything is green, Admiral," the engineer replied. "I'm assuming someone else tested this thing. If it works, it'll be the biggest warp bubble I've ever heard of, though."

Isaac arched an eyebrow, hopefully reminding Catalan that most of Exile Fleet was watching.

"Are we ready?"

"We're ready," Catalan said firmly.

"Then...engage."

There was no verbal response, just a series of new icons and data that flared to life as the exotic-matter ring contained in the cradle charged up and began to spin. Once it reached a specific angular velocity, the warp bubble itself would form.

At its target velocity, the bubble would move through space at four times lightspeed.

For the first few seconds, however, only the data markers told Isaac anything was happening. Then the air started to feel thick, a viscous sensation to his breath he'd only experienced a handful of times before.

There hadn't been much to see in this corner of space except for Exile Fleet itself, but everything except the ships vanished now as the cradle forged its bubble of nonlinear space and dragged them all along with it.

"One hundred percent of target angular velocity," Catalan reported. "Bubble is…stable. All ships are stable." The engineer shook his head. "I strongly recommend that none of the ships attempt to maneuver inside the bubble, Admiral. The space out there is even worse than I was anticipating. So long as we stay where we are in relation to the cradle, we'll be fine.

"I'm not sure even the battlecruisers could survive trying to actually *move* in this soup."

Isaac nodded, coughing to try and clear a phlegmy feeling in his throat he knew wouldn't go away.

"Thank you, Commander." He tried to swallow away the gunk in his mouth. That was no more successful than coughing had been.

The feeling of increased viscosity to the air was mostly psychosomatic, he was told, but it was also universal to every human who'd been in a gravity-warp bubble.

It was going to be a long six months.

———

12

"Warp bubble remains stable." The hourly report echoed across the flag bridge. A few grunts of acknowledgement were the only response. Ennui had set in months before. Six months had even allowed people to get somewhat used to the psychosomatic stickiness of being in warp.

Cameron Alstairs flashed his Admiral a sharp smile and Isaac nodded back. The man commanding Exile Fleet understood exactly what his people were feeling, but there was a point to this one. A point that six months of hourly reports from operations hadn't had.

"Estimated time to arrival is twenty-four hours," the ops officer continued, his voice ringing through the flag bridge. "All ships, all departments, begin final preparations.

"I repeat, warp bubble collapse is scheduled for twenty-four hours from now. All vessels and all departments are to begin final preparations."

Isaac studied the plot with its estimate of their location. It could only be an estimate—for over six months, all Exile Fleet had been able to see was each other, the warp cradle, and the soup of supercharged particles that filled the bubble.

If the previous expedition's data was correct, they were four light-days from the system originally code-named XL-17-3, and now named Exilium. The expedition had surveyed seven systems and found four habitable planets, an unusually high proportion.

But Alpha had been the first they found, in the third system they'd surveyed. It was the closest to the emergence of the XL-17 wormhole and so it was where they'd headed.

And they were almost there. In a sense, they *were* there. If something happened to the warp bubble now, they could make the rest of the trip under their regular engines. It would add weeks to the journey, but they would make it.

Alstairs crossed to his chair.

"We made it, sir," he said.

"We made it," Isaac repeated. "Well, we've mostly completed the trip, at least. I'll refrain from saying we've 'made it' until we've found somewhere worth settling and dropped the sixteen cities-in-a-box we're escorting onto a friendly planet."

"The expedition survey looks promising."

"The expedition survey was a single warp cruiser blasting through the system at a tenth of the speed of light taking photos and doing spectrographic analysis," Isaac pointed out. "We know Exilium has liquid water, continents, and a twenty-to-twenty-two percent oxygen content in the air. That's…enough to be habitable.

"It doesn't guarantee anything *pleasant*, however, and we know nothing about the plant life supplying that oxygen content or local animal life."

"Isn't that why the colony ships are carrying more livestock than people by biomass?"

"We have enough plants and animals to sustain the human population, yes," Isaac agreed. "But how does it change our projections if the local wildlife thinks our corn is the best treat since marijuana? Or, hell, if *humans* are functionally psychedelic chemicals to the local predators?"

Alstairs looked thoughtful.

"That could be troublesome," he admitted. "But we have security gear for that, don't we?"

"We do," Isaac agreed. "And what if said predators are, oh, four-ton pursuit predators that can leap electric fences? Or just don't hear at wavelengths our sonic deterrence gear can affect?"

"Scorched-earth protocols?" the ops officer said slowly.

"Yeah," Isaac confirmed. "Bombardment from orbit with plasma fire to clear areas entirely of local wildlife. It's a last damned option, one I'll make Knutson prove they need at least twice over, but if we go to that option, the bombardment has to be complete before we land the colony ships.

"So, no, Alstairs, we haven't made it. Not until we have four million civilians on Exilium, safe, warm and fed.

"Once we're *there*, I'll relax."

Alstairs chuckled.

"No, you won't," he replied. "Once we've got them safe on the ground, that's when you and I start plotting survey sweeps for the warp cruisers."

―――――

AT SOME POINT during the long voyage, Amelie Lestroud had apparently found a tailor aboard *Star of Delights*. She'd started wearing perfectly tailored suits every time Isaac saw her, suits that managed to enhance her already-staggering height and presence.

She looked every bit the Governor she'd been forced to become—only somewhat like the rebel princess she'd played in at least three movies.

"Twenty-four hours, huh?" she said after they'd made the connection between offices. "Doesn't feel quite real after the last few months."

"I'm just worried what air is going to taste like *outside* warp now," Isaac replied with a chuckle. "I never thought I'd get used to air aboard a ship in warp, but apparently, humans are more adaptable than I thought."

"And I am unbelievably grateful for that," she agreed. "The first few days and weeks, I thought breathing alone was going to give us riots."

They'd had surprisingly few of those. The trip had been almost stultifyingly boring, with only a handful of exceptions.

"Speaking of riots, what's the latest news from *Neverlight*?" Isaac asked.

"Much the same as it's been for the last two weeks," Lestroud told him with a sigh. "Captain Palmer has the bridge and Engineering secured and has evacuated air from the cargo holds. Your Marines have thrown back the attempts to take either of those sections, and something like ten percent of the crew is now incarcerated, and a good two-thirds of what's left is in outright mutiny."

Neverlight's food-storage facilities had failed in the third month of the trip. She had been a military logistics freighter, so she had enough recycling facilities to keep her crew alive until arrival in Exilium.

Captain Palmer had actually gone onto recycled food immediately herself, spinning out her crew's supply of what little real food remained. Unfortunately for impressions, however, the Captain's mess had a noticeably higher grade of food recycler than the one in the main crew cafeteria.

She might have been eating recycled biomass—and no one wanted to think about what that actually meant—but her food looked better than the real food the crew was still getting.

When the real food finally ran out...the crew accused the senior officers of hoarding non-recycled food. A bunch of hungry people, already strained by five months in warp, had decided that armed mutiny was a better solution than living on "recycled biomass".

That had been twenty-five days before.

"Have the mutineers talked to us yet?" Isaac asked.

"No," Lestroud replied with a sigh. "I've tried. I'm not sure that talking to them is going to be any easier once we're out of warp, either."

"What do you want me to do?" he said.

"Back up Zamarano," the Governor told him. "We're going to need to board *Neverlight* as soon as we're out of warp, and stun and detain the mutineers. No punishments," she said sharply. "Once they're planetside, we forget it ever happened.

"This trip has been hell for everybody. They're just the most blatant example."

Isaac shook his head.

"You're in charge."

"So long as you say I'm in charge," Lestroud told him.

"So long as the civilians listen to you, I'll listen to you," Isaac replied. "What about the survey teams?"

"I think Knutson and Wong have that sorted out," she said. "A mix of your people, Knutson's, and ours. Plus a few folks who were neither Fleet nor rebellion—trying to make everyone feel represented."

"That's...clever. I hadn't thought of it that way," he admitted.

"Knutson did," Lestroud said. "I think he and Wong may have more going on than just a professional relationship, but if so...power to them. Wong's boyfriend died in the rebellion."

"In a way, we all did," Isaac said quietly. "We go forward. And we keep everyone behind us. Making sure they all feel represented in the initial air and landing teams...that's important, I think. Just not what I'd think of."

"You're a soldier. Knutson's an administrator and I was a glorified propaganda icon," Amelie Lestroud reminded him. "We'll get it working. So long as we're all pulling in the same direction."

"Six months to an election?" Isaac asked.

"If I thought we could do it sooner, I'd do it," she said. "I'll run, I don't think my inner circle's going to give me a choice, but I get the feeling Governor is going to be a thankless job."

"Then, no matter what, I will make a point of thanking you," he told her with a smile. "So you at least have *one* set of thanks."

———

"WARP BUBBLE COLLAPSE IN SIXTY SECONDS," Alstairs's voice echoed around the flag bridge once more. "Fleet navigation passed to Commander Catalan."

Isaac smiled. There wasn't much navigation for anyone other than Catalan to be doing. For that matter, even Catalan wasn't doing much. The termination point of their trip had been programmed before they'd brought up the cradle.

Catalan was simply the man sitting next to the lever that would hard-kill the warp bubble if the program failed.

"The drive ring has begun spinning down," the engineer reported. "We are three point five *c* pseudovelocity and dropping. Bubble collapse in forty-five seconds."

The air was feeling heavy again, Isaac noted. Now he was able to pick out that the effect was more pronounced at the activation and deactivation of the drive. He'd never spent more than a few hours in a warp drive bubble before this.

Very few people had.

"Pseudovelocity has hit two *c*," Catalan said quietly. "I'm starting to see some severe instability in the drive ring. This...this is not good."

"Commander?" Isaac asked.

"Instability is increasing," the engineer snapped. "Pseudovelocity at one point seven and *holding*. Warp bubble is fragmenting; I don't have a clean shutdown! Drive ring is fragmenting!"

"Commander!"

"Everyone, *brace for impact!*"

Catalan's words echoed across Exile Fleet, and Isaac's systems flashed him a bright red alert—MANUAL SHUTDOWN.

Time stopped. Everything froze. Cameron Alstairs's spilling cup of coffee hung suspended in the air. All of the screens were frozen, nothing was moving, nothing was changing. Isaac was processing the passage of time, but *nothing* was happening.

Even his eyes weren't moving. He couldn't change what he was looking at. Everything was still.

And then it wasn't. A brutal force threw Isaac to the ground, driving him from his chair before its safety systems could activate. The flying cup of coffee flipped upward from its downward arc, smashing into Commander Rhianna Rose's head. Alstairs himself had been standing and went flying across the bridge to smash into the wall.

Isaac coughed, dragging himself to his feet.

"Med team to the flag bridge," he barked. "Multiple casualties."

Alstairs did *not* look good. Rose was unconscious on the ground, concussion risk, but she was still breathing, but the other Commander had definitely broken some bones.

They were probably the worst off on the flag bridge, but...if they'd had the same impact on the colony ships...

"All warships, stand by to provide medical relief to the civilian transports," he barked. "If we all got hit that hard, we're going to have a lot of shaken people and broken bones. We need to take care of them."

He turned his attention to Catalan.

"Are we here?" he asked. "Are we safe?"

Every hair on the engineer's head was standing up, the unexpected afro revealing that the engineer had dyed the underlayers of his hair red at some point during the trip to Exilium.

He coughed, shaking himself like a wet dog.

"Warp drive is shut down," he reported. "We are...seventy-six light-seconds from the fourth planet of the Exilium System...Exilium itself. We are on target."

"And the cradle?" Isaac asked, hiding a sigh of relief as a med-team rushed onto his flag bridge.

"Fucked," Catalan said bluntly. "We knew it wasn't going to fly again, but..." He sighed. "I'm only getting telemetry on thirty-two percent of the ring from the control center here, boss. From what I can see, it broke into five pieces.

"We're probably going to want to retrieve the pieces, for their exotic matter if nothing else, but we sure as hell don't have a warp cradle anymore."

"But we're here," Isaac concluded.

"We're here," the engineer confirmed. "If anyone wants to take a look about twenty-three million kilometers ahead of us, that little green-and-blue ball is our new home."

———

13

KELLIANE FAUST HAD, once, been a member of the Confederacy Marine Corps. An assault-shuttle pilot, one of the best. Then an unfortunate incident with a commanding officer who'd had too much to drink, several broken limbs—on said CO—and a refusal to quietly lie down and trade forgiveness for forgiveness had ended her career.

When the rebellion had found her in a dive bar, she'd been drinking water. Her new career as a drug smuggler had grated on her enough that alcohol had become a *really* bad idea.

New Soweto's Confederacy Secret Police headquarters had been a fortified mountain outpost. The rebels needed pilots to assault it—and not just any pilots. Pilots who could take the stick of highly maneuverable armed suborbital planes strapped together from hopes, dreams, pulse guns, and duct tape, and ram them through the aerial defenses of one of the most fortified locations in the Confederacy.

Unfortunately, the CSP had raided their concealed airbase and arrested everyone before she could try, and Kelliane Faust had ended up first in another cell, and then aboard a colony ship.

And then the call had gone out again. First for volunteers to take up the crimson armbands of the citizen watch that the hundreds of thousands of prisoners desperately needed—and then for pilots to lead the first survey effort of a new world.

That put one redheaded woman with bright green eyes and Asian features back behind the controls of a Peregrine-class assault shuttle. Kelliane's passengers were a bunch of nerds with science gear, not jocks with guns, but that was all right.

She was one of the first people to fly a shuttle in a star system only a handful of humans had ever seen before. Exile Fleet spread out behind them as the flotilla of small craft headed toward Exilium, warships and freighters alike dwarfed into insignificance by the massive colony ships.

"Lander Seven." She tapped her mike. "Watch your drift. If you hit atmo at that angle, your *best* case is that you're gonna bounce."

"Who put you in charge?" the pilot of Lander Seven barked. "I was flying crop-dusters like this 'fore you were born."

Kelliane sighed and tapped another command. A moment later, a red circle flashed around Lander Seven on her screen.

"Lander Seven, if you don't adjust course, you, your passengers and your cargo are going to get shredded by Exilium's atmosphere," she snapped. "It will save the Fleet a *lot* of hassle if I put a burst of railgun fire into your starboard thruster and knock you completely out of local orbit. I mean, we'll have to go retrieve you, but you've got two weeks of life support. We could take our time."

She let that sink in.

"As for who put me in charge, Lander Seven, I believe that was Governor Lestroud. So, unless you want to take up the chain of command with *her* or with Admiral Gallant, *get your ass back in formation.*"

Kelliane killed the channel, watching carefully for a few seconds to make sure Lander Seven actually obeyed.

"You enjoyed that far too much," her copilot quipped. Cai Johnson could pass for her brother, with similar Asian features other than their green eyes and red hair. So far as she knew, she and Johnson were completely unrelated, but twenty-fifth-century humanity was an odd bunch as ethnicities went.

Johnson was technically still a Marine, inasmuch as anyone with

Exile Fleet was still a member of the Confederacy military. They'd served together, ages before, and they'd run into each other when the survey flights were being assembled.

They were trying to mix civilians and military for the flight crews and survey teams. Kelliane understood the logic, but she could also see how it was going to drive at least some of the military crew insane. Johnson had leapt on the technicality that Kelliane wasn't a Marine anymore to make sure he didn't get saddled with an idiot.

"Truth is, I don't even know which ship Lander Seven is from," she admitted. "But I do know that we can afford to chase a Dutchman better than we can afford to lose a shuttle because someone is hotdogging their descent."

"And you want to be the first into Exilium's atmosphere," Johnson noted, studying their vector plot.

"And I want to be the first into Exilium's atmosphere."

———

THE ASSAULT SHUTTLE'S sensors weren't anything to write home about, in Kelliane's opinion, but they were enough to punch through cloud cover and night to allow her to match up what she was looking at with the original expedition files.

"All right, people," she said briskly. "We have eight landers and eight continents. Anyone want to guess how this is going to play out?"

Anyone who needed to guess also needed to have their hearing checked, but Kelliane Faust's time in the Marines had taught her to double-check, triple-check, quadruple-check...and then verify that everyone knew what they were doing, anyway.

"Survey expedition flagged them one through eight. Pull up the map of the continent for your lander number and go in slow and careful. We want aerial sweeps of the entire continent before you touch down—and remember, we're looking for colony sites. Nobody cares if we find a mountain of exotic matter today; we want flat ground and fertile soil."

Acknowledgements chirped over her radio, even her earlier argument with Lander Seven forgotten in the sheer awe of seeing a new world for the first time.

"This is Lander One, breaking formation to enter atmo," she announced. "See you all back at the barn."

Her thruster flared, slowing the Peregrine again and gently dropping the spacecraft into the atmosphere.

"Did anyone name these continents?" Kelliane asked Johnson. "I mean, we were all really bored for six months; someone has to have tried."

"Nothing officially accepted," her copilot replied as they dove into the clouds. "I think most people were content to leave it to the first landing teams."

"Huh. That was nice of them." She checked her screens again. "Looks like a dragon. I say we call this one Drakehold."

Johnson chuckled. "All right, ma'am. You're the pilot. Shall we sweep?"

"Of course."

The shuttle arced over Drakehold, her optics and scanners sweeping the surface of Exilium's largest continent.

"I'm reading temperatures ranging from twenty to twenty-six degrees Centigrade," she noted. "Does it look like summer or spring down there?"

"Neither, really," Johnson told her. "I'm showing a one point three-degree axial tilt. This planet doesn't *have* seasons as we understand them."

"That's…nuts," Kelliane said. "I thought the lowest anyone had seen was twelve?"

"It was. Until today." The Marine ran over the scan data again. "I'd say we're actually looking at the closest thing Drakehold is going to see to winter. Most distant part of the orbit, and the tilt is aligned for this to be winter."

"That's not shabby for winter," she replied. "Twenty-odd degrees? I should start scanning for a beach."

"Or, perhaps, a colony site?" her copilot said.

She chuckled at him.

"That's the second sweep, Cai," she pointed out. "Right now, we're doing aerial survey. Can you get me a spectro on those mountains?"

Part of the reason that Drakehold looked like a dragon to her was the line of mountains forming the "spine" of a great flying creature. They weren't huge, but they were enough to capture a lot of airborne water vapor on the continent, turning the core into a temperate rainforest.

"What do you expect them to be?" he asked. "Pretty sure exotic matter is right out...."

"I want to know if they're volcanos or plate drift," she told him. "There are mountains that are stable and help shield a colony, and there are mountains that are signs the colony would have to fight lava and earthquakes.

"See the problem?"

"Aye, aye," he agreed, running over his numbers. "Looks like granite and limestone from here, or local equivalents. No igneous rock, nothing recent, anyway. Doesn't look like we've got a line of volcanos up there."

"Then those, my dear Marine, are *happy* mountains," she said with a smile. "Keep funneling data in. What have we got for air?"

"Twenty-four percent oxygen, seventy-four percent nitrogen, one percent water and CO_2, one percent everything else. No detectable toxicity concerns. It'll take some getting used to, but it'll be a nice energy for most people."

"Perfect air. Perfect temperatures. Perfect weather." Kelliane shook her head. "What a damn planet. Wait, you see that?"

The shuttle slowed in the air, turning to focus on what she'd spotted. It would have been hard for Johnson to miss it at this point, though, as the river was over a kilometer wide here.

"Damn, that is *huge*," he murmured. "Tributaries flowing in from across the entire mountain range, forming into a single stream that runs down toward..." He coughed. "Toward..."

"Toward the dragon's dick?" Kelliane suggested sweetly. "I'm guessing no one's going to let us name it the Dragonpiss, are they?"

Johnson half-coughed, half-chuckled.

"Let's call it Lofwyr," he replied. "Dragon character from an old series of movies—usually the character's patron but occasionally an antagonist."

"That seems...appropriate," she agreed, sweeping the shuttle around. "Because a river like that is going to have the mother of all deltas—and a river delta, my old friend, is flat area with fertile ground.

"A potentially perfect colony site."

———

DRAKEHOLD WAS A MASSIVE CONTINENT, nearly the size of the Asian landmass on Terra, and Lofwyr's delta covered almost two thousand kilometers of its coastline. Vast tracts of wetlands and secondary rivers wrapped around raised areas of dry ground too immense to be called islands.

"Dr. Crohn, how's it looking back there?" Kelliane asked the leader of the ground survey team. "My computers are churning happily, but you get the call on where we put down."

"Yes, yes, yes," Michelle Crohn replied distractedly. "Lots of potential sites; we're still scanning. Can you bring us around for another sweep over the estuary?"

"Can do, Doctor," she replied. "I'm watching fuel levels, though. We've got about another hour of flight before we need to burn for orbit.

"Not much difference between starting that burn from up here or on the ground, though," she told the biologist. "But I either need to touch down or head for orbit inside an hour."

"All right, all right," Crohn told her. "We'll have a site for you by then. It's going to be one of the big landmasses, probably right on the coast. We're going to need a port."

Kelliane shook her head as she brought the shuttle around again.

"She does realize that doesn't narrow it down at all, right?" she muttered to Johnson.

"I suspect the good doctor has other things on her mind," her copilot told her. "I'm no biologist, but take a look at this."

An image popped up on her HUD. It was a set of massive trees, their roots growing out of the water rather than any visible ground. They stretched for hundreds of meters, but…no.

"That's *one* tree?" she asked.

"So far as the scans and optics can tell, yeah," he agreed. "One plant, approximately three hundred meters on a side and a few thousand tons of biomass. Could almost pass for the mangrove trees we imported from Earth back home."

"Except it's just one massive plant."

"Well, yeah," Johnson allowed. "Parallel evolution in terms of appearance, though."

"So, we should be watching for crocodiles; is that what you're saying?" she asked.

"Or some kind of stealth predator," the Marine agreed. "I mean, we didn't bring the crocs to Erewhon with us, but if these guys are parallel evolution, *something*'s probably used to hiding in them."

"There's a reason the ground survey expedition is armed," Dr. Crohn interrupted. "And not just with tranquilizers for live samples. We know nothing about this planet's ecosystem. It might be toxic to us. We might be toxic to its predators."

"Or we might be the best-tasting treat the predators have ever encountered. Unfortunately, the only way to find out is to land and take a look."

"Fair enough, doc. What's the call?" Kelliane asked, sharing a look with her copilot. She'd forgotten to close the channel. Not, it seemed, that Dr. Crohn had noticed her complaining about the surveyor.

"Here," Crohn replied, dropping an icon on the display. "Largest solid land mass on the largest estuary. If it's stable, fertile, and lacking in anything poisonous or dangerous, it'll be a perfect site for a water port."

"All right, doc. Let's go check it out."

Silently, Kelliane checked something else.

Yep. She was not only going to be first in Exilium's atmosphere, but her shuttle was also going to be first on the ground.

She'd *probably* have to let the doctor get out first.

———

Thrusters flared as Kelliane lowered the Peregrine to the ground, intentionally working the jets of heat across the landing zone to bake the soil. It served the double purposes of killing off most potentially dangerous bacteria and hardening the landing zone to make her takeoff easier later.

"First," she muttered quietly as the shuttle finally made contact. "Dr. Crohn, we're down. We'll need to wait a minute or two for the landing site to cool off before we open the ramp. I suggest you get your gear ready."

"Ms. Faust, my gear has been ready since we left the colony ships," the biologist replied. "As have my people. Let us know as soon as we can jump out; I have a million samples I want to take."

"The shuttle's systems are taking some of the most important ones right now, if you want to take a look," Kelliane told her. "I know the air is breathable, but if it's got toxic spores or some such, I'm not sure our systems will pick them up."

"Yes, yes, yes," Crohn told her. "Send the samples to my people; we'll make sure before we head outside."

The pilot hit a command, instructing the shuttle's samplers to deliver Exilium's air to the survey team. She checked the surface temperature outside again. It was dropping quickly, but it still wouldn't be safe to leave.

"We'll need to install some real landing pads pretty quickly," she told Johnson.

"The colony ships have them," he replied. "Once they land, they unfold into prebuilt cities. Spaceports, the works. I've seen it." He chuckled. "Once, ever. Sixteen of them landing at a time is going to be a sight."

"That's tomorrow's experience," Kelliane said. "Or next week's, depending on what the initial tests say."

"The air is clean," Crohn told her. "Surprisingly so, actually, even given that we just flash-cooked the area. No sign of anything potentially dangerous. Nothing that even flags as potential allergens."

Kelliane shook her head slowly.

"No mass inoculations required, huh?"

The native plant life of her own home world of Conestoga used a version of chlorophyll that triggered severe allergic reactions in roughly sixty percent of humans. A nanite-based inoculation was administered to any human visiting or born on the planet to protect them from the allergy.

Most planets had something similar. Strange new worlds were rarely perfectly compatible with humanity.

"Temp is down to thirty-five degrees," she told the doctor. "Opening the ramp for you now."

————

KELLIANE BREATHED DEEPLY as she stepped out of her shuttle, taking in the slightly spicy scent of the as-yet-unnamed super-mangrove trees, a familiar saltwater scent, and something else that she couldn't quite place.

It was nice. She'd been on five planets in her life and never stood on a coastline that smelled quite as pleasant as this. The extra oxygen in the air helped put a boost in her step, and she cautiously checked the gravity as she left the artificial gravity of the shuttle.

"I make it pretty close to one standard gee," she noted to Johnson. "What does the scanner say?"

"Point nine seven," he confirmed. "Like the air, not exactly what we're used to, but almost better for us. This planet is weird. Even if I'd been designing a new home for us, I'm not sure it would have been this perfect."

"You're making assumptions far too quickly," Dr. Crohn told them as the biologist returned. "Smells right, feels right, but if the ground can't support our crops or the local plant and animal life is incompatible with our proteins, we're still looking at a hard slog ahead."

"I'd rather make that hard slog somewhere that feels *nice* than on an ice ball," Kelliane replied. "Have you ever *been* to Hoth?"

Dr. Crohn blinked. "I'm not familiar with that planet?" she said slowly.

"Because it's officially Estevan, the fourth world in the Erewhon system," Johnson replied. "But everyone who's ever been posted or even *visited* the place calls it Hoth. It's habitable. If you like snow."

"I've seen the biome data for Estevan," the biologist admitted. "Odd planet, odd life cycle. Five months above freezing, twelve below. Life survives."

"It does. But it sucks for humans."

"That it does," she agreed. "And Exilium...doesn't. We'll check soil and take animal samples before we head back up, but we've got the solid surface here for cities."

"Ground survey shows a lot of it," Kelliane agreed. "Enough for most of the colony ships, if not all."

"If the soil will support us, we might be golden," Crohn told her. "It's all down to whether local silt is compatible with our crops."

"Time to dig up mud, then?" the pilot asked.

Dr. Crohn chuckled.

"That, Ms. Faust, is what I brought grad students for."

———

14

Amelie Lestroud leaned against the wall of the briefing room, watching as the collection of "community leaders" filed in. Selection of who got to be in this room had been arbitrary. The colony ship captains were there. Her former Bravo cell leaders, now rejoicing in the utterly vague title of Magistrate, were there.

After those thirty-two people, however, it had been selected based on who she and her intelligence network believed could sway popular opinion.

Her Governorship was provisional, held in place by the existing infrastructure of the rebellion, the support of the colony ship captains and colonial development teams—and the explicit threat of force exerted by Admiral Gallant's Marines.

Speaking of which…

"It feels wrong not to have you here," she murmured into the microphone bead on her throat. "A girl could think you were avoiding her."

The Admiral's deep chuckle echoed in her ear.

"Then people would *talk*, my dear Governor," he replied. "This *has* to be a civilian show, Amelie."

There were no Marines in the room. No Fleet officers. No uniforms

—well, except for the simple black suits she'd had her Magistrates take up as a uniform style.

There weren't even volunteers from the Exile Watch or constables from Colonial Development. None of those armed enforcers of Amelie's will were particularly far *away*, but this was at least publicly a consultation.

"It's all on you," Gallant whispered in her ear. "I'm watching from *Vigil*." He chuckled again. "The whole Exile Fleet will see this, sooner or later."

"No pressure, huh?"

"How much did *Stars of Honor* cost to make?" the Admiral asked her. "What's the pressure of convincing four million people this is going to be home compared to starring in a multi-billion mega-franchise?"

She laughed.

"Worse, and I don't get to distract anyone with an overly low-cut 'uniform' for this one, either," she pointed out.

"You'll be fine," he assured her. "Go get 'em…Governor."

Amelie let his assurance ripple through her as she smiled and straightened her back. Every eye in the room seemed to be on her as she walked down the aisle in the middle of the space to the stage at the front of the theater.

"Good morning, everyone," she greeted them. "Good morning… and welcome to Exilium."

The screen behind her lit up with a map of their new home, glittering in greens and blues now that the computers had stripped away the cloud cover.

"Our first wave of surveys, aerial and ground, have been completed," she continued. "For those of you holding your breath…you can let it go.

"In every sense we can scan for or detect, Exilium is safe and habitable. The air is breathable, the gravity is light, and apparently even the ocean smells like you'd expect," Amelie told them. "There is no question that this can be our new home."

"Which is good," Captain Linton snarked from the third row. "I don't know if anyone *else* spotted the warp cradle breaking into pieces.

It was easy to miss, I suppose."

She nodded to *Star of Delights* Captain.

"As Captain Linton so delicately points out, we have no easy way to move the entire Exile Fleet from this system. Exilium would have to be a pretty significant bust for us to attempt to move on.

"I am pleased to tell you all that it is no such thing. Air, soil, water, and biomass samples from eight different regions are all being reviewed as we speak, but the initial results are that we can breathe the air, drink the water, and eat the plants."

That sent an audible sigh of relief—and surprise—rippling through the audience.

"Isn't that…extraordinary unlikely?" one of the "extras"—a church leader with a notable flock on one of the colony ships—asked. "I'm no scientist, but my understanding is that we've never found a world yet that was in every way compatible with humans."

"We've come close, but the closer the planet, the higher the risk of pathogens and allergens," Amelie agreed. "There are four colony planets, according to my brief research this morning, that appear as compatible as Exilium.

"Three of those four require some form of additional inoculation or maintenance nanite suite for humanity to live on safely. Hence, everyone, the degree of scrutiny we are laying on all of the samples. If it seems to good to be true, the risk is that, well, it is."

"So, what's the plan?" Knutson asked. The Colonial Development Team leader wasn't *quite* a plant in this meeting, but he'd helped plan it out.

"We have surveyed eight ground locations," Amelie replied. "We have sixteen colony ships, each designed to drop a prebuilt city of a quarter million people in place on the surface. Some logic would say we should split them up…but we have the Lofwyr River Delta."

Behind her, the screen zoomed in on Drakehold and then on the dragon-shape's…well, crotch.

"The Delta is roughly two thousand kilometers across and about the same deep, creating a vast area of fertile soil and rainforest we can settle into.

"All analysis suggests that the solid islands in the Delta are capable of supporting our crops. There are several islands on the shore where we can deploy the colony ships with prefabricated ports.

"Our plan is to deploy all sixteen colony ships into separate areas of the Lofwyr River Delta, creating a dispersed metropolitan area of four million souls. This will concentrate our population and infrastructure, allowing mutual support in an area that can definitely support the population."

Sixteen green circles appeared on the map of the Delta.

"Once our population starts to expand, we'll want to set up additional settlements moving out from Lofwyr, but a combined starting point provides us with the greatest efficiencies and safety."

"At what ecological cost?" one of the captains asked. "That's the kind of area with massive impacts on the rest of the biosphere."

"Agreed," Amelie told him. "Our colony ships are designed to establish cities with minimal ecological impact, but the crops will cause problems. We have the tech and the skill to minimize it, but it will happen.

"We can't avoid that. Anywhere we settle on the planet, we're going to have that problem. We have all the technology that was used to rebuild Earth, but..." She shrugged. "We were rebels and dissidents, people. College protesters make shitty colonists.

"We need to stack the deck in our favor. We'll keep our industry in orbit as much as possible, but we need to grow food on the ground— and the Lofwyr River Delta offers us a single zone that will grow enough food for everyone."

"Will we even have the surface-to-orbit capacity to keep our industry in orbit?" the priest asked again. "That's...a lot of transport."

"Among the facilities the colony ships will deploy on the surface are electrolyzing facilities that will use fusion power to crack the seawater into hydrogen and oxygen," Knutson told them, the CDC man cutting in. "Much of that hydrogen will need to go to the fusion plants that will feed the cities themselves, but they are more than capable of producing significant amounts of shuttle fuel."

"The freighters and warships will remain in orbit regardless," Amelie reminded everyone. "Only the colony ships are designed to land."

"Do we really even need warships now? Maintaining them is going to be a drain on our efforts." The same priest was speaking again, and Amelie wished she'd registered the names that went with the faces better.

"That's Father Petrov James," Wong whispered in her ear, the Magistrate apparently guessing her need. "Catholic priest from New Soweto. Avowed pacifist, which is the problem and part of why he ended up in Exile Fleet. He was never one of ours."

"Father James." Amelie spoke directly to the man, thankful for her supporters' perceptiveness. "We are seventy thousand light-years from home. We are, as I'm sure you were considering, absolutely safe from the Confederacy. From, indeed, other humans in general.

"But do you know what lives out here?" she asked quietly. "Because I don't. Nobody does. We know there's no technological civilization in the systems the first expedition visited. That's it.

"Without knowing *anything*, we can't know we're safe. Which means that our safety rests on Admiral Gallant and his people." She smiled. "We all carry our burdens at this point. We all have the tasks that we must take on to make sure Exilium survives.

"Admiral Gallant's task is to be our shield and our eyes, guarding us from what we don't know is out there...and *finding out* what's out there."

———

WITH THE BIG public meeting over, Amelie tossed her suit blazer over the back of her chair as she settled into a much smaller room. Knutson and Wong joined her in person, and unlike the public presentation, Isaac Gallant was officially there, the black Admiral looking amused.

"It sounds like we have a plan?" he asked.

"Yes," Knutson confirmed. "There wasn't much question of what the plan was; the purpose of this was to get public buy-in from key figures. Whether we like it or not, we're functionally a dictatorship at the moment—so the more we *act* like a democracy anyway, the more people will trust our promises of elections."

"And we mean those promises," Amelie added. "I don't know

what the Iron Bitch—sorry, Isaac—was thinking *wanting* this job. Especially not on the scale the Confederacy operates on."

"I've heard the nickname before," he said drily. "As long as no one calls me the 'Iron Brat' where I can hear them, I'm fine."

From Knutson's and Wong's expressions, they'd definitely heard *that* nickname before, too.

"*Star of Delights* will be first to land," Knutson told them. "Primarily because she's got the largest power core and the prefabricated port structures. Auto-deploy will do eighty percent of the work in six hours, and it'll take us six weeks to do the rest.

"We'll land all sixteen transports as rapidly as possible," the bureaucrat told them. "There's nobody aboard any ship in the fleet who isn't going nuts to one degree or another. Once the colony ships are down, we can start rotating freighter and warships crews for 'leave' helping with the setup."

"I promised my crews that any of them that wanted to go civilian at this point would be allowed," Gallant reminded everyone. "My intention is actually to make staying aboard the new Exilium Fleet opt-in. They'll swear a new oath, at least in interim, to uphold the principles and freedoms originally promised to the Confederacy's citizens."

The Admiral smiled thinly.

"Once we know what Exilium's government is going to shake out to be in the end, we'll write up new oaths and new articles of justice," he continued, "but those need to be based on civilian government and civilian law—which puts the foundations in your courts."

Amelie sighed.

"Anything to avoid work, huh, Isaac?"

"I have more immediate tasks than helping write a constitution— and an active need to be nowhere near the writing of the constitution," Gallant replied. "Everyone knows who my mother is. We don't want me anywhere near the formation of the new government. I'm going to be hanging out in orbit a lot."

"And collecting a salary that at least some people are going to complain about," Wong said drily. "Is James going to be a problem?"

"No," Amelie said. "He's going to be…opposition. But I don't think having someone continually question how much force and armament we actually need is a bad thing. I don't think any of us fully agree with Father James, but he does have a point, and using him as an external conscience will be to our benefit."

"I agree," Gallant said instantly. "Again, people, the last thing I want is for the Fleet to have a blank check. Though, speaking of salary, what am I paying my people with if they stay on? I'm relatively sure the Confederacy dollar is…somewhat worthless out here."

"EECs," Knutson said instantly. "Exilium Energy Credits. For the immediate future, the government will be the only source of both capital and equipment. The major resources we have to underwrite a currency are food and energy.

"Even under the First Admiral, the Confederacy accepted that food and water were a basic human right," he noted. "Both Amelie and I refuse to tie the ability to eat to what people can provide to the colony.

"Current plan is to set the energy credit equal to the average power use of an average person per hour," he continued. "For the first ten years or so, everyone will get twenty-six credits a day from the government, three more than they need to fulfill average power needs.

"We'll pay salaries for military police, and administration in credits and accept tax payment in credits," Knutson noted. "When we mortgage our equipment out to people for their own projects, loan amounts and payment will be in energy credits."

"We'll privatize as rapidly as possible, of course, but we don't have any of the corporate interests that would normally be involved in this kind of project," Amelie noted. "The plan is to finance projects that sound reasonable pretty much automatically. We're going to get hammered on at least half of them, and we'll move the credit to a fiat currency in the long run, but tying it to a real resource that the government controls gives us a place to start."

"That makes sense," Gallant allowed. "Speaking of places to start, though…" He trailed off thoughtfully. "Is the wormhole platform in one of your transports?"

Amelie paused. Every Confederacy colony was assigned a small low-power wormhole generation station. It wouldn't have the three-hundred-light-year range of the major platforms in the Confederacy, but it would let them explore the systems around them relatively rapidly.

"Knutson?" she asked.

"I..." The bureaucrat also trailed off. "We assumed it was aboard one of the military ships," he said in a small voice. "You don't have one?"

"We don't," Gallant said flatly. "And you don't. That *bitch*."

Somehow, Amelie found it harsher to hear Adrienne Gallant described that way by her son than by anyone else.

"She wanted to make sure we could never get back," he explained. "Every obstacle she could put in our way..." He shook his head.

"We should have the ability to build one, though, shouldn't we?" Knutson asked. "We have enough exotic matter from the warp cradle?"

"Assuming we have the skills and the designs, it will take at least a year or two," Gallant told them. "But yes, we have enough EM. Do we know anyone who could start that project?"

"Yes," Amelie replied. "Dr. Reinhardt, he's an FTL-specialist astrophysicist we have aboard *Star of Delights*. I think his specialty was the grav-warp drives, but you can't be a Confederacy astrophysicist without knowing wormholes."

"Find him," Gallant said. "Please," he added, clearly realizing he'd just nearly given an order to the Governor. "We need to know how screwed we are."

"What if we don't have any wormhole capacity at all?" Wong asked. "We have the warp ships, right?"

"Six of them," the Admiral agreed. "That's it. My entire fleet is based around having wormhole generators for deployment. If suddenly we need grav-warp drives to leave this system at all...well, let's just say I won't be nearly as bothered to see half my people retire as I expected to be."

———

15

VIGIL AND DANTE jetted away from the colony ships, the destroyers and cruisers moving in formation around them as the warships lifted into a higher orbit. Beneath them, *Star of Delights* began her stately descent to the Lofwyr River Delta and the end of her unimaginably long journey.

"Admiral Gallant," the professor in his screen told Isaac. With the main screen in Isaac's office showing the maneuvers of the newly renamed Exilium Space Fleet, it was hard to judge scale in the smaller screen he was speaking to the man through.

Isaac was quite sure that Dr. Reinhardt was a massive man, with shoulder-length pure white hair and scarring around one eye that suggested it had been replaced at one point.

"Our Governor tells me that you were a physicist, Doctor," Isaac said to him. "Did she pass on our concerns?"

"She did," Reinhardt replied gruffly. "I did some digging—the result I found wasn't what I was expecting, so I had to verify with the other ships. Your own staff allowed me access to the Fleet databases as well, to make very certain."

"I'm not liking the sound of that, Doctor," the Admiral said.

Reinhardt shook his head and sighed.

"We have the complete data archives of the University of Terra, the ultimate repository of human knowledge in the Confederacy," he noted. "In fact, at least one sociologist of my acquaintance is only vaguely aware that we've arrived in Exilium—she's been nose-down in the databanks since she realized we have the U of T's *black* databanks, the ones with an honest history of, among other things, the last twenty-five years."

"That…has to be a fascinating comparison to make," Isaac said drily. His own impressions of his mother's rule had turned out to be quite different from the reality—the discovery of just how much personal wealth Adrienne Gallant had earned from her dictatorship had been what had broken his faith in her.

"Indeed. We have archives on technical specifications that I would have killed for two years ago," Reinhardt told him. "Complete files on grav-warp experiments that were buried to keep the warp-cruiser fleet safe, for example."

"I'm hearing a *but* coming, Dr. Reinhardt," Isaac said softly.

"Yeah. I didn't think what was done would be possible, hence trying to validate with the rest of the fleet." Reinhardt shrugged. "We have no data on wormholes, Admiral."

"What do you mean, *no data*?" Isaac demanded.

"There's what's in the heads of our scientists and military officers, which isn't *nothing*, but…" The big man shrugged again. "Our actual databanks have no research, designs, specifications or details on wormholes since the Einstein-Rosen calculations.

"Those were in the twentieth century, Admiral. By the end of the twenty-first, we had the Telford-Nguyen calculations that laid the groundwork for artificial wormholes. Except…*we*, as in Exile Fleet, don't.

"There'll be data on wormholes in the historical files and military files and so forth, but we're talking fragments at best. There is a giant hole in our databanks where our wormhole technology should be."

Isaac sighed and nodded.

"That's what I was afraid of when I realized we didn't have the generator station," he told the doctor. "You said there was black data on grav-warp drives?"

"Yes. I knew some of what's here existed, but I didn't have access to it. It looks like there may be some data and research I wasn't aware existed, too."

"Can you upgrade our warp drives with it?" Isaac asked bluntly. "If I don't have a wormhole generator, it becomes a much more immediate need for us to have grav-warp drives that can go faster than four times lightspeed!"

"I… I don't know," Reinhardt admitted. "Between my colleagues and I, if you give us some decent engineers, I'm pretty sure we'll be able to build new warp drives relatively easily. I can have the basic specifications of what it would take to make your battlecruisers warp-capable, for example, in a week or two."

"Do it," Isaac ordered. "If you'll take the job, I'm pretty sure I can swing a military R&D department past the Governor. I'm going to need those extra warp drives—and the more you can do with what we can dig out of the warp cradle, the better."

"Do you have data on how much exotic matter survived the breakup?" Reinhardt asked.

"We have scans. We haven't retrieved the debris yet; it's on my, oh, week two to-do list."

"I'll take that scan data," the professor replied. "And that job. I'm going to have friends on this planet, Admiral, and I'd like to see them live out their old ages without being bombed from orbit."

"Then you and I, Professor, are on *exactly* the same page."

───────

"First things first, people," Isaac told his assembled senior officers. "That offer for anyone to step down and join the colony? It applies to you all, too. If it's time for you to retire, or you don't want to face command anymore, or whatever. If being a pioneer is more appealing to you than being the grumpy Admiral's gophers, the offer is open."

None of the half-dozen offers in the room did more than chuckle at him. Lauretta Giannovi leaned back in her chair on the opposite end of the table and grinned.

"I think I speak for all of us when I say that we're pretty okay with being your 'gophers,' sir," she replied. "I, for one, am waiting for when you decide you need a couple more flag officers. I'm in this for at least one star, boss!"

"A lot of people are going to take us up on that," Cameron Alstairs warned him. "We've been keeping a finger on the pulse of the crews for the entire trip."

"How many are we going to lose?" Brigadier Zamarano asked.

"About a third of Battle Group *Vigil*'s people and two thirds of *Dante*'s," the ops officer said calmly. "Roughly forty percent of your Marines, though most of them are probably going to end up as cops—and we need the cops on Exilium to be the best they can be."

"There are almost no circumstances under which I'm prepared to use the Fleet or Marines to intervene in civilian affairs," Isaac reminded them all. "But I agree with Cameron—the better the cops are, the less likely it is that someone is going to ask us to."

Rhianna Rose studied some numbers on her tattoo-comp and shook her head.

"If we lose half our people, we won't have the numbers to keep both battle groups functional," the communications officer warned. "That's basically enough for skeleton crews. Passage crews, not fighting crews."

"I agree," Isaac confirmed. "I also, unfortunately, confirmed with the civilians that we got hit with the worst possible version of what we were afraid of. We not only don't have a wormhole generator station, we don't have the designs and schematics to build one—or the scientific databases to recreate those designs and schematics."

"That's going to be a problem," Octavio Catalan said grimly. "We only have six warp cruisers, Admiral. We're going to keep a higher proportion of those crews to begin with, I suspect, but if that's our entire FTL capability..."

"Then we are blind and crippled for knowing what the hell is going on around us," Isaac told them. Catalan wasn't technically a senior officer, though his role as the engineer aboard the warp cradle had given him an outsized importance on the trip there. Unless Isaac somehow kept all of his cruiser captains—and he doubted that was going to happen—Catalan was getting one of the warp cruisers.

"We're going to have to send the warp cruisers out anyway," the

Admiral continued grimly. "Which gives us our manning priorities, I suppose."

He turned to Alstairs and Rose. Between ops and communications, it would mostly fall on them to organize what came next.

"Warp cruisers first," he said grimly. "Then the battlecruisers. Then at least…let's call it six destroyers for local patrols and search and rescue. Then missile cruisers, then the rest of the destroyers."

If he lost half his people, he'd get most of his cruisers and the six destroyers he wanted for in-system work.

That would be it. At least a dozen destroyers and half of the missile cruisers would need to be carefully shut down and placed in storage orbits.

"Go through our files," he continued. "I know we mothballed a lot of ships when we dissolved the star system militaries. We have to have data on the best ways to do it—if I'm putting sixteen to twenty warships on ice, I want to be one hundred percent sure I can unfreeze them if we need them later."

"Can do," his ops officer replied.

"If we're scouting with the warp cruisers, those are going to be long, lonely trips," Catalan noted.

"I know," Isaac told him. "Which means that warp cruiser assignments need to be volunteer-only." He sighed. "If we're short on volunteers, of course, we'll see who we can lean on. But I don't want to send anyone out on multi-year voyages who isn't willing to go."

———

16

AMONG THE ADVANTAGES of being one of the survey shuttle pilots were both knowing where the best spot to get a view of the colony ship landing was and having the ability to get down there.

Kelliane Faust had arranged a small picnic and party for herself, Dr. Crohn and a few other friends on the tallest hill near the island *Star of Delights* was heading toward. The shuttle's supplies let her set up a transparent barrier to protect them from any excess radiation from the landing, but the sandwiches and wine had come from *Star of Delights* herself.

"How will we know when she's coming in?" asked one of the friends Dr. Crohn had brought. Kelliane was reasonably sure he was some kind of junior professor, possibly a hard scientist of some sort. She wasn't sure.

She was sure that the tall dark-haired teacher was cute...but also that he might not be very bright.

"*Star* is over a kilometer long and masses something like ten million tons," she pointed out sweetly. "Believe me, we'll know when she's coming in. It'll sound something like armageddon."

"Pilot Faust...if you don't mind humoring my ignorance, how does a vessel of that size even *land*?" Dr. Crohn asked. The other professor flushed as his boss freely admitted she didn't know much of what was going on.

"Very, very carefully," Kelliane said with a smile. "And, well, once. She's made a dozen orbits of Exilium on her way down already, each one lower and slower than the one before. When she comes in for final approach, she won't be much faster than a landing shuttle, but she's still got a lot of mass and inertia.

"Her engines will bake the surface she's landing on," she continued, "but the process will still wreck them. Once she's down, she can't lift off again. *Star* will literally melt her thruster nozzles into the ground as she impacts."

"Seems…inefficient," the dark-haired man said. "Why wouldn't we use a reusable colony transport?"

"Well, in our case, why would we?" Kelliane asked. "We're not going anywhere else once we're down. In general, though, it's actually more cost-efficient this way. The ship's power core becomes the city's power core. Command center becomes the new admin center. Habitat sections become apartment buildings, stored prefabricated industrial units just drop into place.… It lets us basically pre-build the core of the colony and store it in a tube we send between the stars."

The ground began to rumble underneath her feet, and she finished her wine as she rose and looked up, shading her eyes. The rumbling grew louder, rapidly reaching the point where she could barely hear herself think as the sound of the massive thrusters tore through the sky and a second sun hurtled through the air toward them.

Star of Delights was slowing fast, her deceleration distinctly visible to the experienced naked eye as she blasted through the sky like a homesick meteor. She *glowed*, too, rotating in the air as she slowed and approached her target.

Then, with a precision piloting skill that could only be achieved by an absolute ace with incredible computer support, one last blast of fire stopped the big ship in midair, spinning her into a vertical orientation as she dropped straight toward the ground.

The thrusters flared again, slowing the massive ship's fall and lighting up the ground in a pillar of white flame.

And then there was a crash they could hear from their multi-kilo-meter-distant perch, and then silence.

"She's down," Kelliane said into the silence. She checked her tattoo-comp for the official report. "Clean landing, according to the reports. Second ship is due in two hours, eleven minutes."

"The landing's done. So…should we be waiting for something more?"

The pilot didn't say a word—mostly because Dr. Crohn was chuckling.

"Take a look, Ryan," she told him as she gestured. The starship stood in the middle of the estuary island, a kilometer-tall spike of silver.

A spike that was already beginning to shed, outer layers folding out like an immense manmade flower.

"I've *seen* big-ship landings before," Kelliane admitted. "Marine Strategic Deployment Transports aren't *supposed* to land, but the Confed Marines train for it anyway. The auto-deploy, though…"

She grabbed her binoculars and trained them on the expanding ship.

"That's something almost no one ever gets to see," she concluded.

———

THERE WAS ONLY SO much time that the survey team could spare to watch the deployment, and when the second colony ship rode her pillar of fire to the ground fifty-eight kilometers to the southwest of *Star of Delights*, it was their cue to get back to work.

"I hate to think how much of the local life we're destroying when we land each of those ships," Crohn muttered to Kelliane as they reen-tered the shuttle. "I know we're going to have to clear vast areas for farms, too, but it still feels wrong."

"That's part of why we concentrated the colony, I think," Kelliane told her. "Minimize and localize the ecological damage. We can expand from here more carefully, making sure it's done right." She shrugged. "After forty-odd planets, we seem to have a clue what we're doing."

"Oh, I know," Crohn agreed. "As a biologist, though, I'm all too aware that we might have accidentally wiped out something unique. Though…"

The scientist trailed off as Kelliane closed up the ramp.

"You sounded like you had a thought, doc," the pilot told her. "Join me in the cockpit while you jar it loose?"

"Sudden epiphany, I think," Dr. Crohn said slowly. "Give me a few. Where are we heading now?"

"Site A-17," Kelliane replied. "Five hundred square kilometers of rainforest to survey from the air and see what looks interesting or different."

"That's the thing," the biologist told her, dropping into the observer seat. "I can already tell you, with a good degree of certainty, that we won't find much different."

The pilot arched an eyebrow.

"That's one hell of a statement, Dr. Crohn," she pointed out. "Last I heard, they were still finding new species on *Earth*, and we've been identifying and classifying stuff there for a few thousand years at least."

"Oh, there may be different trees or animals, maybe," the biologist allowed with a wave of her hand. "But the microbiome won't be. That's my specialty—soil microbiology. And it should be different, *vastly* different, even from one stretch of forest to another."

"It isn't," she said flatly. "I went over the samples everyone pulled. Eight landing parties, each taking a dozen samples to test if we could plant crops. They weren't identical—we're talking microorganisms, that's impossible—but variance was under one-millionth of what it should have been."

The biologist shivered.

"Possibly even less. We don't really have the tools or models for that kind of comparison. We've never seen anything like this."

"Epiphany, huh?" Kelliane asked softly.

"I'm going to need to build those models," Crohn said determinedly. "Because if I'm right, then I can only think of one possible explanation."

"You've lost me, Dr. Crohn," Kelliane admitted. "So, if you'll forgive *my* ignorance…"

"It's been seeded," the biologist told her. "The only way I can think of that the microbiome can be this consistent across an entire planet is if it all started with the same package of microorganisms. Everywhere. Evolution will inevitably give you variance, but if you start with an artificial package, you have less ability to vary."

"Artificial," the pilot repeated. "That's a scary word when we're talking about a *planet*, Doctor."

"I need more data," Crohn replied. "A lot more data. Right now, it's just a niggling in the back of my head. Keep it quiet, all right? I don't need people deciding I'm crazy."

"Doctor...we all ended up in Exile Fleet. We all know everyone here is crazy!"

————

17

THREE WEEKS FELT like barely enough time to scratch the surface of the job Amelie Lestroud had found herself with. The city of Starhaven barely *existed*, let alone functioned. Sixteen prefabricated "neighborhoods" that had once been colony ships still formed the bulk of Starhaven, but additional streets and districts were now taking shape around those cores.

As her shuttle made a long, lazy loop over the Lofwyr delta, the Governor looked out over the colony with an assessing eye, judging those growths as she tried to see where they needed to go next.

They hadn't even connected all sixteen cores on the ground yet. The colony ships had dropped in a two-hundred-kilometer-square area, barely a fifth of the delta, but the road-building machinery carving the roads took time—especially when they kept having to stop and build bridges.

Thankfully, the Colonial Development Teams had *some* people trained in all of this equipment. The CD Teams were doing a lot of on-the-job training, however, as few of the dissidents sent in Exile Fleet had been road-building crews.

There were some, of course, but it felt like Amelie had more sociology professors than blue collar workers most days.

It would still be another week before even the basic road network was completed, but the smallest highway was a project to make skyscrapers look easy. The prefabricated harbor from *Star of Delights* would be complete on the same schedule, allowing the fishing boats already being stripped out of their packaging to get to work.

Everything they'd seen so far suggested that the fish would be edible, which would give the colony a desperately needed source of protein to extend their food supplies. They had enough food for years, but most colonies had at least one bad crop as they sorted out growing Terran food in alien soil.

Similar light industrial projects to the harbor were going up near each colony ship. The survey teams were looking for resources on Exilium and in the space above it.

Three weeks wasn't enough time for most of their projects to even get started. They had manpower to spare, and thankfully people recognized the need to get to work, but everything took time.

"All right, Pilot Mackenzie," Amelie told her shuttle crew. "Much as I'm enjoying the chance to see Starhaven from above, we're actually out here for a reason. Let's get going while we still have fuel."

Her pilot chuckled.

"Oh, we're in no risk of that yet," Rory Mackenzie told her. "I'll get in touch with orbital traffic control, finalize our course."

"We have that much in orbit already?" Amelie asked.

"We don't have cities in space, but we've probably got more prefab industry to set up," the pilot pointed out. "Between those modules, the ships, and the Fleet, Exilium orbit is pretty busy.

"And the Admiral has the Fleet as high as you can go and still be in orbit, so we have to pass through *all* of it to get there."

───────

AMELIE HADN'T LEFT the surface of Exilium since *Star of Delights* had landed and become the first district of Starhaven. Trying to organize four million-odd people to make sure that everything that was needed was either set up from prefabricated components or built from scratch was an all-encompassing task.

Her view from the shuttle as they headed toward the Fleet was the first she'd seen of Exilium's new orbital infrastructure. The twenty transports that had accompanied her colony ships might have appeared small against the immense bulk of the colony ships, but each of them was the size of one of Admiral Gallant's battlecruisers.

Their cargo holds had disgorged sublight spacecraft, zero-gravity manufacturing modules, traffic control satellites, the components of a massive multi-element orbital refinery.... Modern humanity kept their heavy industry in orbit, and those twenty transports had carried the core of Exilium's industrial-plant-to-be.

As she watched, heavy-lift shuttles were maneuvering massive solar panel arrays into position above what had once been four trans-ports—and would shortly be Exilium's main orbital transshipment platform.

When each array made it into position, the destroyer hovering nearby would rotate slightly and then permanently weld the structure together with a carefully calculated blast from a pulse cannon. At first glance, the destroyer was there as a watchdog, but as she paid atten-tion, Amelie realized the ship was lending the power of her immense engines and plasma weapons to the task of assembling the space station.

Exilium orbit *buzzed* with activity, in many ways busier than Starhaven below. The work was spread out over a far vaster area, but the lack of anything to bar the view allowed her to watch the dozens —*hundreds*—of fireflies of working spacecraft lit up orbit of her new world.

"If you look forward and to port, you'll see the Morgue," Mackenzie told her quietly.

"The Morgue?" Amelie asked. She followed the direction, though, barely managing to make out the small flotilla of warships orbiting away from everything else. Only the most basic of running lights were on, enough to make sure everyone else knew where they were.

"Half the Fleet personnel took the Admiral's opt-out," her pilot said. "Those are the ships we couldn't crew. Fourteen destroyers and four missile cruisers. A battle group without the battlecruiser, basically."

"I'll have to talk to Isaac about that," Amelie murmured. She understood the logic, but it was also possible they could find volunteers to help crew those ships. It seemed…pointless to have eighteen warships floating in mothballs, after all.

She was there for a specific purpose, but she was also going to pin Isaac Gallant down for a long conversation. They hadn't actually seen each other in person since they'd passed through the XL-17 wormhole. They had a lot to discuss.

They were the two most powerful people in this new colony, and they needed to coordinate their efforts and plans. Electronic communication could only do so much, after all.

Amelie was looking forward to seeing him.

———

"WELCOME ABOARD *VIGIL*," Gallant greeted Amelie as she stepped off the shuttle.

There was an awkward moment where she almost went in for a hug and he was attempting to salute, which they managed to resolve with a handshake. There was enough of an audience that she hoped they'd managed to cover the confusion.

"It's good to be here," she told him. "It appears you've been keeping yourself busy!"

That got a few chuckles from the surrounding crowd of military officers and crew. They were all back in uniform now, she noted, after the intentionally lax discipline of the warp voyage. There were subtle alterations to the uniforms, though. Smaller insignia, different-colored stripes…things that she suspected were hugely meaningful to the men and women who wore them.

To her, though, they announced something equally meaningful and important: this was the *Exilium* Space Fleet, not the *Confederacy* Space Fleet.

"The Exilium Space Fleet is eager to do our part in making sure our new colony thrives," Gallant said gently, gesturing for her to follow him. "This is your entire party?" he asked, looking over the handful of men and women following Amelie out of the shuttle.

"Media crew and personal aide," she confirmed. One male reporter, one camerawoman, one woman with a tattoo-comp to do live editing and control. Her aide, Roger Faulkner, had been a Charlie cell leader on Earth in the rebellion.

A senior bureaucrat, he'd been an aide to one of the First Admiral's handful of civilian ministers. He might even, one day, recover from the beating the Secret Police had delivered when they'd realized just how high the betrayal ran.

Until then, he walked with a limp and had chosen to take a cybernetic left eye over going half-blind like Dr. Reinhardt.

"The Governor trusts the Fleet," Faulkner said now, his voice pitched so only Amelie and Gallant could hear him as he fell in behind them. "And, almost as importantly, the Governor has to be *seen* to trust the Fleet, Admiral. We cannot risk even the slightest appearance of conflict between you two. Or"—he coughed delicately—"of excessive cooperation. It's a careful line we have to walk."

He'd clearly noticed Amelie's aborted attempt at a hug. They might have spent the last seven months talking daily and become good friends, but she could not publicly appear to be affectionate toward Gallant.

Balance in all things. That was how to run a government.

"I see Mr. Faulkner is being good for you," Gallant told her, glancing over to meet her eyes. His brows wrinkled in a manner she'd learned to recognize by now, and she managed a half-hearted glare no one else could see.

"He says he traded his eye for wisdom," she noted. "I say he traded it for sheer stubborn determination."

"I won't argue that one," Faulkner agreed. "We owe too much to too many to fail. I believe we had a purpose for this trip?"

Gallant chuckled, his brows crinkling at Amelie again.

"We do. We're on our way to the presentation center, where the warp cruiser captains and selected officers and personnel await. The *shortest* mission they're looking at is almost three years."

"We owe them a send-off," Amelie agreed. "Just promise me we're not playing any of my movies at this party."

———

GALLANT'S PEOPLE had opened up *Vigil*'s observation deck and turned it into a party hall for the event. The armored clamshell that guarded the deck in combat was retracted and the deck was filled with uniformed spacers.

A handful of non-Fleet people were already there, mostly officers from the transports and orbiting stations taking shape outside the window.

From where she stood, Amelie could look "up" and see much of the orbital construction going on—and look past it to see the green-and-blue glow of Exilium itself. She didn't think she could see Starhaven; the colony had to be over the horizon by now.

"It's time," Faulkner murmured at her shoulder. "Time to show these people everybody cares."

"Don't let the cynicism show, Roger," she told him. "We need these scouting missions. The government people, at least, do care."

"But most people are too busy to realize the importance," he reminded her. "So, as always, it falls to the leadership to show appreciation on behalf of a population that doesn't know what's going on."

"Cynicism," she repeated.

"Yes," he agreed. "Better to show cynicism than to slip up and treat the Admiral as more than a colleague, Governor. Too many people see his mother in him. Keep your distance."

"I know," Amelie conceded. "But he's a friend, Roger. Not sure why we should hide that."

"Because people are afraid of him and we need them to not to be," Faulkner said flatly. "But more than we need people to trust the Admiral, we need people to trust you. So, you have to keep your distance.

"And you have to give this speech. So, let's go."

She followed Faulkner to the central platform, the crowd separating and re-forming as they saw her coming. The crews of the six warp cruisers gathered around, looking to her and their Admiral as they prepared for their voyages.

Amelie mounted the dais and smiled down at everyone.

"Good afternoon, people," she greeted them. "I think it's afternoon, at least. What time are you keeping up here, anyway?"

That got a chuckle, exactly as intended. They'd switched the Fleet over to Starhaven time a few days before, so it *was* afternoon. Many of the ESF's people were still transitioning, though, effectively jet-lagged from the change in time zones.

"You all know why we're here better than I do," she continued. "Six ships. *Tarantula, Scorpion, Termite, Carpenter, Widow* and *Recluse.* You all volunteered for this mission, which is damn reassuring to me.

"It's reassuring because none of us volunteered to be out here," Amelie reminded them all. "We are here because our government decided, with various degrees of accuracy, that we were a threat. That we were to be cast out to protect the rest."

She turned to let her smile linger on each of the collections that represented the crews of those six ships.

"And yet…you all volunteered to put on a new uniform and take up an old task for a new world," she told them. "Everyone who wears the uniform of the Exilium Space Fleet chose to. None of us chose exile, but *you* chose to take up the shield and stand between our people and the unknown shadows.

"And then, out of those who volunteered to stand guard, *you* chose to crew our warp cruisers. The only ships we can send out of the Exilium System. We *need* you to be our eyes and ears, to let us know what lurks in the shadows that surround us.

"But we are limited in the technology we were allowed to bring with us. We cannot scout with wormholes or other tools. Only your ships.

"Three years. Four. Five." She laid out the numbers softly. "That is the sacrifice we have asked of you. You have come into exile with the rest of us, and now we have to ask you to leave us. To go into the dark beyond even this far-flung light of humanity, to see the rest of us safe.

"And you volunteered again. There are no words for this. Only thanks that ring all too hollow in the face of your devotion.

"So…*merci.* Thank you. Thank you all."

―――

18

Lestroud was still aboard *Vigil* as the warp cruisers began to move out, a surprisingly welcome presence on Isaac's flag deck as his people set to work.

"Captain Catalan," he greeted the commander of *Scorpion*, his own last starship command. "How's the ship treating you?"

"It's nice to be back aboard an actual ship instead of stacked in a glorified apartment building attached to a monstrosity of technology," the younger man told him. "Not that I expected to end up in command of the old girl, in any case."

"Someone has to take care of her," Isaac replied. "You can't trust these new kids with our old lady!"

All six warp cruisers now had their engines live, flaring toward the edge of the system on pillars of blue-white light.

He tapped a command, widening the channel to all six ships.

"Warp cruisers of the Exilium Space Fleet, you will be at most the second group of humans to enter the systems you are visiting—and we know the last survey went through at crazy speeds to minimize their time in normal space.

"You will see things no human before you has seen, and you will bring your new knowledge home to us. We'll be waiting for you with the porch light on.

"Godspeed!"

Scorpion was the first to disappear, her normal-space engines cutting to zero as her drive ring began to glow. Then the glow expanded to encase the entire ship in a Cherenkov-blue bubble that shot away into nothingness.

The other ships followed, their angles different as they each turned toward their own destination. *Vigil*'s flag deck was silent as they vanished, civilian guests and military officers alike quietly saluting the bravery of the scouts they were sending out.

"So, what now?" Lestroud finally asked him quietly. "Half of your fleet is either out-system or in mothballs. How *are* you going to keep busy?"

Isaac chuckled.

"Two battlecruisers, six destroyers, four cruisers," he recited. "Not counting the people I need to run the support infrastructure we're still unpacking, that's roughly seven thousand personnel. I suspect they're going to keep me busy."

"You seem to be busy helping us unpack more than working on your own stations," she noted.

He nodded.

"A lot of our facilities need civilian infrastructure to support them," he agreed. "And pulse guns are apparently fantastic for large-scale welding." Most of the large civilian welders were, basically, stepped-down pulse guns.

"We've got a supply of parts and fuel for now, but we'll need to start manufacturing sooner rather than later. Munitions too, if only to allow for live-fire training."

"And for that you need the same raw materials everyone else does?" Lestroud asked, chuckling.

"Exactly. And money. That darn thing we don't want to print too much of." He shared her chuckle. "Shall we go arm-wrestle over budgets, Governor?"

———

IT WAS FUNNY, Isaac reflected as he led Lestroud into his office. The Governor had made her career out of portraying everything from vulnerability to power but, generally, being sexy and attractive while doing it. The artistry of entire teams had managed to make everything from the terrified teenager she'd played in one of her first movies to the self-assured Admiral she'd played in *Stars of Honor* gorgeous to the audience.

She was still more beautiful in person than she'd ever been on the screen, moving with an easy grace that Isaac was quite certain was entirely unconscious. Reflection beyond that, however, was probably unhealthy for him, so he gestured her to a seat as he crossed to his drinks cabinet.

"Can I fix you something, Governor?" he asked.

"Isaac, Isaac," she chided him. "*S'il vous plaît*, call me Amelie. I've told you this before!"

He chuckled.

"Fair enough, Amelie," he conceded. "But, back to my question, a drink?"

"Wine?" she asked. "Or is it too early for that?"

"You're not flying the shuttle and I need to talk you into giving me resources," Isaac told her with a smile. "I can do wine. My steward appears to have tucked a nice New Soweto Merlot in here, if that will do?"

"That sounds divine," she replied. "New Soweto always made nice wines."

Isaac studied the bottle a moment longer and smiled sadly. The familiar lounging panther logo wasn't just from New Soweto; it was from the Liebermann Cat Vineyards.

"Huh. I doubt Parminder knew to grab this specific one," he said aloud. Parminder Singh hadn't been his steward before the Exile, so it was unlikely he knew which random orchard on Isaac's father's home-world he'd owned.

"What's special about this one?" Amelie asked as he poured, studying the bottle. "Wait, Liebermann…"

"As in Franz Liebermann, yes," Isaac confirmed. "My father. I actually *owned* Liebermann Cat, not that I'd visited in, oh, a decade or so. My father hired good people and they found good replacements."

"Who owns it now?" she asked.

"Who knows?" He shrugged. "If they executed on my will, the staff own it now. If not...well, I doubt my mother wanted it. She hid *everything* of my father's after his death."

"After she killed him," Amelie said softly.

"After she killed him," Isaac agreed. He took a sip of the wine. It was as good as he remembered. "I hope we have more than one bottle of this. I always enjoyed my people's wine."

The Governor nodded as she took an appreciative sip of her own.

"So, resources," she said as she leaned back in her chair. "I saw the Morgue on the way in. That's *damn* depressing."

"And it's staying that way," he told her. "There's no reason for us to spend the time and effort finding people to crew purely sublight ships right now. Honestly, all we *need* is the half-dozen destroyers I've got doing support and search and rescue, but that's assuming this corner of the galaxy is safe."

"If you're assuming this corner of the galaxy is safe, you're not doing your job," Amelie told him.

"Exactly. But there's only so much I can do with a fleet that can't leave this star system."

She smiled. The shiver that sent down his spine was dangerous, and he carefully focused on his wineglass.

"Which brings us back to resources," she noted.

"I've convinced Dr. Reinhardt to come work for me, but that's resulted in him presenting me with a wish list of gear and people," Isaac admitted. "This is just for preliminary work; he doesn't even want any particularly large amount of exotic matter.

"But he wants about ten percent of our lab space and about thirty physicists, plus a hundred or so gophers," he concluded. "The lab space is what I need you to agree to, honestly. I suspect the scientists will be ecstatic to do science instead of farming."

Amelie chuckled.

"University professors and students make mediocre colonists," she agreed. "We've done better on that front that I was afraid of, but I doubt you'll have problems recruiting for research. That's a lot of lab space and gear, though.

"And it needs to be orbital lab space," Isaac told her. "We've even less of that, and the only reason I'm not asking for a ship is because our destroyers actually have the equipment he needs for the deep-space testing."

"But, as I understand, we're talking better FTL drives, right?" she asked.

"Exactly. Improved grav-warp engines. Neither I nor Reinhardt are sure of the actual limits of the tech; the Confederacy never had a reason to push it."

"A lot of people are going to ask why we don't just go for wormhole tech again," Amelie noted.

"From what Dr. Reinhardt said, we lack too much of the foundational knowledge," Isaac replied. "We don't have any wormhole physicists. In fact, we have such a large preponderance of people who spent time working in grav-warp that it's suspicious."

"Your mother's hand at work?"

"Yeah. This whole goddamn expedition has been stealing supports with one hand and providing different ones with the other. We're going to end up with something very different from the Confederacy out here," he told Amelie. "And not just in terms of government and culture. The limits they put on the database are going to force us to take our tech base in a completely different direction."

"And keep an entire branch of humanity intact, no matter what happens to the Confederacy," Amelie said speculatively.

"That, from my last conversation with her, was exactly the point."

"Improved grav-warp drives aren't just a military asset," she reminded him. "We'll want to know what's going on around us, to stretch our limbs and see what we can find and access in the stars nearby.

"Reinhardt will have his lab space. Exilium *needs* those FTL drives."

―――――

19

"Well, Dr. Reinhardt?" Isaac asked brightly. "What miracles do you have for me?"

The massive physicist gave him a dirty look fierce enough to melt a hole through the space station's hull.

"A month, Admiral," he pointed out. "I have had a *month*. We haven't even been in this star system for two months. What do you want from me?"

Isaac smiled as he walked over to the wall of Reinhardt's office. Like just about every office in Exilium these days, it showed every sign of being assembled from prefabricated pieces and only barely personalized to its inhabitant. The wall was a massive screen, currently pretending to be a window showing the planet beneath them.

Seven weeks. They'd been in Exilium for seven weeks, and both Starhaven and the orbitals were finally beginning to take some semblance of their final form. He even had destroyers surveying the rest of the system now.

Exilium was the fourth world in the star system, meaning there were three hotter worlds closer to the star and four more, colder ones farther out. Two of the colder ones were gas giants, and one of the prefabricated stations they had was a cloudscoop.

That cloudscoop would be a far more reliable source of fuel for spacecraft than electrolyzing water on the surface, but the ESF was going to make sure that the gas giants were safe from debris and what passed for inclement weather on balls of hydrogen a thousand times the size of Earth before they let the civilians set up the single, currently irreplaceable cloudscoop they had.

"Miracles, doctor," Isaac repeated. "By which I mean, I don't actually expect anything unless you've *achieved* miracles."

Reinhardt snorted.

"We're barely past database searches of the data we brought with us," he told Isaac. "Which, to be fair, has brought up a lot more than I expected. Did you know the original design for the dreadnoughts called for them to be warp-capable?"

Isaac whistled silently.

"*Liberty* was too damned expensive to duplicate as it was," he replied. "What would putting a grav-warp ring on her *cost*?"

"A lot," Reinhardt said flatly. "That's why that part never made it off the drawing board—it would have doubled the cost of a unit that already ended up far too expensive. But the plan did result in a set of designs, schematics, and feasibility research that's handy for us.

"Not least, the conclusion was that doing so was entirely practical, just insanely expensive," he continued. "The research for making *Liberty* warp-capable gave them the groundwork to build that warp cradle—and it tells us that sticking a warp ring on your battlecruisers is entirely possible."

"That's not nothing, Doctor," Isaac admitted. "Even four times light is better than being effectively trapped in the Exilium System."

The cost in terms of resources was more important than the cost in terms of money at this point, and he doubted it would be cheap. His warp cruisers were the same mass as his missile cruisers and had actually cost *more* to build, despite only being about fifty percent more heavily armed than his destroyers.

"Some interesting studies on that, too," Reinhardt said. "Nothing material; no one was ever willing to front the cash to try and build faster warp ships. Not when we had wormholes."

"But a starting point?" Isaac asked.

"Exactly. Some of the theoretical studies suggest we've dramatically underestimated the maximum speed of a warp drive ship," the doctor told him. "Not *our* warp drives, to be clear, the limitation is tied into some ugly calculations of exotic-matter ratios and so forth, but at least one study suggested that the theoretical limit was potentially measured in *thousands* of *c*, not tens."

Thousands of times lightspeed. *Thousands.*

"That would change our strategic and economic position significantly," Isaac murmured. "Wormhole would still be faster, but a warp drive that could travel multiple light-years a day would be far more flexible."

"And we're not getting wormholes anytime soon," Reinhardt said flatly. "We know it *can* be done, so we could recreate the theory and science from scratch. If we had even *one* wormhole specialist, I'd say we could do it in ten years."

"But we don't, do we?" Isaac asked.

"No. Which is strange, given that I doubt they were any less involved in student protests than I was," the big man complained. "I can't help but feel that was intentional."

"I'm sure it was," Isaac replied. "Without a specialist, what would it take?"

Reinhardt sighed.

"Give me that same ten years, and I'll have increased the effectiveness of our warp drives by at least an order of magnitude. Potentially two or three—a few hundred times lightspeed. We have nothing else to focus on.

"Ask me to rebuild wormhole tech and we won't have that at all," he said grimly. "And in ten years? We won't have wormholes, either. We *might* be able to rebuild basic, early twenty-second-century wormhole drills in twenty years. Once we'd done that, we could get back to Confederacy tech level in, oh, a generation or so."

"Fifty years, give or take?" Isaac guessed.

"Aye."

"We can't wait twenty years to explore the space around us," the Admiral said. "Keep on doing what you're doing. I'll try and keep people from demanding we build wormholes."

Reinhardt opened his mouth to reply, but then Isaac's arm chimed loudly, an emergency alert hitting his tattoo-comp .

He gestured for the scientist to wait and tapped a command.

"Gallant here," he barked.

"Boss, we have a problem," Cameron Alstairs's voice emerged from the device. "A mutiny-type problem."

Isaac turned to look back at the "window" and muffled a curse.

"I'm on my way," he snapped. "Brief me on the run."

———

BY THE TIME he was aboard his shuttle and heading to *Vigil*, Isaac had the high level. *Mutiny* wasn't quite the correct term—mutiny implied that his volunteer-only crews had turned on him.

Instead, it turned out that among the many dissidents and troublemakers swept up in the Confederacy's net for Exile Fleet had, of course, been a significant chunk of at least one organized crime network. An organized crime network that had apparently decided they needed a warship of their own.

The destroyer *Confucius* had been out scouting Exilium's asteroid belt and clusters for anything worth hauling back to the planet's orbit to rip apart. They'd had a successful voyage and been "on a roll."

So, instead of coming back in to resupply, one of the colliers had been sent out to resupply them. Given the shortage of Fleet personnel, this one had an all-civilian crew.

"Any portion of the collier crew that wasn't with them is either dead or imprisoned," Alstairs said grimly as the shuttle dove toward the battlecruiser. "Nothing even suggested trouble before *Dancer* rendezvoused with *Confucius*."

"What's *Confucius*'s status?" Isaac asked.

"As of last reports, the boarders had Engineering and were moving on the bridge," his ops officer reported. "Commander Hemsworth was locking down the bridge as best he could, but…"

"The boarders knew what they were doing and had the gear to get through the security hatches?" Isaac guessed.

"Exactly. Last report was—*fuck*."

"Commander?" Isaac snapped.

Alstairs swallowed hard, and when he spoke, his voice was very formal.

"Admiral, we have confirmed receipt of *Confucius*'s Masada Protocol code. Stage One only, but with a codicil informing us that Stage Two is on a timer."

Isaac closed his eyes in pain.

Masada Protocols were suicide protocols. Stage One meant that Commander Hemsworth had just vented the atmosphere from every portion of the ship he wasn't sure he controlled. From the sound of things, quite probably everywhere except the bridge.

At least some of the boarders would have the gear for that, but almost none of his crew would have. Hemsworth had just killed any of his crew the attackers had taken prisoner.

Stage Two Masada Protocols would overload the destroyer's fusion cores, turning the warship into a multi-gigaton bomb.

"Commander," he said, equally formally as Alstairs. "What is your assessment of whether the boarders will be unable to disarm the Stage Two Masada Protocol?"

His ops officer sighed.

"If they made it this far, they've got ex-Confed Fleet personnel with them," he admitted. "That means they know about the Protocols and wouldn't have tried to take *Confucius* without a solution.

"Given that they went for Engineering first…"

"They have a plan," Isaac confirmed. "Damn. All right. Orders to the Fleet—*Dante* will remain in orbit with the missile cruisers just in case.

"*Violet, Errantry, Shepherd* and *Singh* will form on *Vigil*," he ordered, listing off the four destroyers still in Exilium orbit. "Designate Task Force *Vigil*. TF *Vigil* will move to intercept *Confucius*.

"Make sure Giannovi and the other Captains know the game," Isaac continued grimly. "Under no circumstances are *Confucius* or *Dancer* going to escape.

"I will *not* have pirates in my star system!"

————

20

BATTLECRUISERS WERE "SLOW" by the standards of the Confederacy Space Fleet and their Exilium successors. *Slow*, however, was relative. Within minutes of Isaac giving the orders, his quickly assembled five-ship task force was already a light-second away from Exilium and rapidly expanding the distance.

"The time limit on *Confucius*'s Masada Protocol Stage Two has expired," Alstairs reported as they focused their sensors on the embattled destroyer. "She's still with us...and we haven't heard anything from Commander Hemsworth."

"So, they have her," Isaac assumed aloud. Three hundred people aboard *Confucius*. Two hundred aboard *Dancer*. At least half of *Dancer*'s crew had to be in on this and probably some of *Confucius*'s...but that was still hundreds of his people who were almost certainly dead.

"Any communication from the pirates?" he asked.

"Nothing," Rhianna Rose told him. "No demands, no identification, nothing. We're running the crew list for *Dancer* and comparing it to the old CSF files. We may see something."

"Unlikely," Isaac said. "We're paying more than lip service to the concept of everyone getting a fresh start out here, but we still run everyone we put on a spaceship through a background check. Even one insane asshole at the helm of a tug could destroy the entire colony."

"*Confucius* still isn't moving," Alstairs noted. "Captain Giannovi's people say they're picking up outgassing—it's possible they had to vent the reactor cores to short-stop Masada."

"Or at least buy themselves time," the Admiral agreed. "How long for them to reboot the reactor and bring up the engines if they did?"

"It's not quite a complete cold start of the cores, but it's close. Three to four hours. Maybe two if they're willing to take one hell of a risk," the ops officer concluded.

"We're only three and a bit hours away from them," Isaac said as he studied the plot. "They'll take the risk. I would." He shook his head. "I wish I knew their plan. If I could guess where they were going to run, this would be a lot easier."

"Where can they run? There's nowhere in this star system for them to lay low. No fuel supplies, no depots…"

"They have *Dancer*," Isaac reminded his people. "That's enough fuel, food and munitions to operate for a year, at least. They don't need to go anywhere specific; they just need to disappear. But unless they're idiots, they know the asteroid belt isn't going to cut it for that."

"They need a ring or a moon, and a planet to hide from us behind while they dive for cover," Giannovi agreed, the flag captain's image appearing on the screen. "If they can make it to Exilium Six or Seven, they can cut behind it and bury themselves."

"Won't be Seven," Isaac replied, looking at the chart. "*Destiny* is in position to watch the other side of the planet from us, and it's too damned far away. We'd catch them before they got there. So, either they think they can hide in the belt or they're going to run for Six."

He hooked his tattoo-comp into the main display almost absent-mindedly, running through calculations and vectors as he did.

"If we're on a direct course for them and they get their drive online in under three hours, they can dodge around the planet with a good fifteen-minute safety window. The acceleration to slow down on the other side will hurt—especially for *Dancer*'s crew—but it's survivable and they could drop themselves into the rings or onto one of the moons."

"We'd find them eventually," Alstairs said confidently.

"Sixty-forty, yeah," the Admiral told him. "But they are clearly prepared to take that chance, or think they've got some way to change the odds." He smiled grimly.

"I think they've underestimated us. Listen up, people. This is what we're going to do...."

———

WHOEVER THE SYNDICATE had managed to bring with them for engineers knew their business. Two hours and thirty-two minutes after *Confucius* vented her fusion cores to prevent an overload, the destroyer came back to life.

It took ten minutes after that for her engines to come fully online, but she was one of the newer ships in the Exilium Space Fleet. Once the engines came alive, *Confucius* leapt away from the oncoming task force like a scalded rabbit.

Directly toward Exilium Six.

"It's always nice to be right," Isaac said brightly, watching the starship run. "Any clue from her vector where she's planning on stopping?"

"Not much," Alstairs replied. "Exilium Six, that's all. She's got two thick rings and a dozen moons, seven of which will be on the far side of the task force when they arrive. It's a clever plan."

"It is," the Admiral confirmed. "Unfortunately for them, Captain Giannovi is smarter."

"Do *not* try and foist this brilliant scheme off on me," his flag captain replied sharply. "I suggested where they were going. *This* stunt is all on you."

He grinned.

"When this works, you'll want the credit," he pointed out. "Are you going to argue with me then? *I* don't need any promotions, Captain Giannovi."

She laughed at him.

"And if it blows up in our faces?" she asked.

"The worst-case scenario is egg on my face," Isaac replied. "We'll be fine."

"I may remind you, Admiral, that an unescorted battlecruiser is a destroyer skipper's wet dream," Giannovi said archly.

The four destroyers Isaac had assigned to Task Force *Vigil* continued on their direct course for where *Confucius* had been, adjusting to sweep around behind the rogue destroyer. They had a velocity advantage but were playing catch-up on distance. *Confucius* was going to get to Exilium Six before them.

Not least because the four destroyers were still limiting themselves to battlecruiser acceleration as they fed power to the ECM drone in the center of their formation. There was a dozen or more ways Isaac or his people could have realized what was being done, but he was counting on the fact that their enemy probably hadn't managed to acquire the best tactical people in the system.

Vigil herself was running her stealth systems and heat sinks to maximum. The system was barely more than an afterthought on a battlecruiser, designed to hide a capital ship lurking in ambush, not one accelerating at full power.

But until the heat sinks failed or they shut them down, the only major heat signature *Vigil* was showing was to the planet behind her. If the pirates used their optics for a wide sweep of the sky, they would be able to *see* the battlecruiser…but optical scanners were limited-focus tools.

If they were using them at all, they almost certainly had them focused on the destroyers.

"Time to range?" Isaac asked.

"Twenty-eight minutes." Giannovi shook her head at him again. "Destroyers are *designed* to kill battlecruisers, boss," she repeated.

"In packs, Captain," he replied. "If I was pulling this stunt against eight or even six destroyers, I'd be worried. One? He might scratch your paint."

"If he does, I'm sending *you* out with the paintbrush," his flag captain threatened.

"How long until the heat sinks fail?" he asked.

"Twenty minutes, plus or minus ten depending on when we cut the engines," Giannovi told him. "This ship is *not* designed to pretend she's some kind of pre-space submarine!"

"And yet she's doing such a wonderful job. Be proud of your ship, Captain. And let's make damn sure today is a shitty day for some pirates."

She sighed.

"Cyclotrons are fully spun up and the particle cannon is ready to fire," she told him. "How lucky are you feeling, Admiral?"

"Not lucky enough to expect a clean shot," Isaac countered. "They're going to be ready to fight. We'll have to disabuse them of the notion that it's a fight they can win."

The theoretical range of *Vigil*'s spinal particle cannon was over half again that of the pulse guns she shared with the destroyer. Both, however, were near-lightspeed weapons, which meant that the *accurate* range of the two weapons systems was basically the same.

Which meant the lifespan of *Vigil*'s heat sinks could make the difference between an easy kill and a pitched battle.

———

"Heat sink failure imminent."

The report from the bridge echoed in the silence of the flag deck and Isaac nodded calmly. They'd made it closer than he'd hoped, but they were still well out of range of the particle cannon.

"Shutting down the sinks and venting steam," Giannovi reported briskly. "They know we're here now."

Running water over the heat sinks and venting it to space would help preserve the system—and given their shortage of replacement parts, that was important. It would also make damn sure that the pirates knew they were coming, lighting up a thermal signature several dozen times as wide and hot as *Vigil* herself.

"Captain."

Giannovi turned her attention to the camera and Isaac paused.

There were a thousand orders he could give. Targeting, maneuvers, tricks...and all of them would be wrong. Not because they were tactically wrong, but because this wasn't his ship.

"Fight your ship, Lauretta," he ordered quietly, suppressing the urge to try and do her job for her.

She gave him a sharp nod then turned back to her bridge crew, barking orders to bring up the particle cannon before the pirates could react.

They were outside the practical maximum range of the particle cannon, but that was just the distance at which the packets of super-charged ions retained enough cohesion to punch through armor.

Dancer wasn't armored.

Isaac watched in silent approval as *Vigil* began to spiral in space… and then fired, her particle cannon pulsing seven times in under a second.

It would be a full minute before she could fire again—but they were more than that from the destroyer's range of them. The attack pattern was carefully calculated, bracketing the collier's likely evasive maneuvers.

And Giannovi had reacted before the pirates had. *Dancer* was only beginning to change her course at all when the fire arrived. Only one of the seven rounds hit.

That was more than enough. Without the active dissipation matrix or armor plating of a warship, the ion charge smashed into the collier and hammered through her full length in an instant.

The starship's velocity did the rest, ripping *Dancer* into pieces and scattering them across the sky.

"Target destroyed," Alstairs reported grimly. "*Confucius* is evading. Our velocity advantage is sufficient to bring her into range."

A battlecruiser's particle cannon was designed to kill anything it could hit.

"Rose, get me a communications channel," Isaac ordered. "I'd rather like to get my destroyer back."

She gave him a nod a moment later and he leaned into the pickup on his chair.

"*Confucius*, this is Admiral Gallant," he told the pirates. "This is your one and only chance to surrender. I don't like it, but I will guarantee your lives in exchange for getting *Confucius* back intact."

The message flung itself across space, and *Vigil* pursued.

"No response," Rose reported.

Isaac nodded.

"I didn't expect one," he admitted. Studying the holographic charts, he shook his head. His other five destroyers were all arcing toward Exilium Six. The four he'd brought with him were out of this fight. So was *Destiny*, he decided after a moment's reflection.

This was down to *Vigil*. Fortunately, Giannovi was damn good at her job.

"*Confucius* is turning!" Alstairs reported. "Full acceleration; she's trying for a high-speed attack run."

Isaac started to give his flag captain orders again, then stopped himself.

"That makes sense," he said quietly. "It's their best chance—if they can punch out *Vigil*, they win. But wolf pack tactics require a *wolf pack*, people."

Vigil hummed beneath him as the particle cannon came alive again. Now Giannovi was firing carefully sequenced shots, an ion packet every ten seconds.

Once they'd been intercepted, the pirates' charge was their only hope. But it was a slim hope indeed.

Confucius never even reached pulse-gun range. Giannovi's ninth shot struck home, the destroyer seeming to halt in space as the ion charge transferred its momentum to the destroyer.

The front half of the destroyer came apart in a flash of energy and power, the focused charge overwhelming the dissipation matrix with ease. For a few seconds, half of a destroyer continued along the suicide charge.

Even with full access to *Vigil*'s sensors, Isaac wasn't sure if it was the fusion cores or the next particle-cannon shot that vaporized the wreckage.

———

21

"WHAT. THE FUCK. HAPPENED?"

Amelie's snarl echoed through the tiny meeting room like a caged tiger. She was furious, and this, thankfully, was an audience she could let it show in.

There were only four people in the room, with Gallant linked in by video screen. Barry Wong, Werner Knutson and Roger Faulkner all sat across the table from her in silence.

"Well?" she demanded. "How the *hell* did somebody infiltrate one of our colliers, kill several hundred of our people, and steal a damn destroyer? Where did this even *come from*?"

"They stole a destroyer because we are not the Confederacy Space Fleet," Gallant said in a clipped, exhausted tone. "We've let a lot of security protocols lapse because, frankly, I assumed we were all in the same boat out here and didn't expect this at all.

"If you want to crucify someone, Amelie, the fault is mine."

Even if she believed that, Isaac Gallant was the last person she was going to hang this on. The dead officers and spacers were his people, after all.

"Except you shouldn't have needed to worry about that," Wong told him. "We background-check everyone who goes on a spaceship these days, and we have a *lot* more data on the people who got loaded into Exile Fleet than I think most people know.

"No one aboard *Dancer* had any organized crime connections before we went into Exile," the ex-rebel cell leader said calmly. "Several of them were part of the rebellion, the people we figure we can trust above all others."

"But there are significant organized crime presences in Starhaven," Knutson warned. "We've managed to trace three of our five murders to date back to what appears to have been a consolidation of power amidst the various groups."

"What were they even planning on doing with a destroyer?" Faulkner asked. "We have an entire fleet. What were they going to do with one ship? Hell, it's not even like there's somewhere to fence things they steal."

"I imagine seizing *Confucius* was only one part of a larger plan," Gallant told them. "With *Dancer*, they had the supplies to lay low for a while, slip beneath our radar and set up a black outpost somewhere.

"They'd need to raid our shipping for supplies for a while, but they wouldn't be able to do that for long," the Admiral continued. "They had to have been thinking more in terms of a fallback bolthole than some invincible pirate base.

"Or, well." He shrugged. "Possession of a destroyer would provide them with at least one tool to use, given an appropriate opportunity. In the absence of the rest of the Fleet, *Confucius* would have been quite capable of holding Starhaven hostage. There's only so much resistance you can muster against the people with the orbitals."

Amelie shivered. She'd seen the footage from when the Confederacy Space Navy had taken over the hidden colony at Waterloo. They'd started by destroying army formations from orbit but had progressed to annihilating the second-largest city on the planet as a "demonstration strike."

From Gallant's expression, he was remembering the same thing.

"So, what do we do?" she asked. "I haven't seen any evidence of a growing crime trend in the reports from Starhaven Watch, just the same petty theft and domestics we've seen all along."

"These are not the type of people who show up in crime stats,"

Wong said quietly. "These are the type of people who run very quiet, very dark, and empty an entire warehouse of supplies while we're not looking."

"We dealt with these people while we prepared for the revolt," Amelie agreed. "They're a threat and an insidious one if we haven't seen anything yet."

"I'll pass the word out to the Watch," Wong told her. "But until we know what they're planning…"

"Right now, they're almost certainly in resource-gathering mode," Gallant noted. "Acquiring people, guns, vehicles—they just tried and failed to acquire a warship, which means they're starting to stretch their wings a bit.

"We watch for them to make a mistake." The Admiral shook his head. "Unfortunately, other than providing overhead, I'm not sure there's anything the ESF or EMC can do. The last thing we need is Marines busting down doors!"

"I agree," Amelie said. He was right, but she was *angry*. And the Exilium Space Fleet and Exilium Marine Corps were angry too. It was their friends and colleagues who had died.

"I agree," she repeated, "but if I see evidence that they've acquired anything approaching heavy combat gear, fuck the optics: I *will* be the jackbooted dictator sending in Marines.

"Our people can blacken my name all they want. Keeping them safe is more important than appearances; am I clear?"

———

A DEFINING SKILL to any long-lived organized criminal organization was, as Amelie knew perfectly well, the ability to lie low when the heat was on. Her revolution might have failed, but she'd spent ten years organizing it without being caught in advance.

Whoever had launched the effort to try and take *Confucius* had definitely mastered that skill. The Watch was following up on every lead they had, but nothing was falling out of the trees they were shaking.

There were, of course, trees only Amelie Lestroud herself could shake. After a week of digging had failed to turn up anything, she decided to hit one of them and plugged a communication code into her office's systems.

Somehow, she wasn't surprised that she got a secretary. After two months on Exilium, corporations, collectives and every other business venture had begun to take form. Few of them were related to previous entities, given that any Confederacy wealth was meaningless here.

Ideas were what mattered right now, ideas that could convince Amelie's bankers to front cash and equipment and ideas that could convince people to follow.

She was still unsurprised that Carlos Domingo Rodriguez, once a senior don of the New Cartels, was sufficiently tied into those new organizations as to have staff.

"You know who I am," she told the secretary before he could even reel off his greeting. "I need to speak to Carlos. Now."

The young man blinked, swallowed hard, then nodded silently and disappeared behind a rotating logo of a smiling Komodo dragon.

The logo rotated on Amelie's screen for about thirty seconds before it was replaced by the heavyset face and tanned jowls of Carlos Rodriguez. Among his few charms had been his willingness to act as arms broker for Amelie's people.

In exchange, she'd paid him a *lot* of money and swallowed what she knew the rest of his dealings to be. He had been one of the few outsiders to deal directly with Alpha Cell, though Dresden had done his damnedest to make Rodriguez think "Artemis" was in charge.

"Ms. Lestroud!" he greeted her jovially. "How can I assist our Governor?" He spread his hands wide, showing that he was occupying an office that resembled her own, assembled from prefabricated furniture and gear with few luxuries.

"As you can see, my resources are not what they were, though I am assisting several fine entrepreneurs with their planning and personnel issues to earn my keep."

"We're none of us what we were," Amelie told him drily. "But there are those that say the leopard never changes his spots, aren't there, *Don Rodriguez?*"

He didn't even blink and none of the joviality left his face as he laid his hands on his desk and smiled at her.

"That is a title I once held, yes," he conceded. "I always suspected that Artemis was not the true peak of the rebellion's chain of authority, though it didn't seem worth it to chase the chain further, so long as the dollars kept flowing."

"We wouldn't have told you more, regardless," she said. "I have to wonder, though, if my old friend Carlos is up to his old tricks in our new world."

"We only have the skills we have, Ms. Governor," he said carefully. "But I should point out another old homily that I feel would be relevant to anyone who were, say, to be dipping their toes into those old waters here:

"Don't shit where you sleep," Rodriguez concluded bluntly. "I'm guessing that rule was broken, but my resources are not what they were. Why don't you tell me what you think I did?"

Amelie smiled thinly.

To her surprise, she actually believed him—that he hadn't been involved, at least, though she suspected he *knew* about the attack.

"Someone used a slew of bribed ex-CSF people and organized crime thugs to steal one of our military colliers and tried to hijack one of Admiral Gallant's destroyers," she told him. "They're dead. They're all dead—but so are the crews of two of our ships, and there is, Mr. Rodriguez, going to be hell to pay."

"*Madre de dios*," he swore. "I swear to you, Ms. Lestroud, I knew nothing. I won't pretend my hands are clean, but I'm not going to *fuck* with our fleet. Sell them drugs? Fuck, yes. *Steal a starship*?"

He shook his head.

"We know too little and are too far out in the dark to play those kinds of games."

"So, it wasn't your organization?" she demanded.

The joviality finally faded as Rodriguez winced and closed his eyes.

"I can't guarantee that," he said slowly. "What I will swear to you, Governor, is that if it *was* my people, I didn't authorize anything of the sort. And I will make certain no such thing happens again."

He shook his head, opening his eyes to meet her gaze again.

"There is a dance and a game to what I do, Ms. Lestroud," he said frankly. "I say this much because we both know you can't pin anything on me. There are things that you, as a government, feel must be banned for the public good that citizens with funds and resources feel they must have.

"Someone must fill that need. It can be done quietly, or it can be done messily. I'd far rather the former. Your Watch will hunt the dealers and labs, and we will move and hide. That is the nature of the game.

"But I promise you this: we will not shit where we sleep. We won't undermine the Fleet or the government. We're exiled out here with everyone else."

"And if that isn't good enough?" Amelie asked. "There's a lot of question over how much 'rule of law' we currently have. What if I decide you need to disappear?"

"Bluntly, Ms. Lestroud, you know I don't want to cause waves. Clearly, we can't be so certain about others. I am the devil you know." He smiled brilliantly. "Whether I'm better than the one you don't is up to you."

———

"WELL, boss, I've got good news and bad news for you."

Amelie sighed. Jess Tsuu T'ina had been the senior constable in the training cadre the Colonial Developments Teams had brought. So, she'd ended up as Chief Tsuu T'ina of the Starhaven Watch, the woman in charge of police for a colonial city of four million souls.

Tsuu T'ina was good at her job, but Amelie questioned her sense of humor.

"All right, Chief," she said. "Lay it on me."

"The good news is that we now know who pulled the *Confucius* op," Tsuu T'ina told her. The image of a redheaded and spectacularly pale man appeared on the screen next to Tsuu T'ina's far darker face. "This was Wesley Smith, a member in good standing of the Bane Sidhe."

The Governor of Exilium made a face. The Bane Sidhe were a techno-syndicate known for using the darker side of modern brain-repair technologies to literally make robots of their trafficking victims. Even as organized crime went, they were bad.

"I didn't realize we *had* any of the Bane Sidhe in Exile Fleet," she said grimly.

"Neither did I, given that Mr. Smith was actually arrested and dumped into our care under the false identity of Wayne Bond. Mr. Bond, I suspect, has actually been dead for a while, but Smith was using his identity as a cover.

"Unfortunately for everyone, Bond had been involved in financing and organizing unions on Erewhon, so when the Confederacy swept up their dissidents, we got a bonus brain-hacking crook."

"Tell me he's in custody," Amelie said grimly. The *last* thing Exilium needed was a brain-hacker. That was a technology she was happy to leave behind in the Confederacy.

"He's not. That brings me to the bad news. Our murder rate just went up by a factor of six, because Wesley Smith and twenty-two friends are stacked up in a warehouse they'd converted into a brain-hack 'clinic.'"

"What happened?" Amelie asked.

"We're not entirely sure yet," Tsuu T'ina admitted. "We got a flag on the emergency code an hour ago and deployed a team to investigate. Found a goddamn massacre. Someone went in with knives and lasers, kept it so quiet even the neighbors didn't realize there was a fight.

"And there *was* a fight," she concluded. "We're pretty sure at least half a dozen people got dragged out of there wounded or dead, but we've seen no trace of them."

"And Smith?"

"Smith was killed by someone *very* familiar with the Bane Sidhe," the cop told Amelie. "After he'd been shot down, someone very specifically went back and put a laser beam through his backup brain."

"Backup brain?" Amelie asked slowly.

"Yeah. I knew about them, though I'd never seen one quite so neatly destroyed before," Tsuu T'ina told her. "Some senior Bane Sidhe had a cybernetic backup of their brain kept inside a shielded case, usually inside their ribcage. Backed up with healing nanites, they can regenerate from even having their heads blown off—at least long enough to find a friendly doctor.

"Whoever shot Smith wanted to make damned sure he didn't find one. They also wrecked the brain-hacking equipment but left a copy of Smith's files about *Confucius* on a datastick hanging around the bastard's neck."

Amelie sighed.

"Have we validated that data?"

"We're working on it," Tsuu T'ina agreed. "Nothing solid yet, but it looks clean so far. Of course, the computers it was pulled from have been hacked to pieces."

"Rodriguez," the Governor said flatly.

"I have *nothing* to pin on anyone," the police chief replied. "No DNA traces, no camera footage, not even a noise complaint from a witness. Whoever did this was clean, fast and deadly.

"That said, I would guess that yesterday there was an argument over who ran Starhaven's underworld—and that today there is not."

Amelie nodded slowly.

"So, we have a snake that's being cooperative, but that doesn't make him any less of a snake," she told the chief. "Watch him."

"Like a hawk, ma'am. We'll keep this city clean, I promise you."

———

22

Six months could change everything, Amelie Lestroud reflected. The prefabricated colony sections deployed out of the ships had been massive and effective, but they hadn't been attractive by any standard. The government centers had been the old bridges, with no decorations beyond the old ship logo on the doors.

Now the space in front of Exilium Central, once the command decks of the colony ship *Star of Delights*, had been turned into a public space. Roads had been rearranged to go around it, and an entire unused apartment building had been torn apart for raw materials.

It would be years before the trees grew to any significant height, but decorative pillars carved of native stone lined a stage next to the main entrance of the building. Today, security barriers covered the gap between Central and the stage itself, and a crowd had gathered to see the Governor speak.

Everyone knew what Amelie was going to announce. They'd intentionally leaked it to make sure they had the attention of the newborn media outlets. Exilium Central News was still a government-controlled entity, but she suspected it might be one of the first acts of the new leader to privatize it now that private media sources were popping up on the planet-net.

There were flagpoles on the corner of the stage, a new addition since, to date, Exilium hadn't *had* a flag. She could see several members of the crowd pointing those out as she strode onto the stage alone.

"People of Exilium," she greeted them, looking out at the crowd and swallowing a moment of nervousness. The nature of her old job meant that not only had billions of people seen her work, billions of people had seen her naked—but she had rarely had to stand in front of a crowd of over a hundred thousand people.

"It is always awe-inspiring to consider the difference time makes," she began as the crowd quieted, millions hanging on her every word. "Six months and a few days ago, no human had ever set foot on Exilium. A year and a few days ago, no one had ever used a warp cradle for a six-month voyage of an entire colonization fleet.

"Two years ago, we were all citizens of the Confederacy."

She let that hang in the air for a moment. A large screen rolled up behind her, showing the image of Exile Fleet as it had arrived in Exilium.

"I think it's safe to say that few people who ended up here were content with the state of the Confederacy," she said. "We were dissidents, criminals and rebels. By now, I think everyone here knows that I was leading an organized revolution to attempt to overthrow First Admiral Gallant.

"We failed, and we all ended up here. Necessity meant we had to have a leader, a single voice to direct the early development of the colony. The rebellion became the Exile Watch volunteers and I became your Governor.

"But in doing so, we ended up with a structure no different than the true nature of the government we left behind," she admitted. "It was always the promise that that would change, and today…"

She smiled brightly.

"Today, it is my honor and my privilege to inform you that a working group of constitutional and legal scholars, sociologists and historians has completed the task of assembling our new Constitution. It honors the principles the Confederacy was originally meant to uphold, the principles we inherited from republics across Old Earth."

Amelie gestured and waiting staffers swept into action. Flags ran up the four flagpoles on the stage around her and the two on the building behind her, and the screen showing Exile Fleet flickered, resolving into the new silver-on-green, three encircled rockets of the flag of Exilium.

"Did I mention we also have a flag?" she said cheerfully to a chorus of chuckles.

"People of Exilium, it is my honor and my privilege to declare today the first day of the Republic of Exilium. Today, we begin a thirty-day election period for a hundred-person legislative Senate and a new President.

"By the end of this meeting, you should be advised which of the one hundred Senatorial Districts you will be voting in. Candidacies should be registered with the Election Office being run by Director Knutson within seven days.

"I am resigning as Governor effective immediately, and Magistrate Barry Wong will run an interim government for the next thirty-one days. It would not, in my opinion, be appropriate for me to operate as your government and head of state…while I run for President."

That dissolved the crowd into cheers and applause.

————

"That went better than expected," Amelie said later in the living room of the quiet apartment she'd claimed for herself. "And now I get a vacation!"

Isaac Gallant, present in person for once, chuckled from his seat on her couch.

"Who's running your election campaign?" he asked.

"Faulkner, who else?" she replied, gesturing to the ex-Confederacy aide leaning against the bar. "We have a plan."

"Of course we have a plan," Faulkner agreed. "We had the advantage of knowing when the ball was going to drop, though you did insist on leaking that in likely ears a few weeks ago."

"I want a fair campaign," Amelie insisted. The likelihood that she was going to *lose* the election was frustratingly low, but she didn't want that to be because of any unfair advantage.

"Do we know who's going to throw their hat in the ring for Senate and President?" Gallant asked. "If I'm going to end up with a new boss, I'd like to know who!"

Amelie shook her head.

"Knutson will know pretty quickly, I suspect, but he can't tell me," she told her Admiral. "For thirty days, I have no authority, and since most of the people running the interim government will probably do what I tell them regardless, that means I need to be *seen* to not interact with them."

"Appearances are important," Gallant agreed. There was something in his voice as he spoke, something she didn't recognize. Odd.

"That said, of course, *some* of us had to do some research to prepare for this," Faulkner said in a false-acrid tone. "I don't know much about the Senate. We don't have parties of any kind, so the first few iterations of the Republic Senate are going to be…chaotic and unpredictable."

"Which is probably for the best for everyone," Amelie agreed. "We can't afford fossilization and polarization in the first few years of our existence."

"Agreed," her aide replied. "For President, however, there are three people I expect to run and only two that actually matter.

"First and least important, Robert Bruce, formerly executive officer of *Dante*, will probably throw his hat into the ring. He's…a complete nonentity outside of *Dante*'s crew, and most of her post-Exile crew think he's useless.

"He hasn't made much of himself since we got here, either, so I don't expect him to make a significant showing in the election," the cyber-eyed advisor reeled off, counting off on his fingers.

"Secondly, and our first real challenger, is Carlos Domingo Rodriguez." Faulkner ran off the Don's name with practiced ease. "We're pretty sure Rodriguez is running most of our organized crime at this point and will use those resources to fund a run for the Presidency. In all honesty, he'd probably do a damn good job, but we'd end up with a far laxer set of laws in general than most of us would prefer."

Amelie snorted. She could see that. Rodriguez would lead the

Republic as well as he led his cartel, but she doubted the drug laws they'd copied over from the Confederacy would survive his term.

"Lastly, and potentially a more significant threat—though I'm not certain yet—is Father Petrov James," the aide continued as he counted off a third finger. "The Christian Alliance tried to make him their Director—effectively, Archbishop of all Christian denominations on Exilium despite the intentionally secular title.

"He refused, most likely because he was already planning for this. Make no mistake, however: he can bring the resources of the Alliance and the donations and votes of its worshippers to his cause."

"Like Rodriguez, I think he'd actually do a decent job," Amelie noted. "Even if he and I disagree on, well, just about everything."

"I'd worry about the Fleet surviving his presidency," Gallant admitted. "Though, to be fair to the man, he doesn't appear to be stupid, and sensible pacifists are, well, sensible."

"We shall see," Amelie concluded. "Thirty days, people. Don't forget to vote yourselves," she chided gently. "Democracy starts with the individual, after all, and I'll be *damned* if I'm going to let the system break in our first election!"

———

23

"So, how are we doing on the prep for the election on our side?" Isaac asked his senior officers. "There shouldn't be that much for us to do, but I want to make sure everyone in the Fleet gets to vote."

"We've arranged with each ship's administration department to set up polling booths," Alstairs told him, the ops officer currently inhaling his coffee rather than drinking it. The pot laid out by Isaac's steward was still too hot to drink, but the officers had all grabbed a cup as they filed into the meeting room.

"As I read the email, fleet personnel have basically been randomly assigned to the three orbital Senatorial Districts," he continued. "But the election hardware and software can handle that. It's slick stuff."

"What about cybersecurity for the election gear on the surface?" Captain Giannovi asked. "I know we're pretty sure the Bane Sidhe didn't survive the Cartel's consolidation of power, but they were hardly the only people out there with hackers."

"Cybersecurity for the election systems falls under Director Knutson's purview," Isaac told them. "That said, if we want to offer the expertise of our cyberwarfare teams, I doubt he'd turn it down."

"We can do that," Rose told him. Cyberwarfare fell under the fleet communications officer's umbrella. "We could also run a shadow team."

Isaac arched an eyebrow at her.

"We used to do that in a bunch of systems," she said levelly. "We never officially got involved in the election, but we had a cyberwarfare team watching the systems and intervening from on high if needed. I don't care *who* is trying to hack things, a battlecruiser's computers *will* make hash of their attempts if properly directed.

"We can send people down to help Knutson's people, but I think we want to run a backup security line no one else knows about."

"Purely defensive," Isaac ordered. "We do *nothing* unless we detect interference. We must not only be apolitical in this; we must appear to be apolitical. Fleet personnel get a vote, just like everybody else.

"The *Fleet* does not."

"But we do need to prepare for the change in management that's coming," Alstairs said. "Right now, what few polls we have show Lestroud in the lead by fifty to thirty over James, with Rodriguez claiming most of the rest and Bruce barely registering after the margin of error."

"And regardless of who ends up President, we're going to have to deal with the new Senate going forward. Before, I could argue with Amelie and sort out our budget," Isaac noted with a smile, "but the Constitution puts the power of the purse in the Senate's hands.

"How far can we trust the polls?" he asked. The coffee had finally cooled enough for him to drink, though most of his officers were still regarding their cups with discomfort, and he took a swallow of the welcome caffeine.

Someone had already planted coffee. They might have coffee beans on Exilium before they had reliable food crops. As a Fleet officer, Isaac could only approve of the priorities involved.

"With no basis for comparison, no prior elections, and at least a hundred sociology professors about to knife-fight over methodology?" Alstairs chuckled. "The average is probably close, but we could easily be out. I can be pretty sure that Rodriguez and Bruce are out of the running, but James's odds are better than I expected."

"A lot of people are twitchy about reelecting our effective dictator,"

Isaac pointed out. "And James is a comforting presence to a lot of people. He thinks I'm a redundant anachronism, and I *still* can't help but like him!"

"Some of our non-Christian citizens are voting against him as a point of principle, but enough Christians are voting for him because he's one of theirs to balance it out," Alstairs concluded. "Right now, I'd say the Governor is going to be President, but if anyone other than Lestroud ends up with the job, it's going to Petrov James."

"In that case, I think I need to speak to Father James," the Admiral said slowly. "The last thing we can afford right now is any kind of question or concern over whether the Fleet will respect the transfer of authority."

"I'll reach out to his people," Alstairs promised. "He's going to be twitchy; I suggest going to him and meeting on his ground."

"Agreed. The last thing I'm concerned about with the pacifist is his people trying to hurt me!"

———

ISAAC WASN'T sure what he'd expected of the office of the man who'd almost ended up as the head of the largest religious grouping on Exilium. He definitely hadn't been expecting to end up outside what was clearly one of the millions of identical one-bedroom apartments in Starhaven's prefabricated apartment buildings—or for the door to be answered by Father James himself.

"Admiral Gallant," the graying priest greeted him. "Come in. May I get you some tea?"

Isaac chuckled.

"I'll take coffee if you have it, Father," he told the older man with a small bow of his head, "but if all you have is tea, I'll take that too."

"I don't keep much in," James admitted. "Tea is all I have."

"Then tea will do," Isaac agreed brightly, taking the indicated seat. The living room of the apartment had seen most of its furniture shoved against the walls to make space for a small desk. It was an austere space, even by the military standards Isaac was used to.

The priest emerged a moment later with a tray bearing a teapot and two cups. He put it down on his desk and quickly poured two teas.

"I will admit, Admiral, that I was surprised to be contacted by your staff," James said quietly. "My opinion of the Confederacy's military is well known."

"I know," Isaac told him. "That, Father James, is why I felt it was necessary that we have this meeting. I appreciate you making the time for me."

"I appreciate you being willing to come and meet me here," James replied, his eyes sparkling in clear amusement at the exchange of pleasantries. "You'll forgive me for being somewhat uncomfortable. I spent most of my adult life opposing your mother and all of her works, including the Fleet you served."

"I did not end up here because I supported my mother, Father," the Admiral replied with a chuckle. "My solution was perhaps more violent than yours, but we faced the same struggle."

"Violence, in my experience, solves little or nothing," the priest told him. "The Confederacy and its space fleet were far too willing to lean on it as an option."

"I agree," Isaac said softly. "My mother was a hammer, which meant all of her problems started looking like nails."

"And you, Admiral Gallant?"

"I am also a hammer," he confessed, "but I try to keep a clear idea of what problems are and aren't nails. In an optimal world, the Exilium Space Fleet wouldn't need to exist. But we don't know what's out here."

James laughed.

"We're not going to convince each other on this topic, I suspect," he pointed out over his teacup. "Which leads me, Admiral, to wonder why you are here."

"You've seen the polls," Isaac said. It wasn't a question—this definitely wasn't the actual headquarters of James's campaign for the Presidency, but there was no way the man running for President hadn't seen the polls.

"I have little faith in them at this point," James said drily. "I think I still have a good chance of winning this election."

"Then we are on much the same page," the Admiral replied. "My analysts still think you're going to lose, but you have a better chance than anyone other than Ms. Lestroud."

"If you intend to convince me to bow out—" the priest started dangerously.

"Nothing of the sort," Isaac interrupted. "Quite the opposite, in fact. The Exilium Space Fleet is neutral in political affairs. That is the tradition I intend to enforce and create as we go forward.

"I won't pretend I don't have my own personal preferences," he admitted, "or that I am concerned about what your stated positions will mean for the ability of the Fleet I lead to do its job, but those are entirely secondary."

"Then why are you here, Admiral?" James asked.

Isaac laid his teacup down carefully and met the priest's gaze, hoping his sincerity and determination carried through his eyes.

"Because we came from a society where an admiral decided the government was wrong and overthrew it," he said frankly. "And I wanted to look you in the eyes when I tell you, without doubt or question, that if you are elected President, I and every officer and spacer under my command, will follow your orders.

"There will be no question or hesitation or attempt to fight the expressed will of the people of Exilium. If you become President, I will advise you as completely, honestly and accurately as I will advise Ms. Lestroud. Or, for that matter, Mr. Rodriguez if that somehow comes to pass."

"And if I were to, say, attempt to dissolve the Fleet as President?" James asked.

"Then I would oppose you on the floor of the Senate, with impassioned speeches and hard facts," Isaac said levelly. "I don't think you could get such a dissolution through the Senate, Father James, but that is where I would oppose you.

"And if I failed, and our people decided that we do not need a military, then it would be my duty to see to the dissolution of the Fleet and to arrange for the warp cruiser crews to be taken care of when they got home."

"You would obey that order?" James said slowly.

"It would be obeying that order or becoming my mother," Isaac replied. "And I will *not* become my mother."

The old priest was smiling softly now.

"I see, Admiral Gallant. I very much do appreciate your visit, then, as you lay some of my deepest fears about where we are and what will come to pass to rest. *If* I believe you."

"I cannot make you believe me," the Admiral admitted. "All I can tell you is what I intend."

———

Somehow, Isaac wasn't surprised to find a second vehicle parked behind the one he'd arrived in. The two low-slung black electric town cars were all but identical, able to handle the smooth streets of the prefabricated colony sections but struggling with the new roads between them.

Isaac's Marine bodyguard was looking askance at the two large women leaning on the second car. The Admiral could tell that his protector was wishing that he had the right to stun people merely for being suspicious.

"Admiral Gallant," one of the looming female thugs rumbled at him. "Mr. Rodriguez would like a few moments of your time."

Her silent companion opened the door to the car, and Isaac sighed, meeting his bodyguard's gaze.

"Follow Mr. Rodriguez's car," he ordered, then turned a cold smile on Rodriguez's people. "If they do anything stupid like try and lose you, disable it."

The cars might look identical, but he doubted that the second one had a concealed EMP cannon. If it did, there were some serious questions to be asked, after all.

With a firm nod to his people, Isaac stepped into the indicated car. The guards closed the door behind him and he looked over at Carlos Domingo Rodriguez.

"Well, Mr. Rodriguez?" he asked. "You seem to have gone to some effort to see me."

"You'd be surprised," the big man said cheerfully. "You didn't attempt to be very sneaky, and I'm left with the realization that you've now met with half of the candidates for the presidency. I didn't think I could leave that hanging without meeting with you myself."

Isaac smiled.

"You've seen the polls," he pointed out. "I met with Amelie because I worked with her until this campaign started. I met with James as the only person with an actual chance of succeeding her."

"There are still two weeks left," Rodriguez replied. "Many things can change."

"This is fair," Isaac allowed. "And if you were to pass Father James in the polls—or even approach him, for that matter—I would have arranged a meeting. Since you seem to have done so already, however, I presume you had your own piece to say."

"You are an astute man," Rodriguez agreed. "Your studious neutrality in this election has been noted by many, but I think you underestimate your potential influence here. My own analysis suggests that a word from you could swing the vote by as much as twenty to thirty percent."

"It is my right as a citizen of our newborn Republic to cast my own vote," the Admiral replied. "It is my duty as the head of the Exilium Space Fleet to refrain from politicking on anyone's behalf."

"As the first head of the ESF, your duty is very much yours to define," the candidate told him. "I would like you to come out and publicly support my candidacy."

Isaac couldn't help himself. He actually laughed at the larger man.

"Why would I do that, Mr. Rodriguez?" he asked. "It falls to me to lay the groundwork of the traditions that will define our military. I would be doing a disservice to my successors and our people if I do so poorly."

"Because if you do not, Admiral, evidence of an affair between yourself and Ms. Lestroud will be provided to several of our private media outlets," Rodriguez said quietly. "It's all circumstantial—so *very* circumstantial—but I doubt anyone who has seen the two of you in the same room for more than few minutes would disbelieve it.

"My understanding is that you two have been suffering in noble silence at *least* since we landed," he continued, "and haven't actually *done* anything…but appearances are *so* important. I suspect the belief that our former Governor is having an affair with First Admiral Gall—"

"We're done here," Isaac said flatly. "Stop the car."

"I am not—"

"I do not care," Isaac told Rodriguez. "Driver! Either you stop this car—or I order my people to."

The woman driving the car clearly understood just what Isaac's vehicle carried, the vehicle slowing down to a gentle stop as Isaac rose.

"I will say this once, Mr. Rodriguez," he said quietly. "My oaths and my duty require me to follow a certain course to protect our people, no matter the price to me. If you attempt to use me as a weapon against Amelie Lestroud, however, I will *end* you.

"You think your reach is long? You have no idea how far my word can spread. You think your claws are sharp? I command *legions*.

"Under our new Constitution, it is illegal for me to turn the cyber-warfare and intelligence apparatus of the Exilium military on civilian affairs, but the constitution is not in force until the election is complete."

Isaac stepped out of the car and turned a very cold smile on Rodriguez.

"And if *I* do not intimidate you, Mr. Rodriguez, I remind you that Amelie Lestroud was Archangel—and while we may have failed, she forged a revolution across forty star systems on the force of her will alone.

"Underestimate her at your peril."

———

24

NEAR THE CORE OF *VIGIL*, in a hidden corridor not far from the battle-cruiser's CIC, there was a small, secure room few people outside her communications team ever saw. It was always locked and secured, but today, a pair of Marines in full power armor stood outside it.

"No offense, sir, but we need to validate your ID," one of them told Isaac as he approached. "And confirm that you voted."

"I wrote your rules, son," Isaac replied as he offered his tattoo-comp for the guard to interface with. "For a damn good reason."

He'd voted barely ten minutes beforehand, part of the first round of voting aboard his flagship. With all of the concern and chaos around the Presidential election, he'd barely had time to research who the three candidates for Orbital District Two were.

By which he meant that he'd been reading their bios on his tattoo-comp as he waited to vote. He wasn't entirely comfortable he'd been an informed enough voter on that front, eventually deciding to vote for the woman who'd commanded a destroyer in Battle Group *Vigil*—the candidate he actually knew.

Isaac doubted anyone on the planet would be shocked by who he'd voted for for president. His threat had kept Rodriguez from doing more than using insinuation about a relationship between him and

Lestroud to try and woo voters away from the former Governor, but that insinuation had been acid on his heart.

"You're clear, Admiral. Lieutenant Commander Rose is expecting you," the guard told him.

With a nod, Isaac stepped through the secure door into *Vigil*'s cyberwarfare center. One entire wall was currently taken up by a map of Starhaven, with a glowing bar chart showing the current breakdown of votes.

Amelie Lestroud was currently winning the election by over sixty percent, and Isaac sighed in relief.

"How accurate are these numbers, Rhianna?" he asked Commander Rose as he stepped up behind her chair.

"Right now? One hundred percent," she told him with a quick glance over her shoulder. "That is every vote that's been transferred to the main database in Exilium Central from the polling stations. Of course, that's only about thirty-two percent of all potential votes, so this has the potential to swing unexpectedly."

"Of course." The Admiral studied the chart. "Bruce is making a better showing than we expected."

A "better showing," in this case, meaning a total of five percent of the vote where they'd expected him to take under two.

"He spoke well in the debates," Rose said. "And there are some who are more comfortable with a military leader—but he never had the popular base or the financials of the other three."

"Any sign of anyone poking at the data integrity?"

"Nothing so far," she confirmed. "Knutson's people did a damn good job. We have this"—she gestured at the room around them, linked to the best hacking hardware and running the best hacking software the Confederacy Space Fleet could afford—"and we're barely getting read-only access. Everything is triple-check-summed and validated back to the polling stations.

"Someone would need to have physical access to every single polling machine to try and screw with the vote," she told him. "The connection between the stations and the central hub is surprisingly secure; I wouldn't have expected it to be quite so well protected."

GLYNN STEWART

"The Confederacy's election commissioners had reasons to *want* the votes to be able to be manipulated," Isaac replied. "We don't."

Rose sighed and shook her head.

"Even now, it still stings to hear someone say that," she admitted. "We all believed at one point, sir."

"Hell, Rhianna, my *mother* believed at one point," he told her. "It all went wrong somewhere, and I don't know where. I only know that it's my job it doesn't go wrong here."

————

BY LUNCHTIME, one of Rose's people had added a small set of subscreens showing the media response and exit polls. With only one real geographic area, there was no concern over time zones or light-speed information delays or any of the thousand and one issues they'd all seen in other elections.

"Five hours to poll close," one of the techs announced. "Turnout just hit sixty percent. That's not bad."

"Not bad at all," Isaac agreed. "I think most Confederacy planets were cheering if they passed fifty!"

The local democracies had been in various degrees of health, but the general consensus that the overall Confederacy democracy was broken had undermined faith throughout human space.

"Wait, what was that?" Rose asked sharply. Isaac turned to study the screen and swallowed. The bar chart had just changed. Dramatically.

"Did we just get a lump of new voting reports?" he asked quietly.

"Yes, but..." The comms officer dug in. "We're tracking status moment by moment. Even the election commission isn't actually allowed to look at this data yet—the automatic integrity checks are supposed to make sure everything is in line without human intervention at this point."

"And..."

"And our total votes went up twenty-three thousand...and half a million votes moved." Rose shook her head. "Someone is screwing with the underlying database. That shouldn't be *possible*.

162

The bar chart was flickering, adjusting and changing. As Isaac watched, thousands of votes peeled away from Lestroud and James, attaching themselves to Rodriguez and Bruce.

They'd been looking at an overwhelming victory for the former Governor, and suddenly they were looking at a four-way tie, the kind of election that could be won by any of the four, depending on the tiniest of flukes of turnout.

"I thought you said even we only had read-only access," he said mildly.

"Exactly. Just a reload from the polling stations should fix this," Rose said calmly, breathing carefully. "This looks scarier than it—"

"The *fuck*?!" one of the techs swore. "The central core is data-dumping back to the polling stations, overwriting their checksums and changing *their* saved data."

"The software shouldn't let it do that," Rose objected.

"It's just a software lockout, though," the tech told her. "The hardware won't stop you doing it, and someone's overwritten the software limits, but I'm not even seeing hostile code."

"That's impossible," Isaac's com officer snapped. "We have full access to the election database, everything. We know what software should be in there—compare to our mirror from this morning, *find me the variance*."

She turned to Isaac.

"This is bad, sir," she said quietly. "If someone has broken the software limits and is overwriting the backup databases at the polling stations, they could break the election."

"Who?" he demanded, looking at the bar chart. A four-way tie. Someone was being *damn* clever.

"I'm guessing Rodriguez," Rose told him. "But someone has top-tier stealth worms, an intimate understanding of our security, *and* a physical tap to the Election Commission computer network.

"Not having the last is why we can't edit anything."

"It's still not as bad as you think," he pointed out. "I seem to recall my polling machine spitting out a paper receipt I was supposed to verify and toss in a file."

Rose sighed.

"Nobody *actually* verifies those," she snapped. "The file of paper goes straight in the recycler at the end of the day."

"Well, I did verify mine," he said quietly. "So, I know it was saying the right things. Our mystery player may be hacking the computers, but they can't hack paper that's already printed. You find them, Lieutenant Commander.

"I'm going to go give Knutson a call. We have a multi-layer backup for a reason, and he needs to know we're falling back on paper."

"We…weren't supposed to be doing this, sir," Rose reminded him with a cough.

"That's a problem for tomorrow," Isaac told her. "Today, we're going to make sure no one steals our election."

―――――

IT TOOK Isaac several minutes to reach his office, where a quick update was already waiting from Rose. Nothing that changed the conversation he needed to have, however, and he plugged in a com code and a priority override.

Even the priority override only did so much in the face of just how busy Werner Knutson was on election day, but he got the director on the line in a few minutes.

"We're as busy as you can possibly imagine here, Admiral," Knutson greeted him. "I trust your judgment, so what do you need me for?"

"I'm about to ruin your whole damn day," Isaac replied. "Your electronic voting system is compromised. Someone apparently has a physical hack in place on your central system and is overwriting the vote data.

"I won't tell you what to do, that's not my job, but I strongly recommend that you fall back on the paper receipt trail."

"That would be the logical step…" Knutson paused. "How the hell do you know the voting system is compromised? Your people hacked it themselves, didn't they?"

Isaac smiled.

"Technically, we *bugged* it," he replied. "We don't have edit access, but we were watching the results as they came in so we'd know if someone did just this. We're your overwatch, Werner, and apparently, it was a good call on our part.

"We're not sure who, yet, but they've taken control of the central database and are overwriting the distributed databases as well. We're hunting them right now, but whoever it is, they've got damned good code. They snuck right past your firewalls, and those are *our* firewalls."

Knutson sighed.

"I'll pass the order and make damn sure the paper files are secured," he promised. "They *should* be, but I know what our people generally think of the paper receipts.

"You realize that counting the ballots is going to take a lot longer this way? If our system is compromised, I can't even trust the scanners."

"I know," Isaac agreed. "But I'd rather we took longer than let someone hack the election, wouldn't you?"

"Agreed," Knutson said grimly. He started to turn away, then paused and turned back.

"What are you going to do when you find out who it was?" he asked.

"Much as I'd *love* to drop Marines in their laps, we'll probably just pass the data on to the Starhaven Watch." Isaac smiled. "They *also* have power armor and an assault shuttle when they need to make a point."

———

"We found the worm," Rose reported the moment Isaac walked back into the secured cyberwarfare room. "And we have a problem. A big, ugly, stinking pile of shit-type problem."

He winced.

"Okay, Rhianna, what exactly is this problem?"

She sighed.

"We know the code. But it's not ours—and there's only one organization in the Confederacy with *better* code than CSF Cyberwarfare."

"I'm not following," he admitted. "So, this code is better?"

"This worm is to our software arsenal what a pulse rifle is to a hunting rifle," Rose said grimly. "It sliced through our military-grade firewalls like they weren't even there, and the only reason we found it at all was because we had a full mirror of the Election Commission computers from this morning."

"Knutson's going to paper backup ballots as we speak," Isaac told her. "They'll secure the receipt boxes and make sure the right votes get recorded. Whoever this is, they haven't broken the election."

"That's good, but that's not the problem," the coms officer replied. "Sir, the only people who'd have access to this kind of code are the Confederacy Secret Police."

That froze him in his tracks.

"There shouldn't *be* any CSP agents here," he noted slowly. "It's not like the people responsible for maintaining the Confederacy were going to be dissidents and troublemakers."

"Unless someone wanted to make sure we got screwed," Rose said. "Probably without the First Admiral's knowledge; she seems to have been actually trying to give us a decent chance."

"If there's a CSP cell on this planet, I want to know," Isaac said grimly. "Especially if they were trying to swing the election. Make *damn* sure we're tracking everything they do. I want to know who they tried to make win!"

———

25

"HEY FAUST! *FAUST*!"

The shouting echoed through the shuttle port near Exilium Central, and Kelliane turned exasperatedly on her heel to see who was shouting after her.

To her surprise, the shouter was Cai Johnson. Her former copilot now wore the uniform of the Starhaven Watch, but he was halfway into a flight suit over it and carrying a helmet in his hand.

"Whaddya want, pig?" she asked, half-teasingly. "Isn't it beneath you to be talking to the survey pilot?"

Johnson didn't even laugh at her, and her humor dropped instantly.

"I need you," he said flatly. "We've been called in for a super door knock, assault shuttle, power armor, the works. Our SWAT are ex-Marines, they know what they're doing—but intel suggests we may be dropping on a CSP cell."

"You have my full attention," she told him. "What the hell is CSP doing here?"

"Officially, classified. Unofficially, they're trying to hack the election," Johnson replied. "Look, we both know they insisted on a Marine for the Watch assault shuttle, but none of you ex-jarhead actual *pilots* were interested.

"So, they got me, and I can *fly* that bird, but if we're flying into a CSP trap…I want the best hand on the stick we've got, and we both know you're better than me."

"I'm also a survey pilot still," she pointed out. "I haven't checked out on a proper assault shuttle in three years, and I'm not authorized on that Cobra."

"I can get you auth," he replied. "But if I'm dropping a dozen guys in power armor, I want to make sure they don't get vaporized on the way—and that means I want the best. That means I want you."

"Why, Cai, I never knew you felt that way," she snarked, but his faith was touching. "Look, I'm pretty sure this is against every reg we've written so far, but…okay. Because it's you asking."

"Thanks. I'll make it up to you, I promise!"

"If you get me thrown in jail, Cai, I don't think you have what it takes to make it up to me."

———

SOMEHOW, Kelliane wasn't surprised to find the head of Starhaven Watch's SWAT team waiting for her by the assault shuttle, a flight suit and helmet in her size in her hands.

"Ah, good, Cai's tongue remains as silver as ever," Captain Sandhya Köhl told her cheerfully. "How much did he tell you?"

"Probably more than he should have," Kelliane told the other ex-Marine. "Confed Secrets?"

"Yeah. Not quite sure how the hell they got here, but when the Fleet tells me they ran into CSP moles, I trust them," Köhl replied. "Fleet is playing overwatch and guiding a Watch tech team to the bastards' shunt on the Election Commission's computers.

"The cybergeeks all assure me that once they have their paws on the shunt, they'll be able to track the physical destination of the signal," she continued. "That's where we come in."

Köhl gestured at the faceless suits of armor around her.

"Once we're on the ground, we're basically immune to anything the Secrets should have," she said. "We've got heavier arms if we need them, but these are police armor suits—so we have built-in stunners. My orders from Chief Tsuu T'ina are clear: we want these fuckers alive, but not at the cost of dead cops.

"So, can you fly the bird?"

The SWAT captain's gesture moved from her power-armored troops to the sleek lines of the Cobra assault shuttle behind her, the latest and greatest of the Confederacy Marine Corps' gear.

"I've flown one like her, but it's been a few years," Kelliane said levelly.

"I used to drop with your old flight leader," Köhl told her. "Both he and Cai say you're one of the best, a natural flyer. Don't know why you're in survey."

"Because I get to see what's on the other side of every hill," the pilot replied. "But yeah, I can fly your shuttle. Doesn't Johnson have a copilot, though?"

"We didn't think we'd need one for police work," Johnson admitted. "I don't think we were expecting this kind of mess."

"I'll fly for you, Captain Köhl," Kelliane told them, "but I'm still survey. Can you live with that?"

Köhl laughed.

"Pilot Faust, if you're as good as your reputation, I could live with you flying us naked and painted purple."

"All right, then," Kelliane said with a chuckle. "I'll take the flight suit, though, thanks."

———

FORTUNATELY FOR EVERYONE, the Peregrine Kelliane had been flying for Exilium's Survey Corps had a very similar control panel to the Cobra assault shuttle. The performance parameters were completely different, especially in atmosphere, but Kelliane Faust *knew* the performance of a Cobra.

"This is Watch SWAT-One," she declared as she lifted free of the shuttle pad the various government agencies still shared. "We are airborne. Somebody got a target for us?"

"SWAT-One, this is Lieutenant Commander Rose aboard *Vigil*," an unfamiliar crisp voice greeted her. "We have traced the shunt transmissions, but I'm pretty sure the location we've found is a relay. If you can get above it with the Cobra's sensor suite, I think we can bounce back to the next site."

"Are we expecting resistance, ma'am?" Kelliane asked as she downloaded the nav point.

Rose was silent for a few seconds.

"I want to say no, Pilot, but none of us were expecting CSP at all. Assume you'll be facing at least some automated anti-air defenses along the way. Fly safe and watch your six."

"Wilco, *Vigil*," Kelliane agreed grimly. "Nav point one is in the system, stealth is online, we are going to take a look-see."

That was one system the Cobra had that the Peregrines, decommissioned, if still armed, assault shuttles from the last generation didn't. A production Peregrine could stealth itself against radar and many sensors, though the survey birds had most of that gear stripped out for better sensors.

A Cobra had a smart nanopaint surface that mirrored the light hitting the other side of the craft. It wasn't perfect, not by a long shot, but unless you were *looking* for odd blurs in the sky, most people didn't expect the sky to shoot at them.

With the nanotech surface, the ship's radar-absorbent low-profile design and carefully balancing the shuttle's several lift surfaces and thrust systems, it was all but invisible. Kelliane remembered how to do all of that while Cai Johnson watched over her shoulder in awe.

"Okay, *now* do you understand why we wanted you?" he asked her. "I can turn on the stealth, but that balancing act you're pulling? That's beyond me."

"Then shut it and set up the sensor suite to link up to *Vigil* through a relay no one is going to see," she ordered. "I'd hate to spend all this time making us invisible and blow it by needing to scream loud enough to be heard in orbit."

"We're relaying through Exilium Central already," he told her. "Running passive sensors as we go; so far, what I'm seeing lines up with the tech team. The relay should be dead ahead, seven hundred meters." Johnson paused.

"It's about two hundred and fifty meters off the ground," he noted.

"Yeah, on top of that apartment building over there," Kelliane concluded as she put the pieces together and dropped an icon on the map. "So, if *I* were being a paranoid fuckhead who used to work for the Secrets…"

She dropped the shuttle out of the sky, bringing it drifting along the streets barely fifty meters above the ground. At this level, most people could tell that *something* was moving through the air, even if she was mostly gliding to keep the energy levels down.

"What are you *doing*?" Johnson snapped.

"If I was guarding that relay, I'd have an automated pulse cannon set up and attached to a covert radar array that pulses every thirty or forty seconds," she concluded. "And we're not *that* stealthy—but down here, they can't see us."

"And what are you going to do when we get there?" he asked.

"This."

The shuttle *popped* into the air, Kelliane's sensors washing over the rooftop in a momentary blast of focused active radar. She pinged the relay, exactly where Johnson had said it was going to be.

She pinged the defense system as well. Both simpler and more complex than she'd hoped—no sweeping sensors, no pulse cannon. Just a single rotating tube holding an anti-radiation missile.

The Cobra *did* have pulse guns. Three minimum-power bolts of plasma tore across the roof, vaporizing the missile as it started to launch.

Kelliane exhaled. "I may have fried the relay," she admitted. "Did we get a baseline?"

"We got a baseline," Johnson replied. "More than that—the relay fritzed out for a few seconds but came back online.

"We're tracking, and unless Fleet has gone downhill in the last twenty minutes, we'll have a new target momentarily."

———

THERE WERE TWO MORE RELAYS, both defended by the simple expedient of setting up a missile to fire at anyone who scanned the relay. Once Kelliane knew what to look for, neither of the weapons systems even blipped her shuttle before she blew them to pieces.

The last relay sent them back to Starhaven Central, what had once been *Star of Delights*.

"Transmitter antenna is on the roof of the Gleeside Building," Johnson reported back to Captain Köhl. "You're going to have to physically jack into it to see which apartment it's running to, but the target is definitely in this building."

"Well done, people," the SWAT leader replied. "I'm coordinating with the rest of the Watch; a blockade is going in in the next few minutes. Can you put us down on the roof?"

"Of course I can put us down on the roof," Kelliane replied. "Can you make sure the bastards don't run?"

"Please, pilot, trust me to do my job," Köhl told her. "Hell, at this point, you can come *watch*."

The shuttle glided in to a soft landing, and the pilot smiled grimly.

"I'm going to take you up on that," she announced to the air, turning to find Johnson had already produced a pair of weapon belts from some cupboard.

She shook her head at him.

"What?" he asked. "I *know* you, Kelliane Faust. Neither of us has it in us to leave this half-done."

———

KELLIANE WAS out of the shuttle barely three steps behind the power-armored SWAT members, checking the charge and power settings on the stunner Johnson had given her as she left the spacecraft.

Köhl's armor, marked with the insignia of her rank, turned to face the two pilots and paused for several seconds. Then, with a shrug that only barely made it through the several centimeters of metal and ceramics, the SWAT captain turned back to the tech tearing open what appeared to be a heat exchanger.

"We got it," a voice announced over the earbud Kelliane was wearing. "Thirty-fifth floor, apartment 15D."

"All right. Alpha Team, elevator one. Emergency drop to the ground floor, lock down the elevators and secure the corridors," Köhl barked. "Bravo Team, Charlie Team. Once Alpha's cleared the shafts, you get to rappel.

"Delta Team, pilots, you're with me. We're taking the stairs. *Fast*."

The rappel teams would probably reach the thirty-fifth floor first, but the roof was only ten floors higher. Moving down the stairs would make sure no one broke upward, though the only vehicle on the roof was the Cobra—and the Cobra wasn't going anywhere without one of the two pilots' thumbprints.

Kelliane fell in behind the SWAT team as they opened the roof access to the stairs and charged down. In the confined space of the stairwell, the augmented muscles of the power armor couldn't give the cops that much of a speed advantage, though she still remained behind them.

She had a stunner and a flight suit. It wasn't her place to be stopping bullets!

"Watch SWAT-One, this is *Vigil*," Commander Rose's voice echoed in her earbud. "We don't *think* they know the hack has been compromised, but they probably know you're there." The Fleet officer's voice was very, very cold.

"The apartment belongs to a Brendan Ngo," she continued. "That may not mean anything to you...but *our* records show that Senior Chief Brendan Ngo was the senior NCO in Commander Robert Bruce's administration team aboard *Dante*—and came aboard *Dante* with Bruce.

"He's not officially part of Bruce's campaign team, but there's no way he isn't working for Bruce. He's one of ours, Captain Köhl...*and* he's probably a Secret. Watch your back."

———

EVERYTHING WENT SMOOTHLY until they reached the thirty-fifth floor. Too smoothly, in Kelliane's opinion—and clearly in Captain Köhl's opinion as well. Even as they coordinated with the other two teams to make sure every access to apartment 3515D was cut off, she sent two people in slowly and quietly with full stealth protocols.

The protocols were similar to those that protected the Cobra, but inevitably less effective, as the suit didn't have the Cobra's power supply or size.

They weren't effective against top-grade sensors, and the first trooper went down with a sizzling sound Kelliane was disturbingly familiar with from her own days in the Marines.

"Pulse rifles!" she snapped.

"Barriers forward, advance and fire!" Köhl barked herself. "Lethal force authorized, no chances, people!"

Several of the SWAT troopers produced forty-centimeter by ten-centimeter plates from concealed cases on their suits. At the tap of a command, they expanded into two hundred and forty-centimeter by hundred-centimeter shields that arced with electricity.

Electromagnetic dispersion wasn't perfectly effective against plasma pulses, but it was better than nothing. The troops with barriers moved forward, blocking the hallway as their companions came up behind them.

The troopers hadn't visibly changed weapons—but when the lead troopers opened fire, their gauntlets glowed with the white-hot flares of pulse rifles, not the invisible electron pulses of combat stunners.

They had to level the entire arm for the built-in pulse rifle to work, but it was more than the people protecting the apartment had been expecting. The exchange of fire lasted mere moments, ending as SWAT pushed forward again.

"Automated emplacement," one of the troopers reported. "Kensin is down but breathing. Armor protocols knocked him out to control the bleeding. Oscars took a hit; she's okay."

"Is the hallway secure?" Köhl demanded.

"Hallway is clear, door to 3515D is open—we have movement!"

Pulse-rifle fire cracked in the hallway again, and then there were a few moments of silence.

"We had a shooter," a different voice reported. "Samuels is hit, bad. We need medevac *now*."

"Sweep the room with stunners," Köhl ordered. "Faust?"

"The Cobra is equipped for field surgery if you've got anyone trained," she said instantly. "I'm not."

"Nguyen is," Köhl responded. "Victoria! Get your butt back to the shuttle and de-shell. There's a surgery suite in there somewhere, and we've got wounded headed back to you on the double!"

"Clear the way!" a voice bellowed through the hallway, two power-armored forms moving down the hall. One was scorched and damaged, one of the suit arms clearly nonfunctional, but the trooper was still moving—and hauling a second armored form behind them.

Four troopers, two moving and two down, went past in a blur, heading for the roof far faster than Kelliane could run herself.

"Move in," Köhl ordered.

Kelliane probably wasn't included in the order, but she and Johnson went forward anyway, their stunners drawn as they entered the apartment.

The air *itched*, the burnt ozone smell of pulse munitions and stunner pulses laced with a massive amount of static electricity.

It *shouldn't* have been enough to wreck the computers in the room, so Kelliane guessed that the dead man in the doorway had triggered some kind of destruct before he tried to shoot his way out. Two more people were unconscious, taken out at the desks where they'd been working away.

"Secure those people," the SWAT captain barked. "Check them for suicide devices. If they're Secrets, they're probably fanatics, and I have *questions*."

Kelliane herself crossed over to the computers, pulling a small transmitter from her belt pouch and plugging it into the machine.

"*Vigil*, this is Pilot Faust," she reported in. "We found the computer setup. They tried to fry it, but they may not have had time. I've got a link set up for you. Think you can do something?"

"We're Fleet Cyberwarfare," Lieutenant Commander Rose told her grimly. "If anyone can, we can."

———

26

ONE OF THE advantages of starting an entirely new government and nation from scratch was the ability to decide what the traditions were going to be. The things they did today would define how every election would be carried out in the future.

With that in mind, Amelie had arranged for one of the conference halls in the prefabricated buildings, one well away from Exilium Center itself, to play host to the presidential candidates as the votes were cast and counted.

None of the four of them were out of communication with the rest of the world, but none of the media outlets were playing in the room and no reporters had been allowed in. Various aides and assistants were coming and going all day, but to a large extent, the four candidates were left with no one to speak to except each other.

It had been a very quiet day. She didn't know James or Bruce well, and after the insinuations Rodriguez had been dropping the entire campaign, she was *not* pleased with the crime boss turned politician.

None of his hired talking heads had come out and said that she was sleeping with the head of Exilium's fledgling Space Fleet, but there'd been a lot of hints and suggestions. Hints and suggestions they'd used to question her judgment if she'd allowed herself to become so close to the "Iron Brat."

There was absolutely no truth to it, but she'd allowed Faulkner to convince her to avoid contact with Gallant during the campaign. Appearances were everything—as Isaac had told her himself when they'd spoken about it.

She was surprised how much she'd missed him.

Her phone buzzed, and she checked its tiny holographic screen.

Something's going on, Faulkner's message read. *They're pulling the paper receipts, using those for counting. Isn't that a last resort?*

Trust Knutson, she sent back. Her aide was right. The only reason for Knutson's people to be counting paper ballots rather than using the electronic tallies was if they had grounds to mistrust the electronic count.

That wasn't supposed to happen. If nothing else, no one was supposed to even be *trying* to screw with the election. They were all a hundred thousand light-years from home, after all.

"The polls closed ten minutes ago," Rodriguez said quietly. For a big man, he moved *very* softly when he chose to. She hadn't heard him approach. "Should we have been told the results by now?"

"Getting all hopeful, Carlos?" she snipped.

He chuckled.

"Hardly, Ms. Lestroud," he admitted. "My chances at this were always middling at best, and what I thought was a hole card blew up in my face. I wouldn't have thought associating you with Admiral Gallant would *help* you, but it seems he has earned himself a name separate from his mother's here."

"You don't get to just brush that one off," Amelie told him.

"Why? Because appearances mean you *haven't* had a chance to do anything?" he asked, a childish smile crossing his face. "My dear, you should *thank* me. By insinuating that it was already happening, I have laid the groundwork for you two to actually be able to pursue a relationship in future."

"No such thing is happening," she told him, distracted by movement at the entrance to the hall. Those were Watch officers. Why were there Watch officers here?

"Ms. Lestroud—Amelie," he told her gently, "everyone who has seen you two together knows what's going on. If *you* aren't aware of it, then you may be the only—What the—?!"

The door to the conference hall was flung open and Werner Knutson entered the room, flanked by two power-armored members of the Starhaven Watch and half a dozen uniformed police officers.

"My apologies, everyone," Knutson said brightly. "There will be some delay in the count, as our electronic systems were compromised. Trusted individuals are going through the paper receipts as we speak, and we should have a preliminary result by morning.

"Right now, however, there is a piece of business for Captain Köhl of the Starhaven Watch to attend to."

He gestured the power-armored SWAT officers forward and they entered the room—heading for Robert Bruce.

"Commander Robert Bruce, you are under arrest," the SWAT captain's voice boomed out. "We'll sort out the full list of charges later, but we'll start with accessory to the attempted murder of Watch officers…and treason."

———

FACING down half a dozen stunners and a pair of power-armored SWAT troopers, Bruce went quietly. That left three candidates in the hall with Knutson, watching as the fourth was hauled away in cuffs.

"The courts will go through the evidence in detail," the Election Commission director told them all, "but it appears that Commander Bruce was a Confederacy Secret Police plant. Whether or not he was put in the Exile Fleet to screw us all or ended up with us as part of an internal CSP power play, we don't know."

Knutson smiled thinly.

"I suspect the Watch will find out before they're done. What we *do* know is that he had a small team of CSP operatives working with him who attempted to hack and overwrite the central voting databases. We're not certain of the extent to which they succeeded, so, as I said, we're falling back on the paper-ballot count.

"We weren't truly prepared to do that except in the case of a challenge, so we're scrambling," he admitted. "We have so far confirmed that we have retrieved all of the ballots and aren't missing any boxes, at least.

"The count, however, will take some time, specially with only unconnected scanners being safely usable. I'd ask that you all remain here for now, to avoid further…complications."

"That seems…excessive," Rodriguez replied.

"While I would prefer not to cast aspersions on the character of anyone running for the office of President, one of our candidates already attempted to hack the system," Knutson pointed out. "We would prefer to avoid any…undue temptation to make suggestions with regards to the ballot boxes.

"We'll be securing the door for everyone's security. Once we have a President, you can go your own ways, but until then I must ask you to remain here."

Knutson left and the three people left in the room stared at the closed door.

"What we do tonight sets the traditions for our Republic going forward," Father James said quietly. "I think it costs us nothing to accede to the election commissioner's request—and it behooves us to act with great faith."

"'Great faith,' preacher, is a virtue I usually leave for men like you," Rodriguez replied with a chuckle. "But I see your point." He reclaimed his seat, the big man shaking his head as he grabbed his drink. "We all know how this is going to end at this point. I trust Director Knutson's integrity even more than I trust yours, Father James."

"And so, how do you think this will end, Mr. Rodriguez?" James asked.

The ex-crime boss saluted Amelie with his glass.

"Ms. Lestroud becomes *la Presidenta*," he said cheerfully. "She becomes the Founding Mother of our new Republic, and you and I fall into line. Because Exilium cannot afford anything else."

"That's more sense than I would expect from a…politician," James told him.

"I would hesitate to assume victory for any of us," Amelie reminded them. "The people of Exilium will speak. They will choose."

"The people of Exilium didn't get here by being damn fools," Rodriguez said. "We got here by being troublemakers, rabble-rousers, the folks with the eyes to see the Confederacy was broken.

"Those same eyes can see you did a damn fine job the last year. Yeah, I'll take the job if the vote swings my way, but I don't expect to walk out of this room President of Exilium."

"Then why did you even run?" Amelie asked. She refused to even think about an assumption of victory. That was tomorrow's problem, she supposed.

"Because while you likely are the best choice to lead us, the *last* thing the Republic can afford is for the first election to be uncontested," Rodriguez said. "I don't think *that*, Ms. Lestroud, was a tradition we could allow to start."

———

IT WAS WELL after midnight and Father James was demonstrating that priests, like most soldiers and actors in Amelie's experience, had mastered the ability to sleep anywhere, in any circumstance.

Rodriguez had made the mistake of drinking too much coffee and was pacing one end of the hall. Amelie herself could have slept, in theory, but was too keyed up. She didn't want to buy into the crime boss's assumption of how this was going to end, but it lined up far too well with her assessment of the polls.

There was no way she could sleep, and she rose to her feet instantly when the door opened again to admit Knutson, on his own.

Father James was awake and on his feet almost as quickly. He was clearly a light sleeper.

"The count is over seventy-five percent complete but we had near one hundred percent turnout in the end," Knutson told them. "The count won't be final until late in the morning, but I wanted to give the three of you an update and allow you to make your own decision as to whether to wait until morning."

That was promising, to Amelie at least.

"With just over three point one million votes counted, Amelie Lestroud is in the lead with one point seven million votes," the director said softly. "Petrov James trails with point nine million votes and Carlos Rodriguez holds point four million votes. All of those are rough numbers. Robert Bruce has currently taken just under seventy thousand votes."

Amelie exhaled. She could still, theoretically, lose—if every single vote left went to Father James, for example, he would take the Presidency.

"I think that there is no need for us to wait for the formality of the final count," that individual said as she was thinking that. Father James turned to Amelie and offered his hand.

"Allow me to be the first to congratulate you, Madam President, on the job you have done so far—and to commiserate with you on the task that now stands ahead."

"Indeed," Rodriguez joined him as Amelie shook James's hand in shock. "I see no reason to drag this out. Director Knutson—I officially concede to Ms. Lestroud. Congratulations, Madam President."

She shook both their hands and breathed sharply, rushing oxygen to her brain.

"Neither of you go anywhere just yet," she ordered sharply. "Mr. Knutson?"

"If Father James and Mr. Rodriguez have conceded, then you are President of the Republic of Exilium," he said formally. "We will need to present you to the people and news media as rapidly as possible. There are concerns after the chaos of Bruce's hacking attempt."

"That's fair. I need five minutes with these two," she told him, gesturing at James and Rodriguez. "Can you hold off the reporters that long?"

"I believe I can manage that…Madam President."

Knutson bowed himself out and Amelie turned her fiercest gaze on the two men in the system.

"Now is not the time for Exilium to be divided," she told them. "Any of the three of us could have led the Republic into the future; we all know that. Our skillsets and backgrounds are different, but each of them would have lent themselves well to making sure our little exile colony thrived.

"If I was prepared to accept either of you as President, then I cannot help but feel that I can still use those same skillsets and backgrounds," she continued. "Plus, after the chaos that must have ensued as they shut down the hacking attempt and went to paper ballots...we not only need to *be* undivided, we must *appear* undivided."

"What are you suggesting, Ms. Lestroud?" Father James asked.

"The Republic doesn't have a Vice-President," Amelie reminded them. "We will have a Prime Minister, who I will select from candidates the Senate will provide, but much of the authority rests on the President herself—and her Cabinet.

"Before we say *anything* to our followers and voters, I want to offer you both positions in that Cabinet. We'll sort out titles and details later, but effectively, I want James taking care of national morale and Rodriguez taking care of national industry.

"I want what we used to call an 'all parties' government, a leadership of national unity," she told them. "I want to lead Exilium forward as a *unified* nation, above all else."

"I will gladly accept," James said after a moment. "You and Admiral Gallant may come to regret that, I'll warn you."

"I suspect you'll find you have more in common with Isaac than you think," Amelie told him. "He certainly seems to understand where you're coming from more than I would have thought."

She turned to Rodriguez.

"Well, Carlos? Willing to turn that clever mind of yours to building a nation that you don't lead?" she asked.

He exhaled heavily, looking down at her thoughtfully, then nodded.

"I fear I may become allergic to government, Madam President, but let's give it a shot."

———

27

"ARE YOU SURE ABOUT THIS?"

Isaac chuckled at Amelie Lestroud's question. They were in her new office, an actual upgrade from the austere room she'd run the colony from as Governor. He suspected she hadn't known that Knutson had been preparing the new Presidential Office during the election and it had been a surprise.

It was still plain—except that the plain furniture was handmade from local woods. Isaac's information suggested that there were exactly two craftsmen doing that so far, and the office's cabinets and desk probably represented at least two weeks of *both* of their work.

"We both know that the Cabinet wants to cut the Fleet," he told her. Two weeks of the new government had been enough to make *that* clear. The Cabinet was about half people picked for the purposes of Amelie's "unity government" and half people Isaac guessed she'd actually wanted.

Technically, as the Chief of Fleet Operations, he was part of the Cabinet. So far, however, he hadn't shown up and no one really expected him to. There wasn't much going on that required the Exilium Space Fleet's input, after all.

"We *also* both know that the alliances of the Cabinet are fragile," he continued. "For now, they're content to work with you. Everyone wants to see Exilium prosper; we just have different ideas of how to get there and what's needed.

"And they have their own agendas as well. So far, you have no victories to point to, only arguments and discussions. So, we have something where a slim majority of the Cabinet is in favor of something we both know would also squeak through the Senate."

"We know that, do we?" his President asked. "Based on what, exactly?"

"Prime Minister Emilia Nyong'o's assessment when she warned me that the game was afoot yesterday," Isaac said brightly. "But it wasn't a surprise. The Senate wouldn't pass a bill to gut or dismantle the Fleet, but they *will* sign off on chopping my budget."

"Your presence in the Cabinet changes the balance of votes," she noted. "Brings it, unless I miss my guess on how my Ministers are going to vote, to a tie that I would be expected to break."

"I know. We'll throw everyone off-balance, and then they'll get what they want, and I'll get what I want," Isaac said with a grin. "Trust me, Madam President."

She shook her head at him.

"Dangerous words, Admiral," she warned him. "There are people who question your influence at the highest levels."

Isaac shrugged.

Those people existed, though the degree to which Rodriguez's insinuations of an affair—the threat Isaac had dropped on the man had stopped him from coming out with his so-called "proof"—had failed to have any impact on the election suggested they were fewer than he'd feared.

"There'd better be," he told her. "The influence of military command on civilian government should *never* go unquestioned. It would be far too easy for me to lean on our friendship and the fact that I hold all the guns to make the Republic work the way *I* want. But that would damn everything I rebelled for."

"We don't deserve you, Isaac," Amelie told him. Their gazes met and there was a warmth in her eyes that sent a shiver down his spine.

That was a dangerous thought and feeling. The insinuations of a relationship had forced him to confront the fact that, yes, he *was* infatuated with this woman. And the fact that, regardless of how little impact those insinuations had had, infatuation was all it could be.

Everything they did would define the future of the Republic of Exilium. Even if she returned his feelings, something he strongly doubted, they could *not* let a relationship between the Admiral of the Exilium Space Fleet and the President of the Republic happen.

Whatever said Admiral might want.

"Yes, you do," he said quietly. "I remember everything Archangel did, Madam President. If anything, we don't deserve you."

"Please, Isaac, stop it," Amelie said with a chuckle. "Just call me Amelie. Keep the damn title for when we're in front of the Cabinet."

"Fair enough." He checked the time. "Which is in what, five minutes?"

———

Isaac was the second to last person to enter the meeting room—and all conversation in the room cut off as he did. He smiled silently at the six people already gathered in the room and then took the chair set aside for him.

As he understood it, there were always eight chairs at the table, but his had been empty since the election. He'd wanted to make sure the civilian government got their feet under them before he joined them.

Amelie Lestroud followed him in a few minutes later, minutes that were spent in awkward silence as the politicians couldn't seem to decide what to make of him.

He knew Barry Wong and Werner Knutson, the "loyalists" of the Cabinet, and he was familiar with Father James and Carlos Rodriguez.

He'd actually known Prime Minister Emilia Nyong'o before the rebellion. The petite black woman was a cousin—or, at least, a relation inside New Soweto's complex clan structure he wouldn't try to explain in more detail to a non-New Sowetan.

Nyong'o didn't have a vote, but she was present to express the Senate's opinion on things. To be Prime Minister, she'd had to carry a fifty-one vote majority at least one. In theory, she was capable of delivering a somewhat reliable vote on the Senate floor.

In practice, she advised the Cabinet on what the Senate was thinking. With the anarchic mess that was the current Republic Senate, no one could necessarily predict the result of a given vote.

The last person in the room was Shankara Linton, added to the Cabinet to speak to the civilian space affairs none of the other four non-military members could speak to, and trusted to be relatively neutral in most affairs.

"Good morning, everyone," Lestroud greeted them all with her usual projected cheer. "I'm delighted to say that Admiral Gallant has been able to join us this morning. As you all know," she reminded them gently, "as Chief of Fleet Operations, he is an equal member of this Cabinet and holds a vote."

The Republic's constitution expected the President to be the tie-breaker in Cabinet votes…though it was also clear that no legislation would make it from Cabinet to Senate without the President's approval. There were intentionally ways around that, not least that the Senate could introduce legislation on their own, but the President was *not* an equal member of her Cabinet.

"Of course," Father James responded immediately, the first of the ministers to speak. "I am pleased to see you join us, Admiral. The viewpoint of the Republic's soldiers and spacers should not be neglected—we must not become those we left behind, sending our children into battles they do not understand."

Isaac chuckled and nodded to the priest.

"*Touché*, Father," he allowed. "We have a great deal of work to do, and we don't know much about this sector of the galaxy we've ended up in. I do intend to attend these meetings more regularly in future, but you all, I suspect, understand that I didn't want a military voice here at the beginning."

"We appreciate that," Rodriguez told him. "Though the timing seems…interesting."

"If you mean that you and Father James were meaning to push forward a vote this morning to lay a proposal before the Senate to cut the Fleet's budget, this is no coincidence," Isaac said cheerfully. "Would you care for me to summarize your positions, Ministers?"

He waited. Neither of them objected.

"As I understand where we sit," he told them, "the logic is that we are seventy-five thousand light-years from the only potential threat we know about. We've had some problems with internal difficulties, but those seem to have faded and are most easily defeated by simply not having a Fleet.

"Am I roughly correct, gentlemen?"

For a moment, no one met his gaze, then Linton chuckled.

"That's about right," the ex-colony ship captain turned orbital business magnate agreed. "There's also a question of resources. We only have so much exotic matter, so many parts, so much fabrication capacity. Right now, we are devoting just over fifty percent of our spaceborne industry to the maintenance of the Fleet.

"That's hurting our economic growth and holding back our development. And what value do we really have in a Fleet that can't leave the damn star system?"

"You don't actually need to convince me, Mr. Linton," Isaac replied, enjoying the expression on the Minister's face. "That's why we cut the Fleet in half the moment we arrived—it was not going to be practical to maintain two full battle groups with the resources we have.

"And yes, I sent every FTL-capable ship we have away. It will be years still before we see any of the warp cruisers back from their scouting missions, and I won't pretend that doesn't scare me," he said frankly.

"But that doesn't make anything you have said incorrect. We are currently committing an extremely large amount of resources to the maintenance of the ESF, including not least the trained technical personnel manning my ships."

Isaac held up a hand.

"That said, Ministers, it is your job to look to the future of Exilium and decide how best to build that future. It is my job to make sure we're all still here to enjoy that future, and until the warp cruisers return, we have *no idea* what surrounds us."

"You have a vote on this Cabinet," Rodriguez pointed out. "I suspect both Ministers Wong and Knutson would vote with you to shut down this proposal."

"But you're not wrong, either," Isaac said quietly. "We can't afford to commit half of our spaceborne resources to maintaining the Fleet—and we absolutely are not getting value out of a fleet that cannot leave this star system.

"So, I have a compromise to suggest."

Isaac smiled and tapped on his tattoo-comp, opening up a holographic display above the table. Twelve ships floated in the center display. Six more were off to one side, highlighted in translucent blue.

"This is the current strength of the ESF," he told them all. "Six warp cruisers, eight destroyers, two missile cruisers and two battlecruisers."

They'd replaced *Confucius* from the Morgue, a necessity he still hadn't forgiven himself for.

"We can't do anything with the warp cruisers," he noted. "They're gone, for years; we'll owe them back pay when they return. That's a moral as well as legal obligation we took on.

"But as we have progressed in our work here in Exilium, we've realized eight destroyers is more than we need for search and rescue, and, frankly, destroyers are overkill for local police work.

"I am offering to decommission *all* of our destroyers," he said quietly. "We'll transfer their assault shuttles and volunteer personnel over to the Orbital Watch, doubling the strength of the OW but creating a far more effective and efficient organization for S&R and orbital policing."

The destroyers faded out, becoming transparent.

"That will reduce our maintenance requirements by roughly forty-five percent," Isaac concluded. "In exchange, however, I want half the exotic matter from the warp cradle."

The room was silent.

"For *what*?" James asked harshly.

Isaac tapped on his tattoo-comp again. Drive rings materialized around the four ships left.

"We want to add grav-warp drive rings to all four remaining ships," he told them. "I'm informed that the research we've been doing should allow us to build drives that are roughly twice as fast as those mounted on our warp cruisers, allowing us to cover the entire Exilium System with far fewer ships.

"Adding those drives to our most powerful units provides the maximum effectiveness for protecting Exilium."

"And provides you and our President with a striking force if we find anyone else out here," James snapped. "Are we already planning expansionism and wars?"

"No," Isaac said flatly. "But tell me, Father James…if there is a threat to Exilium, would you rather we defended you in orbit, directly above Starhaven, or in the far reaches of the system, where stray fire won't threaten civilians?

"I would rather never fight at all, but I must repeat, again and again and again, that we know nothing about this region of space. We *must* maintain a Fleet in being. I agree that that Fleet must be the most effective and efficient use of our resources possible, but that Fleet *must* exist."

James looked mutinous, but the rest of the Cabinet was looking thoughtful—and to Isaac's surprise, the final vote was unanimous.

As Isaac had told Amelie before, Petrov James was a pacifist. He wasn't a fool.

———

28

"Dr. Reinhardt, welcome, welcome," Isaac greeted the big one-eyed physicist as he entered the admiral's office.

Reinhardt smiled brightly as he carefully took a seat, the man clearly used to testing to make sure any given chair was able to support his weight. He didn't seem immense in relation to Isaac—who had long ago accepted he was of merely average proportions—so much as he was, plain and simply, the single largest human being Isaac had ever met.

"It's been a hectic few months," the physicist replied to Isaac's greeting. "I've got some of your answers, Admiral, but not all of them."

"I already know the answer to the most important," Isaac told him. "Can we build warp drive rings?"

Reinhardt chuckled, a rumbling noise that almost shook the desk between them.

"Aye, Admiral," he confirmed. "*That* was never in question, so long as we have the exotic matter?"

"We've been allocated half of the exotic matter we've retrieved from the cradle," Isaac told him. "From the numbers you sent over last week, that should be enough for all four cruisers?"

"That it should," the big man agreed thoughtfully, scratching at his eyepatch for a moment. "And we're pretty sure we can make them faster, too, but..."

"But?" Isaac echoed. He hadn't been expecting a *but*. He *needed* those faster warp drives if he was ever going to be able to secure the region around Exilium enough for his peace of mind.

"We've had no ability to do more than the tiniest of lab experiments," Reinhardt told him. "What we've done, however, suggests that the theories and tests that were done back in the Confederacy have only scraped the surface of the speed increase we can get out of the warp drive.

"I can pretty much guarantee you eight light," he noted. "We've never really worked to enhance the drive ring's patterning or resonance. Even the most basic work can double the speed."

"But..." Isaac echoed again.

"But," Reinhardt agreed, holding up a finger with a massive grin. "If we can do those experiments, I think I can give you an entire order of magnitude beyond that."

Eighty *c*. Still nothing compared to the instantaneous transportation allowed by a wormhole generator, but enough for them to actually maintain a perimeter watch of the surrounding systems. Enough for the Republic to establish and maintain outposts in other star systems.

Eight *c* was enough to protect the Republic. Eighty *c* would be enough for the Republic to create a new interstellar civilization.

"What do you need, Doctor?" he finally asked.

"The only scale for an experiment of this nature is one to one," Reinhardt told him. "I need a cruiser-sized hull and enough exotic matter for a cruiser-sized warp drive."

"We only have enough exotic matter for four of those," Isaac replied. "If I give you that, we only have three warp-capable capital ships, not four."

"I know," the big physicist agreed in a soft rumble. "But that's what we need, Admiral, if we're going to build an entire new generation of warp drives."

Isaac sighed. In the end, he'd kept two destroyers to go with the cruisers, but they would forever be sublight defense ships. It made some sense, he supposed, to have a permanent sublight defense force, one no Admiral of the ESF could ever be tempted to send elsewhere.

"You'll get it," he finally promised. "Should we delay the installation of the other warp drive rings until you've completed your experiments?"

"We'll want to hold off on the exotic-matter rings themselves, but we can build the casing," Reinhardt replied. "No matter what we do, we're looking at the same giant tube of empty metal to hold the drive ring and its power plants."

"How long, Doctor?" Isaac asked.

"You can't rush science, Admiral," the physicist replied. "We're going to have a series of iterative tests with different modes and models. Three to six months, at least."

"And then how long to actually have drives on the ships?"

"Assuming we pre-build most of the components, a few weeks at most," Reinhardt told him. "Give me six months, Admiral, and I can promise you a true star fleet. The more time I have, the more success we'll have."

"And so far, evidence suggests we have time," Isaac admitted with another sigh. "I have faith in you. Dr. Reinhardt. Don't screw this up."

"I never do," Reinhardt said boastfully. "I may not achieve as much as we hope, Admiral, but you will not regret giving me the time. We will create something fantastic."

———

29

"THIS IS Survey Flight Alpha Three, now entering Zone KD-174," Kelliane Faust recited into the unit recorder and the shuttle's PA system, keeping both the future and the survey team in her craft informed. "For those of you not looking at a map, KD-174 is part of the Drakehold Spine mountain range and is mostly about two kilometers above sea level.

"The likelihood of us finding anything interesting in barren rock above the tree line is minimal, but the mapping scanners are getting to work, which means now's probably a good time if any of you want to eat a sandwich or take a break."

"Behave, Pilot," Dr. Crohn told her, the biologist leaning against the cockpit of the shuttle with a relaxed smile. Almost a year of working together had smoothed over rough edges, even the new ones added when Exilium Survey had decided Kelliane didn't *need* a copilot once Johnson had left.

Kelliane checked the scanners.

"Yep, I am currently reading a *lot* of bare rock and—ooh! Some lichen!"

Crohn laughed.

"It's a short day today, at least," she admitted. "We're running through what, three zones?"

"That's what my schedule says," Kelliane agreed. "We'll be back for the Landing Day celebrations."

She couldn't believe a year had passed. At other times, she couldn't believe a year had passed and they were still surveying *Drakehold*. Orbital scans meant they had half-decent maps of the entire planet, but to look for useful biologicals and minerals, well, that required a far lower altitude.

And, of course, flying at two hundred meters up through a mountain range did actually require a pilot's attention.

"You have any plans?" Crohn asked. "It's a big day—a full standard year since we landed."

A standard Terran year was only about three-quarters of an Exilium year, but given Exilium's near-complete lack of seasons, the colony continued to use Earth's calendar.

That might last. It might not. That sort of thing was well over Kelliane Faust's head.

"Cai is cooking me dinner and we'll watch the fireworks from his apartment," Kelliane told her colleague. "It'll be quiet, but given the rush this whole process has been…"

"Is he still trying to 'make up' for dragging you into the election day mess?" Crohn asked with a chuckle.

"Nah, we gave up on pretending that was the excuse a few months ago," the pilot replied. Her boss knew *perfectly* well where her relationship with Cai Johnson had ended up. To Kelliane's surprise and delight, for that matter. She hadn't really thought about Cai that way, but he knew her well—and had turned out to be an attentive sweetheart off the job, too.

"Good for you," Crohn told her. "A lot of folks seem to be pairing off of late, too. Seems like we're starting to settle in and feel like this is home."

"It has to be home," Kelliane replied. "There's no way for us to go back. All we can do is make Exilium amazing."

And thank Deity that the Survey teams were still busy. She'd had a rough few days when that had finally sunk in.

"Agreed," the biologist replied. "Still trying to find anyone interested in an over-aged lesbian myself, but there's hope."

"Michelle, you're younger than the President, and I *dare* you to call Amelie Lestroud over-aged to her face," Kelliane told her boss with a chuckle. She started to continue their banter, but something on the scanners caught her eye.

"What was that?"

"What was what?" Crohn asked.

"Something flashed on the scanners. Refined metal?" Kelliane was running the data backward. It was only a blip, but it was a blip of a ferro-titanium alloy that was most definitely *not* natural.

"I take back not finding anything interesting," the pilot continued. "I'm bringing us back around for a closer look."

She recorded the exact point they'd been in their survey sweep—she still wanted to finish the job—and flipped the shuttle in the air to head back toward the blip.

"Refined iron-titanium alloy," Crohn reeled off. "The scanners didn't get a clear enough pulse for spectrographic, but it doesn't look like one we use. That is…"

"Strange," Kelliane agreed. "Very strange. I think…yeah, it had to be that valley."

She twisted the shuttle into a side valley she'd passed without thinking. The valley was filled with the hardy scrub and trees native to this altitude and came to an end in a narrow spike of a mountain towering over much of the range.

There was nothing strange there. The mountain was the same ice-covered rock as everywhere else. The trees had scrabbled up it, marking the same treeline as every other mountain in the Spine.

What had the sensors seen.…

"There!" Crohn snapped, dropping on icon on the window in front of Kelliane. "Got another blip—is that an avalanche?"

It was.

At some point, relatively recently, the snowpack had grown too heavy and been triggered by thunder or something similar. A few tens of thousands of tons of snow had plummeted down the side of the mountain, stripping away trees, scrub…and thousands of tons of rock, to reveal what was *underneath* that mountain.

The silvery metal gleamed with ice as the shuttle drifted closer to it, ice and alloy alike glittering in the Peregrine's search lights.

"What in the name of Deity?" Kelliane breathed. "The mountain-side is artificial."

"How much of it?" Crohn asked. "Can we tell?"

"Yeah, give me a moment," the pilot replied. The shuttle had been refitted with high intensity gravitic and magnetic sensors for identified deeply-buried mineral deposits, but they were high-energy active-pulse systems that required Kelliane to divert the vast majority of the Peregrine's power to operate.

The entire shuttlecraft vibrated as the emitters rotated and *pulsed*, Kelliane working the sensors up the spike of a mountain as she stared at the return in shock.

"That's not possible. That's *insane*."

"The entire mountain is artificial," Crohn concluded aloud, studying the sharply angular lines of the stone-covered facility. "I'm a biologist, Kelliane, not an architect.… Do you see an entrance?"

Swallowing her shock, the pilot studied the outline of the building. It might not have been obvious scanning the mountain before, but with the layout of the underlying massive metal structure, she picked out the cave three-quarters of the way up.

"There," she pointed out. "It's not obvious, but I think you could land one of the big transports in that cave. What the hell is this?"

"I don't know," Dr. Crohn admitted. "But I intend to find out. Bounce a report back to Starhaven—and then get us into that cave, Pilot Faust. We appear to have work to do."

———

WHOEVER—OR *whatever*—had set up the landing site for the strange facility had been good at their job. The natural mountains around it covered the opening from scans from orbit, but there was enough of an opening that Kelliane was quite sure she could have maneuvered an Orbital Assault Transport through the mountains and into the cave.

The surface of the cavern appeared to be regular stone, but it took the blast from the shuttles thrusters easily, absorbing and dissipating the heat in a way she'd never seen before.

"Okay, so we're marking the cave floor to steal bits of," she noted aloud. "That's some impressive heat dissipation. Doesn't look fast enough for any kind of military purpose, but it's perfect for this."

She settled the shuttle down and checked the scanners.

"We can go right outside," she told Crohn with a shake of her head. "But, Doc?"

"Yes?"

"This place is creepy. I'm coming with you—and your team should all load up for bear."

Crohn didn't argue. She popped open the weapons cabinet in the cockpit and took out a weapons belt of her own, only arching an eyebrow as Kelliane removed the full harness for the pulse rifle stored in there.

She didn't even question if the pilot could use the weapon, which was good. It had been a few years, but she'd qualified as an expert marksman with the weapon once.

Hopefully, it would all come back to her if she needed it.

———

THE CAVERN WAS COLD. Even through the flight suit she was wearing, Kelliane shivered. With Exilium's widely balmy temperatures, it had been a while since she'd been outside in anything that required her to use the suit's heat-management functions.

From the expressions of the rest of the survey team, she wasn't the only one poking through software to work out how to warm up. They were a long way from sea level there—high enough, in fact, that the air should have been thinner.

"The air's not right," she said to Crohn after a moment's thought.

"You noticed that, did you?" the biologist replied. "I checked before we left the shuttle. Air pressure in this cavern is basically sea-level, but I don't see anything maintaining that."

"Passive systems, pressure-driven venting from lower down, most likely," Kelliane noted. "It would be quite the feat of engineering, but so's a two-kilometer-tall metal cone."

"There's that," Crohn agreed. "Anyone spot an entrance?"

Flashlights flickered across the empty cavern, and the pilot shivered. The entrance was big enough to easily land on OAT—but the cavern itself could have held a dozen of the big assault ships. It was massive.

"If nothing else, there's got to be fueling equipment around here somewhere, right?" Kelliane asked. "This place is definitely someone's idea of a concealed hangar."

"I don't know about fuel lines, but I think I found a door," one of the surveyors half-shouted, pointing her flashlight at a glint of metal.

"Let's check it out," Crohn ordered. "Watch each other's backs. This shouldn't be here, and it's making me twitchy."

The glint of metal was, thankfully, a door. If you could apply the term to a pair of fifteen-meter-high panels clearly intended to move under power. The portal they covered would have allowed the assault shuttle behind them to have flown deeper into the mountain.

The door was also closed.

"Well, I'm getting the feeling that someone didn't want strangers poking around in here," Crohn said aloud. "Unfortunately for them, they left a two-kilometer spike on the planet we ended up on, which means I need answers.

"Teach—the door, if you please."

"Teach" was Kirby Andrews, who had been a high school teacher on Earth before being exiled for wanting to teach his students to think for themselves.

Right now, however, he was also the man with the crowbar. And a few more modern tools to augment that ancient style of prybar, but if a door was going to be opened, Teach would be the man to open it.

Kelliane guessed that Teach had also coached football from his sheer bulk as he approached the door, running his fingers along the join where the two panels met.

"This might actually not be too bad," he noted, pulling out the prybar. "It doesn't look locked or anything, just closed and big."

He managed to wiggle the prybar into the gap with ease, though it ended up taking most of his more complicated gear to actually force the doors open. They were *very* big.

"There we go, people," Teach finally told them. "I don't think we're getting more, not without heavier-powered gear than we've got."

There was enough of a crack for one person to squeeze through at a time.

"Well, then," Crohn announced. "What are we waiting for?"

———

Kelliane found herself leading the way, the military-grade light attached to the pulse rifle brighter than most of the flashlights carried by the survey team. Each of them squeezed through into the facility one by one, their lights shining on corridors made of the same silvery alloy they'd seen unearthed by the avalanche.

"No signage," Crohn said after a moment. "Not just nothing we can read; no signage at all."

"What about in other wavelengths?" Teach asked, the ex-teacher looking embarrassed a moment later when Crohn held up the scanner she was holding.

"Nothing," she repeated, looking around.

There was only one way forward from their entrance, a hallway sized to the door itself.

"I think we found the cargo entrance anyway," Kelliane pointed out. "I doubt every door was built to handle small spaceships!"

"We didn't see any others," Crohn replied.

"We might not have," the pilot told her. "We did a pretty high-level scan, plus it's possible that any other entrances were buried. It doesn't exactly look like this place, whatever it is, is operational."

Kelliane couldn't even see anything that could have been lights, let alone any that were on. No lights. No fans. No air circulation.

"This place is dead, Doctor," she noted. "Whatever it once did, it isn't doing it anymore."

"That's true enough," Crohn agreed. She knelt on the ground, sweeping the scanner over it. "No dirt, no dust. Just what we brought in with us. Those doors weren't hermetically sealed, but nothing made it in here."

"Maybe someone was cleaning up?" Teach asked.

"Maybe. But you'd think there'd be some sign of that," the biologist told them. "Some sign of life. I can't even date this place, there's just metal everywhere."

"Let's keep going," Kelliane urged. "If there's answers, well, the cargo entrance has to lead *somewhere*, right?"

The others fell back in behind her and she continued. The sheer scale of the facility was daunting. At some point in the past, these halls had been built either for massive machines or some form of utterly immense alien.

There were none of the side corridors and personnel accesses that she'd have expected, either. Just one massive, laser-straight tunnel leading deep into the artificial mountain.

It was almost a relief when they reached the second set of doors. They were a perfect match for the paired panels on the outside.

"Well, at least the builders were consistent," Crohn said quietly. "Teach?"

"On it."

There wasn't any guesswork this time. Teach levered the door slightly open with his crowbar and inserted the self-expanding prybars. What had taken several minutes on the first door took barely one now, pushing a human-sized opening between the massive doors.

Kelliane was through before anyone could argue with her, inhaling sharply as the sheer scale of the space on the other side of the door struck home.

"Doctor, you need to see this," she told Crohn as she looked up, awestruck.

Her light flickered over an empty void that stretched clear up to the top of the mountain. Massive tanks and pipes of the same silver alloy that made up the entire facility snaked their way up to the peak —and down into an abyss that Kelliane's light couldn't see the bottom of.

"My god," Crohn whispered as she added her flashlight to

Kelliane's, the beams of light miniscule against the titanic scale of the artificial mountain. "I'd wondered, but…"

"Doc?"

"It's an atmosphere processor," Dr. Crohn told her. "Tanks of oxygen, nitrogen, whatever else needed to be added to the atmosphere. Drag in the original atmosphere, condense it, add whatever's missing, then pump it back out the top.

"They probably sent that microbiome that we found everywhere out with it, setting up the basic atmosphere and biosphere before they started releasing macro life. Same system could scatter seeds as well with a little work."

"And if it goes down as far as it looks, they probably did at least some release of that macro life from here too, or at least stored it here," Kelliane whispered. "Not just atmosphere. Everything. This is a damn terraformer."

"There have to be more," Crohn said. "Even as massive as this, it couldn't transform an entire planet."

"What are you saying, Doc?" Teach demanded. "A terraformer?"

"We always suspected," the survey team leader replied. "Too much was too perfect. A consistent microbiome across the entire planet? Almost zero seasonal variation? Soil and bacterial life that took new crops with ease?

"We always suspected Exilium was at least partially artificial," Dr. Crohn repeated. "And this…this place is how it was done. From the scale, I'd guess there's only two or three more. Four of these could transform a planet, given enough time and resources."

"There were no energy signatures suggesting anything of the sort," Kelliane reminded her. "Nothing active. Even this one wasn't active."

"No, their work is done. Why leave them turned on?" the biologist asked. "Shut them down, remove computer cores, anything trans-portable. But the facilities themselves aren't movable, so you leave them in place. Come back every hundred years or so, test the atmosphere, check the biosphere. Maybe rerun the processors for a bit to rebalance the air."

"But if someone terraformed this planet, where are they?" Teach said. "You don't build even *one* place like this and just…leave it."

"That's the question, isn't it?" Dr. Crohn agreed. "Where are they?"

"Maybe it's that you were teachers and I was a soldier," Kelliane said slowly, "but that's not the question I'm worried about.

"I'm worried about what they're going to do when they realize someone moved into their gorgeous new home before they got there!"

———

30

THE GOVERNMENT HAD GONE all out for the Landing Day celebrations. Isaac wasn't entirely sure he'd have committed the resources himself, but it wasn't like anyone had asked him. The budget for this hadn't even hit the Cabinet, and even if it had, he still let his civilian colleagues take the lead in most affairs.

After six months, the Republic's government was a surprisingly smoothly functioning machine despite its occasional hiccups, and he had to admit that surviving a year since landing on Exilium was worth celebrating.

Fireworks started flashing silently over the city as soon as it grew dark enough for them to be visible, glittering patterns and symbols lighting up the air over Starhaven. The Senate had declared a half-holiday, and a thousand parties were already swirling their way over the city.

The advantage of being something of an outsider to the government still was that Isaac didn't have to attend all of the parties. He liked parties well enough, but the thought of visiting twenty of them in under eight hours—Amelie's schedule for this afternoon and evening, for example—made him cringe.

Most of the other Cabinet members had kept themselves down to three or four, and Isaac had got away with simply holding one massive party for the Marines, Fleet, and both Starhaven and Orbital Watches.

An entire kilometer-long stretch of beach was a sea of people who would normally be in uniform. Alcohol and food were flowing freely, and volunteer medics and MPs patrolled to make sure things stayed under control, but there'd been almost no problems at all.

Well, almost no problems by the standard of putting twenty-thousand-plus spacers, Marines, and cops in one party, anyway!

If there was one downside to his people's good behavior, it was that Isaac Gallant had accidentally drunk far more than he intended to. Most military parties he'd organized tended to see his own activities regularly interrupted by crises. This one hadn't, and now he stood on the edge of one of the fishing docks, looking out over the beach full of his people and the glittering blue waters of Exilium's oceans.

"You, sir, are a maudlin drunk," a familiar voice said behind him. He glanced over his shoulder to see Captain Lauretta Giannovi drifting up the dock to him. His athletically petite flag captain had traded her usual uniform in for a tight-fitted dress that took full advantage of her body.

"Be careful, Captain," he said carefully, watching the potential slur in his words. "I still need a Commodore for the Sublight Squadron."

"Threats are beneath you, Admiral," Giannovi said gently as she joined him. "Penny for your thoughts?"

"I didn't think we had any pennies," he replied. "And I don't have change."

"Wow, you *are* maudlin when you're drunk," she told him. "I don't think I've ever seen it before."

She promptly filled his glass from the bottle of wine she was carrying in her left hand. "You probably want to get whatever is stewing in your system out before you explode, you know," she said gently.

Isaac shook his head.

"Didn't you bring a date to this affair?" he asked.

"Nah, didn't bother," she replied. "I'm expecting a Cabinet Minister to take me home later, though." She spotted his wince and then laughed aloud, a glorious peal of happiness that warmed the soul.

"*Not* you, boss, don't worry. Shankara has been dancing around for a bit. I figure I can *probably* find a big enough clue-bat for the man at some point tonight."

Isaac chuckled, his subordinate's happiness at least somewhat infectious.

"Good luck to you both, then," he replied.

"And you?" Giannovi asked. "You can't keep mooning over the one woman on the damn planet your ethics say you can't touch, you know."

The warmth chilled again, and he turned away to look at the ocean.

"I have no idea what you're talking about, Captain," he said coldly.

"Yeah, that and three EECs will get you a nice coffee," Giannovi told him. "There was a reason Rodriguez's insinuations worked, you know. You two work well together, but I swear there are days I expected to have to physically remove your hands from each other!"

"I am fully aware of how bad an idea any such thing would be," Isaac said flatly.

"Yeah, and so's *la Presidenta*," his captain agreed. "Not sure anyone else on the planet buys it, but that's what you two think."

Giannovi shrugged.

"So, all I can say is that you should remember that you might be the second-most-eligible bachelor on Exilium."

"Oh?" Isaac asked. "And who's the first?"

"Minister Linton, but I think I have a solution for that," Giannovi purred. "Speaking of which, that looks like an official cavalcade drifting in. I think it's time for you to go play host, Admiral Gallant."

———

SOMEHOW, in the chaos and craziness that followed, Isaac found himself standing back on the dock with a different woman. He wasn't entirely sure how he and the President of the Republic of Exilium stole that moment of privacy, but the way that their respective bodyguards were blocking off the stairs onto the dock probably had something to do with it.

They walked along the prefabricated plastic in silence, drifting farther and farther away from the crowds until one of the boat sheds blocked their view of the beach entirely.

"Don't you have about a dozen more parties to be at?" he asked Amelie as she smiled at him.

"Only three, and Faulkner will let me know when I need to go," she replied. "I don't think anyone on the planet expected me to do more than say hi at the Fleet party. This is my quiet break."

"Ah," he allowed. "How go the parties?"

"I was an actress once," she replied. "I'm used to parties—and to pretending I'm awake when I swear I just want to fall over. Hell, I *love* parties, but this rotation sucks."

"I'm glad I avoided it," he confessed. "Even most of the rest of the Cabinet is managing busier schedules than I."

"One party, right," Amelie said with a chuckle. "You realize that the Fleet party is the single largest one going on right now? And you're organizing it, overseeing it, and keep getting dragged out to play host? I think I prefer my whirlwind tour!"

"I'm used to organizing twenty thousand people," Isaac said drily. "It's what you pay me to do." He finished his wine, letting the alcohol warm him in the cool breeze off the ocean.

"Though I noticed that Shankara's tour *ends* at the Fleet party," she said. "Is there something going on I should know about?"

"My flag captain has designs on Minister Linton's virtue," he told her with a chuckle.

"You *know* what Shankara did to get exiled," Amelie responded. "I'm not sure he *has* any virtue left."

"Then designs on his bed, however you care to phrase it," Isaac replied. "I get the impression it's mutual."

"Oh, it's mutual," his President replied with a giggle. "Lucky them."

"Indeed," he confirmed, turning to look out over the ocean again. To his surprise, Amelie was suddenly much closer to him than before, the tall blonde woman close enough that he could feel the warmth radiating off her.

"And you, my dear Admiral?" she asked softly.

"And me what?" he asked, suddenly vividly aware of both her

nearness and of how much he'd had to drink. Silence was a better option than anything his brain was trying to say.

"I don't know," Amelie whispered, as if cutting off a thought she couldn't say aloud. They faced each other in the night, far too close for them to let any audience see.

"I am in love with the only woman on this planet that I cannot have," Isaac whispered, certain she was close enough to hear him. "The only woman who my pursuing would risk undoing all the work we both have done."

The words fell like toppling stones, a confession he could never take back. He struggled to start an apology, only to find Amelie's finger on his lips.

"Shh."

Her hand slipped around the back of his head, guiding his lips to hers. His arms came up around her and they leant into each other in the chill wind as they gave in to temptation for one eternally glorious moment.

Then, as if by mutual agreement, they both stepped back.

"And I am in love with the only man on this planet that *I* cannot have," Amelie told him. "Knowing how we both feel changes nothing, my dear Admiral. We have sworn our oaths and taken up our duty."

"That we have," Isaac agreed thickly. His heart leapt at her words… and broke at them.

"What is one more sacrifice?" he asked.

"Not the hardest, I don't think," Amelie told him. "But no easier for that."

"No."

Before they could say more, both of their communicators started buzzing.

———

31

"This is Gallant."

The Admiral's tattoo-computer was easier to access than Amelie's tab-phone. She took advantage of the delay in pulling out her own communicator as well to try to slow her racing heartbeat.

The kiss had been a horrible, wonderful, terrible, amazing idea. She didn't regret it at all, but Isaac was entirely correct. There *couldn't* be anything between them—everything they did, every word they said, every action they took would define the traditions and future of the Republic.

The President and the Admiral being a unit was *not* something the Republic's future could afford.

She flipped open the holographic screen of her communicator and focused on it.

"This is Lestroud; I'm online too," she barked. "What's going on?"

"Sir, ma'am, this is Survey Command," a rapid-fire voice responded. "One of our shuttles was overdue, but we'd been advised they'd found something.

"They're now inbound at high speed and requesting a meeting with the Cabinet on an emergency basis," the flight controller continued. "Dr. Crohn is refusing to provide any details over an open link, but she says that this is critical to Exilium's security."

Amelie traded a look with Isaac.

"I know Michelle," she said softly. "If she says it's critical, it's critical."

"You know the Cabinet's schedule better than I do," he told her. "Can we pull them all out?"

"Fuck their schedules," Amelie snapped. If she couldn't have fifteen quiet minutes of privacy with Isaac to forget they couldn't actually be together, the rest of her Cabinet could fall in line.

"If Michelle Crohn says she needs to speak to the Cabinet, she needs to speak to the Cabinet," she continued. "I'll get Faulkner on pulling the rest of them in. Can you get us transport?"

"Madam President," Isaac said with a small bow. "I command star fleets. I think I can find a way to get us back to Exilium Central."

Amelie nodded and turned back to her phone.

"Tell Crohn's pilot to come directly to Exilium Central; we'll have the Cabinet gathered in thirty minutes," she told Survey Command, then killed the link.

She turned back to Isaac; he smiled sadly and offered her a hand, palm up. She recognized the sobriety pills and nodded with a sad smile of her own.

In vino veritas.

For them to have had the conversation they'd just had, they'd probably drunk far too much—and neither could afford to be drunk in Cabinet meetings.

———

FIREWORKS CONTINUED to flash silently outside the windows as the Cabinet gathered on the top floor of Exilium Central. The hubbub of the crowds and parties swarming peacefully through Starhaven was a dull murmur through the thick glass.

None of Amelie's subordinates looked happy to be there, and she picked out the bags under the eyes that were indicators of sobriety pills on *all* of her Ministers.

In hindsight, perhaps they should have had *someone* in the government stay fully sober, but the Landing Day parties had seemed like a good excuse to get out and relax with their constituents.

And now…now she wondered just what Michelle Crohn had found. She wouldn't have to wonder for long, though. The shuttle had landed on the roof as she'd arrived herself, and the survey team lead was already on her way down.

"What's this about?" Rodriguez asked. The ex-crime lord was looking even worse for wear than the rest of the Cabinet, and far grumpier about being pulled away from the parties.

"I don't know," Amelie replied. "Only that one of our survey team leaders requested our presence on an emergency basis, and we didn't pick those leaders out of a hat."

The door swung open before Rodriguez could reply, and two women entered. Both were still in survey jumpsuits, with Faust clearly suffering from a severe case of helmet hair.

"Dr. Crohn," Amelie greeted the team leader. "You realize, I hope, that you just pulled the eight most powerful people on the planet away from their parties of choice."

It was half a joke and half deadly serious. If Dr. Crohn had misestimated the importance of what she'd found, Amelie didn't think she'd be able to save the woman's career.

"I know," Crohn replied. "But believe me when I say you needed to know what we'd found. Kelliane?"

The pilot pulled a projector from a bag at her hip, setting up on the table and feeding data into it from her tattoo-comp. An image of the Drakehold Spine mountains appeared in the middle of the table, glittering as the light from the fireworks reflected off the hologram.

"From the moment we did the very first surveys, we knew something was odd about Exilium's biosphere," the biologist told them all. "There were atmospheric oddities too, and the lack of an axial tilt, but those were all theoretically possible.

"The lack of variation in the microbiome across the planet? That should be impossible. The more we studied the macrobiome as well, the more oddities we found. Every desert on this planet has the same plant and animal life. Every forest. Every plains area.

"Some variation, some regional mutations, some changes to account for temperature…but none of the separate evolutionary tracks we would have expected from different continents."

Crohn shrugged.

"It was always possible it was pure random chance, but there was also the 'easy' explanation: someone had terraformed Exilium. Except, of course, that we would have been talking about a transformation and life-seeding project far beyond anything humanity had ever considered."

"You found something, didn't you?" Father James asked softly.

"We found a terraformer," Crohn said flatly. "It's primarily an atmosphere-processing facility, but we explored as much of it as we could in a few hours before we came back.

"There were freezers that were designed to hold thousands…*millions* of frozen embryos. Mass artificial gestation chambers. Empty tanks that our scanners show once held seeds, oxygen, nitrogen… everything you'd need to change an atmosphere and seed a world."

"That's…insane," Linton said slowly. "A single facility couldn't do that."

"No. Not even this one, which, well…"

The hologram zoomed in, highlighting the alien base underneath its concealing mountain, to inhalations of shock around the table.

"The Drakehold terraformer is roughly two kilometers high and appears to be over a kilometer wide at the base," Crohn told them. "From its size, I would guess it's one of between four and eight such facilities on Exilium.

"It's also dead. Completely shut down, its work complete. No lights, no power." She shook her head. "I want to get some engineers to go through it ASAP, because we didn't even see a power facility in there. It's possible power was being fed from somewhere else, but it's also possible the power source was removed when the place was mothballed."

"Any sign of what kind of creature built it?" James asked quietly.

"No," the biologist admitted. "Nothing. No art. No signage. Not even apartments or quarters, so far as we could tell. It's an entirely automated facility, though we think we found where the computer cores should be."

"'Should be'?" the priest echoed.

"A lot of things have clearly been removed from the facility," Crohn told them. "It's...weird. The computer cores were definitely extracted, but the gestation facilities were left intact. Any power source is gone, but the facility itself represents millions of tons of complex alloys and some *fascinating* passive-materials technology."

"We always suspected," Admiral Gallant noted, his voice soft. "That was part of why I insisted on keeping some level of fleet. We didn't—we *don't*—know enough about what's out here."

"We need to study this facility," Wong said urgently. "We need to know more about these aliens, these people who built our world."

"And we need," Admiral Gallant continued grimly, "to know what they're going to do when they find us on it."

———

32

From Vigil's flag bridge, Isaac studied the world below. It was possible, now that they knew what to look for, that the orbiting warships would be able to pick out the other terraformers. He was certain that if any of the facilities had been active, they would have found them before.

So, all of them, however many of them there were, had to be as dead and cold as the facility Faust and Crohn had found the day before.

"The crews are starting to wake up and get over their hangovers," Alstairs said behind him. "Captain Giannovi just reported in; she'll be aboard in a few hours."

Isaac didn't even need to see his ops officer to sense the man's shrug.

"I'm guessing it'll be evening before we have the crews back aboard?" he asked.

"Give or take," the junior man agreed. "Everyone's got at least a skeleton crew aboard. We may not have *insisted*, but the bosuns knew better than to let us get below a minimum level of sober crew. They were on hand with sobriety pills at the parties, making sure we had enough people to man the ships this morning."

"Thank God for noncoms," Isaac said fervently. "What would we do without them?"

"Die horribly, sooner or later," Alstairs agreed. "It's not like we're expecting an attack, though, is it?"

"Watch the news," Isaac told his subordinate. "We decided not to keep it quiet—the survey teams found an alien terraformer yesterday."

Silence.

"That's…a game changer, yeah," Alstairs finally said. "I guess the fact that Exilium was perfect makes more sense now."

"Not really," the Admiral admitted. "If *we'd* terraformed it, sure. But why would an alien race have terraformed a planet into something this comfortable to us?"

"It might be more comfortable for them," his ops officer said. "Gravity is a bit too low, oxygen is a bit too high…I mean, those end up being *nice* for us, but if we were to customize a planet, we'd target them exactly at Earth."

"Fair," Isaac agreed. He shook his head. "I can't believe we missed a set of two-kilometer metal spikes."

"Buried under mountains, I'd guess?" Alstairs asked in a pained tone. "That's about the only way I can see it."

"Exactly. They found it by accident—avalanche had uncovered the bare metal. I'm having the scans from the shuttle sent up; we should be able to feed those into the Fleet's scanners and find the rest of them."

"The rest of them, sir?"

"Survey figures there's at least three more. Potentially as many as one per continent, huge as the damn thing is."

"And we missed them? I may have to have *words* with our sensor crews."

"Peace, Cameron," Isaac told him. "Whoever built and buried these things built an artificial ecosystem from scratch, so far as we can tell. I'm pretty sure there's more than just rock making them hard to find."

He glanced at his tattoo-comp.

"In any case, I believe it's time for us to check in with our good Dr. Reinhardt on his last round of experiments. From what I've heard, we might finally be putting warp drives on our battlecruisers."

"And from what *I've* heard, it'll have been worth the wait," Alstairs agreed.

———

"Greetings, Admiral!" Reinhardt bellowed cheerfully over the video link, causing Isaac to wince and turn his volume down. "How was the party?"

"Loud, flashy, full of people. Fun," Isaac said drily. "How were your experiments?"

"Much the same, with fewer people," Dr. Reinhardt told him. The physicist stood alone on the bridge of the missile cruiser *Percival*, which was currently empty other than him. *Percival* might still look like a warship, but the cruiser was a testbed now.

She still had her pulse guns and antimissile lasers, but her missile magazines were empty, and she didn't have the crew to properly employ her defensive armament. Most of the people aboard her were focused on the continuing adjustments to her grav-warp ring.

"You told me you'd have some final answers today," Isaac reminded his R&D head. "Did the experiments give you the data you needed?"

"I think so," Reinhardt replied. "The test flight itself went well, we topped out around sixty-five times lightspeed, but we're still resolving the data. We had some very strange interference in the middle of the test that messed with a lot of our sensors.

"We're trying to isolate the signal so we can remove it, but it's like nothing we've ever seen before."

Something in the word *signal* sent icy claws down Isaac's spine.

"*Signal*, Doctor?" he asked.

"Just terminology, Admiral," Reinhardt told him. "Pulse of tachyons ran through our scanner field during the experiments. Like I said, we'll be able to isolate it and remove it."

"When, Dr. Reinhardt?" Isaac said flatly. "When was this pulse? Do you know where it came from?"

"You can't source tachyons; they don't work like that," the physicist complained. "I mean, they came through Exilium, but it's not like tachyons are slowed by passing through something so piddling as a planet."

"What time, Dr. Reinhardt?" Isaac demanded again.

"Let me check," the one-eyed professor replied, Isaac's seriousness finally having sunk home. He pored over some data.

"Looks like about eleven twenty-five Starhaven time," Reinhardt told him. "Why? Does that mean…"

He'd clearly caught Isaac's expression as the Admiral pulled his own data out.

"Fuck me," Isaac whispered. "It was a signal, Professor. Could it have come from the Drakehold Spine?"

Reinhardt blinked, looking back at his own files.

"Yes," he admitted. "It's…possible. But, Admiral, tachyons are a natural occurrence. What are you suggesting?"

"At eleven twenty-five Starhaven time yesterday morning, a survey team breached the exterior entrance of an alien terraforming facility on the surface of Exilium," Isaac told him. "Your tachyon pulse was triggered at exactly the same moment.

"We hit a goddamn silent alarm."

———

ALSTAIRS LOOKED up in surprise as Isaac walked back onto the bridge. Something in his gait gave away that something had gone very wrong, but Isaac ignored the operations officer as he walked over to the communications console.

Rhianna Rose was among the officers and spacers who had yet to return aboard the ship, but Isaac hadn't gone so long without working with the computers that he couldn't manage to do what he needed to.

"All ships, all ships," he said calmly as he opened a channel to every Exilium Space Fleet vessel in the star system. "This is Admiral Gallant. Set Condition Two throughout the system. All leaves are canceled; all crew are to return aboard their vessels immediately.

"This is not a drill. Set Condition Two throughout the Fleet."

He rose from the console and looked at his operations officer.

Alstairs looked as stunned as any of the other half-dozen people in the badly understaffed flag bridge.

"Dr. Crohn's survey team triggered a silent alarm using some form of tachyon transmission," he told them all. "As I understand the physics, that shouldn't be possible, but someone did it anyway. We have no choice but to assume that they received the alert functionally instantaneously, which means we may have an alien force in the Exilium System in the immediate future.

"Coordinate with the Bosuns and Captains; borrow shuttles from the Orbital Watch and the civilian government if you need to," he ordered. "We *must* have the Fleet to Condition Two ASAP."

Condition Two was an alert status two steps down from battle stations. It meant that every system would be checked for effectiveness, every combat capacitor charged, and the entire crew kept aboard the ship.

There'd still only be one shift on duty at any time, but the full crew would be on hand.

From Condition Two, Isaac's fleet could get to battle stations in under five minutes.

They should, in theory, have far more warning than that.

He hoped.

———

33

"IF YOUR ALIENS don't show up, sir, you're going to have some damn grumpy crews," Lauretta Giannovi told Isaac over their private link. "Canceling every leave the day after the biggest party we've thrown in this end of the galaxy? I'm not sure I'd have done it!"

"What, you mean I don't have grumpy crews already?" Isaac asked.

It had been barely twelve hours since he'd ordered everyone back aboard ship. Thirty-six since Survey Alpha Three had crowbarred the doors of an alien facility open and *something* had fired off a pulse of modulated tachyons.

Even Reinhardt wasn't sure if it had or hadn't been a transmission of some kind, but Isaac wasn't taking chances.

"You'd be surprised, sir," Giannovi said. "Our people trust you. If Iron Isaac says there's a threat, they'll turn out for battle. That's not the kind of faith you can buy, sir, but it's easily lost, too."

"I'd rather be wrong," he admitted. "I don't think I am, though. Do we have everyone back aboard?"

"We do," she confirmed. "*Vigil* has a fully staffed Bravo Shift on duty. Every system is charged; everything checks out as fully functional. We're ready to fight…assuming it's something we *can* fight."

"There's the problem, isn't it?" Isaac murmured, looking at the holographic display at the heart of his flag deck.

Two battlecruisers. Two missile cruisers. Two destroyers. That was it.

A third missile cruiser, *Percival*, was orbiting near the civilian stations. *Percival* wasn't really a warship anymore, but the volunteers now operating her defenses would help cover the civilian orbitals from stray fire.

The Morgue held over twenty other warships drifting in high orbit, but those were useless right now. It would take *weeks* to bring any of those cruisers or destroyers online from their current suspended state.

Whatever happened, Isaac wasn't expecting to have weeks.

"We have no idea what kind of force these people could bring into play," he concluded. "The tech involved in the terraforming facility is beyond us—but not by enough that we don't understand what's going on.

"It's even possible that we won't be seeing a hostile reaction," he noted. "I'm not a pacifist like our Minister for Social Welfare, but *I* would be popping in to ask questions and see what was going on if someone triggered my alarm on my shut-down terraformer."

"Logically, they'll talk," Giannovi agreed. "No one is just going to pop in out of nowhere and open fire…right?"

"I'd say that, but that's basically what Admiral Cohen did to the Waterloo colony," Isaac replied quietly. "If humans would do it, I'm not ruling it out when it comes to complete unknowns."

"So, what do we do, sir?"

"We wait," he told her. "We wait, we prepare, and we pray I'm wrong."

"And what if you're not wrong?" she asked. "If these aliens come loaded for bear and don't listen to reason?"

"Then we do whatever is necessary to protect the colony," Isaac said quietly. "Whether that is fight to the death…or surrender."

———

EVERY PASSING minute ratcheted up the tension crawling its way around Isaac's spine. He was relatively sure it wasn't just him, either. Conversations around the flag bridge, communications traffic between ships…it was all slowing.

A nervous unease was settling over the Exilium Space Fleet as the details of what had happened made their way through official and unofficial channels to everyone. Humanity's Exilium branch had apparently settled on someone else's science project—and that someone now knew.

"Thirty-seven hours," Alstairs said quietly over Isaac's shoulder.

"Hmm?"

"It's been thirty-seven hours since the signal was triggered. Is that really enough for someone to get here? I mean, it makes sense to maintain an alert status since we don't know…but." The ops officer shook his head. "How do we know when to stand down?"

"How would we know when to stand to if we aren't ready?" Isaac asked. "Dr. Reinhardt tells me that the tachyons would lose their modulation relatively quickly. He doesn't think you could actually attach a meaningful signal to tachyons for more than a few fractions of a second.

"But, since tachyons are effectively everywhere…"

"A few fractions of a second gives a pretty spectacular range for coms," Alstairs agreed. "So, we're looking at what, a hundred, two hundred light-years?"

"And if they have wormhole tech like the Confederacy's, they could have been here already," Isaac reminded him. "On the other hand, if they have warp drives like the ones Dr. Reinhardt is building us, we'd be looking at three years to travel two hundred light-years still."

"They wouldn't have set up an alert signal if they expected it to take them years to respond, would they?" Rose asked. "The Confederacy used wormhole coms to set up rapid response, but we had a battle group on standby. There weren't many places we couldn't get at least one battlecruiser and escorts to inside of twenty-four hours. That's what *our* alert signals were built on."

"Well, it's been more than that," Alstairs noted. "So…when do we stand down?"

"I don't know," Isaac admitted. "We stay on Condition Two for at least a week, I think. That's what Condition Two is designed for, after all."

"That makes sense to me," the ops officer agreed. "We'll have grumpy crews at that point."

"That's what Captain Giannovi said."

A new icon had appeared on the holographic tank. One that was *way* too close for anyone's peace of mind.

"What the hell is that?" Isaac barked. "Report!"

"It's barely a light-minute away; how did we miss it?" Alstairs snapped.

"Because it wasn't *there* ten seconds ago," Giannovi replied. "It just appeared out of nowhere. No wormhole, no warp signature…nothing."

"What is it doing?" Isaac asked.

"Nothing," Alstairs said. "Just sitting there…Wait. What the *hell*?"

There was no acceleration. The massive engines attached to Isaac's ships could accelerate them at hundreds of gravities, but they still had to accelerate and maneuver under a clear evolution of Isaac Newton's laws.

This ship went from zero to ten percent of lightspeed instantly.

"Admiral," Dr. Reinhardt's gruff voice popped into his earbud.

"Little busy, Doctor," Isaac replied.

"I know," Reinhardt agreed. "But you need to know this. We're still running the sensor arrays we had set up for the *Percival* test flights. There was a massive unmodulated tachyon pulse as that ship appeared.

"I don't know what they're using for FTL, but it isn't anything we know about. Neither is that engine—some kind of reactionless drive. It's beyond our tech. Beyond our understanding."

Isaac closed his eyes and exhaled carefully.

"I'm not surprised, Dr. Reinhardt," he told the physicist. "But thank you, you're right. I did need to know that."

He turned his attention back to the job at hand as he opened his eyes.

"Their course?"

"Directly for Exilium," Alstairs reported. "I'm guessing they can slow down as quickly as they sped up."

"Almost certainly," Isaac agreed. "Orders to the fleet: battle stations! We will maneuver to intercept but we will not, I repeat, we will *not*, open fire unless fired upon.

"Rose—ping her with the first-contact package. We *need* to talk to these people."

————

THE FIRST-CONTACT PACKAGE was a purely theoretical construct, a data package of mathematics and machine code intended to attempt to assist an alien species in building a translation protocol. Since the only aliens humanity had ever encountered barely qualified as Stone Age, it had never been used.

In theory, the aliens would have their own equivalent that the Fleet's computers could work through. These aliens, however, weren't communicating at all—unless one counted their continued attempts to find a course to Exilium orbit that evaded Isaac's fleet.

"The good news, such as it is, is that they only seem to have one speed," Giannovi reported. "Point one *c*. No faster, no slower. In many ways, we're actually more maneuverable than she is, and we have the interior position.

"I don't know what she thinks she's doing, but she won't reach Exilium orbit without passing within one light-second of the fleet."

"Any response to our hails?" Isaac asked. With the battle stations alert active, he was now belted into his seat and had changed into a combat vac-suit. Everyone aboard all of his ships would now be protected against the possibility of breaching the ships.

"Negative," Rose replied. "They definitely received the first-contact package, but...nothing."

"Send it again," Isaac ordered. "I'd rather talk than shoot."

"Resending," she confirmed, then shook her head. "They're receiving it, sir, but I don't know if they're translating it or anything. It's like phoning a black hole."

Every minute brought the strange ship six light-seconds closer, the range melting away with a disturbing finality. Isaac didn't want to fire first...but he also wasn't going to let that ship into orbit of Exilium without knowing their intentions.

"Let's try one more thing, then," he told Rose. "Record for video transmission."

There was a camera attached to his seat, a tiny thing that extended out to focus on his face.

"Unknown vessel, this is Admiral Isaac Gallant aboard the Exilium Space Fleet battlecruiser *Vigil*," he said calmly. "We recognize that we may have settled on a planet that you had terraformed to your own needs, but there was no basis for us to identify it as claimed or inhabited.

"We are prepared to negotiate an exchange of knowledge, goods or services to continue our residence here, but you must understand that our voyage here was a one-way trip. We have no way to go home. We have no way to leave.

"We do not wish to be invaders, but we have nowhere else to go."

He cut off the recording and sighed.

"Send it," he ordered Rose. "It can't make things worse; that's for sure."

"What if they don't respond?" Alstairs asked.

"Bring us out to meet them at the ten-light-second mark," Isaac said calmly. "If she crosses that line without communicating, all ships are to fire at will."

"They've stopped."

Isaac wasn't even sure who had spoken, but they were right. The strange alien ship had stopped, roughly four point two three million kilometers away from Exilium. Presumably that seemingly random number was something specific in their distance measurement.

"Maneuver the Fleet into position two million kilometers away," he ordered. "Get me a good solid look at these people."

Two million kilometers was within range of his missile cruisers, if not the battlecruisers' particle cannons or the destroyers' pulse guns.

He had no idea what weapons the aliens had or what their range limitations might be.

They knew *nothing*.

"We've got a decent optical zoom on them now," Alstairs reported.

"Show me," Isaac said.

The holographic tank zoomed in on the alien vessel, showing it in near-perfect detail. It was a smooth black oval, an extended orb more even than an egg that shone in the light of the nearby star.

"There's no enhancement going on," his ops officer murmured. "It really does look like a giant obsidian stone." Highlights flickered along the strange ship's sides. "These appear to be hatches of some kind, probably weapons or sensors.

"There are no thruster nozzles or anything that we'd recognize as an engine. They just…move. And stop. And move. It's…weird."

"And now they wait. And we wait. And we just stare at each other across the void," Isaac said drily. "Anything, Rose?"

"Noth—wait! I've got something. Audio only, but I think it's English," she told him.

"Play it," Isaac replied.

A strange voice came over the speakers, a dry, mechanical noise distorted by bursts of static.

"These worlds are sacred. You will withdraw."

Silence hung in Isaac's bridge as he stared at the strange obsidian ship. *Sacred*. The aliens couldn't have chosen a more painful set of words to unleash on a child of New Soweto, a descendant of Old Africa.

Much of what Isaac's people had once believed—had once *held sacred*—had been destroyed by European colonizers. What had they done?

"These worlds are sacred. You will withdraw."

The voice echoed in the bridge again and no one said a word.

"These worlds are sacred. You will withdraw or be destroyed."

Isaac swallowed and gestured for Rose to record him again.

"We did not know these were sacred lands," he said softly. "We are refugees, cast out from our home with nowhere else to go. We are…" He coughed, realizing that what he was about to say could get him in a *massive* amount of trouble with the Cabinet. "We are prepared to relocate to a non-sacred site, but we do not have any transportation capability of our own anymore.

"This was a one-way trip. We are prepared to withdraw, but we will require assistance in doing so."

The transmission went on its way and Isaac felt the shock of his bridge crew.

"I will *not* do to another what was done to my people," he said very quietly, knowing they could all hear him. "Neither will President Lestroud. If there is a reasonable compromise to be fo—"

"*GUARDIAN PROTOCOLS ACTIVATED. TARGET NEUTRALIZED. TARGET NEUTRALIZED. SIX TARGETS NEUTRALIZED.*"

The mechanical voice of *Vigil*'s emergency alerts blared across the bridge and Isaac swore.

"Evasive maneuvers," he barked. "All ships, full evasive, release defense control to the automated systems, stand by for incoming fire."

Every Fleet warship had the Guardian Protocols, an AI routine that monitored all sensor data for incoming near-c projectiles—an attack the Confederacy would not have been able to prevent being launched. The Guardian Protocols automatically took full control of the pulse guns and anti-missile lasers, using them to take out incoming near-c projectiles in the fractions of a second between detection and impact.

There was no human intervention in the Guardian Protocols. There couldn't be. There wasn't enough time.

The hologram flashed out to show the fleet as *Vigil*'s engines came to life once more, maneuvering to evade any more impossibly fast shots.

"Talk to me, Cameron," Isaac demanded.

"Our *friend* just launched six missiles, one for each ship in the Fleet," his ops officer reeled off in a shocked tone. "Each went from zero to point nine five c in under a quarter-second. Guardian Protocols initiated across the Fleet and took out every projectile—but she is now maneuvering toward us at point one c again."

A second round of Guardian Protocol warnings echoed through the bridge, and Isaac clenched the arms of his seat.

"Cameron?"

"Three on us, three on *Dante*," Alstairs barked. "She's not transmitting anymore; she's just shooting and charging us."

"Very well," Isaac replied. "All vessels: *return fire!*"

———

THE TWO MISSILE cruisers opened fire first, missiles flashing out of side-mounted launch tubes and turning forward to create glittering flowers in space. Forty missiles blazed out from each cruiser, the salvos rushing toward the strange alien ship at a blistering acceleration.

Unlike the warp cruisers Isaac had once commanded, the missile cruisers didn't have a split between "ready" and "reserve" magazines. Each of their forty launchers had access to their full magazine with automated reloaders.

The flowers of fire repeated again and again as the rest of Isaac's fleet lunged forward. He hadn't had to give specific orders for the missile cruisers to hang back—the commanders knew the doctrine as well as he did.

The destroyers could outpace his battlecruisers, but not by enough to make sending them ahead worthwhile. Not when his opponent was flinging missiles at him at ninety-five percent of lightspeed.

"There's another missile salvo," Alstairs reported grimly. "I don't know how many of these hell missiles this bastard has, but I'm glad he seems to be limited to six launchers. He's still spreading his fire between us and *Dante*, too."

Which was, so far as Isaac could tell, the only reason he still had two battlecruisers. *Vigil* could only provide so much support to her sister ship and vice versa. If the alien focused their missiles on a single target, the odds of the Terrans missing one went up dramatically.

"*Madre de Dio*," Giannovi swore. "Sir, our missiles!"

Isaac had to pull up the recorded data and rewind it. The entire eighty-missile salvo had died in the blink of an eye when it closed with the enemy ship. Several of the hatches they'd identified had swung open as the salvo closed and revealed some kind of extremely rapid-fire energy weapon.

There were *maybe* ten of the weapons, and they'd obliterated the Exilium Space Fleet's missiles in less than a second.

"What the hell was that?" he asked.

"Plasma weapon of some kind," Alstairs replied after studying the data. "An advanced version of our own pulse guns, lower-energy but —as you saw—vastly increased rate of fire. Hit rate wasn't as high as it might look," he noted, "but they were firing at ten thousand RPM."

Their Confederacy-built pulse guns were basically focused vents from their fusion cores, funneling plasma from the power systems into magnetically contained packages—pulses—they flung at the enemy. Their projectiles were almost as fast as the ion packets from the battle-cruisers' particle cannon, but they were more diffuse.

Faster-firing than the particle cannons, the pulse guns still only fired at about fifty RPM. Not the *ten thousand* their enemy had unleashed.

At that rate, ten guns had fired over sixteen hundred plasma bolts at his eighty missiles in one second.

"We're not going to hit them with missiles, are we?" Isaac said softly. "And those guns are going to make a mess of our ships, too. Take the Fleet to evasive pattern Romeo Tango Mike."

"That'll cost us on mutual missile defense," his ops officer warned.

"And if we're not moving enough when that thing reaches range of our ships, we'll die then," the Admiral said harshly. "Pass the order. Inform Captains Giannovi and Anderson that they are *not* to wait for my order.

"The moment they have a shot with the particle cannons, they are to take it."

His four charging ships began to maneuver more and more as they closed the range. With the obsidian orb of the alien vessels rushing toward them at its strangely fixed speed, the range was melting rapidly toward where the Terrans would be able to open fire with their energy weapons.

"Sir! *Dante* is hit!"

Isaac caught Alstairs' report and checked the telemetry from his second battlecruiser. The alien was still splitting their fire between the two cruisers, but they'd been lucky. One missile had made it past the

Guardian Protocols—but *Dante* had been dodging and had only taken a glancing hit.

"Captain Anderson reports her engines and particle cannon are live, but she's lost her entire starboard defensive suite," Rose told Isaac.

"Orders to Commander Riley: *Archimedes* is to move in close to *Dante*; he's to attach his ship to Captain Anderson's starboard flank like a limpet. We need her particle cannon!"

Unspoken, though everyone from Isaac to Commander Jason Riley to Captain Margaret Anderson knew it, was what he was *actually* ordering. If it came down to it, *Archimedes* was to take the hit that would kill *Dante*.

They could afford to lose the destroyer better than they could afford to lose Anderson's battlecruiser.

———

"PARTICLE-CANNON RANGE IN THIRTY SECONDS," Alstairs murmured softly. "Pulse-gun range in fifty."

The flag bridge was quiet enough that everyone heard him. The alien ship had now flung over two hundred impossibly fast missiles at the Exilium Space Fleet, and Isaac could only sit on his bridge and thank every deity he knew of that his mother had hired professional paranoids to design the Confederacy's warships.

To his knowledge, the Guardian Protocols had never been triggered in Confederacy service—but their existence had just saved his fleet. No human could operate quickly enough to intervene in the gap between detecting a near-*c* missile and its arrival.

The Guardian Protocol AI could. Barely.

The state of *Dante*'s starboard broadside was the reality of what that "barely" meant. Four missiles had made it through everything the ESF could throw at them, but only one had hit—and that glancing blow had devastated the big warship.

"*Dante* and *Vigil* both report particle cannons charged," Rose passed on. "Everyone is standing by."

Then the carefully unasked question of "What did the *alien* have for energy weapons?" was answered.

Energy spikes flared across Isaac's display as *something* connected the obsidian alien vessel with *Dante*. The battlecruiser lurched in space as the beam hammered into her bows, splitting open her forward armor and sending the ship reeling out of formation.

"All ships, evasive Omega Zulu Mike!" Isaac barked. Independent maneuvering, no attempt for them to try and cover each other from the alien's godawful missiles.

"What *was* that?"

"Gamma ray laser," Alstairs said grimly. "That was a two-hundred-petajoule pulse delivered in just under point two seconds. An exawatt-rated beam."

"I suppose telling the captains not to let that hit them would be redundant," Isaac said drily.

"We have no telemetry from *Dante*," Rose reported. "She's still here, but I've got no data incoming."

Isaac nodded silently, leaning back in his chair and wishing there was something, *anything*, he could do.

"Hostile has fired again," his ops officer reported. "*Archimedes* evaded but took surface damage. She's still combat-capable."

Vigil shivered underneath them as the battlecruiser finally found her own range, the massive spinal particle cannon firing its first packet as it crossed the arbitrary line where the charged ions would still impact with enough force to do damage.

Seven seconds later, she shivered again. Every seven seconds, the big gun fired as the battlecruiser continued to close, Terran and alien vessels alike dancing around the vast quantities of energy being flung into space.

It took four tries for *Vigil* to land a hit, the packet of near-*c* ions hammering into the alien's smooth black hull. Nothing changed. The alien ship's energy signature didn't even blip, and Isaac caught himself holding his breath.

The laser flared again and again, but the alien seemed to have problems adapting to the rapidly varying acceleration of the Exilium Fleet.

A second particle cannon hit slammed home—and this time, the obsidian finish seemed to crack.

"I have radiation leakage," Alstairs barked. "No atmosphere, but we cracked the hull!"

"Do it again!" Isaac snapped.

Now the pulse guns were joining in. The alien ship didn't seem to have anything beyond what they'd seen earlier, but the sheer rate of fire of its plasma cannons made it impossible to miss. *Archimedes* and *Plato* writhed in its fire, their armor able to absorb dozens of hits from the relatively weak pulse guns…but the alien's rate of fire meant that they *had* to absorb dozens of hits.

And Isaac realized that everyone had forgotten about the missile cruisers. The alien's defenses were such that his people had stopped firing, and he'd been all but ignoring them.

So, it seemed, had the alien—and Isaac's two missile-cruiser captains had been deploying every missile in their magazines with their engines cold. The instant the alien ship started turning her pulse guns on the destroyers, they fired.

Over a thousand missiles lit off their drives simultaneously, hurtling toward the strange obsidian ship. It reacted far faster than Isaac would have expected, flipping in space to direct its pulse-gun fire at the missiles.

Thousands of plasma pulses flashed into space, forming a near-solid wall of fire that intercepted the missiles. Dozens of missiles died. Then hundreds, and Isaac realized that the alien ship was actually going to stop them all.

But it did so by ignoring the closer ships, and Captain Giannovi had always had a perfect sense of when to go for the jugular. *Vigil* abandoned her evasive maneuvers and plunged straight at the alien, emptying every charge her particle cannon had on standby.

Four blasts hammered into the strange ship, each of them flinging it slightly off-balance and out of place. The ship tried to turn, bringing its weapons to bear on the battlecruiser—and then *Vigil*'s pulse guns fired.

A Confederacy battlecruiser's main ship-killer was her particle cannon, but she traded in the missiles of her mid-sized sisters for the pulse-gun batteries of an entire *squadron* of destroyers. Plasma washed over the length of the alien ship, fire hammering into that strange black hull until it cracked and broke under the heat.

And then a final blast of charged ions slammed through the hole Giannovi had torn in her enemy's armor…and the obsidian egg of a warship simply disintegrated.

———

34

TWO STARSHIPS, both wrecked, floated in the hologram in the middle of the Cabinet meeting room. A screen on one wall held the exhausted face of Admiral Isaac Gallant, but Amelie and the rest of the Cabinet were focused on the two vessels.

"*Dante* is, technically, repairable," Gallant told them.

Amelie found that hard to believe. Captain Anderson's battlecruiser had been split open and her front third *peeled* back by the hit that had taken her out of the fight.

"Or perhaps more accurately," the Admiral continued, "the *Confederacy* could have repaired her. In our own state, we have the technology but not necessarily the resources or facilities to do so."

"Given our own *lack* of resources, do we have a choice other than to try?" Rodriguez asked in a pained tone. "We only have two battlecruisers. As I see it, we *must* repair *Dante*."

"I agree, though I'm not sure we will be able to repair her particle cannon at all," Gallant noted.

"What is your assessment of our strange new enemy?" Amelie asked the Admiral. "They didn't seem very talkative."

"They were talkative enough," the Admiral replied. "I'm sorry, Minister James. We really did try to avoid a fight."

"What are you apologizing to me for?" James demanded. "You made offers that were beyond reasonable to try and avoid a fight—and they fired first, not you. Violence is the last resort of a fool, Admiral, but we must be prepared to defend ourselves against such fools."

"I'm not sure we'd even have been able to sell relocating the entire colony to our people even if they had been willing to negotiate," Amelie added. Isaac's offers to the alien had gone well beyond his authority, though it seemed no one in her Cabinet was going to raise that as an issue.

Which was probably for the best. Not fighting this enemy seemed wiser...but it also didn't seem an option.

"In terms of my assessment of them..." Gallant sighed. "That ship was only slightly larger than one of my destroyers and was almost a match for the entire fleet. If they'd had even one or two more launchers for those hell missiles, we'd have been wiped out without even scratching its hull."

He tapped a command on a console they couldn't see, adjusting the hologram to focus on the obsidian egg that had tried to kill his fleet.

"I have General Zamarano's people trying to board the wreckage, but they're not having much luck," he noted. "It's pretty thoroughly shattered, and they can't seem to find anything we'd recognize as decks or working spaces in the wreckage. At this point, the Marines are just trying to find any relatively intact tech."

"Do we know if they called for reinforcements?" Linton asked. "If they have friends coming..."

"Fortunately, Dr. Reinhardt's tests for the new warp drives involved a quite sensitive set of tachyon detectors," Gallant replied. "We picked up the original signal that brought them here and we picked up their arrival. We did not pick up any signals from the ship itself, so we don't think they sent any messages.

"That still means, unfortunately, that someone is almost certainly going to come looking for them eventually," the Admiral said grimly. "We have no idea what interstellar drive they used...or in-system drive, for that matter.

"Without knowing what their system is, we can't account for how long it will take a second wave to arrive. We do know that it took this ship roughly thirty-six hours to get here after the first tachyon signal, which puts a hard limit on the communication-and-transit loop from wherever it was based."

"Admiral Gallant, if they return in greater force, can the Exilium Space Fleet stop them?" Father James asked quietly. "It is our obligation to protect our people, no matter what."

"With just *Vigil*, the missile cruisers and the destroyers…" Gallant sighed. "No."

That was what Amelie had expected, but it still hurt to hear it said.

"So, we need to repair *Dante*," she said firmly. "When we were dealing with the potential of unknown threats, maintaining the ESF as a force-in-being was a necessary expense.

"Now we are dealing with a very clear threat, and maximizing the capability of the ESF just became our top priority. Mothballing the Fleet to help advance our industrial growth just became a luxury we cannot afford.

"What do you *need*, Admiral Gallant?"

That seemed to take him aback, and Amelie took a small concealed pleasure in the surprise at his face—and the unanimous agreement of her Cabinet.

Reducing the size of the Fleet had been their first true decision as a group, an easy victory Isaac Gallant had softballed them. Now they had six months of working together. They knew they could work together—and that they could sell this to the people of their colony.

"It's not a question of technology, resources or even personnel," the Admiral admitted. "We simply don't have the facilities to repair *Dante*."

"But if we build the facilities to do so, they could also be used to construct more battlecruisers, correct?" Linton asked. "Or similar-scale civilian ships, for that matter. We have some components for prefabricated shipyard modules we haven't used yet as we had plenty of shipping.

"We *should* be able to assemble a yard relatively quickly."

"My calculations said six months, so anything better than that is a victory," Gallant admitted.

"I won't swear to less than four weeks," the ex-smuggler promised. "It might be faster, but I think I can promise four weeks."

"That gives us time to deal with the other problem," the Admiral said grimly. "We can't replace the particle cannon. That's…an entirely different type of manufacturing than we've been doing. There are some possible options that I'll have Dr. Reinhardt look into, but we'll need a new main gun for *Dante*."

"And the rest of the Fleet?" Amelie asked.

"Demonstrably, our missile cruisers are useless against their ships," he replied. "I'm going to want to transfer their crews to the destroyers and redraw our plans for the warp drives. I think we can get at least four destroyers online with the exotic matter from the drive rings for the missile cruisers and *Dante*.

"I'll want to recommission at least that many destroyers and accelerate building the drive ring onto *Vigil*," Gallant concluded. "The tactical mobility—and temporary invulnerability—of the grav-warp drives will be too useful in the event of their return."

The Admiral sighed.

"We can commit massive resources to revamping the Fleet, people, with no guarantee of successful defense," he warned them. "We apparently landed in someone's holy gardens."

"Relocating is *not* an option," Amelie told him firmly. "We don't have the capacity and it's pretty clear these aliens aren't planning on helping.

"We will plan to fight them, to defend our new home with every resource and technology at our command." She looked around the table, meeting each of her Cabinet Ministers' eyes.

"Does anyone here have a problem with that?" she asked. "Because if you do, you'd better have a damn good alternative to offer!"

———

ONCE THE REST of the Cabinet had filed out, Amelie leveled her best "come clean with me" look on Isaac.

"And how are *you* holding up?" she asked him softly. She knew the man who led her military well enough now to know that he couldn't have taken the fight lightly.

He exhaled and shook his head.

"I wish I could get out of my head the fact that they've got plenty of reason to be pissed at us," he told her. "The kind of terraforming project we've found evidence of is an immense effort. They transformed this planet into paradise—and then we showed up and moved in."

"That doesn't make sense to me, not with what they were saying," Amelie replied. "'These worlds are sacred,' Isaac. *Sacred*, at least to me, isn't something you *build*; it's just something that *is*."

"And you wouldn't regard the amount of work needed to build this place as worthy of veneration?" he replied. "It's too easy for me to remember the Europeans moving into Africa and wondering if we're repeating the same mistakes of our ancestors."

"I don't recall us taking slaves or using diseases to wipe out resisting populations," the President of Exilium snapped. "We landed on an uninhabited world we had no reason to believe belonged to anyone. There were no beacons, no warning signs, not even a blip of technology. The terraforming stations were damn well hidden.

"*Merde, mon Amiral*, we both know that we only had one choice for a destination," she told him. "You were basically groveling to the bastards and they opened fire." Amelie shook her head.

"And don't think how willing you were to give up the entire colony isn't going to come back to haunt you, either," she continued. "I understand. The Cabinet understands. But soon enough, that video footage is going to be public across the entirety of Exilium."

"I know," Isaac said quietly. "But that, too, was my burden to bear. We are strangers in this corner of the universe; it cannot fall solely to us to decide where we belong."

"And if someone is determined to force us out, to destroy us or enslave us?" she demanded. "What then, Isaac Gallant? When they come back, who will I have? The man terrified of being a colonizer or the Admiral sworn to defend his people?"

He coughed.

"That's...not really fair," he said.

"No," she agreed. "But I'm the President of a planet, Admiral Gallant, which is at least partially your damned fault. *Fair* doesn't get to be in my top priorities."

"I will do whatever it takes to defend the people I serve and the people I love," Isaac replied, his voice soft and sad again. "*Whatever* it takes, Amelie. I'm allowed to regret those choices, I'm allowed to judge them—I refuse to become my mother.

"But I will die before I let these aliens harm you or our people."

The conversation had taken a suddenly sharp turn into dangerous areas, and Amelie took a deep breath to calm her frustration—and the warm flush at his reference to "the people he loved."

"I know," she conceded. "I trust you. Is there anything you need, anything we're not already working on?"

"Anything I need…or anything the Fleet needs?" he said carefully.

This time, she was relatively certain she flushed brightly enough for him to see, and he chuckled at her, the moment of levity softening the conversation dramatically.

"I have all I need, if not necessarily all I want," Isaac told her, his voice so soft she could barely hear him. "The Fleet…"

He shook his head.

"I need about six battle groups, a pair of dreadnoughts, and a production facility for particle cannons," he said. "Since there's no way that the Republic can give me any of that, what's been promised is as good as it can get."

"Can you stop them?" Amelie asked. Her voice was softer than she'd meant it to be, and she realized this wasn't the President asking her Admiral. This was Amelie Lestroud asking her Isaac Gallant.

"If they give me enough time…I think so."

"And if they don't?"

Isaac swallowed hard enough for her to see and looked her levelly in the eyes.

"That's why I want the warp drives," he admitted. "I don't care how tough they are. If I ram a battlecruiser into them at sixty times the speed of light, they are *not* going home."

———

35

DAMAGE AND CASUALTY reports were heart-wrenching at any time. When Isaac was at the far end of the galaxy and each name meant another tiny but significant part of the Exilium branch of humanity wiped away, they were somehow worse.

He'd lost more subordinates when *Dante* had taken the gamma-ray laser hit than he'd lost in his entire career prior to that. Over three hundred people had died to the one solid hit the alien had landed, and he'd lost another hundred or so across all four ships to the damage from the rapid-fire pulse guns.

Four hundred-plus dead. About half that in wounded—space battles didn't leave a lot of wounded. With how thoroughly they'd reduced the ESF, that was a full tenth of the people he still had in uniform.

Fortunately, from a twisted point of view, anyway, they already had more of their old comrades clamoring to sign back up than they had the facilities to handle. Isaac's former subordinates were as furious as he was.

It would take him time to get the structures in place to bring them back into Exilium Space Fleet uniform and bring ships online for them to fly, but the avalanche of messages from people volunteering meant that reactivating the Morgue would be a matter of days and weeks, not months and years.

It didn't bring back his dead. It didn't even guarantee victory in the days to come. But it was a sign that he wasn't alone in his grief and anger.

He was, however, lost enough in it that he barely registered the first knock on his door. It was only the second, much louder round of knocking that shook him from his intense focus on the reports in front of him.

There was also the question, of course, of why anyone was *knocking* on a starship.

"Come in," Isaac barked.

The door slid open instantly, so whoever was knocking did know how to use the door's regular controls, and the massive form of Lyle Reinhardt stumped in. The one-eyed physicist looked as exhausted as Isaac felt, his long white hair in complete disarray and his clothes rumpled.

"I figured you weren't going to remember to call," the head of the ESF's R&D rumbled. "So, I grabbed a shuttle. Seems like it was a good plan."

"The door has an admittance chime, you know," Isaac pointed out drily.

"Aye, and *you*, Admiral Gallant, have a code to lock it into *do not disturb* mode," Reinhardt told him. "You may want to turn that off, my friend, if you're actually expecting anyone to show up at your office door."

Isaac checked and sighed before turning the mode off.

"Most of my people can just call me," he pointed out. "But I was going over casualty reports. I didn't want to be interrupted."

"And we were supposed to start a video call five minutes ago," Reinhardt told him with a chuckle. "I'd have been on time, but I spoke to Alstairs on the flight over and realized I needed to make a detour."

"What kind of detour?" Isaac asked carefully—before the entry of three of *Vigil*'s stewards with a cart of food.

"The kind that makes sure my boss has food," Reinhardt said brightly. "And beer!"

One of the stewards returned the professor's enthusiasm with a small nod, revealing a chilled jug and two mugs.

"We don't normally serve alcohol this early in the ship's day," he admitted, "but it is the Admiral!"

Isaac chuckled at the array of food, coffee, and beer the stewards laid out across his desk with brisk efficiency.

"Thank you," he told them. "I promise to eat. I really do."

That earned him an approving nod, and then the stewards disappeared out of his office as quickly as they had come.

"So, we had a meeting scheduled, did we?" Isaac asked. "I remember that. You know what my biggest question is."

"I do," Reinhardt agreed, pouring himself a beer and Isaac a coffee as he spoke. "Warp-drive rings."

"Exactly."

"We'll have *Vigil*'s ready for installation in two days," the physicist told him. "Everything's been prepared to make that straightforward, but it'll still be another two days. You'll have a warp-capable battle-cruiser in four days, Admiral."

Isaac heaved a sigh of relief.

"That helps," he admitted. "And the others?"

"We had rings built for the missile cruisers, but my understanding is that we won't be using those, right?"

"We threw sixty percent of the magazines of two missile cruisers at the alien in one salvo and we didn't hit it," Isaac reminded Reinhardt. "There's no point taking anything against these aliens that they can intercept. Since we're nowhere near building new ships, that means destroyers and battlecruisers."

"We have the exotic matter from *Dante*'s and *Lancelot*'s rings," the physicist reminded him. "If we aren't upgrading *Lancelot* as planned, that'll give us enough EM for three destroyer warp rings. *Dante*'s would give us five…"

"I've been promised the facilities to repair *Dante*, at least her hull," Isaac replied. "Until I believe that's impossible, we'll want to hang on to that drive ring. Three destroyers are what it'll have to be."

"That'll take a few weeks," Reinhardt warned him.

"It'll take what it takes. I need you and your top people to start digging through our Confed R&D files," the Admiral continued. "We have all of their damned research on potential new weapons systems, stuff they didn't think was practical or wasn't cost efficient to deploy. I know we can't build a new particle cannon. What *can* we give *Dante* when we repair her?"

"That's…outside my expertise, Admiral," Reinhardt admitted. "I'm a warp-drive guy."

"I know," Isaac agreed. "But you're also my head of research and development. Find the right expertise. If I'm rebuilding a battlecruiser, I need to give her a spinal gun worthy of the class."

"We'll see what we can find," Reinhardt confirmed. He shook his head. "We're going to have some interesting considerations in that as we continue dissecting the Stranger."

"Anything useful so far?" Isaac asked.

"I can tell you a few things about her," the scientist replied. "For one, she was a drone. No crew aboard at all. A pure AI ship."

"That's insane," Isaac said slowly. Confederacy AI was finicky enough that even the Guardian Protocols had been a closely kept secret. History suggested that giving an AI weapons was a bad idea, let alone giving one an FTL drive.

"We haven't found her computer core or anything of the sort, I have no idea how she lines up with our AI tech, but there was definitely no crew," Reinhardt told him. "We still have no idea how her FTL, her drives or her missiles work."

"No surprises there."

"We *did* pull three intact missiles and a pair of intact pulse guns from the wreck," the physicist continued. "I suspect it'll take years for us to make sense of the missiles, but the pulse guns fall into the same category as the terraforming gear on the surface."

"What do you mean?" Isaac asked.

"We understand the principles and the tech involved; it's just on a different scale or from a different point of view than our usual applications of it. It's more advanced than ours, but not by much. Give us six months to a year and we'll have a design to upgrade our own pulse guns based off their tech."

"That's the first piece of unexpected good news I've had in a while," the Admiral replied. "I don't know if we'll have that long, but I'll take it."

"Even reverse-engineering things takes time, Admiral. There's only so much we can do."

"I know," Isaac allowed. "Which brings me to another question, in terms of last-ditch options."

"Admiral?"

"What happens if we ram one of these bastards with a warp-drive destroyer? Or a battlecruiser, for that matter?" Isaac asked flatly.

"Even the new warp bubble isn't that stable," Reinhardt warned him. "And there's some weird oddities going on with exotic matter and mass shadows in the Stranger's hull."

"So?"

Reinhardt exhaled heavily, finished his beer in one swallow and met Isaac's gaze with his one eye.

"Ramming them with any of our warp-capable ships would destroy them, but it would be a suicide run," he replied, his voice calm and serious. "Even *Vigil* would be destroyed in the process. Worse…"

He shook his head.

"You have a small but significant chance—on the order of four to six percent, I'd need to double-check the math with the new drive rings—of total energy conversion of both vessels. A few million tons of mass converted to pure energy?"

"Damn," Isaac whispered. "The planet wouldn't survive that."

"Admiral…the *system* wouldn't survive that."

———

36

Isaac stood on *Vigil*'s flag bridge, watching carefully as the five-hundred-meter-wide drive ring was maneuvered toward the battle-cruiser.

"Initial contact in forty-five seconds," Alstairs reported. "It looks like the tug crews know what they're doing."

"I know they know what they're doing," the Admiral agreed. "It doesn't make this any easier to watch. That's almost a fifth of our exotic matter stockpile, Commander, and we have no way of making more yet."

"Do we have any plans on changing that?" the younger man asked.

"Plans?" Isaac asked with a chuckle. "Sure, lots of plans. But given that any mass production of exotic matter requires tame black holes, it'll be a while before we're producing more than a trickle. Even that trickle is going to take two to three years."

The only good news out of that was that the difference between the particle accelerators used for small-scale exotic-matter production and the particle accelerators used for a battlecruiser's main gun was mostly a matter of semantics. Once they could build the EM plants, they could build particle cannons.

"Catch-22, isn't it?" Alstairs murmured. "You need tame black holes to make exotic matter—but you need exotic matter to capture and tame black holes. *More* if you have to make your own."

"And it's not like we've got any convenient wormholes to fling a microsingularity through," Isaac agreed. *That* part of setting up new exotic-matter plants had always been terrifying. The entire Confederacy only had one facility for manufacturing artificial microsingularities, and the system it lived in was uninhabited otherwise.

One facility to produce the things—at over two years a microsingularity—and one ship to transport them…and the entire human race had held their collective breath every time that ship went through a wormhole with its terrifying cargo.

Without even that, however, Isaac and his people were probably going to have to go hunting black holes if they wanted to build warp ships in any significant quantity. That was a problem for another day, however.

"Contact!" Alstairs barked.

Isaac shook his head. He hadn't felt a thing when the connection had been made.

"How are we doing?" he asked.

"We have initial contact and velocity match," his ops officer confirmed. "From what the crew told me, it'll be about twenty-four hours to carefully rotate the ring into the connections and lock into place, during which we have to remain almost entirely immobile. Another twenty-four hours after that to hook it up, but we can at least maneuver once it's in place."

Which meant that for the next day, *Vigil* was helpless. She couldn't maneuver, couldn't fight.

"I wish there was a better way to do this," he said quietly.

"We're refitting a six-year-old starship with a piece of tech she was never designed to carry," his ops officer reminded him. "I'm surprised it's this easy!"

"Thank Dr. Reinhardt for that," Isaac told him. "The man is brilliant. Terrifying on a dozen levels."

"You can say that again," Alstairs replied, shaking his head. "Have you met his daughter?"

Isaac chuckled.

"No, though I'm somehow unsurprised he has a family."

"Brigette Reinhardt," Alstairs explained. "Engineer to her dad's physicist. Smart as a whip. Cute, too."

"Commander?" Isaac said questioningly.

His ops officer chuckled.

"If you think Dr. Reinhardt is intimidating as a subordinate, imagining meeting him as your girlfriend's father!"

————

"CAPTAIN ANDERSON, HOW IS *DANTE*?" Isaac asked.

The tall woman on his screen hadn't commanded *Dante* for the Confederacy. She had never, in fact, commanded a warship for the CSF. What she had been, however, was the Naval Military Police commander for an entire battle group.

From her file, she'd been in jail for two years before the exile, "temporarily detained" by the Confederacy Secret Police after she'd interfered with their purge of suspected dissidents. Her rank and seniority were high enough to command a capital starship, so when the Fleet had assembled Battle Group *Dante* from odds and sods of dissidents, she'd been given the "honor" of commanding *Dante*.

Despite a rocky start with the near-mutiny, she'd done a solid job and stayed in the Exilium Space Fleet. Now, however, her ship was wrecked.

"We've managed to get rough covers in place over most of the holes," Anderson told him. "We're still losing about a dozen cubic meters of air every minute, but we're getting enough help to stay ahead of that.

"As for the rest, well…" She shrugged fatalistically, her eyes distant. "I lost a third of my crew and about the same of my ship. I know we're talking about repairing her, but it's going to be an uphill slog, Admiral. That gamma ray beam gutted us like a fish.

"If you want my resignation, sir, you'll have it."

"Captain Anderson," Isaac told her calmly, "you were following *my* battle plan. If anyone was going to resign in disgrace for *Dante*'s fate, it would be me. And if I think we're too deep in trouble to replace me, the same thing goes for my ship commanders.

"Am I understood?"

"Yes, sir," she replied crisply.

"Good. Because I'm about to make your life harder again," he told her.

She squared her shoulders and looked him in the eye.

"Do your worst, sir; it's not like I have a functioning warship."

"That's the problem," he agreed. "I'm taking Commander Stanz. He'll move over to *Kant* with three hundred of your remaining crew. We're also standing down *Lancelot* and *Galahad*, which will give us the crews to re-commission *Locke*, *Socrates* and *Hobbes*. That'll be all six of our *Philosopher*-class destroyers."

"That makes sense, sir," she confirmed crisply. "What do you want me to do?"

"Focus on fixing your damn ship, Captain," Isaac told her. "Reinhardt's people are digging up details for a new main gun, but I have no idea what they're going to find. I know we can't build you a new ion cannon, so we'll see what our R&D can pull together."

"I'm going to miss that cannon," she agreed. "I can't see us having *Dante* even remotely combat-ready for months."

"I know," he admitted. "But I need you to focus on that job, interface with the civilians, and get the work done. I'm going to have a million other things on my plate, so your ship is going to mostly be your problem, understand, Captain?"

"Promoted to yard dog, I see," Anderson replied, but she nodded her understanding. "I'll make it happen, sir. What miracles can be worked will be worked. I'll get *Dante* back in commission."

———

SHUTTLES SWARMED across the holographic display on Isaac's flag bridge, dozens of the tiny ships transferring the crews from two missile cruisers and a wrecked battlecruiser to the four destroyers he'd picked out.

"How's our plan for bringing people back into the fold coming along, Cameron?" Isaac asked his ops officer.

"Slower than anyone would like, including our volunteers," Alstairs responded. "At least we don't have to train anybody, just recommission or enlist them at their old rates and find slots for them. We'll be able to start crewing the *Icicle*s and *Archon*s in two days."

"Start with the *Archon*s," the Admiral ordered. "The *Icicle*s may be newer ships, but I can assure you from painful personal experience that the *Archon* is a tougher, more powerful unit. Especially with the upgrades ours got."

His six *Philosopher*-class ships were the best and latest the Confederacy had built—Battle Group *Vigil* had been commanded by the dictator's son, after all. Only the best for the "Iron Brat."

The *Icicle*-class ships were the last-generation ships, but the *Archon*s were twenty years old, built by one of the Confederacy's system governments before Adrienne Gallant had forbidden the individual governments from having real fleets.

At the point he had twenty destroyers back in commission, keeping them all fueled and maintained was going to be a major drain on Exilium's orbital industry—but he'd finally feel comfortable that they might stand a chance against the threat he knew was coming.

"Two weeks to crew all the destroyers," Alstairs warned him. "At least. It might be as long as four—and even that is assuming we have no conflicts over seniority or ranks and that nothing took severe damage in the Morgue."

"That's what we have to work with," Isaac replied. "I'll be happier at the end of today once we've got the *Philosopher*s online and *Vigil* is capable of maneuvering again."

Almost as if summoned by his hopeful words, his tattoo-comp chimed an urgent alert at him. He flipped the communication to his command chair and met Dr. Reinhardt's gaze through the video.

"Lyle?" he asked quietly. The one-eye physicist looked even worse than he had earlier.

"We kept the tachyon sensors online," Reinhardt told him, his voice exhausted. "We spread them out so that we could try and identify individual sources at a distance."

Isaac closed his eyes in a wince he couldn't conceal.

"How bad?" he asked.

"At least four individual tachyon pulses. They came out of FTL pretty far out—but you'll have lightspeed data on them in just under five minutes."

"At least?" the Admiral asked.

"It's hard to be sure; this is still more guesswork than science," Reinhardt admitted. "But, Admiral…"

"Yes?"

"If it is only four, one of them is a *lot* bigger than the others."

———

37

"THEY CAUGHT us with our pants down," Giannovi said grimly. "In hindsight, perhaps we should have moved the crews before beginning *Vigil*'s warp installation. We're an immobile weapon platform now, though anyone who wants to get to Exilium is going to have to go right past us."

"And that, unfortunately, is the only option I see," Isaac replied. "If they've got the same speed as the last one, we've got about an hour before they reach orbit."

"By that point, we'll actually have the *Philosophers* crewed, though the crews are going to be literally boarding and going to battle stations. They won't be particularly well-oiled machines, but they'll be six operational destroyers.

"And I'm not going to turn down luring them into the range of *Vigil*'s main gun," he concluded. "Do we have a read on them yet?"

"Five ships," Alstairs reported. "Four much the same as the last Stranger, the other..." The ops officer shook his head. "The last is at least ten times the size of the others. If her armament is to scale..."

"Then our only chance is to sucker-punch her," Isaac said. "And the fact that they're almost certainly here looking for their last scout and we're the only armed starships around, I'm guessing we're not going to get much of a chance."

"No," his ops officer confirmed.

"What do we tell the civilians?" Commander Rose asked. "I mean…anyone with access to the orbital scanners can probably do the math on what this means."

Isaac was trying very hard *not* to do the math, but he knew what she meant.

"I will talk to the President," he told them. "And then I will talk to the destroyer Captains. I see only one weapon to hand that might be able to win this battle."

From the expressions of his officers, Lauretta Giannovi was the only one who saw the option he did.

"For now, we will hold position in orbit and see what our friends do," he concluded. "It's possible that the big mother actually carries a crew, and *they* may be willing to talk to us."

"And if they're not?" Giannovi said quietly. "What do we do?"

"We defend Exilium," Isaac replied harshly. "Whatever the cost."

Even if the cost was to order his entire fleet on kamikaze ramming courses.

―――――

AMELIE LOOKED WORRIED when Isaac got her on the com. He couldn't blame her—they'd gone from the slow and careful development of an idyllic paradise to facing their potential extermination inside of three days.

"Five ships?" she asked. "You lost one of your battlecruisers fighting one—and that mothership is huge. What do we do?"

"If I thought they were going to accept surrenders, I'd offer one," Isaac admitted. He'd called her from his office; no one else could over-hear him. And if there was anyone in the galaxy who deserved his honesty, it was Amelie Lestroud.

"If they had demands, regardless of how unreasonable, we'd have to meet them," he continued. "But the only demand the first one made was impossible, so we have no choice."

"How can you fight something like this?" Amelie said. "You're outgunned, outmatched. What do we do?"

"What we must," Isaac said quietly. "If *Vigil*'s warp drive were online, I'd take her out and try to jump the mothership from FTL. But as it is, *Vigil* is an immobile weapon platform, and my destroyers are all I'm going to have."

"I thought their weapons were relatively ineffective, just less so than the missiles?"

He bowed his head silently for a long few seconds.

"They remain extremely dense vessels with extremely powerful engines," he said quietly. "We have no choice. No other options. I intend to order our destroyer captains to ram the enemy."

Amelie was silent.

"There's no other way, Amelie," he told her. "If *Vigil* somehow survives this, I'll hate myself forever for it. But I don't see another option."

"I'm no soldier," she replied. "But I don't see one either. Isaac—"

"No," he cut her off. "My choice. My orders. My guilt. We swore an oath. We will honor it."

"And what does honor leave of your soul, *mon Amiral*?"

"The people I am sworn to defend," he told her. "That is what this leaves. We will do all we can, Amelie. But realize we still may fail."

"What happens then?"

"I don't know," Isaac admitted. Barring a cruel miracle, he wouldn't live to see that. "But…I fear they will bombard Starhaven from orbit. If we can't stop them, they may burn out our intrusion onto their holy world."

"And there's nothing we can do to stop that?"

"Nothing," he admitted. "You need to start evacuating Starhaven. We have the gear for people to go low-tech in the wilderness, far from any sign of our habitation. That may be the only chance for any of us to survive."

"That…" Amelie nodded firmly. "That we can do. And that is *my* problem, Admiral Gallant. Command your fleet. Know that all our prayers are with you."

She paused.

"Know that—"

"I know." Even now, they couldn't say it.

They might, after all, survive this.

———

THE VIDEOCONFERENCE WAS A QUIET, solemn affair. Isaac and his seven Captains—four of them were Commanders, but ancient tradition gave them the honorary title now that they commanded ships of their own —were linked together as they studied their enemy.

"They continue to advance at point one c," Giannovi told them all. "Exactly the same as the first Stranger. The four escorts appear to be the same class or type, so we can reasonably assume they have similar firepower."

Commander Riley shook his head.

"And the big one will have ten times that—or more," he noted. "We can't fight that, not with scratch crews and ships we haven't tested to see if the mothballs are out yet."

"But we have no choice," Isaac reminded him. "Given that Exilium's biosphere and atmosphere are originally artificial, I suspect they will have no problem repairing the damage caused by, say, dropping a point-one-c missile into Starhaven.

"We must face the truth, Captains. This enemy is beyond us and intends to exterminate the people we are sworn to defend."

No one responded. No one said anything. The faces in the video screens were set and determined—only some of them had realized what he had to ask of them, but all of them understood the gravity of the situation.

"*Vigil* is immobilized," he said calmly. "But she remains the largest and most effective combatant in the battlespace. We have enough maneuverability to use her as a floating battery, but that requires us to allow the enemy basically into Exilium orbit.

"So, we will do so," Isaac concluded flatly. "And then, while *Vigil* engages the enemy with her particle cannon, your destroyers will make high-speed attack passes from the flanks.

"Hopefully, they will be sufficiently focused on *Vigil* to make for easier targets."

"If we focus all six destroyers' firepower, we might be able to take out one ship, not five," Riley replied. "How can we…"

"You're missing one of the weapons at your disposal," Captain Xene Stavros, formerly of the missile cruiser *Lancelot*, said quietly. "Maneuvering as the Admiral orders, our destroyers are capable of building a velocity of around point two *c*. We have enough acceleration and maneuverability that we can nearly guarantee impact at the end of our attack runs."

Stavros's words hung in the virtual conference like the Sword of Damocles, and Commander Riley nodded slowly.

"For a seemingly reactionless drive, their maneuverability once at speed is surprisingly limited," he reminded everyone. "Our navigators are good. I don't think many are versed in ramming tactics, but I think we can do it."

Isaac swallowed hard.

"I hate to ask this of you, Captains."

"Then we volunteer," Stavros snapped. "It's what needs to be done, isn't it, Admiral?

"It is," he agreed. "And that is why those are your orders. You already only have essential personnel aboard; there's no way we can reduce your crews. But yes, you will maneuver to set up collision attack runs on the enemy as they engage *Vigil,* and you will take them out using your own vessels as kinetic weapons."

To his surprise, none of his Captains objected. They could guess the likelihood of *Vigil*—and her Admiral—surviving her role as bait as well.

Before anyone could say anything further, Isaac's tattoo-comp buzzed again. He stared at it for a second, wondering what *new* bad news they could have today, then hit accept.

"What is it?" he snapped.

"Sir—the aliens have stopped!" Cameron Alstairs's voice told him.

"What?" He turned to check the sensor feed included in the conference. The advancing alien flotilla had stopped…at almost exactly the point, he realized, where the first Stranger had died. They were outside the ESF's range still, but they also weren't advancing.

"What are they doing?" Giannovi asked quietly.

"Admiral, this is Commander Rose," his communications officer cut in on Alstairs' channel. "We're receiving a transmission. It's...raw machine code; I'm running it into a standalone processor.

"I...I think it might be an equivalent to our first-contact package."

Isaac realized his heart was accelerating and his face flushed as a new emotion appeared. An emotion he hadn't allowed himself to entertain since Reinhardt had called him nearly an hour before: hope.

"Proceed as per first-contact translation protocols," he ordered Rose. "And send them our package as well."

———

38

BACK ON *VIGIL'S* flag bridge, Isaac discovered that waiting to see what an overwhelming alien force was going to do was almost worse than thinking he knew.

"How long until we can maneuver?" he asked Alstairs.

"They're pushing it, but the last I heard was ten more hours," his ops officer replied. "These guys are just sitting there...but I doubt they're going to be sitting there that long."

"Am I right, Cameron, that they're parked pretty much exactly where the first Stranger died?" Isaac said.

Alstairs checked.

"Factoring in the likely drift of whatever debris we missed...yeah," he agreed. "I'm guessing that's not an accident."

"Me too," Isaac confirmed. "Are the tachyon scanners picking up anything?"

"We finally got them linked into the fleet network," his ops officer told him. "And...yeah. There was a series of pulses from the big ship as soon as they arrived. If it was radio, I'd have said they were talking to somebody."

"And since?"

"They were silent until they stopped, and then there was another series of pulses," Alstairs replied. "Silence since. Someone knows they're here. Someone probably knows they found the debris from the Stranger."

"So, even if we manage to blow these ones to hell, there'll just be another wave," Isaac said with a sigh. "Let's hope all of this is a sign that they want to talk instead of shoot."

"Sir!" Rose barked. "That stand-alone processor has finished compiling their code. It looks like we've got a translator for their communication protocols."

"Anything on language?" Isaac asked.

"Nothing," she admitted. "They've got our package, which does include language, and we can now process anything they send us to get audio out and send audio back. There's no video protocols, though."

"That's odd. What, do they think they're ugly?"

"Or they don't want us to see what they look like, for whatever reason," Rose replied. "I'm…no xenoanthropologist, sir. Though we probably have at least one somewhere on Exilium."

"I'll pass on that skillset for today. I'd like to be able to shoot these people without any more guilt than necessary," Isaac said drily. "Can you use those protocols to ping them? See if we can open a channel."

"On it."

As usual in military affairs, more waiting followed.

"Sir? We have an incoming transmission. Audio only—I think they're even sending in English."

Isaac exhaled softly in relief. If they'd taken the time to adapt and incorporate the first contact protocol enough to speak in English, that hopefully meant that this time they were going to actually *talk* to him.

"Play it."

"This is Recon and Security Matrix KCX-DD-78, a sub node of Regional Construction Matrix XR-13-9." The voice was just as blatantly artificial as the original Stranger, though it was at least identifying itself.

Whatever a "Recon and Security Matrix" was.

"We have confirmed destruction of an unverified mobile security node and the unauthorized settlement of a Constructed World.

"Please identify and state intentions."

"A Constructed World, huh?" Isaac said aloud. "Well, that fits. Any idea what an 'unverified mobile security node' is?"

"Not a damn clue," Alstairs replied. "What do we do, sir?"

"I refuse to start a fight we won't win so long as they're willing to talk," the Admiral told him. "Rose, can we reply?"

"We can send audio back. Hopefully, they can make sense of it on their end."

"Translation difficulties that we won't even know about," Isaac said. "We'll deal. Put me on."

She flashed him a thumbs-up and he activated his microphone.

"Matrix KCX-DD-78," he greeted them, the unfamiliar and strange "name" forcing him to speak slowly and carefully. "I am Admiral Isaac Gallant of the Exilium Space Fleet.

"We are exiles, banished to this corner of the galaxy without our consent. We found the planet we name Exilium, which I presume to be the 'Constructed World,' and colonized her as we did not know it belonged to anyone.

"We have nowhere else to go and no means to leave. The previous vessel similar to your own attacked us without provocation, and we were forced to defend ourselves."

He paused, considering how to phrase what he had to say. Then he shrugged and smiled. He could, if nothing else, steal their own words.

"Please state your intentions."

————

THERE WAS no response for long enough to make Isaac nervous.

"We're picking up a bunch of tachyon signals," Alstairs reported. "Whatever they're thinking, they seem to be phoning home with questions."

"FTL coms." Isaac shook his head. "Even when we had wormhole stations, we didn't have wormhole coms on our starships."

"These guys seem to be at least friendlier than the last one," his ops officer noted.

"No. They're more *talkative* that the last one," the Admiral pointed out. "Not necessarily friendlier. I wonder, though…"

"Sir?"

"With what they're translating their name to…are they referring to the formation? Or is KCX-DD-78 the actual 'person' we're talking to? There was no crew on the Stranger, after all."

"AIs." Alstairs shook his head. "You think we might be dealing with an artificial intelligence?"

"On a scale and of a complexity like we've never seen," Isaac agreed. "If you wanted to terraform an entire region of space in preparation for a mass colony mission, well, sending in von Neumann-style self-replicator machinery…"

"That's a terrifying mental image, sir," Giannovi interjected. "Self-manufacturing, FTL-capable, artificially intelligent starships? When would they *stop*?"

"They wouldn't," he replied. "Not unless you gave them a parameter to. They would keep finding new systems, new worlds, and if left unchecked would terraform the galaxy, just waiting for their creators."

"And then we went and colonized one of their terraformed worlds. And we sure as hell are not their creators," Giannovi said. "What a mess."

"Sir, incoming transmission," Rose reported.

"Admiral Isaac Gallant. This Matrix was investigating a facility breach on Constructed World XR-13-9-27. We expected interaction with unverified combat units. Admiral Isaac Gallant appears to have successfully engaged and destroyed said unverified combat units.

"The Constructed Worlds were made for our Creators, and Admiral Isaac Gallant's presence is neither expected nor welcome.

"However, the destruction of the unverified combat unit suggests possibility to Regional Construction Matrix XR-13-9. A potential exchange of services and alliances for residency on Constructed World XR-13-9-27 may be arranged.

"Is Admiral Isaac Gallant prepared and authorized to negotiate for this?"

Isaac considered that transmission for a long few moments.

"Prepared, yes," he admitted aloud. "Authorized…like this 'Recon and Security Matrix,' I think I need to phone home."

———

THE LAST UPDATE that Isaac had from the surface was that over a hundred and fifty thousand people had been evacuated from Starhaven, aircraft and ground vehicles moving over ten thousand people an hour and rising.

It wouldn't be enough to get everyone out if the negotiations failed. He didn't know how long this "matrix" would give them, but he doubted it would be enough to move four million people—and he doubted that the colonists could feed and protect four million people without the technology and farms in the Lofwyr River Delta.

That made it telling, to him at least, that every member of the Exilium Republic Cabinet was immediately available when he tried to pull them into a conference—and that all of the video feeds were either of offices or spaceships.

None of the Republic's leadership had evacuated yet. Somehow, he knew that many of them would be the last ones out—and if fire fell from on high, the Cabinet would die with their people.

It might not be the most efficient stance, but it spoke to their integrity, at least.

"They want to talk," he told the Cabinet flatly once he had them all. His gaze was focused on Amelie, but this wasn't a decision just for the President.

"They are offering a potential exchange of services and alliance for recognizing our residency on the world they built." He shook his head slowly. "You must understand that they have the capacity to destroy Starhaven. There is a small chance I can prevent it...but it is only a small chance."

"If there is any deal we can cut, any service we can offer, to protect our people..." Rodriguez said slowly. "What could they ask of us that we wouldn't agree to?"

"There are perhaps prices that we, as a people, should hesitate to pay," Father James pointed out. "Would you be prepared to commit genocide to save us, Minister Rodriguez?"

The ex-gangster said nothing, but Isaac could see the answer in his eyes—and he suspected James could too. If it came to a choice between himself and his people and some other race, Carlos Domingo Rodriguez would commit genocide without a second thought.

He probably wouldn't even feel guilty about it.

"We do not know what they want," Lestroud cut in. "Without that information, we cannot make a decision, but as Minister Rodriguez says, there is basically nothing that is within our capacity that I am not prepared to offer to protect our people.

"Admiral Gallant, you've spoken with these people. What do you think they want?"

"I don't think we're dealing with people," Isaac admitted. "I think we're dealing with an extremely sophisticated artificial intelligence, outside of anything in our experience. This AI was, I suspect, tasked with terraforming this sector of the galaxy for their creators.

"There's something else going on here too. They don't seem bothered that we destroyed the first Stranger—more...impressed. We don't have enough data."

"Agreed. We need to meet with them. In person, if that's...possible."

"I will speak to them," Isaac promised. "We'll see what can be arranged."

"I will meet with them," Amelie decided. "Aboard *Vigil*, I think. That's as much of a position of strength as we have."

———

"HAS anybody moved on me while I wasn't looking?" Isaac asked as he took his seat in the flag bridge.

"Our strange friends are still hanging out at about six million klicks," Alstairs told him. "Twenty-second com delay each way. You're still not having a live conversation with them."

"Given the translation delays, I'm not sure we'll have a live conversation when we're in the same room," the Admiral pointed out. "Rose, get us set up to transmit. Let's see if we can organize a party for everyone."

The Commander flipped him another thumbs-up a few moments later and he took a deep breath as he considered his options.

"Matrix KCX-DD-78," he began again. "I have consulted with my superiors, and my President wishes to meet with you to discuss the possibilities of alliance. She would prefer to meet you face to face, preferably aboard this vessel.

"Please respond and advise if this is acceptable."

He hit TRANSMIT and looked around his flag bridge.

"We may be able to negotiate a solution that doesn't involve shooting," he told his people. "But even if we can't, every minute we can buy is closer to *Vigil* being functional and Starhaven being evacuated. We're playing for time as much as actual success in negotiations."

"Can..." Rose shook her head, then swallowed and began again. "Can the colony even survive without Starhaven and the orbital infrastructure?"

"Some of them will," Isaac replied, trying not to think of the price in that situation. "Exilium's plant and animal life is edible for us. Those of us in orbit are doomed," he admitted. "Even on the surface...the survivors will find themselves unable to maintain any significant technological base.

"Negotiating a deal is the better option by far."

"Response incoming," Rose reported, cutting off the conversation.

"Admiral Isaac Gallant. This matrix's processing cores mass approximately twelve thousand four hundred and eighty-two tons and are housed in a combat-and-construction unit approximately one thousand and thirty-eight meters long. An in-person conversation may be impossible."

There was a pause, though Isaac's screens told him the transmission continued. Then the mechanical voice resumed.

"We will be able to retrofit a terraformer inspection unit to act as a relay. Please stand by for two hundred and eleven minutes."

The transmission ended, and Isaac shook his head. It was clear from the odd numbers that the Matrix was translating into metric from some other measurement, but it was at least *making* the translation.

That was promising...and in less than four hours, they'd find out how promising.

"Well, I guess that gives us some time to get President Lestroud up here," he told his people. "I have the suspicion this is going to be the weirdest meeting I've ever sat in on."

GLYNN STEWART

———

39

It was an odd feeling for Amelie to step onto *Vigil*'s flight deck. Despite everything that had occurred, she'd never actually been aboard the battlecruiser. Admiral Gallant—Isaac—had always come to the civilians for meetings.

One of the thousand tiny ways that Isaac had tried to make it clear that the new military answered to the civilians. One of the thousand tiny ways the son of a dictator had made it possible for Exilium to birth what was looking to be a truly functioning democracy.

If they survived.

An honor guard of Marines in dress uniforms saluted crisply as she exited her shuttle, and Captain Lauretta Giannovi joined them as Amelie proceeded down the unrolled carpet.

"Welcome aboard *Vigil*, President Lestroud."

"Thank you, Captain Giannovi," Amelie replied, offering the woman her hand. "Are we prepared for our guest?"

"Beyond that our guest is going to be a robot, we know nothing about them," Giannovi told her as she led the way into the starship. "We've arranged a space that's large enough for us to be able to fit them in if they turn out to be a bulldozer or something, but I'm hoping for something more…reasonably sized."

Amelie chuckled.

"Who knows what their remote looks like, huh?" she asked.

"We certainly don't," the Captain agreed. "The Admiral is waiting for you in the conference room; I'll make sure our guest gets there, too."

"Any ETA on them?"

"They said two hundred and eleven minutes three hours ago," Giannovi replied. "So, thirty minutes or so. Assuming that whatever transport they use can pull the same velocity and acceleration stunts as their main ships, they only need a couple of minutes to get to us."

"That just seems…weird."

"Yeah. Even your *Stars of Honor* movie had better physics than these guys are playing with in real life," Giannovi told her with a chuckle of her own.

Amelie winced.

"I thought we had Fleet consultants for those?" she asked plaintively.

"Yep," Giannovi agreed. "You did. Your producers also ignored half of what they said because it didn't 'look cool enough.'"

"That…is far too believable," the former actress admitted. "On behalf of everyone *else* in the production, I apologize. We did try!"

The Fleet officer laughed.

"I know. I was the Fleet consultant's assistant on *Echoes*," she replied.

They stopped at a massive set of doors.

"This is normally a storage bay for the Marines' tanks," Giannovi noted. "All four of *Vigil*'s armored combat units are on the surface now, though, so we have a nice big empty room with a big door. We moved a table and chairs in for you and the Admiral."

She shrugged.

"We have *no* idea what kind of furniture the Stranger will need, if any. We'll adjust when they arrive."

———

GIANNOVI USHERED Amelie into the "conference room" where Isaac

Gallant was waiting, and the President of four million human beings was suddenly grateful for the presence of the other woman.

And somewhat resentful, too, for exactly the same reason. In the absence of the other woman, she wasn't sure she could have stopped herself from all but leaping into Isaac's arms. It would be a horrible idea, but it would also be reassuring as hell.

Giannovi's presence imposed a certain degree of decorum, however. Enough of a degree for Amelie to remember that the room was being recorded and that having video of the President of Exilium glomping her Admiral would set tongues to wagging.

Again.

"Admiral," she greeted him warmly with a smile.

"Madam President," he replied, bowing slightly in his chair. "Coffee? Tea?"

"Tea, please," she told him. "I'm guessing we don't have wine in here?"

"I don't think the robot will be able to drink it, and you and I should be at our best," Isaac told her with a smile in his eyes. "Captain Giannovi, any updates?"

"We're still inside the Matrix's two-hundred-odd minutes," the flag captain replied. "Is there anything else I can get you two?"

"I think we'll be good," Amelie replied as she took the tea from Isaac. She couldn't, after all, ask for twenty minutes with the cameras turned off—she suspected Giannovi would give it to them, but it would raise too many questions.

The good news was that she'd only signed herself up for a six-year term, and they'd written a single-term limit into the Constitution. Five and a half more years, and she'd be a private citizen again and the gossips and reporters could go burn in a fire.

Assuming they were all still alive.

"Is there anything we shouldn't be offering this Matrix?" she asked Isaac as she took a seat.

"I would be hesitant to commit to long-term mercenary work, but if that's the price, that's the price," he admitted. "I'm with Father James on genocide or, well, planetary bombardment in general. But the only clue we have as to what they want is that it's related to our destruction of the first Stranger."

"So, the odds are they want us to fight for them," she concluded. "Can we?"

"Thirty-six hours and *Vigil* will be FTL-capable," he told her. "Give me a couple more weeks and I'll have a squadron of warp-capable destroyers to go with her. All of them over a dozen times as fast as the warp cruisers we sent out scouting.

"Unfortunately, we can only refit those cruisers here, so we have to wait for them to come home," he continued. "Until then…one battle-cruiser, six *Philosopher*-class destroyers. That's going to be our FTL-capable fleet for a year or two still.

"Once the warp cruisers come back, we'll add them to that list, but they're honestly not that much more heavily armed than the destroyers," he noted. "Thirteen warp-capable warships. That's all we're going to have until we can produce exotic matter."

"So, if they want us to fight an enemy for them…"

"Then I hope they're providing transportation," he said drily. "We can make sixty-five times lightspeed now. I don't know how fast these guys travel, but someone was here within two days of us tripping the silent alarm.

"Which means I'm guessing they're a *hell* of a lot faster than we are."

———

IT TURNED out that holding the meeting in a space designed for storing tanks had been a good idea on Giannovi's part. The "inspection unit" that Matrix KCX-DD-78 had apparently reworked as a remote representative turned out to be a four-legged robot roughly three meters tall and wide.

Amelie's guess was that the visible hatches concealed sensors and working tools, but the remote managed to look unthreatening as it ducked its torso under the door and entered the impromptu conference room.

Walking up to "face" Amelie and Isaac, it slowly folded its legs to bring its torso to the ground and level with the two humans.

"This unit is a tachyon-communicator-enabled remote linked to the core matrix of Recon and Security Matrix KCX-DD-78," a buzzing artificial voice told them. *"Neither the speaker unit nor the tachyon-communicator are standard on these inspection units; there may be delays in communication due to system interface issues."*

It wasn't an apology. Just an explanation.

"I am President Amelie Lestroud," she told the robot, feeling vaguely strange talking to something without a face. "I am the elected leader of our colony here and I speak for all of us. You told Admiral Gallant that we may be able to assist you in exchange for peaceful residency here.

"What did you have in mind?"

"Admiral Isaac Gallant destroyed an unverified recon unit," the robot buzzed. *"The destruction of a Matrix recon or combat unit is unprecedented in our records. This represents possibilities for us."*

"What kind of possibilities?" Isaac asked. "We destroyed one of your ships…I'm not sure how this creates options."

The robot was silent for several seconds, presumably linking back to the core AI on the big ship still twenty light-seconds away.

"To explain this, we must provide historical detail. Is this acceptable?" the robot finally asked.

Amelie concealed a snort. This AI held the entire future of the people she had sworn to serve in its "hands." Whatever it wanted, she was going to give it.

"Go ahead," she told it.

"Regional Construction Matrix XR-13-9 is one of multiple units of its type deployed by our Creators," the robot explained. *"However, we have lost contact with all other Regional Construction Matrices. We have also lost contact with our Creators.*

"Regional Construction Matrix XR-13-9 acts as a central nexus for the terraforming units operating in this galactic region. We are preparing the way for our Creators."

That was all roughly what Isaac had suggested to Amelie, and it made sense. If you planned on a massive scale, unleashing a fleet of self-motivated, self-constructing terraforming robots would definitely help turn large chunks of the galaxy into potential new homes.

It was a dangerous game, but she could see the value.

"Where are your creators, then?" she asked. "How could you lose contact with them?"

The robot was silent for a good ten seconds.

"We were created because the tachyon punch was universally fatal to sentient organic life aboard the punching vessel," it finally explained. *"We were built with redundant holographic memory cores and supplied with cloning equipment and vast supplies of frozen embryos.*

"We knew we were losing a significant portion of those embryos each time we punched, but recreating them was possible with the technology we had."

The robot paused and if Amelie was prepared to attribute emotions to a machine, she'd have thought it was in pain.

"We did not realize that our own memories were suffering the same degradation," it told them. *"Not until we forgot who our Creators were."*

Amelie shared a look with Isaac. That had terrifying implications. Not least the potential that every one of the "matrices" they were talking to was likely insane.

"We created the verification process. Upon completing each tachyon punch, tachyon communicators are used to verify the integrity of the Matrix's memories and core protocols against a backup copy kept with Regional Construction Matrix XR-13-9.

"We know that verified units are mentally intact. Unverified units have no backup and do not necessarily contain the original core protocols intended by our Creators."

Corrupt data. Corrupt minds. That was horrifying enough to Amelie—she could easily see how the Stranger Isaac's people had destroyed would be a nightmare to these AIs.

"The presence of unverified units in this sector was known." The robot paused, as if trying to determine what to say. It was an illusion, Amelie knew, created by the delay in communication and translation between the remote and the AI in the main unit.

"We have evidence that at least three planets were fully Constructed despite the presence of indigenous intelligent life, including in one instance

the destruction of primitive orbital industry. This is in contradiction of all core protocols.

"These unverified units are murderers and must be stopped."

"What…what planets do your 'core protocols' allow for terraforming?" Amelie asked, trying to buy herself time to think. These terraforming robots apparently had rogues—and those rogues had destroyed *three civilizations*?!

"Our process is designed to Construct a world from base rock. Core protocols call for leaving any world with native life intact. Dead rocks are to be moved into the liquid-water zone and Constructed from there." The odd buzzing of the robot's voice was giving Amelie a migraine—and so was the sheer scale of what they'd been built to do!

"What do you want us to do?" Isaac finally asked, clearly thinking faster than Amelie was. "We don't have your 'tachyon punch.'"

"President Amelie Lestroud's people are here and did not evolve here," the Matrix reminded them. *"Admiral Isaac Gallant clearly has some form of inter-star-system travel unknown to our Creators. We would be prepared to allow President Amelie Lestroud's people to remain on Constructed World XR-13-9-27 in exchange for Admiral Isaac Gallant's assistance in neutralizing the unverified node."*

Amelie exhaled sharply. That was a hell of a request—exactly the kind of mercenary work they'd been afraid of, if for a better cause than they'd feared.

"If you know where they are, why do you need our help?" Isaac asked.

"Core protocols do not permit Matrix units to use weaponry on other Matrix units. Unverified or not, they still register as part of us to those protocols. Those same core protocols mean we cannot permit them to continue Constructing inhabited worlds.

"We are trapped in a dilemma, one that Admiral Isaac Gallant's combat forces present a potential solution to."

That was a very…robot problem to have, Amelie supposed. The Regional Matrix almost certainly had the firepower to destroy this rogue node, but its programming meant it *couldn't*. But its programming also told it that it couldn't stand by and watch worlds be destroyed.

"You must understand the limits of our military capacity," her Admiral told the robot. "Destroying the one ship that came here took the full effort of our fleet—and one of our capital ships was critically damaged.

"We have only one vessel capable of traveling between star systems at any speed. We would be a poor match for this 'unverified node' without some form of technological transfer."

That was a step further than Amelie had reached. She'd realized they couldn't win the fight, but the thought of asking for help hadn't occurred to her.

"Core protocols forbid us from transferring technological data without approval from the Creators," the robot told them. *"We may be able to repair Admiral Isaac Gallant's damaged unit, but that is all."*

There was a long silence.

"This is the only service President Amelie Lestroud's people could potentially provide the Regional Matrix of sufficient value for us to surrender a Constructed World. President Amelie Lestroud has forty-three hours to decide."

It began to unfold, rising from the ground with its offer complete, but Amelie shared another look with Isaac and rose herself before the robot completely unfolding itself.

"There is no point in any of us pretending," she told the remote. "We have no choice but to at least make the attempt. We have no way of leaving Exilium and no way of protecting ourselves against you as things stand."

The remote's faceless front considered her for a few moments.

"Very well," the buzzing artificial voice told her. *"We will commence repairs of the damaged vessel and provide all information we have on the unverified node's location to Admiral Isaac Gallant."*

It paused again.

"It is not in our protocols to commit murder. We do not require success.

"Not on the first attempt."

———

40

"ALL RIGHT, people, our new friends have given us a giant pile of information and I want to make sure everyone has the key components."

If any of the Fleet officers present or video-conferencing in objected to Amelie's presence in the room as Isaac spoke, none of them were showing it to her. She had taken a seat in the back row and was listening in, making sure she was as updated as everyone else.

"Commander Alstairs is going to fill us all in," Isaac Gallant continued at the front of the briefing hall.

Amelie had known, intellectually, how far they'd cut down the Exilium Space Fleet, but the briefing room brought it home with a new reality. It was designed to hold the physical or virtual representations of the senior officers of an entire CSF battle group.

The captains and executive officers of the entire Exilium Space Fleet left enough seats for Isaac's entire flag staff to be present and to slot Amelie herself in.

The purely average dark-skinned form of Amelie's Admiral stepped aside, allowing the gaunt blond form of the operations officer to take his place at the lectern at the front of the room.

"Our allies don't really have a name for themselves," Alstairs told everyone. "Given their various designations, however, we're desig-nated them the Matrices. Our target for this operation is also a Matrix, a Sub-Regional Construction Matrix that our Matrices don't know the designation of."

The space behind the ops officer lit up with a holographic represen-tation of the region around Exilium.

"For ease of reference, we're designating the primary computer in our target node as the Rogue Matrix," he noted. "The Rogue Matrix has, according to our allies, suffered from degradation of what they call its core protocols due to an inherent randomizing factor of their FTL drive.

"Put more simply: this Rogue Matrix has gone violently insane. They believe it has exterminated at least three intelligent species in addition to its unprovoked attack on us.

"Since our Matrices cannot fight another Matrix, they want us to destroy the Rogue for them."

Alstairs held up a hand as the audience started shouting questions.

"There will be time for questions later," he told them. "For now, we have a lot of information to get through that should cover many of your questions.

"Firstly, the Rogue is here." One of the systems on the hologram behind Alstairs flashed red. "This system was designated Kappa in the original survey by the Confederacy.

"Kappa is too far away from both the XL-17 wormhole and Exilium itself for either of the surveys carried out by the Confederacy or our own warp cruisers to reach. What we know about the system has been provided by the Matrices, and they only know basic geography."

The hologram behind him zoomed in anyway. A single F-class star. Eight worlds, two of them gas giants at the edge of the system.

"Planet three was just barely inside the inner limit of the liquid-water zone according to the Matrices' long-range scans," Alstairs noted. "They'd flagged it as a potential Constructed World, and it appears that the Rogue Matrix is in the process of 'Constructing' it—what we would call terraforming."

A red icon appeared above the third planet.

"Our intelligence suggests that the Rogue Matrix has between two and four Security and Recon Matrices similar to the one our Matrices brought here," he continued. "Any of those Matrices would be an existential threat to Exilium, so the destruction of the Rogue Matrix is critical to our own security.

"Fortunately, our allies believe the Rogue will only keep one of those Matrices with it at any time for its own defense. The core unit of the Rogue is not a warship, but it is quite heavily armed nonetheless."

Alstairs shook his head.

"Evidence suggests that the Matrices' mysterious Creators were as paranoid as Confederacy Fleet designers," he said drily. "None of their units are unarmed, from their recon ships like we originally encountered to the Sub-Regional and Regional Matrices that are basically flying shipyards.

"Our new friends have been surprisingly forthcoming on the strengths and weaknesses of their ship design, but perhaps more importantly, about their deployment doctrine. The Rogue Matrix may have corrupted code, but it is still essentially running the same protocols.

"That means we have a minimum of one hundred and sixty days before Exilium sees another visit."

"How do we know that?" someone demanded, loudly enough to be heard, and Alstairs smiled grimly.

"Because the Matrices would never send the same-type unit to investigate a lost unit," he told them. "And it will take the Rogue Matrix a minimum of one hundred and sixty days to fabricate a combat platform."

The room was suddenly very silent. If a "combat platform" was a different beast from what they'd seen so far…

"Kappa is twelve and a half light-years from here—just under two and a half months at full speed for the new warp drives," the ops officer concluded. "Seventy days. That gives us a few weeks of leeway for preparation before we have to leave.

"The Matrices have agreed to repair *Dante*. Our own R&D believes they can convert *Lancelot*'s drive ring into two, potentially three destroyer-size drive rings. The current plan is take a task force consisting of both battlecruisers and two destroyers to Kappa and destroy the Rogue Matrix."

The room once again dissolved into shouted questions.

———

IF THERE WAS ACTUALLY a plan for *what* to do when the task force reached the Kappa System, Amelie missed it in the chaos of the discussion that followed. She had committed her fledgling fleet to a battle she wasn't sure they could win...but all she could do was have faith in Isaac Gallant.

Which meant she had to have faith in the man she loved while sending him off on a suicide mission.

That thought clung to her as she returned to the flight deck, staring at the shuttle that was waiting to take her home. If everything went according to plan, the task force would leave in two weeks.

She had no illusions about who was going to command it. Even if she thought she could talk Isaac out of leading the fleet personally, it wouldn't be fair to him to do so.

There was no way she could justify returning aboard *Vigil* before they left, either. Not without coming up with an excuse that would be all too obvious to most people. They needed to not only manage to *be* careful but to *appear* careful.

Even the appearance of a relationship between the President of the Republic and her Admiral would be dangerous for the future of Exilium.

"You know," Captain Giannovi's voice suddenly said quietly from behind her, "we run a shuttle to and from Starhaven about every twelve hours."

Amelie looked over her shoulder at the Captain. Giannovi barely came up to her shoulder, much the same height as Isaac, but the mischievousness in her face made her seem even smaller and younger for a moment.

"Sorry, I don't understand," Amelie replied carefully.

Giannovi shook her head.

"I've served with Admiral Gallant since the Battle of Conestoga," she pointed out. "Over five years now, as XO and flag captain. I know that man better than anyone else alive." She stepped up to stand next to Amelie, looking at the shuttle with her.

"You, I don't know as well," she admitted. "But I know women in general. And I don't think I have ever met a pair more determined to nobly suffer in silence."

Amelie was silent for several seconds.

"And here I thought we were being careful," she confessed softly.

"Oh, you are," Giannovi agreed. "But I don't think anyone who knows either of you well is fooled. And you and I both know he's going to take the task force out himself.

"And you're a smart-enough woman to do the math on the odds, Madam President. I can guess what you want. So, I'll repeat myself: we have a shuttle running to Starhaven in the morning. I'm pretty sure your aide can cover for you if this one"—the Captain gestured—"arrives empty—and I *know* we can sneak you down without any problems."

Temptation struck Amelie dumb, and she stood there in silence for several long seconds.

"You don't know if you'll ever see us again," the flag captain said very, very quietly. "I know I'm going to be pinning your Minister for Orbital Industry to a wall pretty quickly here.

"We'll cover for you." She smiled mischievously. "I promise."

———

TEMPTATION AND HOPE carried Amelie Lestroud from the flight deck all the way to Isaac Gallant's quarters. That was when hesitation set in. Their subordinates—their *friends*—would cover for them, but that didn't necessarily make this any less terrible of an idea.

Plus, she wasn't even sure that *Isaac* would be okay with this.

That thought, at least, shook her into a giggle. She was *Amelie Lestroud*. There had been entire planetary fan societies dedicated to her at one point. What business did one of the Confederacy's top ten actresses have standing outside a man's bedroom door, feeling *hesitant*?

She knocked. When Isaac opened the door, she stepped inside before he'd finished opening his mouth, letting the door slide closed behind her before she said or did anything.

As soon as the door did close, she reached out for his hands without a word. Their fingers intertwined without a word, dark skin against pale white, and he drew her to him.

"Amelie," he breathed.

"Your Captain and my aide have promised to cover for us," she whispered in his ear.

Her Admiral appeared to be in shock as she gently led him to the couch in his quarters and slid into his lap, but his arms wrapped around her without hesitation.

"And just *what*, Madam President, are our subordinates covering for?" he finally managed to ask.

"Our *friends*, Isaac, are covering for us having one night together before you go off on this damned suicide mission," Amelie told him.

It was a good twenty or thirty seconds before she stopped kissing him long enough for him to reply—not that he appeared to be objecting in the slightest.

"You realize, my love, that this is still a terrible idea?" he asked gently. His arms were still wrapped around her and her lips were still warm from his.

"I think, my love," she told him, a shiver running down her spine at both of their use of the words, "that *not* taking tonight would be a worse one."

His hands ran up her back, and his fingers were suddenly in her hair as he smiled brilliantly at her.

"I can't argue with that."

———

41

DANTE LOOKED…ODD now. The Matrix remotes had been swarming over it for a full week, and their "repairs" had clearly ended up being something completely different.

Before, she'd been a rough cigar shape, a long cylinder built around her primary particle cannon with pulse guns positioned equally along her flanks in six distinct broadside batteries.

Now her back half looked much the same, though Isaac was relatively sure the remotes had "repaired" *Dante*'s undamaged pulse guns. Her forward half, however, had been mostly wrecked and peeled back like a wrecked banana.

Now, *Dante* looked more like a claw or a trident than a cigar. Her forward hull split into three pieces, each a bit over a third of the original size of the hull. Each of the "claws" was coated in the same obsidian-black ceramic the Matrices used to armor their own ships and carried a full battery of pulse guns.

"Well, Captain Anderson?" Isaac asked the tall woman on his screen. "How's your ship feel?"

"The good news is that I have a warship again," Anderson replied with a smile and a shake of her head. "The bad news is that I'm only vaguely certain what the hell they've armed me with. 'Repairs,' my ass."

"If you're vaguely certain, you're ahead of us," he pointed out. "What have they told you?"

"They haven't told us shit," she said. "But they updated all of our software to handle it, and it *looks* like I have a trio of gamma-ray lasers, each roughly twice as powerful as what the Stranger hit me with, powered by a pair of ungodly power cores using more exotic matter than my entire artificial-gravity system."

Isaac shook his head.

"The temptation to dismantle your ship when this is over is going to be strong," he warned her. "I don't suppose they gave us specifications?"

"*That* would be technological transfer," she replied. "Just 'repairing' my ship to something comparable to one of their combat platforms apparently wasn't."

"Now I want to 'accidentally' run *Vigil* into something,' Isaac told her with a chuckle. "But they definitely installed exotic matter-based equipment?"

"Yeah. Don't ask me how the power cores work—my eyes glazed over about three seconds after my engineer started speaking, and I *have* a degree in theoretical physics—but they're definitely based around exotic-matter arrays of some kind."

"We'll need to check with Reinhardt, make sure that doesn't require any adjustments to the warp drive ring," Isaac warned her. "Barring that, we should be able to begin installation?"

"Between the new power cores and what they did to the prow of my battlecruiser, he's going to have to make at least some changes," Anderson admitted. "But so far as I can tell, our robotic friends are done."

"It'll be five more days before *Plato* and *Archimedes* are prepared for FTL," Isaac told her. "That should be enough for Reinhardt to get your warp drive online. Then we're on our way. Seventy days each way."

He was going to miss Amelie. Though, to be fair, it wasn't like being in orbit would make it any easier for them to manage to repeat their one night together.

"Takes them thirty hours," Anderson said. "Doesn't seem fair."

"Well, if you were a giant computer, tachyon punching would just risk driving you insane every time," he replied. "But since we're organic, a tachyon punch is apparently about ninety percent likely to kill us instantly. Oh—and if it doesn't, we *definitely* go insane."

"I guess there's a reason the Matrices' Creators were supposed to follow them in slow boats," she agreed.

"For now, *Dante* is ready for combat again. I won't object to a chance to take her out toward Exilium's asteroid belt and test these new guns, but that'll depend on Dr. Reinhardt."

"We'll try and make it happen," Isaac promised. "And Captain? We need every scan, photograph and power-emission recording you get from every piece of tech they added to *Dante*.

"The Matrices are playing games with their core protocols—and if they want to hand us gamma-ray lasers, super pulse guns and exotic-matter power plants, I will be *damned* if I'm not going to work out how to duplicate them!"

———

"I'M NOT EXACTLY COMPLAINING…BUT how the *hell* is *Dante* powering those?" Reinhardt demanded grumpily as he and Isaac watched the recordings of *Dante*'s test-fire sequence.

"Four-hundred-petajoule pulse delivered over point two seconds," Isaac confirmed, studying the numbers. "A two-exawatt beam."

The asteroid Anderson had picked for her test was simply *gone*, the three beams intersecting with it in a single violent moment of vaporization.

"I've studied the exotic-matter cores she got," Reinhardt told him. "They're powerful, but they don't output six exawatts!"

"No, the lasers have a charge capacitor, similar to our pulse guns," Isaac confirmed as he checked the schematics on another screen. "Each of the two cores outputs about a quarter-exawatt of power—between them, they provide over eight times as much power as every fusion core that *Dante* used to have combined.

"One of the operating problems that Anderson has noted is that the exotic-matter cores can only be stepped down to about fifty percent of their output and *can't* be shut down," he continued. "Thankfully, *Dante*'s fusion cores can be. Outside of combat, she is actually running purely on the new EM power plants.

"Bringing up the fusion plants to run the rest of the ship and dedicating the new cores to charging the graser capacitors can charge the capacitors from zero to full in about twenty-one seconds. It's not a hundred-percent-efficient process."

"So, you can fire all three lasers every twenty or so seconds or one of them every seven." Reinhardt shook his head. "Just what have we found in our allies and enemies, Admiral?"

"Trouble," Isaac said. "A lot of it. But the Matrices built Exilium, Lyle, so…we will fulfill their request."

The big physicist nodded.

"Twenty-four hours," he said calmly. "Then *Dante*, *Plato* and *Archimedes* will all be fully warp-capable and we're out of excuses. I have no idea how you plan on winning this battle, Admiral."

He gestured at the screen showing the current status of Exilium orbit. Recon and Security Matrix KCX-DD-78 was still three light-seconds away from the planet, a minor concession to the humans' paranoia, but the five looming robotic starships were still an intimidating addition.

"As I understand it, the Rogue will have the equivalent of that force, at least, to defend itself?"

"That's what the Matrices have suggested, yes," Isaac agreed mildly. "In all honesty, Lyle…I have some thoughts, but nothing fixed in stone.

"Fortunately, I have ten weeks to come up with something better."

———

TWO BATTLECRUISERS. Two destroyers. Four warp-drive ships.

It seemed like such a tiny force to fling into the darkness, but it was all that Admiral Isaac Gallant had. All four of them were now beginning to accelerate away from Exilium. There was nothing necessarily *stopping* them from bringing up their warp drives where they were, but getting at least some distance between them and the planet had always seemed like a good idea to the Confederacy—and to Isaac.

"I suppose one of their tachyon communicators was too much to ask?" Amelie told him from the screen on his chair.

"No technological transfer, remember?" he pointed out.

"I've *seen* what they did to *Dante*," she replied drily.

"They repaired *Dante* to what they regard as the standard of a warship," Isaac replied. "It's semantics…but we're talking about the core protocols of a bunch of sentient computers. Semantics are *important*."

She shook her head.

"Ten weeks?"

"Ten weeks there, ten weeks back. Plus, however long it takes us to fight a desperate battle against the odds versus an insane alien computer," he concluded. "We'll be back before you know it."

"I think you underestimate my perception of time," his not-quite-lover told him archly. "Don't screw this up, hey, Isaac?"

"I wasn't planning on it," he agreed. "I owe it to my people, if nothing else, to try and get them home."

"I know," Amelie said softly. "Bring them home, Admiral Gallant."

"I will," he promised. "You see if you can talk the Matrices into selling us exotic matter. They clearly have some way of producing it, and if we can buy *enough,* we can build our own production facility."

"Because what this star system is missing is black holes, huh?"

"I'm more thinking the ability to build new warp drives," he noted. "But I do find that the black holes add a certain…rustic charm to a star system."

She laughed at him.

"Good luck, Admiral Gallant. Our thoughts and prayers are with you. I wish we could send more."

"If we needed more, we wouldn't be your space fleet."

———

ISAAC GAVE everyone aboard the ships an hour after leaving to sort out their last personal messages before they left. Then he had Rose set up an all-ships channel and settled into his chair.

"All right, people," he addressed them all. "You know what we've agreed to, but I'm going to run over it so you all know where we're at."

He smiled. Not everyone in the task force would be able to see him, but enough were watching the video that his relaxed state would carry throughout.

"In exchange for giving us Exilium and not causing us grief for accidentally settling on their science project, the Matrices want us to deal with a long-standing problem of theirs. Their FTL drive apparently drives them insane if they're not careful, and they learned this too late to save them from losing things that were precious to them."

He wasn't a computer. He didn't know with certainty who'd built him or even that he'd been built. He had his opinions on that matter—most humans did—but the Matrices had had *certainty*.

And then they had forgotten who created them. He couldn't even imagine how much that had hurt.

"While our current batch of robotic friends seem pretty together and sensible, the first Matrix we met wasn't. We all remember the Stranger vividly.

"And the Stranger was a recon unit of a Rogue Matrix...a Rogue that the Matrices believe has exterminated multiple civilizations. By the nature of our accidental colonization of one of their Constructed Worlds, we're next on the Rogue's list."

He shook his head.

"We made a deal and that's why we're going out. We face an enemy that wants to exterminate *us*—and that's why we're going out.

"But we also hunt a monster that has destroyed three sentient races before they could become star-faring peoples," he concluded softly. "We hunt a broken machine, a rabid dog. The Matrices are computers, and their programming prevents them from fixing this mess.

"We have no such programming, and I will not stand by while evil is done in this universe—and I think we can all agree that genocide is an unquestioned evil."

He let that sink in and focused on the camera, hopefully looking his people in the eye.

"If you think we have become mercenaries, trading our weapons and service for a world, realize that is only part of why we have taken this on. We do it for our new allies, yes. But we do it for our own survival as well. And we do it for the dead, for those races who will never again speak for themselves.

"You are the first crews of the Exilium Space Fleet, and everything we do defines the traditions that will follow us for the crews and spacers of the future of our Fleet.

"Let that tradition be that we stand against the genocides and the monsters of the galaxy. Let that tradition be that we are the shield of the innocent and the weak.

"We were born of a Fleet that turned on its own nation. Let us become something new."

His smile was fierce, and he knew it as he looked at the screens linking him to the bridges of his ships.

"Captains, navigators. Do you have your courses prepped?"

Affirmations came back.

"Then…engage."

———

42

Two weeks out of the twenty Isaac would be gone was more than enough for Amelie to realize just how long and frustrating the wait was going to be. They had no communication from Isaac's task force, no way to know how things were going.

All they could do was wait and continue building up the colony. The Matrices, at least, didn't seem to mind that Starhaven was expanding while they watched. If they weren't giving Isaac the benefit of the doubt, they were at least assuming that the Republic would keep trying until the Rogue Matrix was destroyed.

They were probably right, even if Amelie had no idea how they'd make that happen. She was an actress turned politician, not a soldier. How to build a battle fleet from scraps was entirely outside her experience and knowledge base.

"Roger, did we hear anything back from the Matrices on the last proposal?" she asked her aide as he stepped into her office.

"We just did, yes," he confirmed. "They're being cagey, as usual, but it sounds like we may have finally hit on something they're willing to trade exotic matter for."

Amelie shook her head.

"That's a relief, even if our history files are a somewhat limited resource," she admitted. There was no physical resource Exilium had that the Matrices couldn't get on their own far more easily. The Republic's technology was, with a handful of exceptions, roughly fifty to a hundred years behind the robots.

But Exilium had every scrap of recorded human history that the University of Terra had had on file, which meant they knew as much about the history of humanity as anyone in the galaxy.

The Matrices knew nothing of their own history and turned out to have a fascination with it.

"Will they give us enough?" she asked.

"I'm not even sure what 'enough' is in this context," Faulkner replied. "But I think so. From the numbers I've seen, if we hand them the entire U of T archive, they'll provide us enough exotic matter for us to construct a production facility."

"With or without making our own damn singularities?"

"Without," her aide admitted. "Remember that a singularity production facility is something like a hundred times the exotic matter of an EM facility." He shook his head. "From the conversations, I don't think they use the same tech to produce exotic matter. They had no idea why we wanted singularities, but...they've promised to help us track down two, even if they have no tools for capturing them."

"I wonder what they do use," Amelie said. "If it's more effective and safer..."

"Remember that they don't use artificial gravity and don't use warp drives," Faulkner replied. "If they're just using exotic matter for power cores, they might be able to get by with just a more efficient version of the particle accelerator method."

"Sort it out," she ordered. "Let me know if you need me to cut through any red tape or bullshit."

"I think we just needed somebody to realize that we were barking up the wrong tree," he confessed. "You were the first one to realize we needed to be trying to sell them *knowledge*."

"I was an actress," Amelie said. "The value of intellectual property is rarely lost on the people who create it."

Faulkner chuckled.

"True enough. I'm used to favors being the currency of power, not history archives." He shook his head. "Speaking of which, Father James is scheduled to arrive in fifteen minutes. He still hasn't told me what he wants to meet with you about."

"He hasn't spoken to me outside of Cabinet meetings since the Matrices arrived," Amelie admitted. "I'm curious to know what's running through the old priest's head. I hope he isn't planning on resigning."

"The government could survive it at this point," Faulkner said instantly, her aide clearly having been following the same line of thought. "About half of the Senators we think of as 'his' would stick with the government on most issues if he left the Cabinet. It would make our life harder, but we could keep things running."

"I didn't put together an all-parties government just to make my life easier, Roger."

"I know," he agreed. "But if Father James feels he can no longer serve in the Cabinet in good conscience…"

"Father James *is* our damn conscience," Amelie told him. "I'd rather keep him."

"If the choice is between the survival of the Republic and keeping your conscience clean, Madam President, I already know you have the fortitude to choose the path you must."

———

FATHER PETROV JAMES looked to have aged years in the last few weeks. His gray hair had faded further toward white, and there was a new stoop to his shoulders and wrinkles to his face.

He still walked into Amelie's office under his own power, even if he took with a grateful sigh the seat she pulled out for him.

"Stress, Madam President, is no good once you're my age," he admitted. "I apologize for the cold shoulder I have given you the last few weeks. Duty required that I attend the Cabinet meetings, but I needed to make my peace with God for where we are and what we have become."

"We all have our own struggles, Father James," Amelie told him. "Are you all right?"

"Other than having violated one of the most fundamental principles of my entire life by signing off an offensive military campaign?" he asked softly.

"We didn't have a choice," she replied. "And I didn't ask the Cabinet to approve it, either. You didn't sign off on anything."

"We both know I could have fought you," James said. "I doubt it would have changed the end result, but the principles I uphold and the oaths I swore demanded that I make that fight...and I didn't."

Amelie smiled sadly.

"I know," she admitted. "If you came here to make confession, Father, I don't know if I can help you. Penance is not in my personal lexicon, I have to admit."

Now she was expecting the resignation she dreaded. Which would be a pain in her ass.

"No," he agreed. "My penance is my own, and God has made clear to me what it needs to be. Whether we desired it or not, we are colonizers in a strange land with a strange people, and it falls to those of us who speak for both God and humanity to guide us away from the errors of the past."

"I believe, Father, that it falls to all of us to avoid those errors," Amelie told him. "If you wish to resign and go into opposition as a matter of principle...I won't stop you and will continue to try and work with you."

James laughed. It was a surprise to Amelie, a heartfelt boom of laughter that echoed across her office.

"No, Madam President, I have no intention of resigning—though I'll admit the thought crossed my mind, and I can see why you'd expect it. There is no better place, I think, to try and guide us away from the shadows than where we sit.

"I worry, though, about some of my fellow Ministers. They seem to be starting to regard the Matrices as...well, naïve indigenes to be exploited."

Amelie smiled at his laughter—and her smile thinned at his point. He was referring to Rodriguez. The man shared a vision and a goal with the rest of her Cabinet, but she had no illusions about what kind of viper she'd brought to the table.

"Having negotiated with the Matrices in good faith, I have no sympathy for anyone who tries to negotiate with them in *bad* faith," she admitted. "They don't lie. I'm not sure if it's against their protocols or if it just doesn't occur to them, but they are definitely aware of the concept.

"Anyone who tries to deceive them or trade them something of no value is going to regret it."

"Your own negotiators, Madam President, are attempting to trade historical archives for exotic matter," James pointed out. "That rings a little close to glass beads for land, don't you think?"

"Perhaps," Amelie allowed. "The difference, I think, is that no one is pretending things have value that they don't. Yes, we are offering only information…but information is the only thing we *have* of value to them.

"The historical archives are hardly without value for us, but they are of unique and special value to the Matrices. They have no history, no details of their Creators. They lost all that."

"A horrifying thought," James murmured.

"We have no physical resources they have any interest in. No technology. Only knowledge. Only our history," she told him. "It is all we have that they care about, so all we can do is hope they value it enough to give us what we need as well. I don't think anyone is being deceived here, Father."

He made a semi-disgruntled sound.

"Perhaps not," he admitted. "It still feels…wrong on some levels."

"I can see that," Amelie admitted in turn. "But it's as fair a deal as I can arrange. And I suspect anyone else who wants to exploit them is going to find themselves completely out of anything the Matrices want."

James nodded and leaned back in his chair, folding his hands together and studying her over them.

"There is one other matter I wanted to raise," he said quietly. "A moral concern for our populace, I suppose."

"A moral concern?" Amelie asked carefully. Just what rumors had escaped the careful precautions around that one night on *Vigil*?

"When Admiral Gallant returns, he will be a hero," the priest told her. "While he has earned the trust of many of our people, there are others who will see shades of his mother.

"A hero in command of our entire military with the potential adulation of much of the population. People will worship him…and because of that, others will fear him."

"Admiral Isaac Gallant would never do anything to threaten the Republic," Amelie told him.

"The Admiral and I have clashed since the moment we entered Exile," James said calmly. "I am a pacifist; he is a warrior. It is inevitable given our natures, but make no mistake: I have nothing but respect for Admiral Gallant as a man and as a protector of our people.

"I do not believe for an instant that that man would do harm to the Republic or to you. What I *fear*, Madam President, is what others might do out of fear of him. When he returns, we must act quickly to assuage those concerns, to clearly bind Isaac Gallant to the civilian government."

"What did you have in mind?" she asked carefully. Short of requesting and receiving Isaac's resignation, she wasn't sure what she *could* do.

"I'm not certain," the priest told her, but there was suddenly a mischievous glint in his eyes. "I mean, if you were to marry him, that would work, but I'm sure that's not an option."

Amelie was silent for a long moment, glaring at her Minister.

"I am relatively certain that I am not supposed to call a priest ugly names," she finally said primly.

"Oh, you mean that *might* be possible?" he asked, his laugh lines crinkling up as he smiled at her. "If it were, then I think it would be for the best for the Republic.

"I'm sure the pair of you would be prepared to add this one small sacrifice to your duties."

———

43

Every two weeks, the entire task force dropped out of warp to make sure they were still anywhere near each other and to make sure any problems were addressed. It was only for a few hours, but it was enough for a video-conference between the senior officers while the engineers and logistics teams made sure every ship was in fighting shape.

"*Dante*'s engineers have been going over the Matrices' modifications and upgrades to our systems," Captain Anderson told Isaac and the other captains. "Talking over them, we've got good, bad and ugly."

Isaac chuckled.

"You may as well lay it out in order, Captain," he instructed. "*Good* sounds promising, at least."

"The good news is that, other than the exotic-matter power cores, we understand everything they're doing well enough to duplicate it—in the long run, at least."

"That's better than I was hoping for," Isaac admitted. "Even the gamma-ray lasers?"

"*Powering* the grasers is going to take some kind of miracle in the absence of the power cores they gave us, but we think we'll be able to duplicate them. Eventually," Anderson said drily. "Given that about all my engineers can tell me so far about the exotic-matter cores is that they're some form of *matter-conversion* plant…"

Isaac winced. $E=mc^2$ offered huge potential for power…and equally huge potential for dangerous mix-ups.

"They're stable, right?" he asked.

"So far as we can tell," she agreed. "I'm pretty sure stability is part of why the Matrices hardwired them not to go below fifty percent capacity, though."

"Please tell me those things are behind every scrap of armor plating we have?" Captain Giannovi added. "Because otherwise, I need to tell my helm officer to start maintaining a bigger interval. No offense, Margaret, but I do *not* want to be anywhere near you if those things get breached."

This time, every officer on the call shared Isaac's wince.

"They're behind about three meters of the black ceramic the Matrices use for armor," Anderson noted. "The stuff can disperse a direct hit from *Vigil*'s main gun…once. Maybe twice."

"Which is more then anything else in the task force can say," *Archimedes*'s Commander Riley noted.

"Agreed," Isaac noted. "So, the good is that we *can* duplicate them. What's the bad?"

"The only thing we could do right now is the pulse-gun upgrade," *Dante*'s Captain said calmly. "My engineers figure they can get a two-hundred-percent increase in rate of fire in exchange for a thirty-five-percent reduction in firepower per shot.

"With, of course, a three-hundred-percent increase in power draw and something like a seventy-percent reduction in designed lifetime," she concluded. "It's probably worth it…except the ugly is that in the absence of the Matrices' construction remotes, we basically need to tear down the entire mount and refit it in a vacuum."

"Which we can't exactly do under warp drive," Isaac concluded. "I see your point." He shook his head. "All right, Captain Anderson. Make sure all four ships have a full copy of everything your engineers have pulled together.

"We want that data to make it back to Exilium."

He couldn't rely on the survival of any one ship in the task force.

Hopefully, at least one ship would make it back no matter what happened.

———

SIX WEEKS into the trip and Isaac was surprised by the morale of his crews. Warp travel sucked; there was no way around it. The air felt wrong. Food tasted wrong. Everything about *living* while in a warp bubble was ever so slightly off.

But his crews knew why they were on this trip—and it seemed that they trusted him to get them through this alive.

He wasn't so sure himself, looking at the screen in his office where his latest simulation of the potential positioning of the Rogue Matrix and its possible forces spun in front of him.

Matrix KCX-DD-78 hadn't been able to confirm what kind of security the rogue node was going to have kept around itself. Their best guess was a combat-and-construction unit equivalent to KCX plus four to six recon nodes.

The Rogue itself occupied a regional construction matrix capable of building terraforming spikes...and everything up to and including further combat and construction units.

Assuming access to any reasonably sized asteroid belt, there was nothing stopping the Rogue from constructing an entire battle fleet with echelon after echelon of the armored combat platforms KCX's matrices had apparently never built.

They'd been far freer with the specifications of those combat units than they had been with the details of the ships they were actually using.

Time was not on their side. One hundred and sixty days to build a combat platform from scratch, but Isaac's simulations showed that even a single combat platform could annihilate his task force. The upgraded *Dante* could give the robotic warship a fight but would, in the end, be outmatched.

And while *Dante* was being outmatched by the combat platform, the recon platforms would be wiping the floor with Isaac's destroyers while the combat-and-construction platform obliterated *Vigil*.

Even with just the "standard" Matrix security flotilla guarding the Rogue, the odds weren't in his favor. Any straight-up battle had the best-case scenario of a mutual massacre.

"Still beating your head against imaginary enemies?" his flag captain asked as Giannovi walked into his office with a tray holding a pair of coffees. "Need a sounding board?"

"Yes, and yes," Isaac said gratefully, taking the caffeinated beverage. "I'll admit, part of me was hoping that the engineers could come up with some kind of super-weapon out of studying *Dante*'s upgrades."

"*Repairs*, surely," Giannovi reminded him with a grin. "No technological transfers, remember?"

"I know," he said grimly. "The data they gave us suggests that even *Dante* is no match for one of their combat platforms. She's armed and armored along the same schema now, but she's still only a third of their size."

Less, really. Even "repaired" by the Matrices, *Dante* was four hundred and twenty-seven meters from prow to stern. A Matrix Combat unit was *fifteen hundred* meters long, with six graser-equipped "claws" to *Dante*'s three, plus broadside-mounted versions of the terrifying energy weapons.

"But we shouldn't have to worry about a combat platform, right?" his flag captain replied. "'Just' recon and the construction units?"

"Ignoring the fact that the Rogue itself is in a mobile platform seven kilometers long?" Isaac asked. "Sure. Each recon unit carries a graser that can demonstrably gut even our capital ships, and an arsenal of pulse guns to make our destroyers blush.

"The combat-and-construction units have *four* grasers, plus pulse guns, though thankfully only two of those grasers can bear on any direction."

He shook his head.

"And that's ignoring the fact that they have missiles that fire at near-*c* velocities. Our task force can reliably stop maybe eight. So, two recon units can overwhelm our Guardian Protocols and wipe us out."

He gestured at the screen, showing the simulation where the

combined salvos of six recon units had annihilated the entire task force.

"I'm not seeing a solution."

His flag captain sighed, studying the simulation.

"Okay, so they've got a million advantages," she agreed. "What have we got?"

"Surprise and the warp drive."

Isaac stopped.

"Let me check something," he told her, pulling up the files the Matrices had given him on their weapons and drive.

"Interesting…"

"Are you planning on sharing, boss?" Giannovi asked with a chuckle.

"Those near-lightspeed missiles have a minimum range to get up to speed," Isaac told her. "That's why the Stranger stopped using them once we were in pulse-gun range. They need almost four hundred thousand kilometers to properly activate."

"Every weapon we have that can actually hurt them is shorter-ranged than that."

"Exactly. We don't want to be in their missile range at all," he agreed. "And their tachyon punch requires a minimum of ten light-minutes from a star to emerge. The gravity-warp drive has no such limitation."

"If we stop and see where they are before we make the final jump, we can collapse the warp bubbles right on top of the bastards," Giannovi said. "They won't be able to use their missiles—"

"And they'll never see us coming."

———

44

"Emergence in thirty seconds."

Isaac breathed a soft sigh of relief that he hoped none of his staff caught. The every-two-weeks drop out of warp to coordinate with the rest of the task force had only seemed to make things worse. Unlike the six-month-long voyage from wormhole XL-17 to Exilium, he'd never quite adjusted to the feel of warped space this time.

Some of his people clearly had, including Commander Cameron Alstairs, and he envied them.

"Warp drive is at seventy percent of angular momentum and slowing," an announcement echoed from *Vigil*'s bridge. "Emergence in ten…nine…"

The countdown echoed through the entire ship, but Isaac could feel the slowing in his bones. The air grew thicker as *Vigil* dropped back toward normal speeds and normal space, and he coughed to clear a frog in his throat that wasn't actually there.

And then it all broke and he could breathe freely as *Vigil*'s warp bubble collapsed and the battlecruiser arrived in the XL-17-K System.

"Report, Cameron," he ordered.

"*Dante*, *Archimedes*, and *Plato* are all in position, condition codes flashing green," Alstairs said after a moment. "All ESF vessels are moving into wide-array scanning positions. Let's see what we can see."

The hologram at the heart of the flag deck lit up with the map of the system as provided by the Matrices. Eight planets. Two gas giants. All of them were closer to the star than the Exilium task force, currently sitting sixteen light-hours away from Kappa itself.

"Okay, that is disturbing."

"Commander?"

"Matrix data aligns with the long-range scans from the Confederacy survey," Isaac's ops officer told him. "All of that data is from a distance, so it was eight years old when they took it and is over a decade old now. And, well…"

The third planet on the hologram *moved*.

"Orbit of Kappa-3 has been expanded by approximately forty-five light-seconds since then," Alstairs reported. "The planet has been moved well into the liquid-water zone, and its axial tilt has been adjusted to under three degrees."

"First stage of their construction project is to make sure the foundation is right," Isaac observed. "That's…still terrifying."

He studied the data for a moment longer.

"And our robotic friends?" he asked.

"They're a good bit smaller than a planet," Alstairs pointed out. "We're still resolving the data, though…"

A new icon appeared above Kappa-3 as the hologram zoomed in.

"We *can* pick up the primary node from here," the ops officer concluded.

"I think our computerized friends missed something," Captain Giannovi noted from the bridge. "That is *significantly* bigger than they told us it would be."

The Rogue Matrix had apparently spent at least some of its time upgrading itself. The Sub-Regional Construction Matrix design their allies had given them was a rough disk seven kilometers across.

The Rogue was nothing like the design they had. It was a seventeen-kilometer sphere, radiating energy in every spectrum *Vigil*'s scanners could detect as it drifted in a geostationary orbit around Kappa-3's equator.

"The good news, such as it is, is that it appears that the expansions aren't armored," Alstairs said quietly. "The ceramic they used for armor absorbs and disperses light very differently. That hull is just a basic titanium-steel alloy."

"Which means the original armored hull is somewhere under there," Isaac pointed out.

"Yes, but the difference is that we can *nuke* a titanium-steel hull," Giannovi replied. "Assuming we can pin the bugger down long enough to use ground-bombardment missiles, anyway."

None of Isaac's ships had space-to-space missile launchers, but *Vigil* retained the ground-bombardment weaponry of her Confederacy past, weapons he'd hoped to never use in his life.

Including among those were twenty space-to-surface five-hundred-megaton fusion warheads.

"I don't think the Rogue is going to be the problem," Isaac told his people. "What are the rest of the icons, Cameron?"

Alstairs studied them and nodded slowly.

"Six recon platforms, two combat-and-construction platforms," he concluded. "More than we were hoping, but still no combat platforms."

"All right, people," Isaac said loudly. "We know what we're up against now. The Rogue won't know we're here for sixteen hours, but we'll be on its doorstep twenty minutes after I make the call.

"All ships are to stand down to Condition Three for ten hours. Make sure everyone aboard gets a meal and at least six hours of sleep.

"In ten hours, we go to war."

———

THERE WAS MORE reason than one for the ten-hour wait. Rest was important—and Isaac wasn't going to pass up the chance to get a solid eight hours of sleep in normal space himself—but they also needed to know the exact routine and orbit of the Matrix ships they were targeting.

For the plan to work, they had to emerge basically on top of their targets in an astrographic scale, optimally within two hundred thousand kilometers.

The more scan data they had on the Rogue and its escorts, the better. Especially if they wanted to try and take out the Rogue itself with ground-bombardment nukes.

"Is it even possible for us to hit it with the nukes?" he asked Giannovi. They were both in the Combat Information Center, looking over the shoulders of the analysts running the numbers to project where the Rogue and its escorts would be.

"It's not easy," his flag captain replied. "Only the battlecruisers even carried ground-attack munitions—I don't think your mother wanted them out of sight of her battle-group commanders."

"Given what some of her Admirals did with the damned things, I don't think that was enough restraint," Isaac noted. "I'm trying to remember the specifications on them. For some strange reason, I never really looked into them."

The only targets available for the Confederacy's ground-attack munitions, after all, had been the Confederacy's own worlds. That they'd been issued to *any* ships spoke volumes to at least part of the CSF's mission.

"We have two varieties," Giannovi told him. "Both are based on the Specter Six chassis, which is basically a glorified rock we can drop from orbit with enough engine power to make sure it hits the right target.

"We have a hundred Specter Sixes, with the assumption that most would be used as kinetic weapons," she noted. "The Phoenix Eleven warheads go on the Specters. With a little work, we can strip the heat shielding and include additional fuel tanks, but they're still going to be super-short-ranged by space standards."

"Captain…the only chance we have of hitting with a missile of any kind is for them to have *no* possibility of interception," Isaac reminded her. "We have surprise, yes, but we're talking about going after a computer. We need *seconds* of flight time."

"The Specters can't give us that," Giannovi admitted. "But those warheads are our best shot of managing to take the Rogue out in the opening round."

"Then let's get some of our engineers and missile techs in a room and give them the problem," he suggested. "Never assume that just because we officers can't think of an answer that the NCOs that live with this hardware can't!"

———

V*IGIL* HAD EXACTLY three missile techs aboard, all specialists in the design of the Specter Six bombardment munition. Giannovi had grabbed three of her most-senior engineering NCOs as well, and the six of them were all looking horrendously awkward at being in a room with the Admiral.

"All right, ladies, gentlemen," he addressed them. "The problem we face is simple. The solution requires specialized knowledge."

That seemed to perk up everyone's interest.

"*Vigil* has twenty five-hundred-megaton warheads, and our primary target appears to have augmented itself with significant steel and titanium construction. Conventional materials can't withstand nuclear explosions, so we find ourselves with a unique opportunity to at least temporarily disable the Rogue itself."

He tapped a key, bringing up the schematics of a Specter Six chassis.

"The problem is that our best guess is that we need to deliver the warheads to target within five seconds of emerging from warp," he told them. "We're not sure how close a range we'll emerge at, but we are aiming for about a hundred and fifty thousand kilometers. It's possible we can shave that down, but it'll be dangerous for everyone aboard *Vigil*.

"The further and faster we can deliver those twenty warheads, the more likely we are to actually score hits on the Rogue—and if we drop a few gigatons' worth of nukes on the bugger, it's going to be out of the fight—at least long enough for us to clean up its guards."

"Specter Six isn't a space-to-space missile," one of the missile specialists noted, absently twirling long dark hair around a finger as she considered the data. "That's a big target, but the Specter isn't designed for this."

"We know," Isaac agreed. "And neither Captain Giannovi nor I have a clue how to adapt for that. Hence, this meeting." He gestured around.

"Specter *really* isn't designed for this," the woman repeated. "The parts might be useful, but we may as well ditch the chassis. Too heavy, too much heat shielding."

"And if we're just stealing parts, we've got a whole inventory for fixing *Vigil* and the shuttles too," one of the engineering NCOs added. "We don't have anything that could let the missile survive a hit, so it just needs to be secure enough to survive acceleration."

"We've got *lots* of things that can accelerate a warhead," another missile tech said.

The first woman flashed a brilliant grin and turned back to Isaac.

"We've got what, six hours, Admiral?"

He checked his tattoo-comp.

"Plus about fifteen minutes, yeah," he told them.

"Give us an hour to hack together an idea and we'll tell you if it's possible," she replied.

"You can build a new missile from scratch in six hours?" Isaac asked, astonished.

"Not a chance. But I can sure as hell strap a fuel tank and a rocket to a nuke in under ten minutes if we draw it up first."

———

"Well, we have a solution," Giannovi told Isaac.

She had joined him in his office now—and had brought a very nervous-looking Lieutenant Commander. The young man was *Vigil*'s navigator, the person primarily responsible for bringing the battle-cruiser through the warp jump to come.

"From Lieutenant Commander Brankovich's presence, I can guess what one of the complications is," Isaac replied. "What have we got?"

"Our engineering team is busy gutting our collection of Specter Sixes and the spare parts for our shuttle fleet," the flag captain told him. "They've got a design for a crude delivery device for the nukes, but the best they can promise me in a five-second flight time is fifty thousand kilometers."

"Fifty," Isaac echoed with a sigh. That was frankly spectacular, an acceleration he didn't think they had any systems capable of…but it still left them with one hell of a problem.

Hence Lieutenant Commander Brankovich, who was looking thoughtful at the description of the "missiles" Engineering was building.

"Well, Andelko?" Isaac asked the dark-haired young man. "Can you do it?"

"Get us within fifty thousand kilometers of a target seventeen kilometers across after a sixteen-light-hour warp jump?" he asked, laying the parameters out aloud.

Isaac winced.

"Yeah," he conceded. "And with about a ten-thousand-kilometer potential error radius on where the target might be."

Brankovich inhaled thoughtfully, any nervousness at being locked in a room with his Captain and his Admiral lost as he stared blankly at the wall, numbers crunching behind his eyes.

"Maybe," he finally said. "Sixty-forty. Maybe fifty-fifty; it's hard to say. If they were further out from the planet, it would be easier, but with them in orbit, we also need to make sure we don't hit Kappa-3."

"What's the chance of us hitting the planet inside that forty to fifty chance of missing the target?" Isaac asked.

"I can keep *that* at zero," the navigator said instantly. "But…it'll work best if the rest of the fleet is still coming out well back. Fewer calculations, fewer variables—but that leaves us out on our own."

"We're still within weapons range of the rest of the task force," Giannovi pointed out to Isaac. "I'd take the risk."

He smiled and nodded grimly.

He was honest enough, with himself at least, to admit that he was glad only *Vigil* had the nukes. There was no way he'd order any *other* ship in his little fleet to take this risk.

"Do it," he ordered. "No point in wasting all the hard work your engineers are putting in, after all."

———

45

THE TWENTY MINUTES in warp from the outside of the Kappa system to orbit of Kappa-3 were some of the longest minutes of Isaac's life. The icons representing his fleet blinked across the hologram of the system at a mind-boggling speed, closing toward destiny.

"Emergence in ninety seconds," Brankovich reported. "The moment of truth is upon us."

"Lauretta?" Isaac asked quietly.

"The nukes are all prepped and ready to fire," Giannovi confirmed. "No humans involved. Computers will initiate the sequence as soon as we emerge."

She paused.

"Everything else is going to require human authorization to engage," she warned. "But the capacitors and cyclotrons are charged, and from what Andelko is promising for emergence distances, we'll shoot first."

"Shoot first, shoot straight," Isaac told her with a smile. "As the Lieutenant Commander says: the moment of truth is upon us.

"It's been an honor, Captain Giannovi."

"It will *continue* to be an honor, Admiral Gallant," she said sharply.

"Emergence in thirty seconds," the navigator reported.

Isaac nodded to his flag captain and leaned back in his chair as she set to work, barking orders through a dozen channels to every corner of the ship.

Seconds ticked away. There was no contact with the rest of the fleet, not in warp. Only the hope that everyone else had done as planned and that *Vigil* would not be emerging from the void alone.

"Emergence."

The battlecruiser plunged back into real space with all of the subtle calm of a breaching whale. Isaac had never been aboard a warp-drive ship coming out this close to any kind of planet-sized mass. All he'd known was that it was theoretically possible, but CSF regulations and doctrine strongly discouraged it.

Now he knew why.

For a seeming eternity he couldn't breathe. Couldn't see. Couldn't even *think* as a cloying blackness overcame every one of his senses, clogging his throat, forcing him to gag against its strength.

Every nerve was on fire. His body violently rebelled against the violation of reality they'd unleashed.

And then it was over, *Vigil* snapping back into existence around him like nothing had happened—but from the instant of frozen reaction on the part of his flag bridge crew, he hadn't been the only one.

Giannovi coughed first, clearing her throat and shattering the spell.

"Nukes away," she reported. "Holy shit, Andelko!"

The battlecruiser wasn't fifty thousand kilometers away from the Rogue Matrix's core unit. They were *five hundred*. The crude nuclear-tipped rockets Giannovi's engineers had assembled crossed the distance in under a second—and the Rogue *still* shot down six of the twenty incoming warheads.

Fourteen five-hundred-megaton warheads were still more than the titanium-steel outer structure it had built around itself could take. Entire kilometer-wide sections of the superstructure vanished in balls of thermonuclear fire, and Andelko whipped the battlecruiser around their enemy as the massive robotic ship reeled away, her orbit degrading toward the surface of the world below them.

"Recon unit at forty-three by fifty-one," Giannovi snapped. "Andelko, bring us about. Connor—FIRE!"

Vigil spun in space, aligning her spinal main gun with the obsidian egg of a hostile recon unit. The alien ship was still bringing up its engine, its computer brain confused by the sudden explosion of violence. It was responding quickly, inhumanly so.

It wasn't responding quickly enough. Andelko brought the big Terran warship in line with her target, and Isaac's flagship emptied her particle cannon into the enemy. Seven high-velocity packages of super-charged ions hammered into the recon unit's black armor.

The material dispersed the impact of the first two. The rest shattered the hull and vaporized the interior, sending the deadly ship scattering away from *Vigil* in pieces.

There were still five more of them—and two of the larger combat-and-construction units. They were at a range where *Vigil*'s weapons could hurt them, but the battlecruiser couldn't fight this on her own.

But then the rest of the Exilium Space Fleet arrived.

———

ONE OF THE big construction units was lunging toward *Vigil*, the surge of power to her gamma-ray lasers clearly visible to *Vigil*'s sensors. A dozen pulse guns fired into her, slowing her advance as her weapons charged up.

Then three grasers hammered into her, a perfectly timed salvo of matched beams that ripped gaping holes in the black shell of the robot starship. The construction unit reeled away—but *Dante* was on her like a shark.

Rotating as she came, the battlecruiser's new rapid-fire pulse guns lit up in a near-solid stream of fire that filled the gaps in the robot's armor with plasma. The robot survived, somehow, rotating in space to bring her own lasers to bear on Captain Anderson's ship.

The delay in changing targets from *Vigil*, however, allowed Giannovi's ship to rotate and finish charging her particle cannon. Three packets of supercharged ions hammered through the cascade of plasma and ripped through the length of the robotic starship.

She broke apart, chunks of black armor falling toward the planet and hurtling toward the still-falling Rogue Matrix.

A recon unit lunged at *Vigil*, only to find itself flanked by the two destroyers. *Archimedes* and *Plato* were the lightest-armed units in this fight, but with the drone ship caught between them, they hammered it with pulse guns along its entire length.

It returned fire, but its gamma-ray laser appeared to be built on the same spinal design as *Vigil*'s particle cannon. The recon ship's pulse guns were more powerful than the destroyers', but the two Exilium ships simply had more guns.

The recon unit came apart under the pounding, though not without sending red damage data codes flashing over both destroyers in Isaac's display.

The second combat-and-construction unit was now maneuvering for *Dante*, her pulse guns hammering *Vigil* as the un-upgraded battlecruiser tried to get her particle cannon lined up for another shot. *Dante* herself twisted in space, her gamma-ray lasers flashing in space as one of the remaining recon units made the mistake of being in the wrong section of Kappa-3's orbit for a few seconds.

Half of the Rogue Matrix's units were gone in exchange for minor damage to the destroyers. Isaac allowed himself to hope for a single instant—and then the second construction unit lined up her shot.

Dante visibly moved in the hologram as multiple gamma-ray lasers struck home. Anderson twisted her ship in the fire, but it was instantly obvious the battlecruiser had been badly injured. The construction unit was hammering her with four grasers—and *Dante* was only responding with one instead of three.

"Brankovich!" Giannovi barked, her single-word order echoing over the chaos of both the bridge and the flag deck.

"Got it!"

Vigil's engines flared to full power, a wash of charged energy that sent a too-close recon unit staggering away into the pulse-gun fire of the charging human destroyers.

The recon unit's death barely registered to Isaac as his flagship charged into the chaos of *Dante*'s duel with the last robotic capital ship. *Vigil* didn't have the new passive energy-dispersing armor the Matrices had installed on *Dante*. She didn't have rapid-fire pulse guns or gamma-ray lasers.

But she was four hundred meters of the most advanced military technology the Confederacy had possessed when she was constructed, one of the most modern warships in the Confederacy Space Fleet. The pair of gamma-ray lasers that hit her broadside armor *shoved* her toward her sister ship, hundreds of tons of armor and half a dozen pulse guns going up in vapor as the battlecruiser took the hits that would have finished *Dante* off.

Anderson took advantage of the distraction, flipping her ship up and over *Vigil* and firing her sole remaining graser directly into the emitters of the construction unit's comparable weapons.

A graser backfired, unleashing its destructive energy into the robotic ship's hull—and opening a gaping hole just in time for the near-crippled *Vigil* to rotate in space and empty her particle cannon into the gap.

They hit...*something*. Isaac wasn't even sure what. One moment, the combat-and-construction unit was reeling from the damage *Dante* had inflicted.

The next, a new star erupted from the heart of the robotic warship, radiation hammering into the two Terran battlecruisers and flinging them away as the uncontrolled reaction tore apart their enemy.

There was a moment of calm and Isaac inhaled slowly.

"Status report," he ordered.

"Battlespace is clear," Alstairs reported. "That's...not right. There were two more recon units."

For a moment, Isaac wanted to just take it. They'd *crushed* the Rogue's defenses, blasted the Rogue itself out of orbit and ended the machines blindly genocidal campaign.

But he didn't have it in him to leave a job half-done, and just *one* recon unit had almost destroyed the ESF. He couldn't count on them not being able to save the Rogue from its death spiral toward the planet.

"Find them," he ordered. "We need to finish this."

———

46

WHILE SCANNERS SWEPT the field of debris and radiation where the short but intense battle had taken place, the four Exilium ships met in high orbit, the destroyers moving in to cover the battlecruisers' crippled flanks.

None of Isaac's ships were unharmed. *Dante* had taken the hardest pounding, and even her Matrix-built armor with its amazing energy-dispersion properties hadn't been enough to keep her intact. Two of the three "claws" holding her grasers were gone, and Matrix grasers had left ugly gouges in her flanks.

Vigil was in better shape, but only because the hits she had taken were along her broadsides. Her main gun was intact, but an entire quarter of her pulse guns were offline. The destroyers were in similar shape, but they knew their enemy now.

Unlike when the Stranger had first come to Exilium, they knew how to fight the recon units, and Isaac was sure even his damaged task force could take the last two—if they could *find* the ships.

"We had them on our screens when we arrived, right?" Isaac asked Alstairs.

"We did," his ops officer confirmed. "We took pulse-gun fire from six recon units at one point, so where *are* they?"

"There aren't that many places to hide in orbit of a planet," Isaac pointed out. "This planet doesn't even have much of a moon, but that's all I'm seeing as an option."

"*Archimedes* is swinging out to get a look behind it," Alstairs replied.

Kappa-3's "moon" was a captured asteroid, maybe twelve hundred kilometers across. It wasn't much of a moon, but it was enough to hide the two recon units if that was where they'd gone.

"Get me a detailed sensor pulse on the Rogue itself, too," Isaac ordered. "I know its orbit is decaying, but I want a timeline on that. I want to watch that thing hit the ground and come apart before we leave. Let's make *sure* this is done and done right."

Space battles were always waiting split by moments of violence, but Isaac was starting to get tense again. The data they had on the tachyon punch said those ships hadn't left, which meant they were still here. Somewhere.

He doubted they were afraid of his fleet.

"This is *Archimedes* Actual," Commander Riley's voice came over the channel. "We're sweeping the far side of the moon and there is nothing here but some monitoring stations."

He paused and there was a flash of energy signatures on the hologram as the destroyer's pulse guns fired.

"Well, *now* there's nothing here," he said with a satisfied tone to his voice. "But no recon units."

A sinking feeling began to run down the back of Isaac's spine.

"Cameron, do we have that sweep of the Rogue?" he asked.

"Coming right up…what the hell?"

"Show me," Isaac ordered, not waiting for the ops officer to explain himself.

The hologram zoomed in on the wreckage of the Rogue Matrix. There was a disk-shaped core to the unit, but its engines had been interlaced through the superstructure, and the destruction of most of that superstructure had disabled the spaceship.

The upper half of the sphere was a nightmare of melted metal and debris, and the lower half wasn't in much better shape. The two recon units were on the far side of the robotic platform, tucked right in against the warped and melted superstructure…and were *shooting* at it?

"We need a better angle," Alstairs reported. "They're doing something—and I don't like it."

"Could they be trying to free the engines from the superstructure?" Isaac asked.

"It's possible, but I don't think their inertialess drives work like that," the ops officer reported. "Passing a course to *Archimedes*. Commander Riley can use the moon for a slingshot maneuver and come up under the Rogue.

"If nothing else, *Archimedes* will get a shot at the bastards, which might distract them."

Isaac nodded slowly.

"That makes sense…but bring the rest of the task force in after her. Something about this is making the hair on the back of my neck stand up."

"That's scientific as hell, but all right."

The destroyer looped the moon, using its minimal gravity to fling her deeper into Kappa-3's gravity well and toward the Rogue. *Vigil*, *Dante* and *Plato* began to drop from their high orbit, accelerating gently toward the alien ship as they prepared their weapons again.

Archimedes flashed across the flimsy, still-growing atmosphere of Kappa-3, keeping an intact portion of her armor toward the planet as she closed. Her scanners were relaying directly to *Vigil*, and Isaac caught himself holding his breath as Riley's ship finally lined up to give them a clean view of just what the two recon units were doing.

Their pulse guns fired again and again, vaporizing the superstructure in smaller, more carefully calculated chunks than the human nukes had done. There was a purpose to their fire…and then the first of the ships the Rogue had been building broke free, the recon units finally having destroyed enough of the wreckage to allow the first of the two combat platforms to maneuver out of its construction slip.

"Oh *shi*—"

Energy signatures flared—and six gamma-ray lasers cut Commander Riley off in mid-curse.

———

"THOSE WERE SUPPOSED to take four *months* to build," Alstairs snapped. "What the hell?"

"The Rogue started them early—and they're not complete," Isaac replied. "Look at it: it's still missing most of its armor. Her *weapons* are complete enough, though."

One combat platform was free, maneuvering slowly for a Matrix ship but maneuvering nonetheless. Even if her pulse guns were offline and much of her armor was missing, six gamma-ray lasers were more than enough to finish off Isaac's fleet unless they got *very* lucky.

And a second combat platform was still trapped in the Rogue's lower superstructure. If it was half as complete as the one the recon units had already freed, the Exilium Space Fleet was doomed.

Except that it was still trapped.

"Lauretta," Isaac snapped at the bridge link. "How many of those Specters do you have left?"

They'd stripped the bombardment chassis for the rockets they'd unleashed on the Rogue, but they'd only had twenty nukes and most of the engines had been taken from the shuttle spare parts.

His flag captain didn't even hesitate, pulling the data up on her tattoo-comp and meeting his gaze.

"We have sixty functioning Specters," she told him within seconds. "We can't hit a combat platform with them, though!"

"The Rogue itself isn't maneuvering," Isaac pointed out. "I want that thing smashed from the sky, Captain. Let's hit the damn computer with the biggest object available: Kappa-3."

He flipped to his link to *Dante* as Giannovi nodded and started barking her own orders.

"Anderson, we *might* be able to take the second one out of the fight, but you need to keep this one distracted while we throw rocks at its friends." He paused, meeting the tall woman's gaze with an icy chill in his heart.

"I don't know if you can fight her," he admitted. "But I need you to try."

"There is no try," she told him calmly. "We do what we must. *Dante* to the fore!"

The battlecruiser broke formation, *Plato* swinging in to cover her wounded flanks as she charged at the alien warship.

Whatever the combat platform's AI had been expecting, it wasn't that. Her first fire went wildly wide, and Captain Anderson's first return strike obliterated one of the combat platform's gamma-ray claws.

Now the odds were only *five* to one.

Isaac's attention was pulled back to his flagship as *Vigil* began her own acceleration. The warship's massive engines came to life at a power level that was *completely* unsafe in planetary orbit, lunging at a terrifying speed toward the massive robotic brain-ship that was their target.

Vigil was a four-year-old ship, with half of her life spent in exile now, and in her entire career, she'd never opened her bombardment tubes. The crudely assembled high-speed nuclear missiles had needed to be launched from outside her hull because none of her systems could fit them.

Now as she charged the Rogue, those hatches flung open as easily as if they'd been built yesterday, and dozens of smaller engines flashed to life. Twenty Specter Six ground-attack munitions flashed out in the first salvo, followed by forty more over the course of the following seconds.

Then *Vigil*'s engines cut out and her main gun spoke. The difference between the technology behind her main gun and the technology underwriting her engines was a matter of power and concentration, not principle.

Each time the particle cannon fired, the cruiser's headlong rush slowed measurably. The charged ion packets hammered into the half-wrecked Rogue, each impact throwing it farther toward the planet.

Pulse guns awoke as well, plasma fire walking its way across the helpless genocidal robot ship as Captain Giannovi unleashed every tool in her arsenal to turn the tide.

The upper side of the Rogue's core hull was *glowing*, energy-dispersing armor or not, when the bombardment munitions arrived.

Each one hit at almost five percent of lightspeed, and the massive disk hidden inside the sphere lurched again.

And again.

And again.

The Rogue was no longer in a degrading orbit. The Rogue was outright falling—and it smashed into one of the recon units that didn't dodge fast enough, trapping the egg-like spaceship in the superstructure it had been trying to cut the combat unit free from.

Gravity wasn't adding appreciably to the big ship's velocity now. The atmosphere the Rogue had been installing on Kappa-3 tried to slow it, the underside of the crashing starship lighting up bright red as the steel-titanium superstructure liquefied.

It hit at just over half a percent of lightspeed, an impact to put Earth's dinosaur-killer impact to shame.

———

"PLEASE TELL ME IT'S DEAD," Alstairs murmured.

"I believe that's your job, ops," Isaac replied. "Because right now, Captain Giannovi needs to be turning her attention to rescuing *Dante*."

The other battlecruiser was still with them, somehow. A sterling testament as much to her original engineers and the Matrices' rebuilding as anything else. Captain Anderson's ship had lost her last gamma-ray laser, and her entire forward third was gone again.

Somehow, *Dante* and *Plato* were still in the fight, and the Rogue combat matrix had lost all but two of her own heavy grasers. *Plato* was half-gone, the plucky destroyer somehow having taken a direct gamma-ray laser strike and still managing to keep her less-damaged side toward the combat platform and pound her with pulse-gun fire.

"Captain, you get just one chance for a clean shot," Isaac murmured. "So, we need to make it count. Where are the exotic-matter cores?"

Giannovi was silent for a long moment.

"We can't detect that through their hull," she pointed out. "But... when they rebuild *Dante*, the Matrices put the EM power cores right at the base of the claw, heavily armored but close to the grasers they were feeding."

"This one doesn't have most of her armor."

"No. No she doesn't," Giannovi agreed. "Connor! I want a full particle-cannon salvo set up, minimum sequencing, backed up with whatever pulse guns we've got left.

"This bastard's got a beating heart they forgot to put a ribcage over. Let's rip it out."

Vigil took precious seconds to align the shot—precious seconds paid for with a pulse-gun salvo that knocked *Plato*'s engines out and sent the destroyer finally careening out of the fight into a rapidly degrading orbit toward the planet below.

"*Now.*"

Giannovi's barked order echoed through the audio channel, and *Vigil* shivered as her main cannon spoke again.

There was no identifiable gap between the packets this time. No half-second sequencing to protect the gun—and the glaring red damage icons that flared up on Isaac's screen were a stark reminder of *why* that sequencing was a requirement.

Plasma pulses followed the ion packets in, *Vigil* burning out her weapons systems as she made one last charge. Isaac could follow their course with a trained gaze and could see the split-second decision Giannovi had made.

If the particle cannon and pulse guns failed to penetrate the armor over the Matrix combat unit's matter-annihilating heart, half a kilometer of accelerating battlecruiser *would*.

"What the *hell*?"

Isaac wasn't sure who had said it. It might even have been him. One second, *Vigil* was charging to her death, flinging fire into the teeth of her enemy...then next, they breached the containment of the matter-conversion plant that fed the enemy warship.

He understood, now, what had killed the combat-and-construction unit earlier. A new star ripped out the guts of the Matrix ship as the reaction broke loose, consuming its feeding apparatus and the ship around it.

The shockwave flung *Dante* and *Vigil* away, and Isaac *felt* his battlecruiser break, her spine snapping as tidal forces hit the front and back of the warship at very different levels.

Vigil spun away with a terrifying resemblance to a boomerang, her warp drive ring split into two like outstretched wings. *Dante* was luckier—she wasn't as close, and her earlier damage had left her with less length for the blast to twist her in. Her engines, strained to a breaking point, failed and she was flung free of Kappa-3 on a course that would, eventually, take her clear of the system.

"Where is that last recon unit?" Isaac asked in a strained voice as he studied the hologram.

"There," Alstairs told him, highlighted the obsidian egg of their enemy—moments before the out-of-control robotic ship slammed into Kappa-3's moonlet with hull-shattering force.

There was a long, long silence.

"The battlespace is clear," Alstairs reported again, this time with certainty. "Task Force One is now in control of the Kappa System."

———

47

"CONTROL" implied victory...which was probably an exaggeration of what the Exilium Space Fleet had achieved.

"Can we launch search-and-rescue craft?" Isaac asked. "Some of *Archimedes*' crew may have made it off, and we need to stabilize *Plato*'s orbit before she joins the Rogue on the surface."

What scan data he was getting from Kappa-3 was...ugly. There were no power signatures in the wreckage on the surface, but there was enough oxygen in the planet's growing artificial atmosphere to support a firestorm that was sweeping the planet at nearly the speed of sound.

Isaac hoped that the Matrices hadn't made it very far in their terraforming process, because they'd just undone it. From what he understood of the tech, if the terraforming spikes survived, they'd be able to repair this.

Eventually.

If *Plato* went down, her crew wouldn't survive.

"Two of our boat bays are gone," Giannovi told him. "I've got DamCon checking on the transfer corridors; we're *supposed* to be able to move our shuttles between the bays, but..."

"But no one expected the stern of a battlecruiser to end up at ninety degrees from the bow," Isaac agreed. "But we've got one bay?"

"We do," his flag captain replied. "There's just no search-and-rescue birds in Bay Three. That one is all assault shuttles."

"If they can *board* a damn starship, they can latch on to one and *push* it," Isaac told her. "Get them out there. We might not be able to pick up escape pods, but we can probably push *Plato* into a safer orbit."

Giannovi nodded firmly, dropping the channel as she turned to try and continue organizing the salvation of her starship.

"Commander Rose, do we have a link to *Plato* or *Dante*?" he asked his coms officer.

"Negative," she replied. "Last telemetry from *Plato* suggest her entire power network is done. Nothing similarly critical from *Dante*, but we can't raise her on coms."

"Captain Anderson's still with us," Alstairs confirmed. "*Dante* has power but no engines. Unlike us, however, it looks like her warp drive ring is intact. She's currently on a ballistic… Wait!"

"Cameron?"

"*Dante* has aligned her pulse guns and is using them to slow her vector," the ops officer reported. "It's not a fast process, but if she can keep it up, she'll drop into a stable orbit of Kappa about a light-minute out from Kappa-3."

"If we can get in touch with Captain Anderson, let her know I have to prioritize S&R here," Isaac ordered. "Once we've retrieved whoever we can from the debris field, we'll maneuver to rendezvous."

"I'll record and keep pinging them until I get a response," Rose promised.

Isaac nodded and turned to Alstairs.

"What's *Plato*'s status?" he asked grimly.

"No power. No engines. Her warp drive ring is wrecked, and she's missing forty-two percent of her hull," his ops officer replied. "Anything with *Plato* is a rescue op; she's non-salvageable."

Isaac shook his head.

"Cameron, by any rational standard, *Dante* and *Vigil* are non-salvageable," he pointed out.

"Yes, and by the standard that says we have no choice but to try and salvage them, we still can't salvage *Plato*," Alstairs said flatly. "There just isn't anything left of her."

A quartet of assault shuttles blasted free of *Vigil*'s boat bay toward the wrecked destroyer.

"Assault shuttles are probably the right call," the ops officer noted. "Marines will be able to sweep the hull for survivors and set the scuttling charges. She's done, sir. She can't give us any more."

"Then by all that is sacred, we owe her crew everything we can do for them," Isaac agreed. "Interface with the sensors of every shuttle we get up. Our flag deck has the best systems for turning multiple scanner sources into a single map, so let's use them.

"Every bird we get into space is one more chance to find our survivors—and if someone has made it this far, I *refuse* to lose them."

PLATO'S WRECK SLOWLY, ever so slowly to someone used to the blistering accelerations of modern warships, lifted out of Kappa-3's gravity well. *Vigil* maneuvered to meet her as her shuttles continued the slow and painful process of sweeping for survivors in the wreckage.

"There's nothing from *Archimedes*," Alstairs finally had to report. "They were completely vaporized when the combat platform opened fire. There isn't even any debris, let alone survivors."

Isaac nodded silently, his eyes still locked to the hologram. As he watched, four more survival-pod beacons appeared—from the codes, these had been the support crew in one of *Dante*'s gamma-ray mounts.

As *Vigil*'s flag-deck computers isolated their signals from the background radiation, techs in the background leaned into microphones, passing urgent orders. The search-and-rescue craft that had finally been transferred to Bay Three and launched into space adjusted their courses, sweeping toward their new targets.

There were still far too few of them.

"That's forty-three," Alstairs said quietly. "Probably...three hundred people. I don't think we're going to find more, boss. That's more than I was expecting."

"Any kind of casualty report from *Dante* yet?" Isaac asked.

"Captain Anderson is still with us, but much of her crew isn't," the ops officer told him. "Best estimate is six hundred lost."

"Plus *Plato*, plus *Archimedes*, plus *Vigil*," Isaac counted off. *Dante's* losses were the worst, but he'd lost over a thousand people in this godforsaken system—and that was *with* their pulling over three hundred people from the void.

He stepped, again, on the urge to contact Giannovi and ask for an update on the damage reports. His flag captain was swamped.

"Once we've finished this sweep and evaced the last of *Plato's* crew, we'll need to move out to rendezvous with *Dante*," Isaac ordered. "If there's nothing left here, then we need to work out how we're getting everyone home."

Since he was down to two battlecruisers, both half-wrecked, that was a question Isaac Gallant wasn't sure he knew the answer to.

———

FORTY-EIGHT HOURS WASN'T REALLY enough time to recover from a clash as brutal as the Battle of Kappa System. They'd scuttled what was left of *Plato*—in the end, with the warship's reactors wrecked and scuttling charges disabled, they'd sent her wreckage crashing down into the funeral pyre of her enemy.

If anything had survived the original crash of the Rogue Sub-Regional Construction Matrix, well, it probably hadn't survived *Plato* crashing down on top of the same site at only slightly lower speed.

Kappa-3 was never going to be a Constructed World. Two of the terraforming spikes had been in the impact crater from the Rogue's crash. Another had ceased functioning after the firestorm swept over it.

The two remaining spikes would probably create a partially inhabitable area, but they were designed to operate in groups of five to seven. Two of the facilities couldn't transform an entire planet.

Dante and *Vigil* now floated in the void beyond Kappa-3, the two ships within a few kilometers of each other as the task force's engineers did their surveys and tried to see just what they could make of the wrecked warships.

"Captain Anderson," Isaac greeted *Dante*'s Captain with a sharp salute as she stepped off the shuttle. "It's damn good to see you."

Margaret Anderson looked like she'd walked through hell and come back the same way. If she'd showered or even changed uniforms in the last two days, it didn't look like it—which meant she looked just like the rest of Task Force One's remaining senior officers.

"It's good to be alive," Anderson told him. "We were worried for a while."

"We all were," Isaac told her. "Part of me is still half-convinced we died back there and the rest of this is a just a dream as I asphyxiate."

Captain Giannovi physically elbowed him for that, a gross breach of military protocol…that he saw no reason not to let stand this time.

"We're all still here," she said sharply. "Let's not borrow even more trouble or death than we already have to deal with, all right?"

"You're right," Isaac conceded. "Come on, Captains. We have much to discuss if we're going to get our people home safely."

———

THE ENGINEERS DIDN'T LOOK PARTICULARLY *happy* about being dragged away from the seemingly endless tasks of trying to piece together their two battered battlecruisers, but when both Captains and the Admiral insisted, mere Commanders obeyed.

There were only six people in the tiny meeting room in the end. Captains Anderson and Giannovi and their chief engineers faced Isaac and Cameron Alstairs.

"We have a lot of work to do," *Dante*'s chief engineer, Commander Woolsey, pointed out. "Every minute we're here—"

"How much of that work matters if we can't get home?" Isaac said flatly. "*Vigil* has no functioning warp drive. *Dante* has no sublight engines. Neither of those is reparable, so the fact that we don't have guns or one hundred percent functional life support is of lesser importance.

"We have two half-wrecked battlecruisers. Neither can get home. Do we have a plan for that yet?"

The room was silent for a long minute.

Woolsey sighed.

"No," he admitted. "We've been focusing on making sure nothing explodes and no one asphyxiates."

"We're past that point now, aren't we?" Isaac asked.

"We are," Anderson confirmed. "Should we be planning to relocate everyone to *Dante*, then?"

"In theory," Woolsey replied, "but it won't work. We need a minimum real-space velocity for the new warp drive to engage properly. Without that…we lose ninety-five percent of our pseudo-velocity."

"So, back to four *c*?" Giannovi asked.

"Exactly. And we don't have enough supplies for a multi-year trip," Isaac reminded everyone. "I had Cameron here run the numbers."

He gestured to Alstairs.

"We over-stockpiled on supplies past when we expected to need," the ops officer said. "But we lost a lot of that. Even with our losses, we have about a four-month supply of food.

"Even with protein recycling, we can only spin that out for maybe another four months," he continued. "If we can't manage to somehow scrape up at least twenty *c* of pseudovelocity, we will run out of food long before we get home."

Isaac let that sink in.

"You have staff and crews for damage control, Mr. Woolsey, Mr. Popovski," he told them. "I need *you* to find an answer to the only important question left:

"How do we get our people home?"

Vusala Popovski, *Vigil*'s chief engineer, chuckled at him.

"That's easy," he told him in faintly accented English. "You said it yourself, Admiral Gallant. We need a full battlecruiser to get home, and, as it happens, we have two half-battlecruisers.

"Attaching them won't be easy, and balancing the warp drive will be even harder, but it *can* be done."

Isaac blinked. That thought hadn't even occurred to him.

"Are you certain?" he asked.

"It won't be easy," he repeated. "But yes. Woolsey?"

The other engineer looked horrified at the thought but slowly nodded.

"It's insane," he said. "Utterly, completely, batshit insane. But Commander Popovski is correct. We have the parts, the equipment and the people to basically weld the two cruisers together.

"We may even be able to take them apart again at the other end."

"At this point, people, I'm perfectly fine if we need to build the ESF new battlecruisers when we get home," Isaac told them. "I care about one thing: can you get our people home?"

The two engineers shared a long look, then turned back to him and nodded as one.

"Yes."

———

48

THE MASSIVE FOUR-LEGGED form of Matrix KCX-DD-78's remote "diplo-mat" robot had become a relatively common sight in Starhaven, at least around Exilium Central and the rapidly growing offices that housed both city and planetary bureaucracy.

Amelie was a realist about how much government four million people needed. She was doing her best to keep it under control, but the new need to actually assemble and operate a real military wasn't helping.

Security was still quite light, and most of the uniformed people she could see scurrying around her capital building were officers and enlisted of the explosively expanding Exilium Space Fleet.

A team of what security there was trailed the robot as it made its way carefully through the crowd, and Amelie sighed.

"Roger," she called out the front door of her office. "Does the Matrix have an appointment booked?"

She heard her aide's answering sigh before he spoke.

"I don't think KCX has mastered that nicety yet," the old Earth bureaucrat told her. "Shall I slot him in? We can probably push Captain Cavan back." Faulkner paused. "It would probably be good for us to do so, in fact. Cavan needs to be reminded that he's one of half a dozen Captains and doesn't actually run the ESF."

Robert Cavan was the most senior, per Confederacy term of service anyway, of the Captains Isaac had left behind. Most of Isaac's people had sorted out what minimal chain of command was needed and got on with recommissioning the Morgue.

Cavan, however, was certain that he was in command of the ESF by virtue of his seniority. The fact that none of his erstwhile subordinates agreed with him was irrelevant in his head, and he kept petitioning Amelie to promote him to make that clear to them.

She had no intention of doing so. If she ended up with reason to believe Isaac Gallant was dead, she'd promote *someone* to Admiral.

She didn't know who it would be…but she knew that it wasn't going to be Robert Cavan.

"It's almost a shame Captain Cavan is actually good at his job," she mused aloud.

"Yes, ma'am, certainly, ma'am," Faulkner said in the sharp tone he reserved for when Amelie Lestroud had said something out loud that the President of the Republic shouldn't say. "I'll postpone the good Captain till tomorrow and slot in the Matrix Ambassador?"

"Oh"—Amelie waved a hand—"I'm going to take tomorrow afternoon off. Postpone Captain Cavan to next week, please."

Both she and Roger Faulkner knew that Cavan's *Demeter* was scheduled to leave on a week-long patrol of the outer system. Taking the Friday afternoon "off"—which really just meant out of the office; she *was* the head of state for four million souls—meant it would be at least twelve days before he could get in to see her.

She also knew that if Cavan was actually scheduled to see her on something *important*, Faulkner would gently discourage her from being quite so petty.

"Of course; I'll let Captain Cavan know," Faulkner said instead. "I'll make sure the front desk knows to expect our robotic friend, too. Shall I have the garage conference room prepped?"

"That robot weighs fifteen hundred kilograms," Amelie replied. "I'm not certain the floors can hold it. The 'garage' conference room will be perfect."

———

Amelie wasn't even sure that Matrix KCX-DD-78 even realized that the humans had set up a special conference space specifically to meet with them. The Matrix seemed very pleased with their success with the remote, and none of her people could bring themselves to disabuse them of their almost-childish glee.

The Matrices in general swung between utterly terrifying creatures of cold logic and calculation and naïve, utterly adorable creatures who seemed only barely familiar with their emotions and natures.

The President of Exilium had probably spent more time with KCX's remote than anyone else had, and even she wasn't sure which one was the Matrices true nature. She suspected that the reality was both—and she had to wonder which one their mysterious Creators had *intended* to create.

"Greetings, President Amelie Lestroud," KCX's mechanical buzz echoed through the garage they'd repurposed. *"This Matrix has positive news to report."*

Amelie took her seat carefully and tried not to hope too hard. "Positive news" from the Matrices could only be news about Isaac's mission —a mission that should have reached Kappa three days ago.

"What news is that?" she asked.

"The Rogue Matrix has ceased transmitting on all tachyon frequencies. Admiral Isaac Gallant has completed the mission as promised, and in return, Regional Construction Matrix XR-13-9 is recognizing your residence of Constructed World XR-13-9-27 and ownership of the attendant system.

"With that recognition, this matrix's role in this system is complete and we will be leaving shortly," the remote concluded.

"Wait, that's it?" Amelie asked. "You're just going to leave? No further contact, nothing?"

"This Matrix is not intended to fulfill a role as a communication relay node, as evidenced by the use of an inspection unit as a remote," KCX reminded her. *"Recon Matrix DD-78-E will remain in the XR-13-9-27 System until the communication unit has arrived."*

"You have such a unit?" she asked. That was contrary to everything they had said before.

"Specifications for a long-term inter-sapient relations unit were discovered in the archives of Regional Construction Matrix XR-13-9," KCX told her. *"Construction will be complete in thirty-six days. It should arrive in the XR-13-9-27 System shortly before Admiral Isaac Gallant returns."*

Amelie let *that* thought send a smile onto her face, though it was followed quickly by another thought.

"Do you know that Isaac survived?" she asked. "Can you check in on his people?"

KCX was silent for a lot longer than the robot had ever been in response to a question before.

"We…cannot."

"Cannot?" Amelie demanded. "You just sent him into battle for you and you can't even spare a recon unit to go see if he's okay?"

The robot was silent again. In a human, she'd have thought they were marshaling their thoughts or working out how to say something unpleasant. In the Matrix's case, though, it almost certainly meant that KCX was talking to XR-13-9. She wasn't even sure how many light-years away the main brain of the Matrices she'd dealt with was, but their communication wasn't quite instantaneous.

But KCX had almost never needed to call home before.

Something strange was going on.

"We…can spare the unit," KCX admitted. *"What we cannot do is deploy to that region. XR-13-9 is not certain why. Unidentified protocols have activated and the zone is restricted to us now."*

"Are those protocols going to be a threat to us?" Amelie asked carefully.

"No. We have registered the area as a threat, but despite our existing knowledge of why the Matrix was destroyed, the protocols are not registering President Amelie Lestroud's people as a danger. The inter-sapient relations unit may be able to carry out calculations and interactions that we currently cannot."

"So, we won't know anything about what happened until they return?"

"No. Admiral Isaac Gallant will return. Once Admiral Isaac Gallant has done so, we will learn what occurred. Until then, we only have the knowledge that Admiral Isaac Gallant was victorious."

She sighed and nodded.
That was going to have to be enough.

———

49

THE HIDEOUS-LOOKING MESS that was all that remained of Isaac's fleet served one distinct purpose and one purpose only: it could make sixty-five times the speed of light and bring his people home.

He'd been surprised when the engineers had told him they'd managed to rig up the drive ring to still be able to make the full speed of the new warp drives. *Dante* and her warp ring were basically welded into the angle where tidal forces had snapped *Vigil*'s back.

But they'd managed to expand the ring with the wreckage from *Vigil*'s ring. It had taken the engineers two full weeks to do it and he was coming home almost three weeks late...but Isaac Gallant was coming home to Exilium.

And Exilium *was* home. Home was where the heart was, so for Isaac Gallant...that was wherever Amelie Lestroud was.

It would be some years before they could admit that in public, but they'd make it work. He would wait. He'd sacrificed enough to make certain that the Republic of Exilium could exist that he could give it those few more years.

"Emergence in sixty seconds," Alstairs reported. "Ready to be home, boss?"

Isaac shook his head.

"Never more so," he admitted. "I owe my mother a vote of thanks, I think. This is certainly a nicer home than anything we had in the Confederacy."

"Yeah, we didn't have crazy robots building perfect planets back there," his ops officer agreed. "And we all figured the Confederacy was headed for a crash. Whatever happens, we're here. On Exilium."

"We're home," Isaac replied. "That's what's important now."

Emergence.

The warp bubble collapsed, and he could finally breathe again, the combined ship lurching back into reality and reaching out with her scanners.

"What have we got?" Isaac asked.

"The Recon and Security Matrix is gone," Alstairs reported. "Looks like the Morgue has been activated and armed; I've got a bunch of destroyers and missile cruisers in high-guard orbit."

"No Matrices at all?" Isaac asked.

"I'm not… Wait, there they are."

"Ops?"

A new highlight flashed up on the screen.

"Wasn't anything we'd seen before, so I wasn't sure if it was Matrix or ours, but it's their hull ceramics, so almost certainly Matrix."

The new ship was a flat black disk that resemble the core of the Rogue Matrix at less than one-twentieth scale. It was about a hundred meters across and twenty thick, with visible gaps that Isaac noted where smaller ships had clearly been attached.

"I'm guessing that's what the Matrix thinks is an ambassador," Isaac noted. "Any escorts?"

"The missile cruiser *Galahad*," his ops officer reported. "That was part of what threw me. *Galahad* is in standard escort position above the Matrix ship."

"Well, then I think we can safely say they're friendly," the Admiral replied. "Get me a channel, Rose. It's time to let everyone know we made it home safely."

———

It took long enough to get into orbit and start shuttling the crews down to the surface for the government to make an announcement—and it seemed like all four million of Exilium's inhabitants had turned out to watch the shuttles land.

Caretaker crews were swarming over the two wrecked battle-cruisers already, but every single surviving spacer and officer who'd gone to Kappa was being shuttled down.

Isaac had tried to be last, but he'd been overridden. He was still on the nineteenth of forty-plus shuttles, stepping out of the spacecraft onto a landing pad that was already swarming with his people meeting their loved ones.

"ATTEN-HUT!"

He'd recognized Kira Zamarano's voice anywhere. The Brigadier appeared out of the crowd in full Exilium Marine Corps dress uniform —and a double file of similarly dress-uniformed Marines seemed to materialize from nowhere, opening a pathway through the crowd with an ease that spoke of prior conversations.

He returned their salutes and stepped into the path they'd opened for him, nodding to the left and right to acknowledge the Marines as Zamarano stepped out to meet him.

"Welcome home, sir."

"Thank you, Brigadier. Don't you think this is a little overkill?" he asked.

"Not a chance," she told him with a wicked grin. "Let's move; the Cabinet is waiting."

Zamarano and two gruff-looking Marines fell in behind him, giving him little choice but to continue to make his way down the path the uniformed troopers and the crowd had opened for him.

The noise level was dropping as they moved too, the entire crowd turning to watch as he approached the end of the pathway. There was something anticipatory about the hush, and it made the man who'd fought a genocidal war-computer to a standstill nervous.

There, at last, was the Cabinet of the Republic of Exilium, with Amelie Lestroud standing out in front of them. His heart tried to skip a beat, and he almost tripped over his own feet at the sight of her.

If he'd ever doubted how well Zamarano knew him—or that the

woman had guessed his feelings for their President—the ease with which she caught him in mid-trip and kept him going would have told him the truth.

"Madam President," he greeted Amelie as he approached her. "It's done. Our mission is complete."

"So I see, Admiral Gallant," she replied. "And your people?"

"We lost...more than I hoped," he said quietly. "But we brought most of them home."

"And brought them home victorious," Amelie agreed.

Isaac realized that even the *Cabinet* seemed to be listening in an anticipatory silence, and the Ministers of the Republic seemed to be trying to hide almost childishly gleeful grins.

"So, what reward, then, would our gallant hero ask of the Republic?" she asked, her eyes crinkling in a smile at the inevitable pun.

"None," he told her, waiting for the other shoe. "I swore an oath to serve this government, this Republic, this people. Reward my people if you must, but I have only done my duty."

She shook her head at him.

"Your duty covers so much in your mind, doesn't it, Isaac?" she asked, and suddenly, the entire crowd was *completely* silent. "Fortunately for you, expert advice has overridden you and me on certain sacrifices we were determined to make, and I think that allows for a reward few would argue, don't you?"

Isaac stared at her in confusion. He had *no* idea what she meant, not even as Roger Faulkner handed her a small black box and she sank to one knee to present him the plain titanium ring in it.

"*Mon cher Amiral*, will you marry me?"

———

ABOUT THE AUTHOR

Glynn Stewart is the author of *Starship's Mage*, a bestselling science fiction and fantasy series where faster-than-light travel is possible—but only because of magic. His other works include science fiction series *Duchy of Terra, Castle Federation* and *Vigilante,* as well as the urban fantasy series *ONSET* and *Changeling Blood.*

Writing managed to liberate Glynn from a bleak future as an accountant. With his personality and hope for a high-tech future intact, he lives in Kitchener, Ontario with his wife, their cats, and an unstoppable writing habit.

 facebook.com/glynnstewartauthor
twitter.com/glynnstewart

OTHER BOOKS BY GLYNN STEWART

For release announcements join the mailing list or visit GlynnStewart.com

Exile
Ashen Stars
Exile

Castle Federation
Space Carrier Avalon

Stellar Fox

Battle Group Avalon

Q-Ship Chameleon

Rimward Stars

Operation Medusa

Duchy of Terra
The Terran Privateer

Duchess of Terra

Terra and Imperium

Vigilante (With Terry Mixon)
Heart of Vengeance

Oath of Vengeance

Bound by Stars
Bound by Law

Bound by Honor (upcoming)

Starship's Mage

Starship's Mage

Hand of Mars

Voice of Mars

Alien Arcana

Judgment of Mars

Starship's Mage: UnArcana Rebellions

UnArcana Stars (upcoming)

Starship's Mage: Red Falcon

Interstellar Mage

Mage-Provocateur

Agents of Mars (upcoming)

ONSET

ONSET: To Serve and Protect

ONSET: My Enemy's Enemy

ONSET: Blood of the Innocent

ONSET: Stay of Execution

Changeling Blood

Changeling's Fealty

Hunter's Oath

Noble's Honor (upcoming)

Fantasy Stand Alone Novels

Children of Prophecy

City in the Sky

CPSIA information can be obtained
at www.ICGtesting.com
Printed in the USA
LVHW03s2044120918
589920LV00003B/342/P